William Morris Davis

Nimrod of the Sea

The American Whaleman

William Morris Davis

Nimrod of the Sea
The American Whaleman

ISBN/EAN: 9783744715423

Printed in Europe, USA, Canada, Australia, Japan

Cover: Foto ©Andreas Hilbeck / pixelio.de

More available books at **www.hansebooks.com**

NIMROD OF THE SEA;

OR,

THE AMERICAN WHALEMAN.

By WILLIAM M. DAVIS.

NEW YORK:
HARPER & BROTHERS, PUBLISHERS,
FRANKLIN SQUARE.
1874.

CONTENTS.

CHAPTER I.

CHAPTER II.

CHAPTER IIL

CHAPTER IV.

CHAPTER XV.

CHAPTER XVI.

CHAPTER XVII.

CHAPTER XVIII.

CHAPTER XIX.

CHAPTER XX.

CHAPTER XXI.

CHAPTER XXII.

CHAPTER XXIII.

CHAPTER XXVIII.

CHAPTER XXIX.

CHAPTER XXX.

. CHAPTER XXXI. .

CHAPTER XXXII.

CHAPTER XXXIII.

CHAPTER XXXIV.

ILLUSTRATIONS.

NIMROD OF THE SEA;

OR,

THE AMERICAN WHALEMAN.

CHAPTER I.

Story of Ohther and King Alfred.—First Whaling in America.—Work
proposed in this History.—My Owner.—The young Candidate.—Papers
signed, and we sail.—The first Reef.—Going Aloft.—The *Chelsea.*—The
Crew.—The Outfit.—Food.

My story of whaling, to begin at the beginning, should
tell how King Alfred, of blessed memory, listened to the
wondrous stories of whaling told by "Ohther, the Norway
man," and how he was so charmed by the recital that he
published, for the benefit of his subjects, information to the
effect that Ohther "coasted along the country of the Fins
(Lapland) until he passed the North Cape, and penetrated
the great White Sea—the same which washes the icy barrier
of the Arctic Pole—wherein he found great whales of forty-
eight and fifty elns in length, the same being so exceedingly
numerous and tame that Ohther, with the help of five men,
could kill sixty of them in two days." The average Englishman is not impulsive, and he slept over the good Alfred's
hint for six hundred and ninety-three years, when, in 1593,
some English ships made a voyage to Cape Breton for the
morse and whale fishery. Such was the beginning of this
brave and adventurous business by people who think and
speak in our mother-tongue. The same adventurous spirit,

transplanted in America, struck deep root, and brought forth a rich harvest from the sea.

The first recorded agreement concerning the capture of whales in America commences in this wise:

"Ye 5th day of ye 4th month, 1672. James Loper doth ingage to carry a design of whale-catching on the island of Nantucket. That is to say, James ingages to be a third in all respects, and some of the Town ingages on the other two-thirds in like manner, etc."

Behold in the wonderful history of American whaling how great a flame this little spark kindled. The practical mother-wit, or gumption, which characterized the early American found expression in this first adventure in this most perilous profession. In this agreement we find that subdivision in interest, that co-operation of capital, skill, labor, and courage which ultimately secured a prosperous career to the Americans, made them masters in the business, and drove the men and ships of all other nations from the whale-fishery.

Just two centuries from the date of the above contract, or about "ye 5th day of ye 4th month," 1872, my good angel wrote to me, saying: "Overhaul your journal of a whaling voyage to the Pacific, and give us a history of American Whaling by pen and pencil. Fling yourself into the work; write of that strange life as you saw it from the forecastle and the mast-head, from the boats and the quarter-deck. Put into it all the poetry and rapture, the danger and the deviltry, the enjoyment and the suffering, with all the history you have in your memory or have access to. To be statistical and tedious is a felony; but history can be made as charming as romance, without losing any of its value." Such were my directions, and, sailing by that chart, I open the old oil-stained pages of my journal, and therein find that on the 11th day of ye 10th month, 18—, I, Bill Seaman,

"BEEN ABOARD THE CHELSEA YET?"

bow-oar with divers others, including captain's mates and harpooners, did "Ingage to carry on a design of whale-catching" in the Atlantic, the Pacific, and all other waters to the uttermost ends of the earth, wheresoever whales did swim; and "some of the town of New London did ingage with us in like manner, in proportions" as set forth in the ship's articles of the good bark *Chelsea*, Major Thomas A. Williams, owner. And·here, before I begin my narrative, I wish to bespeak indulgence toward one of its features. It is based on the well detailed journal of a foremast-hand, who rose to boat-steerer; therefore it·is written from the stand-point of the forecastle, and the quarter-deck is treated of as an object of a laudable ambition. My journal is used as a cord on which are strung the experiences and advent-ures of others, such as I have been enabled to pick up in the form of yarns on board the *Chelsea*. Omitting a date to my voyage, I am thus enabled to give the experiences of a quarter of a century. About the internal economy of our ship I write as the boyish sailor; and I ask you old captains, in imagination, to sit barefooted on an old sea-chest as you read my story as I sat to write it.

Is it necessary that I should recount how complaisant the major was before I signed the ship's articles? It appeared that the major was anxious to fill up his crew, that the ves-sel might not be detained when her fitting was completed; and doubtless, as he regarded the tall, slender, and rather weakly youth before him, he deemed it necessary to throw in an encouraging word to strengthen good resolutions:

"Ah! you're from Pennsylvania. Very good place that: a little too far from salt-water to be wholesome, I guess. Salt air will soon put color in your cheeks. You think you'll like the sea? of course you will. Nice life—very, if you take to it right. Been aboard the *Chelsea* yet? Yes; good ship the *Chelsea*, and such a sailor! A regular Baltimore clipper; easy times aboard that ship. You've trade-winds most of the way to Cape Horn: trade-winds, you know, are steady; as fixed, sir, as the needle to the pole, as the poet has it. And then there's the Pacific! Grand sea that; all about Juan Fernandez, Magellan, and the Southern Cross it's as calm and smiling as a mill-dam—so smooth that the illimitable sea seems a boundless oil-tank; where you see reflected in it the belt of Orion and the Pleiades. The thought almost tempts me to run out on a voyage, just to see that whaleman's heaven.

"Do you know that you get fresh beef at sea? Yes, sir, you do. Porpoises are to be had for the catching. Porpoise has muscle in it; you'd stiffen up on porpoise. And albatross too, big as geese; a little oily, but you'll get used to that. It makes a man water-proof to eat albatross."

The good man never dreamed that this moment was the fulfillment of the dreams of my short life. When I was a little boy, I had rigged and sailed my toy boats; and when a few years older, I had devoured Cook and Delano, and was happy in the library of Mavor, looking forward to the time when I too should visit the strange seas and scenes I had pictured in imagination. I took joy in the major's persuasions, as I knew that he would accept me, and allow me to go in his ship. Let me say it was no freak of a child, no sudden whim, which led me to this point. Twice I had been disappointed in going to sea. Once I had shipped in the *Globe,* East Indiaman, when a severe accident kept me confined for weeks after she had been under way. On a bed of sickness my young heart followed that gallant ship on her course, and I found consolation only in the promise of my fatherly brother, that when well another berth should be found me.

Then I shipped on board the saucy little free-trader, *Star,* bound for the coast of British India. She was armed, and carried a very heavy crew. My kit was purchased and taken on board, and one drizzly dark morning I went on board in my gay shirt and spotless ducks. When examined by the surgeon, he pounced on my wrist, left crooked from fracture in the late accident. It was still tender : he gave it an awful wrench; I flinched. "You won't do," was his awful verdict. In vain I told him that it was getting well very fast, and would soon be as sound as the other. He saw my heart was in going, and, being a kindly man, he said, "I can't pass you as sound; but go on shore now, and thank God that a weak wrist stands between you and this voyage." I did not know what he meant, but I went home to the quiet country almost heart-broken; and had no peace of mind until a letter from my friend, Mr. Lorenzo Draper, of New York, brought the glad tidings that he had secured a place for me on the *Chelsea.* And in a few days, with great joy in my heart (for which God forgive me), I kissed the tearful faces which bade me farewell for the long and, to them, fearful voyage which lay before me. Little did the good major know how little I needed the kindly encouragement he was extending; and lest I might again be disappointed, I made haste to append my name to the articles.

"Ah! you've signed. That's a good Bill; there's a captain's berth ahead, if you earn it. Now run down to Mr. Strong in the basement; he'll finish your outfit in a jiffy. Take good advice: he is as sharp as he's Strong; make him take off fifteen per cent. for cash: he will get rich faster than you or I at that. Get a good outfit; spend your money for clothes, and not for tobacco, so that you may keep clear of the slop-chest. You have a week before you sail: look about you, and make the most of New London; for a three years' voyage is no trifle, and you won't see a better place the other side of the land. Good-morning."

I did not again speak to the major for forty-five months.

Eight days afterward, I was standing, a cold, wet creature in red flannel and duck, looking back at a low bank of cloud-like land, as Montauk Point was fast sinking from sight.

> "So Juan stood, bewildered, on the deck:
> The wind sung, cordage strained, and sailors swore.
> And the ship creaked, the town became a speck,
> From which away so fair and fast they flew."

It seemed a wide Rubicon I was crossing. Heart and landscape sunk together. I was now in fitter mood to bid a proper good-bye to those I had so lightly left, so lightly thought of—bah! what a miserable substitute is the rough flannel cuff for a linen handkerchief: it leaves the eyes so red that the jolly brutes about me, in sympathetic tone, inquire if my "head is running on shilling calico already." The first night at sea is ever memorable, especially when a stiff north-west gale whistles a double-quick over the starboard quarter. Such was our welcome; but running free, we made good progress on a course. By some mysterious election I found myself in the starboard watch, Mr. S——, the second mate, heading it. I very soon found a prejudice against my superior, and a serious doubt arose as to the right of his claim to be a gentleman. The matter came out in this wise: in the course of his duty, I suppose, it became necessary to order a reef in the foretop-sail. The yard was lowered away; the reef-tackles hauled out, with much unnecessary "Yo, heave oh'ing," and the old salts flocked up the weather shrouds. I was deeply interested in their movements, never suspecting that a green hand would be required to go aloft the first night out, and in such rough weather; so I studied the endless tangle of braces, halyards, reef-tackles, clew-garnets, falls, and purchases by which I was surrounded. I wondered at the strange music of the storm-harp, the infernal confusion of creaking yards, the flapping of the sails away overhead: all this was food for the mind of the lad fresh from the little saw-mill quietly nestled in the shelter of the Gulf Valley. But presently, as I held some secure rope, admiring the agility with which the sailors squirmed out of sight into the whistling, howling darkness overhead, I saw the mad second mate coming for me with a rope's end in his hand, and with some ugly expletives, in sea lingo, between his teeth. I took in the whole situation in a moment, as S—— again yelled to me, "Lay aloft, and reef top-sails, you infernal lubber!"

The turmoil and confusion of the gale had subsided before this new storm came, and unhappy I found it comparatively easy to creep up the ratlines. My pride then led me to avoid the "lubber's hole" and to mount the terrible futtock-shrouds. Here, in some way, I found myself close in to the bunt on the weather foretop-sail yard. The roll, pitch, and sway of that yard, and the gyrations of the foot-rope supporting me; the darkness, wet, and howl, the hoarse orders and naughty oaths of the men, banished the little sense which the premonitions of sea-sickness had left me. I wonder if any sailor ever forgot his first reef at night. I don't remember to have knotted a point. In sheer desperation I hugged the shivering spar, repeating the beautiful prayer, "Here I lay me down," etc.

I was very loath to let go, and even allow the impatient sailors to lay in from the yard-arm. "Goodness gracious!" thought I; "can I ever go clear out on that yard in such a night?" By some means all hands got safely on deck, all was bowsed taut, and we stood on our course again. For the remainder of this miserable night we were hauling and letting go, belaying, making fast, coiling, reefing, and furling, and doing many things which I never so much as heard of in the whole twenty-seven volumes of Mavor's voyages. The pitch of our little uneasy bark, the spraying seas which overleaped our low bulwarks, and the growling oaths of moist humanity grew worse and louder, until I thought we were in for a terrible gale, and would have so described it, had I not overheard an old salt remark that it "blowed a stiffish breeze." Then I took courage and thanked God, though I should have preferred, with Paul, "to land at the Three Taverns" to do it. Such was the opening of the young landsman's journal of a voyage round Cape Horn in a three years' cruise for sperm-whales, Captain B—— commanding. In passing, let me state that, as the names of our officers are not material, I omit them for reasons which will appear hereafter.

If you follow me through the rest of my wanderings, it is proper that you should know and love the good ship which bore us. She was beautiful and good—beautiful in the calm, swift in the breeze, and staunch in the storm; sharp as a clipper; graceful in every line as the frigate-bird; wide-spread in wing as the albatross; and, in riding the waves, like a Mother Cary's chicken. She was sharp in the bow, broad in her beam, and clean in her run; small in her hold, with broad and roomy decks. A woman's head graced her cut-water, and half the gods of heathendom, in alto-relievo and high colors, decorated her stern. In fact, in rig and hull she was a prince's pleasure yacht, rather than a blubber-hunter, although she was built expressly for such service. "Give her speed," was the major's order; for speed in a whaleman is as wisdom was to Solomon—it includes all things. She had the proud habit of the blood-horse in tossing her beautiful head in the face of a gale, and if the martingale was not of the truest and strongest she would toss her jib-boom over the top-sail yard. Then she would nestle her woman's head so deep in the bosom of the leaping waves, that the foam of their crests would kiss the feet of her master on his quarter-deck. Gay and lively, brave and safe, was my old pet and mistress; for I came to love her in my long life of safety aboard her.

Our ship, bark-rigged, and registered 400 tons, could stow 300, equivalent to 2400 barrels of oil. We carried four boats on the cranes, and three spare boats on the spars above the quarter-deck. To each of the four boats was assigned a crew of six men—viz., a boat-header, a harpooner, and four oarsmen. Besides the twenty-four men assigned to the boats, we had a carpenter, a cooper, a cook, a steward, a cabin-boy, and three spare men, or thirty-two all told. The captain, cook, steward, and cabin-boy did not stand regular watches; they aided as ship-keepers when the boats were off. This gave the starboard and larboard watches each fourteen men, sufficient to handle sails in nearly every emergency.

The crew was composed of a captain; a mate, who headed the larboard watch; a second mate, who, with the third mate, headed the starboard watch; four harpooners, and the trades mentioned before, with greenhorns and old salts, who were known to be, and shipped as, able seamen. The strong force on board a whale-ship and the duties in the boats give an importance to the under officers unknown in the merchant service. With us the second mate was the officer of the deck during his watch, and he never left it to furl or reef: he exacted as respectful an "Ay, ay, sir," in answer to his orders as did the captain himself. The harpooners were divided, two in each watch, save when we were on cruising grounds. Then we reefed down every night, and each boat-steerer headed his own boat's crew's watch during the night, and became officer of the deck.

Our outfit consisted of extra sails and rigging, spare spars, and a store of tar, paint, etc., for repairs to ship; cedar boards and light timbers for the boats; a large quantity of admirably made whale line; a store of harpoons made of

the softest and toughest iron, with lances of a quality of
steel and capacity of cutting edge that might excite the envy
of a diplomaed "sawbones;" also cutting-in spades, boat
hatchets and knives; casks for the oil, stowed with water,
food, or clothing; and all the very many necessaries to cover the wear and tear of long years of arduous service. An
important and peculiar feature in the equipment of a whale-
ship is the "try-work." This consisted in our ship of three
large iron pots, built in brick-work, and so supported by iron
stanchions, that a body of water was maintained between
the hearths and the deck to intercept the heat of the furnaces. For stores we carried as a staple, ship-biscuit, pork,
and beef, with coffee, tea, molasses, rice, beans, Indian meal,
flour, and pickles. Our worthy major was a professor of
religion, and I am quite sure that on the day of final account
he may safely call upon the *Chelsea's* crew to testify to his
liberality in our outfit. We might confuse the accountants
if we gave our entire list of luxuries, which included "dough-
boys," "choke-dog," "lobscouse," "dough jehovahs," and
"menavellins." Each day of the week some one of the
above delicacies accompanied the inevitable salt-junk; and,
believe it who may, we had pork every day, not two or three
days a week, as some unfortunates have it. Furthermore,
access to the bread cask and the molasses tank was never
denied. Perhaps there is no single article, I may say in pa-
renthesis, in which the superiority of the American whaleman's outfit is more manifest, than in the excellent ship-biscuit which all carry, the greatest care being taken to exclude
dampness or decaying influences. It will be noticed at once
how well we were provided for.

CHAPTER II.

Uneventful Passage.—Captain's Inaugural.—Mast-head and Place in Boat.
—Discipline in Boats, and first Whale raised.—Awkwardness of Crew,
and Whale lost.—Music and Song a Necessity.—Hinton, the Nightingale.—The Yarn as Mental Food.—Forecastle Philosophy.—Burrows's
Theory of the Gulf Stream.—Whales pass under the Isthmus of Da-
rien.—Ben Coffin.—His Idea of Luxury.

THE whale-killing historian and poet, Obed Macy, says
very truly, that "The sea to mariners is but a highway: to
the whaler it is his field of harvest; it is the home of his
business." The passage, or voyage, to the harvest-field occupies little of the mind of the whaling man; it is to the
harvest-field itself that his thoughts turn. Green hands,
women, and men-of-war's men may find material for a journal and a book, mayhap, in the incidents of travels about the
blue sea. But the whaleman steps on board his full ship,
bound home from Behring Strait, and battered and rusty
from a four years' cruise, with the expectation of no more
noteworthy incidents than a tired bank-clerk might encounter in a voyage from the Chestnut Street wharf, Philadelphia,
to Camden, *via* Smith Island Canal. I was verdant, and
the old journal was well filled before we reached the Brazil
Banks, *via* the Cape Verds, which we sighted and passed.
The notes taken were mainly personal, however, and imma-
terial to this history, except, perhaps, one referring to the
captain's inaugural speech. In this speech there was the
stereotyped bluster, threat, and insult deemed necessary to
place the captain and officers in their proper places, and to
put the crew in sailing trim. We were duly informed that

the captain was to do all the fighting and swearing on board the *Chelsea*. Green as I was, the deprivation of these two sea luxuries was of small account, but some of the old salts took it greatly to heart. To stop the grog on board our whale-ships is of slight moment, but " to clap a stopper on honest swearing is a lubberly go," was the general verdict when the men went forward. Very soon after leaving home the mast-head lookout was established. This consisted of an officer, or boat-steerer, at the main, and one of the crew at the foremost top-gallant cross-trees or royal yard. The mast-head was manned at daylight, and continued until sunset, and was relieved every two hours, the crew taking the watch, as they did the helm, strictly in turn.

We were assigned to our places in the boats. I was placed at the bow-oar in the starboard, or captain's boat, in which position service was likely to be seen, as Captain B—— was an ardent whaleman, skilled with the lance, and proud of helping his mates out of a tight place by pitching his lance into the life of their whale. Our boat-steerer, Elisha Chipman, was a fine specimen of manhood, as will appear hereafter.

At times, when the ship had moderate headway, the boats, with their green crews, were lowered, and we manœuvred around a dummy whale—a spare spar towed astern. Thus we were continually drilled in lowering away, shipping oars at the word, "pulling in chase," "going on," "starning," "pulling two oars starn three," until our hands were sorely blistered, and something like discipline was established among the crews. Now we were fairly launched on our cruise, and the captain was ready for whale. The injunction was given to keep our " eyes skinned at the mast-head, and sing out for every thing you see." And thus we ran through the tedious calms and sudden squalls of the "line" into the south-east "trades," which blew us to the Banks

"THERE SHE BLOWS!'

of Brazil. One day the cry came from aloft, "There she blows!" "Where away?" shouted Captain B——, his gray eyes snapping with excitement. "Three points off lee bow; blows; blows; four miles off, and sperm-whale." All hands were now alive, the watch from below came on deck, the captain sprang aloft, and a long-drawn shout came from above, "There goes flukes!" as the whale went down.

The excited crew were in the lee rigging, keeping a sharp lookout, the boats having been cleared for lowering. The captain ordered the maintop-sail aback.

"Stand by to lower," he cried. "There she blows, close aboard."

The boats were awkwardly launched, the willing crews tumbled in, and great confusion of oars ensued; but in good time we settled down to the work, and were fairly off in pursuit of our first whale. A long chase it proved, and fruitless, although we had two fair darts. The mate's boat was first on, and ours was second; but the hump seemed under my bow-oar as we ranged across the corners of his flukes. Owing to want of nerve, or awkwardness in the crew, however, the iron dart came back straight; and so this fine whale was left in the South Atlantic, to blow in peace. The captain took his failure in good part, and scolded less than we expected. The evening's watch was an excited one. As hunters track back on the sport of the day, so we sought reasons for our failure. The knowing ones were wise about spermaceti, and we green hands learned much of forecastle natural history in the evening's recital. Every mother's son who had ever gone on to a whale had a yarn, and some of those told were indeed "wonderfully and fearfully made."

The enjoyments of the voyage—these I will describe, as they show something of a whaler's life—in no slight degree depend on the crews having some one skilled in the violin to stir the dance on calm evenings. Generally the accomplish-

ment is considered necessary in the "doctor" (*i. e.*, cook)
of the ship; and if the cook is a black, the chances are that
a fiddle is stowed in his sea-chest. We had a *beau ideal*
"doctor" and fiddler, and his enlivening medicine went far
to banish scurvy from the ship. The second in importance
is the "minstrel boy." He must have considerable range
of expression, that he may sing of love, war, and the storm;
to soothe us with the sentimental and cheer us with the
comic. He must sing with Castillego:

> . "How could we love, if woman were not:
>   Love, the brightest part of our lot;
>   Love, the only chance of living;
>   Love, the only gift worth giving."

Or, with Dibdin:

> "Yet, come but Love on board,
>   Our hearts with pleasure stored,
>   No storms can overwhelm;
>   Still blows in vain,
>   The hurricane
>   While Love is at the helm."

Touching on the known constancy of Jack, and the temptations of this wicked world:

> "Some with faces like charcoal, and others like chalk—
>   All are ready one's heart to o'erhaul;
>   'Don't go for to love me.' 'Good girl,' said I, 'walk;
>   For I've sworn to be constant to Poll.'"

He will shock our native modesty by singing of the sights
prepared in the ballet:

> "And she hopped, and she sprawled, and she spun round so queer—
>   'Twas, you see, rather oddish for me;
>   And so I sung out, 'Pray be decent, my dear;
>   Consider I'm just come from sea.'"

He sings the joys of virtuous love thus:

> "No gallant captain in the British fleet,
>   But envies William's lips those kisses sweet."

And of the sterner duties of our hardy profession:

> "Cease, rude Boreas, blustering railer!
> List ye landsmen unto me,
> Listen to a brother-sailor
> Sing the dangers of the sea."

If need be, he must, handspike in hand, mount the windlass and, in deepest bass, lead the chorus,

> "With a stamp and a go,
> And 'Yo, heave oh!'"

In brief, the "minstrel boy" must have a fitting song for all moods and every occasion. He is an attraction in the carouse on shore, and in the night-watch in calm and storm. Such a treasure we had in our mulatto boat-steerer, Harry Hinton. Brave and faithful, he never shrunk from a duty below or aloft, or a danger in boat or port. He stuck to the *Chelsea* through good and evil, and was one of the six who remained to drop anchor from our old ship in New London harbor.

The sailor is an insatiable lover of the yarn, and his passion is still strong after he has put aside his sea-legs and settled in the peaceful home, away from the blue water. The marvelous narrations of the forecastle and the quarter-deck have as wide a range as the songs. One of our crew had mastered Mavor's voyages, Walter Scott, Cooper, and Marryat; and being blessed with a memory that held all the wonderful and beautiful of his earliest readings from the "Good Book," he was able to hold the watch in breathless attention through many bells—now with the matchless story of "Ivanhoe," now with the "Talisman," now with "Peter Simple" and "Snarleyow," or with the adventures of the old terrors of the seas on which sailed the English buccaneers. The wild extravagances of Hackett's Nimrod Wildfire and Forrest's Metamora were recited in minutest detail, regardless of time, as Time was an enemy to be led captive by the cunningly meshed yarn.

"Come, Jack, now for a long yarn," is the request of the watch, as we gather about the windlass and the forehatch.

"Oh, Lord bless your souls! I haven't time for a long yarn, as it's my 'trick' at the helm at four bells."

"You don't get out that way, Jack;" and some one agrees to take Jack's trick, so that he has a clear three and a half hours to drone over an old-fashioned yarn, the requisites being that it shall be of "love and fun, with some murder in it"—the more improbable the better. Jack consents, and is conscientious enough to stretch the yarn out to eight bells, as per contract. Should he find himself, at the end of half an hour, ahead of time, he resorts to an expedient worthy of a professional novelist. The hero is taken home, and friends crowd around him anxious to hear his latest adventures. Jack refreshes himself from a black bottle, and boldly repeats the yarn he has just told us. We then lay awake to watch that his memory is perfect, and that he does not trip, or omit the slightest detail. Should he do so, he is at once stopped, to account for the kink we have detected. If he makes many slips, the impression becomes general that he has been playing on our credulity. This is pretty sure to breed a row, to be settled at the first port we make, as Captain B—— will not allow any fighting on board. Thus we are thoroughly awakened, and in great good humor we strike eight bells and call the larboard watch.

The theories and philosophy of the landsmen are accepted with a very liberal discount by forecastle savants. "How could those lubbers ashore be expected to know the real facts of deep water, when they squat ashore and take the dead shells and waifs which the live sea tosses to their reaching hands? A dead whale floats ashore, and they make drawings that would stand as well for a Dutch galiot, and put it in their picture-books as one of the living, beautiful facts of God's creation!"

Reasoning much in this way, Jack takes a landsman's theories with a grain of allowance, deciding that much learning tends to madness. His own philosophy is sometimes astonishing — certainly original; and I may cite the theory of the Gulf Stream proposed by Mr. Burrows, our Mexican third mate, as an example. He started our greenhorns on a new track, by declaring the old theory of a concentration of Atlantic currents insufficient to account for all the phenomena attending this stream, and also that the influence of the north-east trade-wind blowing into the Gulf of Mexico was incompetent to produce such a result; for, said he, the violent interruptions of contrary gales and hurricanes would not affect the general velocity or volume of the stream.

"The fact is," said Burrows, very learnedly, "there is an under-ground channel between the Pacific and the Gulf of Mexico, through which a great river of the warm water of the Pacific is poured to the lower level of the cool Atlantic. In evidence, the pretty weed which floats in great fields in the Gulf Stream is found growing on the Pacific shore of the continent, and not on the eastern side. To be sure, great masses are met north of the islands, but it is the bruised, half-killed weed which has passed north in the stream and has been swept into the great return eddy. The little crabs and the peculiar creeping fish found in the weed belong to the Pacific shore. But the best reason is the fact that whales do pass from sea to sea in a time too short to allow of the long journey around Cape Horn. Whaling skippers tell of sperm-whales that have been killed in the Pacific carrying in fresh wounds the bright irons bearing the stamp of ships then cruising in the Atlantic. On after comparison of the logs, it became apparent that but few days elapsed between the escape of the stricken whale in the one sea and its subsequent capture in the other."

The interest in this view lies in the existence of the inter-oceanic canal; but the sperm-whales are close-mouthed (as we afterward learned), and keep their own secrets. One of the men remarked that the idea was " too simple and rational to be believed," and he went into a scholarly yarn on the subsidence of a great part of our continent, the lofty finger-prints of which he said yet remain visible in the mountain heights of Cuba, San Domingo, and the chain of the Carib-bees. And he told of a civilization in this Western World older than the Pyramids, and in existence before the learned Brahman Menou recorded, in Sanscrit, the dawn of human history. But the incidents of the day indisposed us for subjects so scientific, and all knowledge concerning the Gulf Stream was voted a whaleman's yarn.

Old Ben, one of our crew, was then called on for his yarn about the first time he went on a sperm-whale. This story was as nuts and cider to the green hands, inasmuch as it was an honest confession that an old hand had been "gal-lied" (frightened). The fellow-feeling made us wondrous kind. But you should know Ben Coffin in order to ap-preciate the fun of the story. Ben, in his youth, might have sat for the picture which Dibdin sang:

> " His form was of the manliest beauty,
> His heart was kind and soft,
> Faithful below he did his duty,
> But now he's gone aloft."

Ben, as he begins, says he is a rich farmer's son, and that he came to sea to wear out his old clothes. When he gets through with the job, he is going to play the rôle of the Prodigal Son, and go back to the old Vermont farm, and say, "Father, I have whaled," which involves all of sinning, and then eat fat veal all the rest of his days.

" When that port is made, and I am safe anchored, and rich, and all that kind of thing, and can do as I please, I am goin' to ship a bosin-mate from the biggest seventy-four in Uncle Sam's blessed navy, and I'll give him a silver call; and his duty shall be to pipe all hands at eight bells (4 A.M.) in the morning, and to rap a handspike ag'in the mahogany (inlaid with whale ivory) door of my state-room, and rouse me out with, ' Starbo-a-r-d watch, a-h-o-y—oy !' Then I'll sing out, ' *Watch be blowed!*' and go to sleep again. . What's the gain of bein' rich if you can't blow the starboard watch at eight bells ?"

Ben is about sixty-five, and has a chestful of old clothes yet. Fifty - two years he has spent at sea, with short intervals on shore. He never married, "because his mother was particular on the score of daughters-in-law." Ben is bruised, battered, and warped in body; seamed and wrinkled in brow, by fire, by ice, and shipwreck. The few fingers which the frosts of Labrador have left him are corrugated and doubled in, to fit close to the rope and the oar he has tugged at for half a century. During the war of 1812 he served in the *Constitution*, and labored faithfully and successfully in shooting some new ideas through Mr. John Bull's head. Growing tired of the humdrum and peaceful quiet of man-of-war life, he came whaling, as he expressed it, to " see life, to sweat the weeds from my figure-head, and to rub off the barnacles which deadened my headway; and, by the great hokey! I got in the right place in the *Chelsea* under old Captain Davis. I'll tell you green hands about that first whale I went on in the captain's boat."

CHAPTER III.

Ben's first Whale.—Struck on a Breach.—Cedar cracking, and Ben goes
up.—As he rises from deep Water he meets Captain Davis coming
down.—He takes a Departure, and strikes out for New London.—Chipman confirms the Yarn.—Albatross, and one sent homeward as Messenger.—The Pilot-fish, and its long Passages.—Work of the Watches,
and learning the Rigging.—Washing, Mending, and other Accomplishments of the Sailor.—Lessons taught on the Forehatch of the *Chelsea.*
—My Crony Posey.—His Love Story.—Why the Nobility of Nantucket
go Whaling.—Posey's Ambition.—The Secret of Nantucket's first Success.—Successful whaling Co-operation.—Obed Macy's Description of
Whaling.

"WE was a-runnin' down the trades, in lat. 13 S., right
about this very spot as it might be, and Lish Chipman
there, he was at the mast-head, and raised whale. We ran
down with the ship convenient, and lowered four boats.
Captain Davis was real hungry and cantankerous for a
whale, for he hadn't been in a fight for nearly six months;
howsoever, the whale soon turned flukes and staid down,
so that I thought he'd never come up ag'in. The captain
was mounted on the gunwales, and Lishey was on the box;
and we was a-lookin', each man over the blade of his own oar,
to catch the first spout, when suddenly Lish uttered a cry that
almost made one's marrow creep. 'Bill,' said Ben, addressing me, 'you're in his boat, and you'll hear him whisper that
way some day, and you won't grow any more after hearin' it.'

"Well, however, as I was sayin', Lisha, with a quiet yell,
not much above a whisper, said, 'Look out for breakers,
captain; take your oars, all of you, and don't speak for your
lives.' He grabbed his iron, when, quick as a white squall,

STRUCK ON A BREACH.

there was the whale's head on a clean breach, not two iron's length from the head of the boat. We couldn't stir hand nor foot for the life of us. Up, up, not fast, the whale kept going. It seemed there was no end to him. The old man was gallied a little I think, but he let Lish have his own way. I don't think one of us breathed, or even winked, as we watched that awful black mass shootin' into the sky. I tell you, boys, you'll never really know how big a critter a whale is until you see him eclipsing the sun, as I did that blessed day.

"And there stood that Chipman, his back to us, and at that minute, I guess, to all the world, with his iron and hand away back over his shoulder, a-waitin' and waitin' till the hump showed itself, and full fifty feet of black skin was in the air! It looked as if it hung right over our heads, when, holy Moses! Lisha clapped the iron in right up to the socket, and yelled out so they heard him aboard the ship, 'Starn for your lives! Starn all, I tell you!' At the same time he planted his second iron in the falling whale. Didn't we obey orders that time, I wonder! The boat had jumped its length, when the whale fell crashing right across our bows, nearly swampin' the boat in the swell he raised, and more 'n half filling us with white water.

"I never was at the Falls of Niagara, and, at my time of life, don't believe I'll ever go there for the express purpose of listenin' to splashin' water, as I have heard one uproar that showed what might be done.

"The whale thought that blow between wind and water was foul, for he cut such infernal canticoes that we could not get on to him. He sounded out half the line, and then ran under water, and provoked us in that way till the old man got real mad, dashed down his hat, and let out one of his rip-stavin' swears. Old B——, you know, wouldn't swear to save his soul, let alone a whale! But our old man, Jerusalem! how he could swear when there was honest life-and-death need of it! Well, while the old man was a-cussin', I heard cedar a-crackin', and when I looked around I was goin' up to the sky fast, with Captain Davis about half a boat's-length ahead of me. We parted company up there, for he kept on his course when I turned. I come down head first as in course, and went down into dark water like a bower anchor; I was kind of wire-drawn, and felt long as the main-mast. Bime-by I turned a sharp corner and glanced up, most as fast as I went down, and was gettin' purty well into daylight ag'in, when all at once it was dark ag'in. I looked up, and there was the whale, like a comet with a tail of sea-fire a-streamin' behind him, a-headin' right for me. Good Lord, how I sculled out of his course! He shot by me like a rocket, and when I came up on a half-breach, I was just dead-beat for breath. I spouted like a whale, and blowed out the surplush water, and got a good long breath. Oh, how good the blessed air comes to a famished, chokin' man!

"Just then I heard something splash in the sea; I turned quick, and obsarved that the boat keg had just come down. 'Stand from under!' said I, and, I looked up, and believe it or not just as you please, but there was Captain Davis a-comin', end over end, makin' the tallest kind of headway to his nat-ural level. This whirligig made me kind of sea-sick, and turned my stomick ag'in whalin'. I thought I'd carry out my old plans, and git to Vermont jist as quick as I could; so I got the sun well over my larboard shoulder, and struck out north, two points east, for New London. But the mate's boat overhauled me before I had swum far, and took me back to the ship, where the captain gave me a stiff can of grog, to qualify the salt I'd swallowed in my deep-sea sound-ings.

"Now, boys, I never could make out exactly whether the captain went up very high, or I came up quicker than I thought for (I allowed that I was down about a half-hour), but, maybe, I only dreamed the dreams of the drowning, and saw sights which flit through men's heads in their last minutes. I asked Captain Davis once how long he'd been kiting that time. The old chap grinned, and said he hadn't looked at his watch, but he could now believe that the 'cow jumped over the moon' about the time when 'the little dog laughed to see the sport, and the dish ran away with the spoon.'"

"How about Ben's yarn?" we inquired of Chipman, who sat quietly smoking his pipe on the end of the windlass.

"Ben is about right in the main features of the case. I happened to look straight down from the head of the boat, when I saw the whale right under us, coming on a breach. He glimmered as bright a blue in the deep water as my sweetheart's bonnet. There was no time for thought, so I only acted on instinct and followed mother's last advice, never to let black skin go by the head of my boat without putting an iron in it, which the dear creature gave, illustrating it by throwing a fork at the black cat. But say, Ben, I was mortal feared the old man might order you to starn off before I could get my irons in. The whale didn't act so ugly as Ben thought; Ben was green then, you know, boys; but the durned critter did smash things when he hit us. But, then, nobody was hurt, although some were mightily skeart; and the old man himself owned that he got confused in his whirligig passage from the stern-sheets of the boat to the water."

Such were part of the yarns called forth by the adventure of the day; and we young fellows retired to our virtuous straw, in the main pleased that we had passed the first ordeal without mishap, but sorry, of course, that we had missed this first chance for oil.

After this, long days passed as we sped southerly. Many

false alarms were raised from the mast-head ; ships were seen
and passed ; none spoken. We watched the little pilot-fish under the bows, and the great albatrosses as they sailed about
the ship or floated gracefully on the water. About the Brazil Banks several of these great birds were taken by baiting a
floated hook with fat pork. As the "Antient Mariner" hath
it : "It ate the food it never had eat ;" and, in consequence,
it fell into the hands of those who had not the awful warning of the slayer of albatross before their eyes. We caught
and killed them to obtain the long, hollow bones of the wings,
for ornamental needle-cases for the " girl I left behind me."
One grand old fellow, whose stretch of wing was guessed as
twelve feet, and whose great, hooked beak seemed little injured by his capture, we preserved from death to convert
into a messenger. Writing the words "*Chelsea*, of N. L.,
Captain B——; all well; lat. 27° S., long. 36° W.," we secured
the paper in oiled silk. This was waxed, varnished, rendered perfectly water-proof, and secured by a cord around the
base of the bird's neck. A red ribbon streamer was attached to attract attention. All being prepared, we headed our
messenger by compass a true course for our " sweethearts
and wives," and launched him on the wing with a loud hurra. Forty-two months from this time we learned the conclusion of our venture. Five months after we had released
the bird in lat. 27° S., it was shot from a pilot-boat off the
harbor of New York, and our dispatch, with the manner of
conveyance, made an item in the papers of that city. This
was the first news our friends had received of the wild wanderers. Thus the albatross had come like a voice from the
sea to many anxious hearts, bearing a welcome message five
thousand miles, and, like the messenger from Marathon's
bloody field, dying in delivering it. As I have anticipated
in the case of the albatross, let me do the same with the little pilot-fish which leads our good ship on her way. From

the neighborhood of the Cape Verd Islands, where it joined us, until we lost headway in the port of Callao, Peru, it accompanied us. Undaunted by the cold and the storms of the cape, it led the way into lat. 62° S., and during a fearful scud before a south-east gale, which drove us for forty hours at an average of nearly fifteen miles an hour, we carried it into the shoal and perhaps too foul waters of a Peruvian harbor. The whole distance run by this little fish, allowing for traverses, was over 14,000 miles; time 122 days, or a daily average of 115 miles. In all these days, there was not a moment when the ship had such headway on her that our pilot might not be seen distinctly in front of the cut-water. By day, we could see it near the surface at our rising and falling bow; by night, in the phosphorescent seas it shot along, a gleaming flame, just in advance of the scintillations caused by the spurt of the cut-water. Our little companion obtained the interest of the crew, and word that it was still with us was passed from watch to watch. It finally entered into the superstitions of our ship, and its leaving us would have caused concern to many minds on board. Among men and officers there was no doubt that it was the same fish that joined us on the coast of Africa, and followed us south 77 degrees of latitude, thence north 50 degrees, making west 60 equatorial degrees, boarding itself meanwhile, without a watch below for sleep or rest. Let any boy or girl turn to the map of the world, and trace this long track of a fish not over twelve inches long, and think how wonderful are God's ways even with the smallest creatures—ways so wonderful that they are past finding out by grown men, even professors in natural history.

In the days that gradually grew longer as we approached the cape, the time of the watch on deck (or half the crew in turns of four hours each) was employed in pulling old rigging into yarn, knotting the yarn and winding it into convenient balls, or, by a simple wheel and axle, spinning it into rope-yarn for rigging again. The finer and evener yarn was neatly woven into mats to prevent the yards from chafing. The old sailors would neatly point ends of rigging or work the various knots of the "rose," and "double rose," the "wall," and "wall and crown," each having a special place and service. To "man-rope," "bucket-rope," "stoppers," etc., etc., are the accomplishments of the able seaman, next in order to reefing and steering. Inability to place the appropriate splice or knot in the appropriate place is deemed lubberly. Endless were the lessons patiently given and received in this intricate and important part of a sailor's education. Long were the discussions, and countless the authorities quoted to establish diverse views as to the placing of some knot, splice, point, or seizing. Things were simplified to me, however, when I learned that in all the tangle of taut, strained, or swinging lines, there were only three ropes in the ship—viz., man-rope, monkey-rope, and bucket-rope, with a rope's end to every piece of standing or running rigging. The first piece of rigging my poor brain located was the clew-garnet; its mineralogical association fixed that. From this little point I soon got over the lubberly habit of asking some one to "cast off" or "make fast" this or that rope, and began to chatter in the best sea-lingo about "swifters," "fore" and "back stays," "braces," "halyards," "falls," "purchases," "jewel-blocks," "ear-rings," "chains," "forefoot" and "taffrails," "binnacles" and "lockers," and to respond promptly to "bowse, taut, and belay all," and to "cast a bowline" or "double hitch." The mystery of the short and long splice, the "grummit" and "thole mat," the "thrum" and the "point," afforded play to the fingers which had practiced with the trout-flies and lighter tackle of the gentle art taught by Izaak Walton, of most worshipful memory. The useful art of washing and mend-

ing was not neglected, and we collected our *rents* as faithfully as did the closest landlord of the dry land. A sailor
should be able to direct the building of his ship from
royal-truck to keelson, and rig her with his own hand from
a rope-yarn to the "hawser bend." But he must also know
the altitude of the sun which will cast a true forked shadow on a piece of duck, as pattern for a pair of trowsers; he
must work the American eagle and a true-lover's knot in
blue yarn, to quilt his flannel shirt against the cold of the
cape; he must plait the split palm-leaf into pointed sennit
for his tarpaulin hat; he must never want protection for his
feet against cutting rocks, when his club can secure him
a seal or sea-lion; he must stand by a shipmate in trouble;
jump at the order of his officer, never "sodger," of all
things, never question about.God and his ways on deep
water, and never flinch from the tallest kind of a row when
the honor and good name of his mother or country are called in question. Such was the teaching on the forehatch
of the *Chelsea,* as we scudded past the mouth of the La
Plata, and made preparation to meet the old Storm King
who has his home in the Antarctic.

As the days lengthened and the nights grew less dark,
the more exact history of the business we were engaged in
occupied many of the idle hours of the night-watch, our ship
bowling along, without labor or care other than that of the
man at the helm and the lookout on the bows. In this lore
my special crony, Posey, delighted. To question him on
the history of Nantucket, New Bedford, Sag Harbor, or New
London, and of the famous captains who had fished in these
beautiful towns, was to open the flood-gates of his knowledge. Often, on the quarter-deck and on the forecastle, he
would talk to delighted audiences about the antiquity of our
craft, and the high honor in which it had been held by great
princes and powerful nations of the earth. Posey was a

great favorite with officers and men. Never in the way, his
hand and voice were always present when they were needed.
He had auburn hair, and blue eyes, set in a broad, sanguine
face (hence unaccountably, it was said, the ship-name of Posey), wearing an expression of sadness. Posey was a scholarly man ; his hands were delicate, and he had a stoop which
neatly fitted him to the low ceiling of our forecastle. He
was not at all the beauty of the crew, and he had not come
to sea to escape the "fool-catcher." He pulled the bow-oar
in Mr. F——'s larboard quarter-boat, and so was in direct
line of promotion. His heart was in his work, and he used
all his energy to win his way to the harpooner's place. No
boat was lowered to practice on black-fish in which he was
not a volunteer, and he was always on hand to aid in coiling
line in the boat-tubs and in mounting and grinding harpoons
and lances. In fact he was a ready hand for the hundred
little details which go to complete the gear of a whale-boat.
In a night-watch he confided to his companions the inspiration which sustained him, cheery and unwearied, in the hard,
uncongenial life in which he was immersed. I was young
and heart-whole, with my love in the wild, wandering life
before me, and was amused, rather than interested, in the
story which told of a young scholar from Vermont, who
found home and occupation as master of a school in Nantucket.

The old, old story it was—old as the Garden of Eden. A
man met the woman he loved, and found, too late, that he
could only win the daughter of a long line of the nobles of
the island—the whaling-captains—by winning his knight-
hood at the head of the whale-boat. A true daughter of the
land, the girl desired the security of a home founded on the
traditional harvest-field of her ancestors. How could it be
helped? She had been taught to refuse to dance with one
who had not been fast to a whale, and never to accept a

hand which had not planted a harpoon. So, in due course, when he avowed his love, Katie, with a smile of encouragement, replied, "Dear Garvin"—that was his proper name—"sing that song to me after you have struck a sperm-whale, and it will sound more real." How could the bonnie lassie do otherwise? In her home she had been severely trained.

NANTUCKET SCHOOLING.

One day she saw her good mother throw a loving arm around her father, and say,·

"Jack, dear, one of us must go a-whaling, and I can't."

"Why, what's up now, Dolly?" the briny old man asks.

"There's low tide in the bread-kit, and another mouth is coming."

The dear old fellow stows his kit, kisses Dolly and the little ones, and, leaving a kiss for the coming stranger, goes to sea for a four years' voyage.

Katie, with a daughter's love, looks into the mother's eyes, and says,

"We're lonesome, now that father's gone."

"Lonesome, dear? not a bit of it. We have a clean hearth and a husband at sea. What more can woman desire?"

In such a severe atmosphere no school-boy love could flourish, but Posey had heroic stuff in him. The idea never entered his head to slip his cables and drift out of action. He recalled the servitude of Jacob for the woman he loved, and he said, "It is a little thing to serve one voyage for Kate; and if I am only lucky enough to have Mr. F—— put me on a whale, I won't miss, be right sure." Such was Posey, the banished school-master.

The starboard watch was on deck one day, when Posey gave us the following "key to Nantucket's success in the whale-fishery:"

"From the first, our people clubbed their means to build or buy the vessel, and many of the necessary branches of labor were conducted by those immediately interested in the voyage. The young men of the island, with few exceptions, were brought up to some trade necessary to the business. The rope-maker, the cooper, the blacksmith, in brief, the workmen, were either the owners of the vessels, or were connected with the families of the capitalists. While the ship and part of her owners were at sea, the remainder in interest were busily employed at home preparing an outfit for the succeeding voyage. The cooper, while employed in making the casks, took good care that they were of sound and seasoned wood, lest they might leak his oil in the long voyage; the blacksmith forged the choicest iron in the

LIGHT-HOUSE, SANKATY HEAD.

shank of the harpoon,
which he knew, perhaps from actual
experience, would be put to the severest test in wrenching and twisting, as the whale, in which he had a
one-hundredth interest, was secured;
the rope-maker faithfully tested each yarn of the tow-line,
to make certain that it would carry two hundred pounds'
strain, for he knew that one weak inch in his work might
lose to him his share in a fighting monster; the very women
and girls who made the clothing remembered in their toil
that father, brother, or one yet dearer to them, might wear
the garment, and extra stitches were lovingly thrown in to
save the loss of button and prevent the ripping of a seam.
Thus the profits of the labor were enjoyed by those interested in the fishery, and voyages were advantageous even
when the price of oil was barely sufficient to pay the outfit, estimating the labor as part of it.

"How could the British capitalist, who required a net profit, compete with this industrious hive of co-operationists? His Government aided him by a bounty equal to $10 per ton on the burden of his ship, protected him by excessive duties on American oil, and granted immunities to his seamen. All was in vain, and he was compelled to yield the field. Listen also to the words in praise of our whaler, penned by a hand that wielded harpoon and lance as successfully as the pen. Obed Macy, of Nantucket, tells us: 'His youth and strength, his manhood and experience, are devoted to a life of great labor and much peril. His boyhood anticipates such a life, and aspires after its highest responsibilities, while his age delights in recounting its incidents. For deeds of true valor, done without brutal excitement, but in the honest and lawful pursuit of a means of livelihood, we may safely point to the life of the whaleman, and challenge the world to produce a parallel. The widow and orphan mourn not over his success; oppression and tyranny follow not in his paths; his wife and children reap the reward of his toils and danger, and his prosperity is his country's honor.'"

"Every word of that is true," said the captain, who was listening to Posey, while his thoughts were doubtless soaring beyond the snow-capped Cordilleras, to a quiet home, and wife, children, and friends, near the distant hills of New England.

CHAPTER IV.

A brave, righteous Man first Settler of Nantucket.—Early English and
Dutch History of Whaling.—Bounties and Immunities granted by Britain.—Captain Wilkes's Picture of American Whaling.—Preparation to
weather the Cape.—Able Seamanship of our Whale Captains.—Constant Vigilance of Captain B——, and slight Toss of Whalemen.—
Where the Whaleman shows to best advantage.—Run to 62° S. latitude, and meet a favoring Gale.—The "Lay" and Fibre of a Cape
Yarn: Hinton's last Passage around.—The great icy Barrier, and Home
of Mother Carey.—A Gale of Wind in the Ice.

THE first white who settled the island of Nantucket was
Thomas Macy, a brave, righteous man, a hater of tyranny,
a contemner of religious bigotry, a hero in every particular
fibre of his being; right worthy of founding a community so
virtuous, hardy, and adventurous, whose members by their
lives have made their desert island a monument of human
enterprise more enduring than bronze or marble.

"Having my hand in," said the school-master, "I would
like to reach down into the ages and show you how ancient
is our craft, and how honorable it was held above all other
commercial enterprises by the rulers of the Old World, and
how desirable was the business to the governments of great
nations. I would like to show you how princely bounties
to the merchant, and privileged exemption to the mariners,
have failed in hiring England's sea-dogs to hunt the grandest
of ocean's game. Thus you may realize what the American
has done, unaided save by his natural attributes, in winning
unexampled success in this grand and hazardous vocation.

"That our craft excited a lively interest in the English at

a very early period in their commercial history, is shown by Alfred's account of Ohther's adventures; and we find in Hakluyt's voyages that, in 1598, an honest merchant requests, in a letter to a friend of his, 'to be advised and directed in the course of killing a whale.' The answer conveyed the information that 'all the necessary officers were to be had from Biscay, whose people had pursued the hazardous business since A.D. 1390.'

"The English went on, from 1598, unrivaled with their whale-fishery in Greenland, until 1612, when the Dutch first resorted thither; whereupon the English-Russia Company's ships seized the oil, fishing-tackle, etc., of the Dutch, and obliged them to return home, threatening that, if they were ever found in those seas thereafter, prizes would be made of their ships and cargoes. The English whalers claimed that their master, the King of Great Britain, had the sole right of the fishery, by virtue of the first discovery thereof. The natural result of this peculiarly English proceeding was, that in 1613, while the English sent thirteen ships, the Dutch sent eighteen ships, four of which were men-of-war of the States, and they fished in spite of the English companies' pretensions.

"In 1617 the quarrels ran very high between the English and the Dutch. The former persisted in seizing one part of the oil; and this is the first time mention is made that the fins or whalebone were taken home with the blubber, although probably before this date it came into use for women's stays, etc., through the Biscay fishermen. The whales, never having been disturbed, resorted to the bays and the seas near the shores, and their blubber was easily landed, and the oil extracted in boilers which were left standing from year to year. But after the violation of their sanctuary the whales became less frequent in the bays, and commonest among the ice farther from the land. The ships followed them thither, and the blubber could no longer be landed, but had to be cut from the floating whale in small pieces, and brought home in casks for boiling. The new method of fishing was often found dangerous to man, and perilous to shipping. So discouraged were the English adventurers, that they soon afterward relinquished the fishery, until the time of Charles II. In 1618, with respect to the whale-fishing of Holland, De Witte quotes Sievan Van Aitzma, who says 'that the whale-fishery to the northward employs about 12,000 men at sea.' Anderson, in his 'Annals of Commerce,' treats this as an exaggeration.

"In 1634 'The Dutch Greenland Company' made an experiment of the possibility of human beings living through a whole winter at Spitzbergen, till then believed to be impossible. They left seven of their sailors to winter there, one of whom kept a diary from the 11th day of September to the 26th of February following. The men were then down with the scurvy, and their limbs were benumbed with the cold, so that they could in no way help themselves. They were found dead in the house they had built for themselves, on the return of the ships in 1635. In 1670, Sir Joseph Child, in 'Discourses on Trade,' informs us that in 'the Greenland whale-fishery the Dutch and Hamburgers have annually four or five hundred ships, and the English only *one* ship last year, and none in the former one.' In an account of the Dutch whale-fishery for forty-six years ending in 1721, we are informed that the 5886 voyages made had secured 32,906 whales, valued at £16,000,000, a clear gain out of the sea, mostly by the labor of the people.

"In 1740 England made a determined effort to establish the business in her dominions. To this end she granted an additional bounty to those formerly established; making in all thirty shillings per ton for each voyage on the ships employed; and to induce her mariners to engage in the business it was enacted 'that no harpooner, line-manager, boat-steerer, or seaman in that service should be impressed into the naval service.' Such immunity from the odious tyranny of the press-gang, we should think, would have flooded the whaling service with seamen; but no! the perils of this fishery were more terrible to the English imagination than forced service under the thunder of great guns. Eight years later, the bounty was increased to £2 per ton on the ships employed, and the foreigner was invited to do for England that which British seamen failed to do. The following was enacted: 'Foreign Protestants who shall serve three years on board British whale-fishery ships, and shall take the usual qualification oaths, shall be deemed natural born subjects of Great Britain to all intents and purposes, as far as other foreign Protestants can so be.' Such is the evidence that the 'jolly British sea-dogs,' the 'hearts of oak,' had no hankering for the whale fight, and that Britannia could not rule that wave at least. Now the hand of the American whaleman is first felt in the markets of the world. Nantucket, in the year 1761, employed ten vessels of one hundred tons each; in 1762, fifteen vessels; in 1763, above eighty vessels; 'whereupon,' says M'Pherson's Annals, 'the increase of the quantity of whalebone imported from New England to Britain reduced the price of whalebone from £500 to £350 per ton.' From these annals we also learn that in the thirty-nine years to 1788 the whaling voyages made from Britain numbered 2874, and the sum expended from the treasury in bounties amounted to £1,687,902.

"The British Government continued to manifest the liveliest solicitude in the development of the fishery, and in 1795 the following additional bounties were granted: 'To the vessel proceeding to the Pacific Ocean, continuing four months upon the fishing-ground, and, after being sixteen months out, having the greatest quantity of clear sperm-oil,

£600; to each of the seven having the next greatest quantity, £500.' And it was further provided by the act of June 22, 1795, 'that foreigners, not exceeding forty in number, who had previously been employed in the occupation of fishing for whales, and were owners of vessels, should be permitted to come to Milford Haven, in Pembrokeshire, with their families and vessels, not exceeding twenty in number, each vessel being manned by at least twelve seamen accustomed to the fishery. They were allowed to import their goods, furniture, and stock, duty free, on giving security for their residence at least three years in Great Britain. They were then entitled to the premiums granted to British fishermen, and in general to all the rights and privileges of natural-born subjects.'

"Opposed to this picture, I quote Captain Wilkes: 'The American whaling-fleet now (in 1840) counts six hundred and seventy-five vessels, the greater part of which are ships of four hundred tons burden, amounting in all to two hundred thousand tons. The majority of these vessels cruise in the Pacific Ocean; between sixteen and seventeen thousand of our countrymen are required to man them. The value of the fleet is estimated at not less than twenty-five millions of dollars, yielding an annual return of five millions, extracted from the ocean by hard toil, exposure, and danger.' This wonderful success of our whalemen has been achieved in the face of an almost complete destruction of the ships in the two wars with Great Britain, and entirely unaided by any particular encouragement by Government in the form of privileges or pecuniary aid."

Having transgressed the directions of my good angel, and remembering that to become statistical is felonious, I beg your pardon, good reader, and promise to abstain therefrom most religiously hereafter. Posey has had his scholarly say, and we will clap a stopper on his tendency to figures.

Approaching the cape, the inexperienced were somewhat daunted by the preparations our prudent captain made to meet the boisterous nature of this passage from the eastward. All the spars above the topmasts were sent down, the anchors taken from the bows, the stocks removed, and the ponderous iron securely lashed to the deck ring-bolts forward. Our boats were taken from the cranes and secured on the over-deck spars, spare topmast, and yards; scuttle-butts were double-lashed; and the cook's house was strengthened by the proper disposition of the lighter spars. Merchantmen and hide-droghers may smile at such precautions on the part of whaling captains, especially considering the strength of their crews; but it must be kept in mind that we came to get oil, not to risk the ship in boastful display of fancy sailing. We frequent seas where repair of damage is difficult or impossible. Our resources are within ourselves, and we husband our strength until we arrive on the actual field of operations.

A man-of-war's-man may anchor in the rollers in the bars of well-known harbors, and be held to her surging cables, with imminent risk to the ship and death to part of her crew, although, confessedly, to retrieve the error, they have but to slip their cables and drift into the calm harbor in full sight. Such was the case of the *Vincennes* on the bar of San Francisco; and another such lubberly feat sent the gallant *Peacock* to the bottom on the bar of Columbia River. No captain of a whale-ship would again sail in command who was guilty of such manifest ignorance of seamanship. The officers in this service are held to such strict accountability for the safe return of the ship, after the longest voyages, and the greatest actual sea-service, that their vigilance is incessant and unexampled. Loss by fire, or the powerful drift of currents during calm, or by the crushing of floating ice, may be shown to be unavoidable cause of wreck; but seldom may a whaling captain plead stress of weather or error in reckoning, ignorance of entrance to harbors, or the dangers of bars, as a valid defense for the loss of his ship. · I was continually impressed by the unceasing vigilance of Captain B—— to keep the exact run of the ship. The log was as regularly kept as though we ran by dead-reckoning; and we were running almost in mid-ocean, with land hundreds of miles from our known position. Yet every clear night, or whenever a break in the clouds admitted the observation, the captain would glide silently on deck, sextant in hand, and, taking his seat at the head of a quarter-boat, would abide his time to get his meridian by the passage of some star of the many brilliant constellations in the southern heavens. Not once, but perhaps several times in a night, he sat star-gazing and full of anxious care, while the thoughtless youngsters were listening to the song and the yarn, thinking of the good time the "old man" had, and wondering why captains grew gray-haired so early. The highest testimony to the seamanship of our whalemen is that the rate of insurance on the American is just one-half of that on the British vessels engaged in the service. In illustration of this point, Macy informs us that the whole number of Nantucket vessels lost, exclusive of captures in war, since the settlement of the island to 1835, is 168; viz., 78 sloops, 31 schooners, 18 brigs, and 41 ships. Yet for many years Nantucket had 150 ships at sea, on voyages of great length, and in distant, dangerous, and unexplored seas, unaided by correct charts or sailing directions. The loss of lives by wreck in this time was but 414.

Unquestionably the seamanship of the American whaling captain is of the highest order in every respect, and many of the most successful and adventurous commanders of packet and clipper ships graduate in this school. The seamen educated in whaling have no superiors in the substantial el-

3*

ements of the sailor, although they may lack the jaunty tie of the cravat, the saucy cock of the new tarpaulin of other sailors, and may make less parade of their peculiarities on shore. To be sure, they are clumsy and rough as the walrus on dry land, but they only need the wash of deep blue water and the excitement of the chase to bring the true elements of their character to the surface. No one can witness the change which attends actual service in the boats, without astonishment. The dull, sluggish, and sleepy become full of animation, dash, and endurance.

Fortunately our careful preparations were needless. We made what was considered a good passage going west, head-winds and the set of a head-current forcing us into 62° S., when a cape gale from the south-east sent us scudding "norrard" at railroad speed. The log reported fifteen miles an hour, continued with a nearly equal rate for forty hours, and left us fairly round the cape with the broad Pacific before us. Many were the stories of prolonged storm and terrible suffering endured in the passage of the cape. At certain seasons the great south-west storms buffet the outward-bound ship for weeks, and she drifts before it, laying to, and becoming unmanageable from the accumulation of ice on her hull and rigging. We youngsters had the benefit of a relation of these experiences, and consoled ourselves with the thought that it would be at least three years before we would again encounter the stormy cape.

The following gorgeous and mythical story by Hinton will give an idea of the "lay" and fibre of a Cape Horn yarn:

"We had made a good voyage. The *Chelsea* was full of oil, and we were homeward-bound. We had mounted a new suit of sails in Talcahuana—stay-sails, double-stitched —and the old beauty was in perfect trim, except that her copper was rolled up, and the grass and barnacles fouled .

her bottom, causing us to lose about two or three knots' headway. We got pretty well up with the cape, when a south-east gale struck us and headed us off. We battered against it for eight days, when we found ourselves in 68° S., and about 130° W. Here we came in sight of the great ice-barrier, extending far as the eye could reach, plumb up and down, two hundred feet or more. This was the great shining wall, beyond which, we are told by the scientists of a couple of hundred years ago, lies the great open sea of the Antarctic, where dwell nations of mermen and maids; krakens, with 'amethyst and golden antennæ, of power and scope to entangle and draw down great ships; and sea-serpents of hideous mien, and fathoms in length;' where, in a wondrous palace of ice, dwells the southern ice-king, who drives the frost-fiends to labor on icebergs, and store treasures of the hail and snow; where the marmicle and marmate gambol in fields of the giant kelp, and herd the countless shoals of mackerel and herring; where the ivory-toothed walrus and the shag-maned sea-lion keep guard over the nests of the uniformed penguin and the albatross: a sea, in whose calm waters the wounded whale finds sanctuary against the pursuit of the hunters of the open ocean. Here the worried whales find peace, and grow in blubber on the crimson carpets of medusæ. There are no threshers there to club the old backs; no sword or saw fish to stab and scarify; no Nimrods to harpoon and lance, to mangle, tear, and boil. Above this sea a six months' sun has four or five counterfeits, and paints the leaden sky with rings, and crosses, and crescents of colored fires; and the six months' night is illumined by the coruscations of the aurora borealis.

"In the centre of this sea is a circular marble throne, whose base has three hundred and sixty divisions, from which meridian lines run out and span the great world;

ana from its centre rises a pole of electric light reaching
upward into the heavens to the constellation of the Southern Cross.   On this throne sits Mother Carey, the fashioner
and maker of millions upon millions of new creations of
more varied shapes, colors, qualities, and functions than

any but little children ever dreamed of. She sits quite still with her chin upon her hand, looking down into the sea with two great, grand blue eyes, as blue as the sea itself. Her hair is as white as the snow, for she is very, very old—in fact, as old as any thing which you are likely to come across, except the difference between right and wrong.

"Such is the sea beyond the ice-barrier, as our fathers believed it to exist, even after Columbus taught the world how to make an egg stand on its end.

"To come back to my story, however," Hinton continued: "As we stood by the ice-wall, the weather thickened, and a heavy snow shut out the ice. We were standing along under close-reefed maintop-sail, reefed courses, and try-sail. The spray of the sea went right to ice as it touched the deck and rigging. We were heading aslant the wall; it was still light enough to see that we were among floating ice, and we could catch glimpses of the cloud-like outlines of great bergs, which it would be destruction to touch. The captain stood under the lee of the mainmast, his clothes covered with ice, giving orders to the men at the wheel. The wheel was double manned, and the mate stood by to see that the helm was well served. The wind was piping its strongest, and the combing seas were such as are only to be seen off Cape Horn. The drift and ice islands came on us thicker and faster. Once we passed to the windward of a great iceberg, higher than the mast-heads, and we held our breath as we listened to the thunder of the great waves, which one moment tossed our little craft, and the next burst with awful force against the ice under our lee.

"We suffered very much from the cold; our clothes were stiff with ice. We were dashing blindly on, but with good steerage-way, and the ship answered quickly to her helm, although she ran deep by the head on account of the accumulated ice on her bows and head-hamper. Now the cry came, 'Ice ahead!' Then, on the weather or on the lce bow, the pounding and grinding of the rocking bergs, the roar of the breakers, and the awful tone of the wind as it cut through the strained rigging, almost drowned the hoarse orders of the captain as they came through his trumpet. So we dashed through the darkness and blinding snow, every eye awake to watch for ice; every ear expecting the crack of doom.

CHAPTER V.

The Aurora Borealis, and Explanation.—Coleridge's Mistake in the "Antient Mariner."—The Mother Carey's Chicken.—Ben moralizes on this little Bunch of Feathers.—Captain Folger's Luck.—The Devil no Match for a Gale of Wind off Cape Horn when the Skipper is bound to carry.—The Cape doubled, and we come on Cruising-ground.—Boats' Crews Watches established.—Idle Time on Cruising-ground.—The Length of Cruises.—Fasten to our first Whale.—Crew behave well; the Whale killed.—Disappointed in Size of Whale.

"At times the ship was almost on her beam-ends, and the sea was making clean breaches over the bows and waist. Great surges would leap in the air and drop on her deck, making our timbers, to the very keelson, twist and tremble. The poor ship groaned and complained like a sick man. Masses of ice, too, swept across with the water and carried away the rail and planking of the bulwarks. Suddenly the overborne ship righted and rolled easily on an even keel. So close were we under the lee of a great iceberg that we rode as if we were in a harbor; but the roar of the storm was all around and above our heads. We drew slowly ahead, and came out into the storm again, but as far as we could see there was open water, and we felt as though we were saved. Toward morning it cleared away, and in the lull of the storm we could hear the puff of whales as they were making south for the icy wall. Now and then a gleaming light would play along the front of the great wall, and bring every crag and peak into radiant relief against the jet-black sky. Old Captain Davis said it was a beacon-light to guide every creature that sought its shelter.

"The next day, with wind north-west, we stood for the cape, and saw no more of the ice-wall; but the following night we saw a bow of shooting lights, reaching a great distance across the sky, shooting and waving tender colors, now opening and shutting like a fan, now lighted up with crimson fires. Oh, man alive! you should see this glory of the southern sky as we saw it that night, and you would dream, with John, that you were looking into the gates of the New Jerusalem! I heard the old man say that these lights only reflected the brilliancy of the crystal palaces, and the colors of the bright waters of the sea beyond the shining wall."

As Hinton concluded, some one recited from the "Antient Mariner:"

> "The ice was here, the ice was there,
>   The ice was all around;
> It cracked and growled, and roared and howled,
>   Like voices in a swound.
>
> At length did cross the albatross,
>   Thorough the fog it came;
> As if it had been a Christian soul,
>   We hailed it in God's name.
>
> "It ate the food it ne'er had eat,
>   And round and round it flew;
> The ice did split in a thunder-fit,
>   The helmsman steered us through."

This started a discussion among the savants about the curious mistake the poet had made in attaching this superstition of a protective guidance to the great albatross, instead of to the little floating, skimming "Mother Carey's chicken."

"Why, you see," said Coffin, "the albatross carries such a spread of sail that he's busy enough takin' care of himself in a gale, and you find him huggin' close to the ship in good weather only, and then he's lookin' for grub. But the worse the gale the more chippy is this little black butterfly of a Mother Carey, and no man's heart feels lost while he sees the little specks finding a safe lee from the hurricane right under the comb of the breaking rollers. You young 'uns may laugh at me for soft, but I tell you when you get as old as me you'll know a darned sight less than you do now. In the worst gale I ever was in off Cape Horn, where the gales are the worst of any place in this world, a great sea ran from under the keel, and let the ship down so fast that you could hardly keep with her, and you'd grab the rigging to keep along. And when the ship struck the bottom of the trough with a chuck that made her tremble as if she had an ague fit, and the on-coming sea, high as the mainyard, was a-rollin' down us with a hissin' comb, and the dark wall of water was so straight up that I thought it would breach thirty feet over us—in the very worst of this a whole flock of Mother Carey's chickens came down, hovering close under the breaking white-cap, safe harbored from the blast. I thought of the promise that as the sparrows are cared for so would we be; and whenever I saw these little bunches of black feathers playin' safe in the hollow of the sea, I never could get up much of a scare as to what would happen to me." Our men all felt that bad fortune would attend the killing of one of these little birds, and I found something of the same feeling among the sailors of other ships.

Among the yarns of the cape, a favorite one with our crew was "the dismasting of the *Ironsides* under the lucky Captain Folger."

"He was always lucky," said Harry, "and never more lucky than the night off Cape Horn when he lost every spar to the stumps, ten feet above deck. I'll tell you how it was. Ours was the luckiest ship that sailed from Nantucket, and the captain was the luckiest man that ever trod shoe-leather. He had made five voyages to the Pacific; come home full, 'Chock-a-block;' never over two years out; and he never lost man, boat, or spar. There was not a boat-steerer but was glad to go on a one-hundredth 'lay,' and he'd get rich at that. I went with Folger on his sixth voyage, and steered Mr. Starbuck, the first mate. In twenty - one months we were off the cape, homeward-bound, try-works overboard, and every thing that would hold oil—case-bottles, captain's boots, and medicine-chest—was filled with head matter. We hadn't a man hurt, not even the skin scraped off a man's shin in the rigging, and that, you know, is extraordinary. Nor had·we a plank started in a boat, or a spar sprung. The whales would seem to spout thick blood if they were struck forrard of the hump, and the main course would seem to furl itself in a gale. Something was wrong about the ship, and our good luck frightened us. Well, we were off the cape; the night was as black as my hair, a stiffish breeze was over the quarter, and we headed free on a course, every sail drawing.

"We were makin' a splendid run, when Mr. Starbuck ordered top-gallant sails in; but before we started halyards or sheets, Captain Folger put his head up the companion-way and sung out, 'Stand fast there; belay all, and let her run. Excuse me, Mr. Starbuck, but I've the cards in my hand to-night, and mean to play the game out. Please crack on her as long as she'll carry.' So we forged on for half an hour, when the wind hauled abeam, and we braced the yards forrard. This brought us down, scuppers under. The captain was on the weather quarter-deck holding on to the mizzen rigging; Mr. Starbuck was opposite to him, leaning against the companion-way. Two men were at the helm. The old ship was brought to her best bearings for a run, and was plowing a wake of foaming light through the dark waves. The whistle of the wind was changing to a hoarse growl that meant business. Every thing was terribly strained, when the old man called across to the mate, 'This is heavenly, Mr. Starbuck; heavenly breezes, sir; more heavenly than you have any idea of. Hold on to every stitch, but keep a sharp lookout to windward, and if you see any break in the gale, keep her off a point or two and get out stormsails.' We were gathered close to leeward, and thought the old man was clean daft; but we had no help for it.

"The wind piped stronger and stronger. Great white-combed seas burst out of the darkness to windward, smote us broadside on, and went roaring over the bows into the night. The snapping of the rigging and the creaking heard in the very heart of the mainmast told of the fearful work aloft. We stood every man alone with his fears. The only face we could see was the captain's, as a gleam from the binnacle-light fell on him. We were more frightened by his insane joy than by the gale, as every now and then he repeated 'Heavenly breezes, Mr. Starbuck!' At this time it seemed as though nothing made by man could stand the strain. The ship seemed actually to leap from sea to sea, as you see the dolphin chase flying-fish. She never pitched, but, right flat to her work, she hissed through the water as though she were red-hot iron. Just then a new sound was heard away up in the darkness. It was like the angry snort of a locomotive on an up grade. Sharp and mad it came above the howl and rush of the storm. We could hardly help screaming as we looked up and saw two lights in the air right over the royal-yard. From this out my telling takes more time than the happening.

"A voice, shrill as a steam-whistle, hailed from aloft:

"'On deck there!'

"'Ay, ay,' replied old Folger, calm, but glad as a boy.

"'Is Captain Folger on deck?'

"'At his post.'

"'Captain, I can't hold on much longer.'

"'Belay all, and hold on.'

"And we dashed on, the crew gallied almost to death.

"'How do you head?' shouted the captain to the man at the wheel.

"'Steady on her course, sir?'

"'How does she steer?'

"'Easy as in a calm, sir; haven't shifted the wheel two spokes in the last hour!'

"'Good; keep her steady; and you to leeward there, keep a stiff upper lip and trust to me!'

"And he called Mr. Starbuck over to him, and said:

"'I know the ties that are towing your thoughts homeward to-night. Now if you love that wife and your children, as you hope to see them again, don't fail me now; keep your eye to windward, and watch the wind; if you feel a lull to the moving of a feather the less, let me know it somehow, but don't speak it aloud for your soul's salvation.'

"Again came the voice:

"'On deck there!'

"'Ay, ay.'

"'Captain, release me. My punishment is more than I can bear.'

"'Remember your bond, and hold on.'

"Here a broad flash of lightning illuminated sails, masts, and every line of the rigging, and the wild seas. Every thing for an instant was white in light, save a giant shadow which seemed to hold the span, from the flying jib-boom to main-royal, in its wide clutch. This horrible thing stood black against the lighted storm; and in the bellowing thunder came the voice, 'I am dead beat!' At that moment the mate pointed a break to windward.

"'May I let go, Captain Folger?' came from aloft in a choking sob, like the spout of a sperm-whale when he stran-

CAPTAIN FOLGER'S LUCK.

gles with thick blood. The captain, with a wild scream, cried,

"'In the name of God let go, and my soul is saved!'

"And with a tearing crash the stays parted, and masts, sails, and the whole top-hamper of the *Ironsides* swept away to leeward, and were swallowed in the darkness, our poor ship rolling helpless in the trough of the sea. All of which goes to show that the de'il himself can't hold to a bargain, if he has a Cape Horn gale against him in it.'"

Having made a good offing of the dreaded cape, we slanted along the coast of Patagonia and Chili, until we reached the southern limit of the "off shore" ground, in lat. 38° S., when it was announced that we had reached whale-ground, after a run of about three months. The passage accomplished, and the cruising begun, my journal becomes more regular, and the business of whaling will now occupy our attention.

Feb. 7. Up to this time the crew has been divided into two watches. Now that we are on cruising-ground, a new disposition is made of our forces. Cruising on whaling-ground consists in running over as much space as the wind will permit during the hours of day, and remaining as immovable as possible during the night. For this purpose we carry sail in the day, and at sunset take in sail, lying under jib, doubled-reefed top-sails, foresail, and spanker, with the mainyard aback. Thus a small force is required on deck during the night, and as the toil in the boats is excessive, the men are allowed all the rest and sleep that the nature of the service will allow. The crew is divided into four boat's-crew watches, headed by their respective boat-steerers. A single boat's crew has the deck by night, and two crews by day, strengthened by the cooper, carpenter, and cook, who do not stand night-watches. This gives the men three-fourths of the night below and one-half the day, when they are not in the boats.

No unnecessary work on sails and rigging is done on the cruising-ground, as all energies are husbanded for the emergencies which arise in the toilsome chase. Thus, after a long cruise, a whaler presents a woefully bleached and ragged appearance, with her ragged or well-patched sails and loose ratlines flying in the the wind, until scarce foothold is left to shin aloft. The seizings and servings are frayed and crazy, the canvas is blackened with the sooty smoke of burning scraps in the try-works, and the poor hull, with the damaged paint of her fancy work, is but a sorry ghost of the neat ship which left port perhaps eight months ago. In this condition, as she creeps into port to refit, our whaler is a subject of merriment and sport to green hide-droghers and simple merchantmen, who are seldom at sea long enough to soil the paint of their ships, or to get their sea-legs and the manners of deep soundings aboard. But think, dear reader, of eight long months with sea and sky alone above and about us! Three-quarters of a long year, and not a glimpse of God's blessed land! Might not these ephemera of the sea make allowance for us communicants with the wildernesses of the ocean?

> "Oh, wedding guest! this soul hath been
> Alone on the wide, wide sea:
> So lonely 'twas, that God himself
> Scarce seemed there to be."

This 7th of February the life of the voyage commences. The morning watch washed down decks, manned the mast-heads, made sail, braced forward, and kept a lookout for whales—all the sharper, since yesterday we struck into great numbers of the floating mollusks, the "Portuguese man-of-war," and had great schools of fish (the albicon) about us. These are evidences that we are at such a meeting of the great oceanic currents as constitute the feeding-grounds of

IN A SCHOOL.

the sperm-whale. As the daylight revealed a sail to windward, the captain, thinking the neighborhood too populous,
ordered, "Up with your helm, and square in the yards,"
and we ran off to leeward. At 8 A.M. we raised sperm-
whale on the starboard beam, luffed to the wind, and at 9
lowered away all four boats. After a long following to leeward for twenty miles, the mate and second mate got iron
into a fine bull whale. After a fierce struggle, he ran out
one line and wrenched out the irons of the other, then coming to windward head out. The two unfortunate boats
made desperate efforts to overhaul the flying game, but the
whale made two miles to their one, and we should have lost
him but for a favorite manœuvre of Captain B——, who lay
well to windward for just such flying chances. We worked
across so as to intercept the whale's course, and with sails
and oars we stood directly in a line with his great square
snout, which was thrown eight feet in the air at every spout.

Tugging away at the bow-oar, I had no share in the sport
until his great black head rushed into sight just outside my
oar-blade, and his polished, glistening body rounded out as
we swiftly passed. A slight backward check of the boat
told that Chipman was at work, and two planted iron poles
under the hump told us that we were fast. The thundering
flaps of the whale's flukes, and the quantity of white foam
and spray, are all I can recall of the instant preceding the
rapid whirl of the boat, as it swung to the tow of the line,
and followed the mad whale. Long John, midship oarsman, a little white about the gills, was disposed to be funny,
and in a rather tremulous voice remarked that "his quid
was shifted to the wrong side by the sudden jerk, and that
was the reason he didn't trim the boat." The fact is, John,
with some others of our crew, thought it was in order to
jump overboard as soon as the irons were in the whale.
But, on the whole, we did creditably, and Captain B—— had

a word of encouragement for us. He said he had hopes that in time we would be steady, and to be depended on.

A great many things were done with boat and lance incomprehensible to me. I was alone responsible for the bow-oar, and I pulled and starned, as the rapid orders came from the captain or boat-steerer. In good time, thick blood was spouted, the flurry followed, and a dead whale, floating fin out, was lying ahead of our boat. We were still to leeward of the ship. She ran down, and luffed to the wind, with the foreyard aback. This brought the whale on the weather-side, with the tail toward the bows; and then, by a curious arrangement of buoy and line, a heavy fluke-chain was secured around the small at the junction of the body with the flukes, while the other end, through a side hawse-hole, was brought to the windlass bitts. The cutting-in falls for the morrow's work. I had time to look over the side, and try to study a sperm-whale; but as he lay alongside, exposing but a small part of his bulk, I was disappointed in his apparent size. My notions regarding the leviathan had been somewhat loose, and I had a general idea that a whale was as large as a Pennsylvania barn. I set this fellow down as a baby, perhaps, but was disenchanted by a remark of the second mate that we would see few larger. Our capture was estimated at eighty-five barrels. That night we turned in with blistered hands but easy consciences.

Feb. 8. The ship we had seen to windward ran down to speak us. As she approached it was plain that a whaler on the cruise could not be mistaken in her calling. The large number of beautiful boats on her cranes, the cumbersome try-works amidships, the two enormous blocks lashed to the mainmast-heads for " cutting-in " (or *flensing,* as the English writers term it), and the men at the mast-head, all proclaimed her occupation.

CHAPTER VI.

The *Phœnix*, of Nantucket. — "Cutting-in" first Whale. — Boat-steerer goes over the Side to hook on.—Choice between drowning and Sharks. —Immense Power required.—Blanket-piece.—Misapprehension regarding Size corrected.—Deep Surgery.—The Head.—The Junk.—The Case, and the Bailing.—The Spermaceti Bath.—Contents of the Case.— Trying-out, and Ship drifting.—Bill in the Blubber-room.—Night Scene in trying-out.—The Suffering of this first Night.—But we will soon harden to that.—Want of Sleep.—Sleeping at Wheel and Mast-head.— Always tired, and never wide awake.—Moralizing on the same.

THUS equipped, the *Phœnix*, of Nantucket, ran under our stern. She was commanded by Captain Huzzie, sixteen months out, with 1100 barrels of oil. On Saturday last she took two whales, making 170 barrels. We reported clean hold, but grease alongside. We had no time for civilities, and, hastily touching hats, we parted company, she, with mast-heads manned, luffing to the wind as we turned to the hard work of cutting-in the whale.

> "Roused from repose, aloft the sailors swarm,
> And with their levers soon the windlass arm ;
> They lodge their bars, and wheel their engine round,
> At every turn the clanging pawls resound."

The "cutting-in" of a large whale is truly a formidable undertaking. It is surgery, or dissection, on a gigantic scale, and the appliances are of corresponding magnitude and power. From the head of the mast two great sheave-blocks depend, through which is run a Manila rope of about eight inches circumference. This passes through a corresponding traveling-block, to which, in the commencement of the operation, a heavy iron hook is attached by a clevis and bolt.

The fall leads from the upper or fixed block to the windlass, around the smooth, hollowed end of which the necessary number of turns are taken—all the men, save the cook and the men at mast-head and wheel, standing by to lend a hand. The whale is floating on its side on the starboard beam of the ship, and is hauled forward until the eye comes opposite the gangway. The rail and side-planks above the deck having been removed, this brings the first point of attack directly under the tackles. Two narrow stages are slung over the side, on which, secured by waist, belt, and monkey-rope, the officers stand to cut, as may be needed, with sharp, broad-edged spades mounted on poles sixteen or more feet long.

We begin by cutting a round hole in the tough formation termed "white horse," about the eye. Then, by a semi-circular cut above, and to one side of the eye about two feet in radius, the first cut is prolonged toward the ship, so as to form a flap of about four feet in width. Now one of the boat-steerers appears, rigged in an old woolen suit, with woolen stockings — a material that grips the smooth skin of the whale and prevents the wearer from slipping. He has a monkey-rope about his waist, and when the tackle is overhauled until the hook is at the proper height, he descends on to the whale, and inserts the hook in the hole by the eye. This is drowning work when the sea is rough enough to wash heavily over the partly submerged whale; it is arduous when the irregular roll of the mast-head sways and jerks the ponderous block and hook; it is dangerous when the roll of the ship and whale may catch the man between them; and, lastly, it is unpleasant from the proximity of half a score of hungry sharks intent on blubber, but which are liable to mistake a floating head, leg, or arm for a part of the whale, and claim it as legitimate toll. Against these inconveniences the spades of

"CUTTING-IN."

the officers and the management of the monkey-rope are guards.

The hook is inserted and the order given "Haul taut and heave away." Sixteen men double manning the hand-spikes, responsively heave away at the powerful windlass, while the spades are busy under-cutting to free and tear up the eye-flap. The great surge of the rolling ship greatly aids in this effort, and soon the strip of blubber, termed the "blanket," slowly moves upward. This is the moment seized by the artist in the illustration. The floating whale is shown with head partially dissevered, and with the spiral cuts which are to lead the unrolling of the blanket. When the cry of "To blocks" announces that the head of the blanket has reached three-fourths the height of the mainmast, the order is given to "Board blanket-piece." Now a boat-steerer, with a long, double-edged sword, mounted by a long, straight handle, and termed a "boarding-knife," makes a lunge at the swinging mass, cutting out an oval plug of blubber, through which the eye of the strap to the second tackle is thrust, and secured by a heavy oak toggle. Then the order is, heave away on the second tackle, and as soon as the strain is fairly taken by it, a second cut of the boarding-knife detaches the upper blanket-piece, which is swung inboard, immediately over the main-hatch. Here it is lowered into the blubber-room, where a man awaits it with a hook to send the slippery end away to leeward, and pack the long pieces to the best advantage. Thus alternated, the two tackles relieve each other, and the windlass travels almost continuously until four hundred and fifty or five hundred feet of blanket, from four feet eight to eighteen inches in thickness, have passed from the symmetrical form of the whale into the confused, disagreeable mass in the blubber-room.

While the huge carcass is being turned in the water by the unrolling of its valuable blanket, the officer on the forward stage is carrying forward the spiral cut which regulates the width of the blanket, and the older and more experienced officer on the after stage is delicately amputating the head with his sharp spade. He slowly cuts his way through several feet of dark, red, coarse-fibred muscles, rope-like tendons, and blood-vessels through which a little boy might be propelled, and artistically cleaves his way to the junction of the vertebra with the head. Finally, he severs the thick coating of tough integuments, the head separates, and turns, curiously enough, the bony jaw upward, and the case and blow-hole below. Now is revealed the joint of the vertebra, like an exquisitely polished sphere of whitest ivory, in diameter equal to a barrel. This great joint most impressed me with the monstrous proportions of the creature we had been tearing at with windlass, tackles, and spades all this long day. The head thus severed constitutes nearly one-third the length and a greater proportion of the actual bulk of the whale. It is allowed to float under the main-chains until the body is disposed of. After the body of a large whale is stripped to the vent, a second transverse section is made, and the great carcass, a mass of red flesh and white integuments, drifts slowly to windward, soiling the clean water with its slowly-oozing blood, and smoothing the surface with exuding oil. Accompanying it are flocks of albatross ("mollemokes") and other birds above, while the surface of the deep appears cut and fretted by the high, sharp fins and lashing tails of troops of sharks, which ravenously bite at the mountain of food we have provided for them.

The body disposed of, the head occupies our attention. The general form of this immense mass may be better seen in the different illustrations than from description. To obtain the valuable spermaceti with which it abounds, we dissect it into three parts — the " case," junk, and bony part. The latter, containing the skull and lower jaw-bone, is gen-

BAILING THE "CASE."

erally allowed to sink at once (save when teeth are needed to furnish ivory for "skrimshoning," or to trade with the islands). By reference to Fig. 3, page 168, a general idea of the parts may be obtained. The upper part of the head, *a*, is termed the case; between this and the skull-bone is the great wedge-shaped mass, *b*. This is the junk; *d* forms the rejected part; and in this figure the spiral cuts of the blanket are shown. The junk is first hauled in bodily, and thence aft out of the way until the case is bailed. This mass is surrounded, as is the entire head on the outside, by the tough, almost impenetrable white horse, several inches in thickness, which proves a secure armor against the harpoon. Its interior consists of a cellular formation, the walls of the cells running vertically and transversely, varying in thickness from a half-inch to two inches, and being formed of the same closely interlaced fibres of beautiful satin lustre and alabaster whiteness that constitute the white horse of the external head. The cells are of varying size, generally about four to eight inches between the separating layers of white horse, and are filled with an oily substance of a faint yellowish tint, translucent when warm, and rivaling in delicacy of flesh the interior of the ripest water-melon. The clear sweet oil follows every cut which is made into it. The oil-bearing flesh forms about one third of the mass, and in a large whale has yielded twenty-eight barrels—equal to three and a half tons. This would make such a junk about ten and a half tons' weight.

The case has, besides the respiratory canal (which is about twelve inches in diameter), a cavity about twenty feet in depth, filled with oil, which we bail out with buckets. To this end the iron hooks are again attached to the cutting-in tackles, and are inserted in the white horse of the sides. The end of the case is then hauled up to keep the seas from reaching the opening made in it for bailing.

A whip-block is placed directly over the opening; a long, narrow bucket is attached to the end of the fall; and a man stands on the square-cut end, with a long, slender pole to push the bucket into this well of flesh.

On being withdrawn, the bucket is filled with transparent spermaceti, mixed with the soft, silky integuments, and possessing the odor of the new-drawn milk of our home dairies. With our hands blistered yesterday by the oar, and all on fire to-day by the harsh friction of the handspike, it was luxurious to wade deep in the try-pots filled with this odorous unguent, in order to squeeze and strain out the fibres, which, if allowed to remain, would char with the heat, and darken the oil. No king of earth, even Solomon in all his glory, could command such a bath. I almost fell in love with the touch of my own poor legs, as I stroked the precious ointment from the skin.

A case has been known to yield twenty-three barrels of this purest of spermaceti—equal to nearly three tons. As it constitutes less than one-sixth the mass, a case may be estimated at eighteen tons' weight. Add to this the weight of the junk, the skull, and jaws, and an idea may be gathered of the head of a sperm-whale. I would remark that in modern ships the increased power of the patent windlass enables the fortunate possessors to heave the case inboard and bail it on deck by opening it longitudinally, thus saving much precious oil. By our system of bailing, the depth of the bucket was left in the bottom of the well. However, the utmost power of the *Chelsea* could not have brought this case on to the deck. When the case is bailed, the hold is cut away, and, with a solemn plunge, the great mass sinks into the sea, the white-marble surface changing to a purest azure until it sinks from sight.

Now the try-works are brought into play. The boat-crew's watch of yesterday gives way to starboard and lar-

TRYING OUT.

board watches, and the watches on deck and below are prolonged to six hours each. The works are started on the oil of the head, which is termed "head matter." As this was our first whale, it was necessary to use wood as fuel, until we could get the brown doughnut-looking "scraps" out of the remains of the blubber after the oil is boiled out. These scraps are the proper fuel of the try-works, and are always more than sufficient to cook the oil of the whale, so that a quantity remains, and is carried forward to start the works on the next. At six bells in the evening, one watch of tired men hurry below, "to sleep, perchance to dream;" and the other, just as wearied, have before them six hours of labor. The mainyard is aback, mainsail furled, topsails reefed, and the ship rolls lazily on a drifting course to leeward. The duties of the watch are thus divided: One man is in the blubber-room with knife and spade to cleanse the skinny parts and flesh from the blanket, and to reduce it into long narrow pieces, say six by twenty-four inches, termed "horse-pieces." These are tossed to the deck above, and conveyed by another man to the "mincing-horse," where they are sliced into thin leaves, which adhere by the tough inner integument, and are called "books." In this form the blubber passes to the try-pots. The duty of the boat-steerers and the mate, who heads the watch, is to attend to this boiling, as the value of the oil is materially affected by the care used in preserving its light color.

The night scene on the deck of a whaler while she is engaged in trying-out is weird-like in the extreme. The black smoke from the burning scraps, lighted by the red flames which issue from the flues; the tracery of masts, spars, and sails, sometimes brightly lit up as in the roll of the, ship the boiling oil overflows into the furnaces, and sends a broad flame half-mast high; the blood-red reflections from the sea-caps; the diabolical appearance of the stokers

and deck-hands, make a picture which might grace a vision
of Dante's "Inferno!"   Oh, the horrible memory of that first
night's trying-out!   The soreness and fatigue of the long
hours of extreme toil; the deathly drowse that comes over
one while standing, or mechanically performing some mo-
notonous duty; the sliding of the bare feet over the greasy
deck in pools·of greasy and foul water; the dirty clothes,
cold and clammy from the saturating oil; the glare of the
fierce flames, with the impenetrable gloom of the night beyond—hell before, and heaven shut from view, as it were;
the acrid, choking smoke; the sooty deposit in nostril and
on palate; the harsh commands of officers, and the fierce im-
precations of overtasked men — all tended to fill six hours
with wretchedness greater than I have ever since experienced.

But they tell me one soon gets bravely over such sentimental tenderness, and the fatigue, the smear of blood, oil,
and dirt.   The stench and the foul oath will become a matter of course.   I am promised that I shall be habituated to
all, save the tyrannical hold of the awful drowsiness which
pours lead through the veins of the sailor:

> "Oh sleep! it is a gentle thing,
> Beloved from pole to pole!
> To Mary, Queen, the praise be given,
> She sent the gentle sleep from heaven,
> That slid into my soul."

It may appear that we have time enough for sleep, standing watch and watch, or half our time below; yet remember that our best sleep is in snatches of four hours each,
and that even these intervals are broken by the crowding
thoughts of the past.   The tired sailor, as he tumbles into
his coarse, straw-lined bunk, loses precious moments in
dreams of home and of love, so much at variance with his
bitter surroundings.   As a consequence, awaking at mid-

night from his short nap to the duties of the steersman, his nodding head bows to the dancing compass, and the ship luffs, to wake him by the flapping of the sails aloft. Up goes the helm, and he again sleeps until aroused by the cry of the mate, "Mind your helm there, and keep her steady." "Ay, ay, sir;" and, in spite of the mate's little thunder, the sailor has another nap, and the sails again shiver in the wind. The drowsiness is also felt in other ways. One may sit across the slender swaying "royal-yard," with the bare feet dangling in space a hundred and twenty feet over the sea, the thin shroud-stay fitted in the groove of the shoulders, and one arm hooked in the halyard. Thus the sleepy "look-out" swings, "rocked by the billows to and fro," and, in spite of the awful danger, his eyes close. Wrapped in oblivion as sweet as in bed of down, he sleeps, preserved from positive danger by the self-poise and wakeful instinct of the perched bird (perhaps). No officer observing a man in this position will call to him, lest, with the habit of instant obedience, the unfortunate should, with the routine "Ay, ay, sir," start from his narrow perch to almost certain death. The feeling of nervousness and sleepiness is chronic in the whaleman's life on an active cruise over hunting-grounds.

Consider their hardships, you good souls who are truly concerned for Jack's temporal and spiritual welfare, and don't give him over to perdition for his thoughtless carouse, when he is first thrown from the privations of the sea into the allurements and temptations of the shore. Remember that he has endured long months, in which the disagreeable has only been varied by the dangerous, in which he has ranked next below the captain's dog. Make allowance for this poor waif of the sea, when the land-sharks, the keeper of the grog-shop or the brothel, entice him with false smiles, and with open hand of cheery welcome lead him through the gates of hell. Now, I ask you, why should he not enter? All other gates are hermetically sealed to him. A simple glimpse or hope of heaven is shut out from him by the coldness of even Heaven's ministers, and the gates of the Inferno seem inviting, when viewed from the forecastle of many a whale-ship just in from an eight-months' cruise. Good temperance-man as you are, would you dash the cup of temporary oblivion from this poor wretch's lips? You say "it steals his brains." Exactly; that he desires. With a shilling's worth, he becomes a man; with twice that quantity, the old boyhood is with him again; with thrice that, he staggers down the street, and, with his thumb in his armpit, tips his tarpaulin to his captain, bites his thumb-nail at the port admiral, and votes the President a lubber. He feels, for the time, "every inch a man."

Your warning that "he endangers life" has no weight with a being who lives hourly with his life in his hand. Don't plead the joys or duty of life to him who, to save his life, will not waver a step from the line of duty. You preach never so well of Heaven, and plead for his soul in the accepted ways of the churches; but your good words and ways fall weak and meaningless on the ear of the man who lives habitually in the presence of God's mightiest works, and who, in the lonely nightwatches of the silent sea, is forced into communion with the Divine Authority for all things. Careless, thoughtless, and wicked as the sailor may seem, it was not a bad impression I received in my discourses with many seamen in the nightwatches.

CHAPTER VII.

How to save Jack.—Mr. Deil, of Honolulu, tried successfully.—Run down the Coast.—View of the Cordilleras.—Disappointed in the first View of Peru.—Touched at Callao, and ran on to Payta.—Captain ran counter to the Laws.—Chipman prepares to defend the Boat.—Pistol and Lance drawn.—Liberty on Shore, and Effects of Aguadiente.—Adjourn to the Calaboose.—Africa against Peru.—Chips joins the Company in poetic Mood.—The good Captain's Advice and Warning.—Sail from Payta, and anchor at Galapagos.

To save Jack from himself, we must better his conditions of existence; to save him from the evils that beset him on shore, we must reform ourselves, and be willing to reach out the brotherly hand to welcome him on land, and to a better life. We must develop his manhood and self-respect, and thus lead him to a life of decency. These views are strengthened by the remembrance of the services of the good and truly Christian seaman's chaplain at Honolulu, Sandwich Islands, the Rev. Mr. Deil, and the very marked effect his labors had among the crowds of whalemen who frequent that port on their passage to the distant grounds of Japan. He boarded every ship in advance of the sharks, and extended the welcome of a brother to the humblest and worst. Sitting on a chest in the forecastle, he would inquire about the voyage and the men's needs, informing them that a good library and a quiet, comfortable reading-room, with facilities for writing home, were provided ashore. He not only invited the men to these privileges, but also to his home, where he said he would be glad to see them, and he generally left a Bible for each man desiring one. And let me here alarm the Christian hearts of the American people by informing them that in no other Christian port on the west coast of America was there a door to welcome or a roof to shelter the sixteen thousand souls engaged in whaling, other than that of a gaming-house, a grog-shop, or a brothel. The influence of this good shepherd was remarkable, and gave me an opportunity to contrast the partial decency and good behavior of men in this port with their reckless abandonment to the extremes of wickedness in other Pacific ports. I believe he labored, nevertheless, under discouragement, caused by the wrong-doing surrounding him. He has gone to his sure reward, gratefully remembered by many a sailor, on whose path he shed a ray of genial light.

The whale stowed us eighty-five barrels of oil; and when the first part of our work was complete, we scoured down the decks with sand from America and the alkaline cinders remaining from the burned scraps of the try-works. We rubbed and scrubbed, and drenched decks, stanchions, and bits, until there was not a suspicion of grease to tell the story of the pandemonium of last week. We now proceeded on our cruise down the coast of Chili and Peru, keeping quite close in. Standing off shore during the day, we headed in during the night, a course which afforded us several magnificent views of the mountain chain of the Andes. In the early morning this lofty range, rising to sixteen or eighteen thousand feet, intercepted the rays of the sun, and its broken, rugged outline stood in bold relief against the luminous sky. As the sun climbed higher, the cloud colors softened the sharpness of the mountain summits; and a moment later, when the sun appeared above the heights, the whole magnificent scene, volcanic peak and snow-clad cliff, seemed to melt into thin air, and was lost to us until the following morning. The first view of the varied sandy and rocky shore of Peru was a bitter disappointment to me. Ignorantly I had clothed all parts of the tropical world with luxuriant vegetation, while here, for hundreds of miles, not a trace of leaf or shrub was discernible from the ship's deck: a great desolate stretch, without a sign of life. And this was the home of the Incas!

We passed leisurely down this coast, much enjoying the tranquillity of the seas, the constant clear, dry weather, and the grand panorama of mountain scenery. But we saw no whales. Touching at Callao only to send a boat in to communicate with the *Brandywine,* frigate, we stood down the coast for the port of Payta, crossing several schools of whales without making a single capture. In running into the harbor, we spoke the *Washonk,* of Falmouth, whose tragical history will fill a future page. We hailed, " Five months from home, with eighty-five barrels of oil."

These five months seemed interminable to the youngsters. We longed for the land—for any land in any clime. A veritable homesickness it was that came over us. We were of the dust, and unto dust we would return. But the cruel captain said " nay " to our pleading looks, for he was not unnaturally anxious to report more than a single whale before the anchor went down. Yet, good soul that he was, he could not refuse his " merrie men " a taste of the earth's fruits; and while we were lying-to he sent a boat on board a whale - ship at anchor, and bought a load of onions and sweet - potatoes. His proceeding, it seemed, however, was contrary to a port regulation requiring vessels to come to anchor and pay port dues before purchasing supplies.

The captain, after his trifling trade, proceeded to shore, and left us to take the vegetables on board, and then return for him. Our proceedings were watched from a Peruvian armed vessel, the *Libertad;* and when we were returning for the captain her boat put off with evident intent to intercept us. But it was not in the timber of any man-of-war's boat to hold her own in chase with a whale-boat. Chipman stood in our stern, and sprung on the after-oar, in order that we might gain all time possible in getting the old man aboard before our pursuers could reach the shore. We passed across their course at full spring, as though we were going on to a whale, inattentive to the Spanish hail that came after us. Chipman could not "sabe Spanish," and he consigned the men-of-war's men to regions more torrid than Peru, at the same time urging us to pull faster. It was but a mile's distance to the shore, and we had time enough, if the captain was only on hand. We shot up to the pier in a few minutes, but he was not to be seen. A man was hurried to the consul's house to find him, and meanwhile the mud-turtle in chase hauled alongside. A Spanish sailor laid his hand on our gunwale, as though to seize the boat. "Put your boat-hook through that hand," said Chipman, coolly; and, in obedience to orders, the point of the hook was struck deep into the wood, from which the frightened señor hastily jerked his hand. The lieutenant in command of the Spaniards, with a "carrajo," tumbled from his stern-sheets clumsily to the pier, and drawing a pistol from his belt, more by his motions than by the clearness of his lingo, gave us to understand that we must surrender the boat. Chipman had quietly obtained a lance, and had slipped the wooden sheath from the head, and when the officer gave a dangerous direction to his pistol, the whaleman's favorite weapon was poised in the air, in the hand of a cool, determined fellow, who seldom missed his mark. The Spaniard cocked his pistol, and in broken English said, "Get out." In very excellent and time-honored English, Chipman bade him "go to Jericho!" With hurried aim, and a visibly trembling hand, the trigger was pulled, a cap snapped, and the Spanish officer's billet for Paradise, signed and sealed, was almost delivered from the point of a whale lance, when the voice of Captain B—— was heard shouting, "Put up that lance, and surrender the boat."

The capture of the boat and the detention of the captain necessitated the anchorage of the ship, much to the contentment of the writer and all the rest. How the captain settled with the authorities was none of our business. We were too busy for a fortnight in repairing ship to trouble ourselves with international difficulties and treaties. At the end of this time, with hull new painted, rigging set up and tarred down, masts scraped, and yards squared by the lifts, man-of-war fashion, the *Chelsea* rode at anchor again in all her yacht-like beauty. The port of Payta is a favorite resort of the offshore cruisers, as the harbor is good, the supplies of vegetables reasonably abundant, and not high-priced. We took in a large supply of sweet-potatoes, onions, yams, and pumpkins, and fruits for immediate use. After this we were allowed liberty on shore, and had an opportunity, as far as a few dollars advance-money would go, to realize the fleas, dirt, discomfort, and vice which characterize a Spanish refuge for recruiting whalemen. The women are homely, the men beneath contempt; and what more could a captain desire for the safety and enjoyment of thirty-two free and enlightened citizens a-pleasuring in the Pacific? Perhaps I ought to draw a pen through this page of the journal, but honesty and truth require the confession that the first day's liberty of the starboard watch was a little given to riot.

May 8th my journal reads: "Got up with a swimming in the head. It seems to me that the smooth water of the harbor produces sea-sickness in all deep-water fellows. As I don't feel like writing, my Hinglish friend, Charlie, volunteers to write up my day's work. Thus runs his entry: 'Starboard watch on liberty. Up to four bells last night, Bill was right as a trivet, when the boys at the "mizzentop" toasted the "Philadelphia bar, where choice spirits do

THE PRISONER.

abound." Bill, as in duty bound, responded as follows—' But I will not give Charlie's quotation from my worthless speech, which I was sorry for afterward. From the snug quarters of the mizzen-top I believe the meeting described adjourned to a dimly-lighted calaboose (or watch-house) in the town. It was not clear to us how matters came about; but some yarn about the American consul's wanting us brought us to the door of the barrack and calaboose. After a little row with the armed soldiers, we found ourselves inside a bamboo house on one of the usual flea-ridden, dusty floors common in this town. In the stocks to the right of the entrance were three *pisanoes*, who had brought the fruits of their little gardens to this morning's market, and had been seized by a press-gang, and destined for transfer to-morrow to the decks of the *Libertad*, to serve as sailors. The poor fellows were sad enough. Perhaps their people would never learn their fate. As the prisoners were Indians, one of our boys, a black, became sadly afraid that he might be spirited away also. Our mischief-loving Smith, who "sabe'd Spanish," primed the guard with the yarn that the black was a desperado, and had been the death of "Indianos muchos." As the frightened fellow unintentionally slanted toward a pile of spears, the soldiers thought his bad fit was coming on strong. The scene came to a head in our black boy's gradually backing against an arms-rack, and watching the soldiers as closely as they watched him. At last his drunken, frightened brain thought that he was surrounded and entrapped, and he plucked down a lance, with a wild yell charging for one of the frightened Indians. We interfered now, and quieted the excited fellow by promising to see him safe on board the *Chelsea*.

Late in the night, or early morning, as tolled by the bell of the cathedral, we heard our mother English in plaintive, maudlin tones in the street, and made it out as old " Chips," the carpenter. In a boosy sing-song he was pleading his cause. The door was thrown open, and his venerable head nodded to us as he leaned against the door. There he stared at the poor fellows in the stocks. He had us very much mixed up evidently, and he staggered helplessly, hopelessly forward, and threw himself on the low platform where the sergeant of the guard was trying to sleep. The worthy officer took umbrage, and then ensued a wonderfully confused intermingling of English and Spanish maledictions, as the mad Spaniard and the tipsy Yankee squirmed for possession of the narrow shelf. We interfered to keep off the soldiers from molesting our old shipmates. " Blood will tell, the world over," and Don Emanuel was tumbled out of bed much as the callow sparrow is by the unfledged cuckoo. We sprang in and seized the arm of the furious don, to prevent him from carving the figure-head of Chips with his sword, the carpenter himself meantime sitting on his conquest, and crowing like a game-cock. After this incident, until morning, on some pretext or other, we managed

to keep up a row, and gave the "Spanioles" not a moment
of rest. At times things looked serious, but Payta soldiers
are slow to push a quarrel to extremities with a party of
sailors as strong as ours was. As morning approached, we
learned the secret of our arrest. It proved to be a little
private speculation of the little garrison of the place. They
had arrested and brought us to their barrack-room in the
hope that we would offer them a dollar or more to be let off.
As we made no advances in that direction, they gave us
to understand that "une peaso" would open the door to the
donor; but we could see in a dollar more enjoyment than
winning an early morning's walk in the empty streets of
Payta. Therefore, in the gentle terms of our nation, we
declined, much to the disgust of our hosts.

At sunrise our worthy captain appeared in the market of
the Plaza on which our calaboose fronted, and catching a
sight of so many of his crew through the open door, he
went off in one of his pious tantrums, using so few strong
words that his spiritual health was more endangered, perhaps, than if he had freely used his breath in sea-lingo.

Such was my only night in a Peruvian calaboose, and the
experience may account for the lapses in my Payta journal.

The good captain called me into his cabin soon after, and
said,

"Bill, you were brought up a Quaker, weren't you?"

"Yes," I answered, shortly.

Flushing up, he demanded,

"How's that? Yes, *sir*, is the answer I expect in this
cabin."

"I beg your pardon, sir, I forgot. I was thinking I was
a Quaker again."

He smiled good-naturedly, and then lectured me thus:

"I sent for you to warn you against rum. You risk your
soul sure, and you lose all chance of promotion in my ship.

If you are not man enough to keep clear of rum entirely— *entirely*, mind—I won't have you at the head of my boat. Now, go forward."

"Captain B——," I replied, "I am very much obliged to you for manifesting such interest in me. I will remember and profit by your advice."

"All right; I believe you," he added; and so we parted. For the first time I had the thought that my good friend Draper had not only secured me my berth, but had bespoken the care of the worthy captain.

"*May* 12. Having had our fill of this wretched land, we weighed anchor and stood out from the arid, treeless shores of Payta, bound for Cocos Island, in 10° N. lat., for water, stopping at the Galapagos Islands, *en route* to secure a store of terrapin. The second day from port we took two whales. No peculiar incident lent an interest to the capture, but they increased our oil to one hundred and forty barrels. In a few days we dropped anchor in the harbor of Porter Islands, a favored resort of Commodore Porter, commanding the frigate *Essex* during the last war with Great Britain."

CHAPTER VIII.

Volcanic Desolation.—To Black Beach for Terrapins.—We reject Green
Turtle.—Strange new Life.—Town ho!—First Terrapin.—A live Knap-
sack. — Grandfather as an Angler. — Supper in Camp. — Terrapin and
Iguana. — Jim Sellers's Philosophy, and probationary State for Captains.—Watch by the Camp-fires.—Breakfast, and proper Stowage of
Grub. — A Cruise up into the Island.—The Voice of the Terrapin is
heard in the Land.—Brown and the Sculptor.

THE appearance of these volcanic islands is the extreme
opposite of my prior conceptions of tropical scenery, but
they fully realize the desolation of an earth born of fire.
The jagged peaks shoot into the air almost devoid of vegetation.   In places the sky outline is broken by gigantic cylindrical, or flat-stemmed cacti, whose rigid forms and blunt
terminations are only suggestive of dead, branchless trees.
Along the shores at intervals are stunted growths of brownish
foliage, and at the projecting points black, shapeless masses
of lava.   My dreams of the verdure and bloom of the tropics
seem as though they are never to be satisfied.   But, as
Posey remarks, it was not for scenery we came in, and we
will find the best fruits of this paradise running on four
feet, and packed away in shells.   The old hands long since
whetted our appetites by toothsome talk of the land-terra-
pin of these islands, and we cheerfully lent a hand in preparations for an early start to Black Beach, a few miles from
the anchorage, to seek the delicate game.

Two old boats were selected, stored, and swung alongside.
Long before day-dawn, the call of "all hands turn out for
shore duty," started the crew into active life.   A hurried

breakfast disposed of, the two mates, with ten men, were soon bending to the long, sweeping oars of the whale-boat. A pulling song and chorus marked time to the stroke, and awakened echoes in the lava-cliffs of the near shore, and seemingly responsive cries in the sea-birds and seals. As day revealed the jutting rocks, we kept nearer inshore, and on the points and beaches saw numbers of seals and large turtles, the former so fearless that they took no alarm at the passing boats. Philosophic-looking pelicans, perhaps brooding over piscatorial theories, crowned the rocks, and great gatherings of gannet and boobies flew screaming over our heads. A narrow beach of dark olive-colored sand marked our landing-place, where we ran the boats ashore, unloaded them, and drew them up out of harm's way, erecting a shelter out of an old top-gallant sail. We left two men to prepare camp, while the rest started for the back country to hunt terrapin; the order being to prepare the first one captured for our dinner. We became very fastidious on terrapin-ground, and were above green turtle—considering them somewhat coarse food, suitable, no doubt, for aldermen and others of the shark family. So we left the flat-shelled fellows sprawling on the beaches behind us, with the hope that at some time they might be made into soup for hunters less epicurean than we.

After getting on our stout shoes, the first worn since we left the shores of America, we clambered over a rocky way which skirted the beach, and struck into a pathway tramped upon first, perchance, by Sir Francis Drake. A short distance inland we spread abroad among the scant bushes to hunt our slow-going game. Every thing about was so strange that each step revealed new objects of interest. The purely volcanic nature of the rocks and soil; the enormous spiny cactus; the broad-palmed prickly pear; the aromatic foliage; the great iguanas nodding good-morning to me, or running noisily through the dried grass to a neighboring hole; the multitudes of curious, bright-colored lizards skipping over the burned rocks, and the tameness of the pretty doves which confidently alighted on my shoulders—all gave a charming variety to my first walk on this prolific field of new life, and my disappointment at the rugged coast passed away. I had proceeded perhaps a mile, when the cry of "Town ho!" was heard a short distance off. This announced game afoot, and I hurried in the direction of the cry. As I was ambitious to vindicate myself as a hunter, having spun many a yarn about fox and coon hunts in the woods and over the hills of Pennsylvania, I kept a bright lookout under every cover, ignorant of the character of the game, much as a rabbit-hunter might, and often stumbled over the stones in my eagerness, the cry of "Town ho!" coming again and again. Presently, to my surprise, I saw our happy darkey, 'Zekiel—the same whose ferocity alarmed the Peruvian guard—sitting on the rear of an enormous terrapin about the size of a wheelbarrow, and much the shape of my mother's forty-gallon apple-butter kettle.

'Zekiel was shouting "Town ho!" for the necessary help to tote this great meat-chest to the shore. Good heavens! thought I; is this the animal I was "peeking" to find under the stones, much as Handy Andy did when ordered to look up the unlikely places for the lost cows? Here was a "baste" that would weigh three hundred pounds at least. In the vicinity were numbers of others of more manageable size, and we selected two of perhaps fifty pounds' weight. We tied the fore and hind legs of each, so as to leave convenient loops through which to slip our arms, intending thus to carry our capture home, knapsack-fashion, on our backs. The great cavity in the bottom shell fitted nicely to our shoulders, and, aiding each other in adjusting the load, we made for the beach. All went pleasantly until my terrapin got it into his stupid brain that he was being "sold," and, tired of his position, he drew his legs within his shell with tremendous power. I found he had caught me most foully. How he pulled! I imagined my shoulder-blades must crush under the strain, and I cried out with the pain. A life-long stoop was straightened out, but I could not get the brute from my aching back. Sinbad, with his "Old Man of the Sea," had a comparatively good time; for no old man's knees could squeeze as that fifty-pound terrapin did. And I happen to know as much about the strength of an old man's knees as Sinbad did.* I was almost fainting as the men at the camp cut the cords and released me from my bondage.

---

* My grandfather was ninety-three when I left home, but still was able to take his end of the cross-cut saw in dividing a three-foot log in the old mill, as well as to canter the friskiest gray three miles to First-day meeting. He was a lover of the gentle art from his youth upward, and retained the inclination, having a wonderful ability for tempting the speckled trout from the musical waters of our wooded hills. But early stiffness in the joints and the twinges of rheumatism forbade his wading our cold brooks. The wiry feather-weight old sportsman therefore converted his mischievous grandson into a pack-horse, to carry him dry-shod from side to side of the shallow streams. The old gentleman's sense of touch was delicate as in youth; the hand struck surely on the faintest rise at fly, or a nibble at caddis. And when he hooked a fish, how tenderly, yet certainly, did the old angler lead the resisting beauty from the deep tangle of the alder-roots to bed of moss prepared for it in the creel! But the suns of ninety-three summers had somewhat hurt his eyes, and at times he failed to mark the position of the hook so cautiously dropped from a fern-covered bank. In boyish glee the by-standing urchin would shout, "Why, grandfather, thy hook is a foot from the water!" The touchy angler would drop his tip-a-wee, tempt a rise, and land the trout. But the boy had the laugh at the master, and he must pay for his whistle of course. And when we next crossed the rippling shallow, the old bony knees played hard on the wind-organ between them. As good a horseman as the old man was, his grip was too much for the barefooted biped roaming over rolling rocks; but with a teasing tweak of the ear, and a "Dodrabbit thee, thee laughs at my fishing, does thee?" he put on his best squeeze. The next moment the irate angler

The true way to carry a terrapin is to form a hand-barrow with deal clubs, or, for the largest, of the steering oars. Such a contrivance, manned by two or ten men, will bring down the capture with comparative ease. I have not a certain idea of the weight these creatures attain, but think I am within the mark in placing them at four or five hundred pounds. A somewhat hasty dinner of fried terrapin scarcely interrupted the coming and going of the carriers, and an hour before sunset a boat loaded to the water's edge with our spoils was dispatched to the ship. We who remained ashore prepared beds of dried grass under the tent, while the cook made a savory mess of terrapin-meat, with the sweet, golden fat, the rich, melting liver, potatoes, and onions. As the savory odors swept athwart my nose, I almost lost heart and appetite in the roasting of an iguana nearly three feet long, and as thick around as a man's leg. As I turned and basted the horrible beast, it was with less and less stomach for the feast.

Part of the crew had started on a hunt for a sea-lion (male seal), as we wanted the thick hide for moccasins, our leather shoes having been cut to pieces in this single day's tramping over the *scoria*. Others found amusement in killing the great conger-eels in the shallow pools left by the receding tide. These spotted, snake-like fish are bold and vicious, not hesitating to dart at you, and fasten to the naked leg or foot. It requires nerve to stand the charge of the ugly creatures without flinching.

Luxurious dogs that we were, to our roast iguana and terrapin stew we added the conger-eels, and craw-fish as large as our lobsters, and equally good. At the going down of the sun, a ravenous crew, seated on the convenient backs

and young nuisance together were gathering their sprawling limbs from beneath the laughing waters, which carried the joke to the tickled trout in the pool below. Ah! lackaday! Such days and such grandfathers are not now with us!

of terrapin, gathered about a feast to be treated by fork and spoon, not by stupid pen. Man's capacity for good living is fortunately limited; but for this night's work each man's appetite seemed endless as my neighbor, Tetty Worrah's, parsnip, which penetrated so deep into the earth that a strong smell of tea came up through the hole it bored.

After the feast came the soothing pipe; but the more thoughtful remarked the continued absence of the two sealhunters; and as the sudden darkness of the tropics settled upon us, strange tales of adventure in these islands were told by the older men—stories of lost seamen, never found, who probably had fallen into the volcanic pits and traps. Jim Sellers, learned in the lore of deep water, averred that these were enchanted lands, differing in all respects from other islands. Of the hundreds of islands which shoot out of the deep blue water, he said there is not one that was not born in volcanic fires. All that we tread upon has been a bottom of the sea, and there has been a fight through the ages of fire against water. The wild imagination of a Western tourist suggested the picture of Niagara pouring into Vesuvius—a grand tournament of the elements, surely, yet baby's play compared to the scenes in which these islands had their birth. Jim held further that Fiddler's Green could not be enjoyed by good sailors were "hazing captains" allowed to anchor their souls in its happy port without a thorough overhauling of life's log; and he showed that the islands we were in must be the probationary cruising-ground of the misdoers. In these rainless deserts, in the forms of terrapin, they do penance for their rancorous sealife, and their only liberation and clean bill of health comes through the sea-pie, and the satisfied hunger of the sailor whom they once hazed and bedeviled. Old Jim avers that he well knows the wicked, winking eyes of an old terrapin lying staring by the hour into the glimmering embers of the cook's fire. But he had lost the run of old Captain Springer for years, and did not know he was dead till he now met him here at Porter Islands. He pounced upon the terrapin at once, intending, as he said, to have the only good dinner that he ever got out of the "stingy cuss." Old Jim may be right; on a fair vote, a majority of mankind would agree with him in his doctrine of transmigration, and our boat's crew would count with the winning side. It will be rather a pleasant relish to fat pork and plain boiled rice to have fivescore of captains looking on for the next six months through hungry terrapin eyes. Jim bestowed a blessing and a kick on Springer's senseless shell, knocked out the ashes of his pipe on his obdurate brow, and rolled over in the inviting grass to dream of home or Fiddler's Green. We followed suit, first taking the shoes from our blistered feet, after our habit of sleeping barefooted on board ship, and turning into the luxury of a clean bed without cockroaches. Who among men has kept a journal of his dreams? Surely in my sea-life the hours in dream-land were the most enjoyable, and quite as good in a business way as fussy waking-time. Yawning, and terribly asleep, I answered, "Ay, ay," to the midnight summons of "Watch on deck." This setting a nightwatch on a fast anchored isle, arose from the fixed habit of sea-life; for in the sailor's existence he must count sure on two things—the watch on deck and death at the end of it.

The glint of the moonlight from the rippling water troubled my dry, heavy eyes, and with the constitutional growl of the forecastle I blessed the eyes of my disturber, and took a seat on the back of a terrapin, and found it cooler than the surrounding lava. Now came waking dreams in the novelty and silence of a land-watch. The brawling brook and old saw-mill, the *kreetching* cider-mill, and ranges of barrels with convenient straws. And then the dear old—

Ah me! Silly thoughts these for a rough being keeping lone-watch on an ash-heap of nature's laboratory. Next my mind turned to mischief. The spirit of the solitude invited me, and then came the desire and the resolve to see more of the interior than was usually penetrated in the terrapin hunt; and I returned to bed at the relief of my watch, determined to play lost next day.

In due course came the dawn, and with it an ample breakfast on the warmed-over remnants of supper. Eight hours' sound sleep had exhausted all we ate last night, and had cleaned out our lockers for the stowage of more unknown quantities. Old Lisha, the boat-steerer, advised a "proper chinking between the solid *menavellines* with the mushy lobscouse, to prevent shift of cargo in the rolling country we were to hunt over." He claimed there was much judgment necessary to stow "grub," so as to carry it well in a rough sea, "as Jack discovered in," he added, "his voyage from Groton Hill to Stonington on a kicking horse. The heels and taffrail of the infernal craft were in the air overhead all the time, and the brute pitched bow under at every jump. It was awful goin', and the more Jack dug the craft amidships with his heels the more it wouldn't sail on an even keel. So Jack hauled up at a road-side inn, and ordered two bushels of oats, saying, 'Look here, hostler; mind you stow that grub well aft, as he sails too much by the head to steer well.'"

Our seal-hunters had returned in the night with the hide of a sea-lion. This we cut into moccasins, and laced on our feet to a neat fit, the fine hair inward, forming a perfect shield against the cutting edges of the rocks.

Charley Lings wished with me to push for the interior and find the enchanted castle that might be there, and our desires were forwarded, when word came that we should remain on shore another night. We secured a boat, hatchet, and fire materials, and then set out from camp, striking from the path directly for a notch we observed in the range before us. We had no means of carrying a supply of water, and we trusted to our luck. After walking several miles, we reached a district where, in all likelihood, human foot had never trod. The face of the country was gloomy in the extreme, broken into abrupt walls of flinty lava, the valleys being floored with scoria. There was no vegetation or evidences of life other than the little lizards. Following a narrow defile which the rolling pumice made tiresome walking, we next met many walls, or dikes, of vesicular lava thrown across the gorge. We had to climb these under the intense heat of the sun, and attained a summit overlooking a plain several miles in extent. Our altitude was considerable, and we could discern a number of the surrounding islands, and the ship lying quietly in her nook. Inland stretched a plain of greater beauty than we had expected to find, or had hitherto met. The grass was green, and the trees and bushes comparatively luxuriant.

Finding an easy descent, we hastened onward to seek the refreshing shade of the trees, and with a faint hope that we might obtain water. Great numbers of terrapin were about, some of them of immense size—very much larger than any seen on the shore plains. Here we first heard the deep bellowing of the male terrapin — not unlike that of an angry bull. But wherefore this cry was a mystery to us, as the creatures seemed deaf to any sounds which we could make to alarm them. Possibly the male felt that it was good to bellow, though none might enjoy the music, or he may have bellowed, as some flowers grow and some men work, unseen, for the love of God; and, I might add, as an old sculptor chipped marble in dark places. This reminds me of a story, which I told to my companion as we trotted on. In a cathedral of Italy, so old that the finger of Time was tracing growing lines on its marbles, a tourist's ear caught the tiny clink of a sculptor's hammer behind a frieze in the lofty interior. Searching for the sound, he mounted upward until he stood before the wondrously graceful stone wrought by genius seemingly superhuman. In the increasing gloom of the back galleries, his ear alone became his guide as the louder clink of the hammer invited him on. At length, by the feeble glimmer of a lamp suspended from the sculptured stone, he discovered an old, bearded man, patiently drawing and perfecting curves of beauty in yielding marble. The worker was partly hidden behind the frieze, where human eye might never see or be instructed by his labor. The tourist drew near the solitary artist, all the reverence of his nature stirred by the scene. Uncovering his head to the courteous salutation of the old man, he inquired, "Wherefore?" "For the love of God," responded the old worshiper. So, it may be, the poor misshapen terrapin sang his untuneful, unheard song from the mysterious love which dwells in his cold heart; the love of God may be even there. Who knows? Who dare say nay?

CHAPTER IX.

WITH the established inconsistency of moralists, we took
the head off the largest terrapin we could find—one great
enough to furnish a feast for a hundred men—as we stood
in sore need of refreshment. We were exceedingly thirsty,
moreover, and had tried to satisfy our craving with the
warm, insipid juice obtained from the trunks of the giant
cactuses, but in our capture, in our terrapin, we found the
living spring of this wilderness. An ample supply of pure,
limpid water was discovered in the pearly sack placed at
the base of the animal's neck. There were some three gallons of water here, and, wonders of wonders! it was cool.
The temperature of the animal is but 62°, but that of the
country may reach 110° in the sun. Thus we carried our
water in the bottle of classic ages, only that this was Nature's own water-bottle. Such is one of God's providences
for man in dry places.

Heartily refreshed by the drink, we built a fire under the
branches of a tree of fragrant foliage out of wood whose
smoke was incense, and we toasted great slices of the terra-

pin liver, which is sweeter than the almond. This dainty, served on our excellent ship-bread, made a feast fit for a prince. Our cookery was entirely novel; and as it may happen that the reader one day will be enabled to obtain two pieces of lava and a pound slice from the tenderloin of a four-hundred-pound terrapin, I will let him into the secret. Place two such pieces of lava, with spoon-like cavities to catch the gravy, before the blazing fire, until they become frying hot. Then place the meat upon the stone with the largest cavity; lay a piece of sweet fat on top, sprinkling a little salt over it, and cover all with the second lump of lava. In a short time you will have a dish that none but good whalemen or honest landsmen deserve to eat. Having thus dined, and lighted our pipes, we threw ourselves at length on the bosom of our kingdom, and were willing that crowned kings of earth should draw up to dull mahogany, and eat the best of the coarse fare their possessions afforded; better, we thought condescendingly, that they should eat salmon and venison than starve. Another tenderloin from between hot stones supplied us with a night-cap; and after another solacing pipe, and dreamy talk of homes in England and America, we fell into a peaceful slumber, under the enchantment of a moonlight glimmer on the broad floor of an extinct volcano.

The morning broke on us, refreshed and transported with the wild romance of our surroundings. We discussed the possibilities of existence in the heart of this island, and almost persuaded ourselves that such a chance of life would be preferable to much that we had seen in the back alleys and slums of crowded cities. We were at a loss to account for the verdure, and comparative fertility of this elevated plateau, but concluded that its elevation was sufficient to cause heavy dews—perhaps to condense the clouds to rain—while the coast beneath was parched by nine months of un-

interrupted drought. Making another inroad on our store
of flesh, and slinging our water-bottle over the shoulder,
we retraced our steps to the camp, which we reached about
noon. We were made more of as lost and found than we
really deserved. But we took the petting kindly, and promised to be careful thereafter. With one hundred and fifteen terrapin of all sizes secured, we then returned to the
ship, whose decks were crowded by our sleeping captives,
and the cook's galley steamed with a new and savory odor.
But no artful mess of the "doctor" seemed to equal our
home-made dish on the mountain top.

On the following day all hands had liberty on shore—fishing, hunting seals, to be used in future caps, gathering beau-
ful small shells for a sweetheart's work-basket, and swimming, forming the staple amusements of the day. With improvised spears, we pierced and captured numbers of large
skates, or "stingarus," and on a small island to weather of
the anchorage we found numbers of large, clumsy land-
crabs. The sailors claim that these creatures have power
in their claws to strip the husk from the cocoa-nut; but
why they should amuse themselves thus is more than I can
understand, as they surely can not crack the shell.

On the next morning, to the song,

> "The windlass ply, the cable haul;
>   With a stamp and a go and a Yo-heave oh!
>   Our sails to the winds let fall.
>   Joys of the shore we must forego,
>   To brave the storms, and to seek the foe,
>   And win the spoils of victory,"

we brought the anchor to the bows, and stood to the north
for Cocos Island, to take in water. The second day out we
lay top-sails aback, with two good whales alongside; and
after cutting-in, we braced forward and stood on such course

as we could lay in these calm latitudes. We sighted the cloud-capped heights of Cocos, but were three days in working up to an anchorage in the beautiful bay.

This solitary island is touched by the southern skirt of the south-east trade-winds. Its mountains serve to condense the vapors borne by the hot winds, which here meet the upward currents of the equatorial belt, and consequently the island is enveloped in clouds, its climate bearing the character of constant rain. The whalers run from great distances for water supplies from the pure stream which flows into the head of the bay. We towed our water-casks ashore in long snake-like rafts, and filled them directly on the beach, leading the water by a spout from the ravine to the edge of the sea. In this manner four hundred barrels of water were obtained in a very short time. After this duty was done, we had liberty on shore. On the beach at the head of the bay are many detached rocks, of such softness that they may be easily cut with a carpenter's chisel, and on their surface are carved the names of many ships, and persons who have visited the spot. We soon became in a degree inured to the rain; and notwithstanding the thoroughly soaked condition of every thing, we plodded through the marvelous ferns and mosses, over hill and valley, to feast our sea-tired eyes with the beauty of a miraculous vegetation. Now, for the first time, my anticipation of tropical growths was exceeded, and I wandered from beauty to beauty with a pleasure alloyed only by the enveloping clouds and pouring rain.

A deep, fertile soil, held in place by the fibrous roots and mosses, covers the steep hill-sides, and everywhere we see an endless variety of strange plants, urged into the wildest luxuriance of growth by the extremes of heat and moisture. It seemed a vast conservatory, in which every growth was perfected and uninterrupted, decay being instantly covered by new accumulations of beautiful life. My poor language is

too feeble to convey the wonders of nature's productiveness
to minds schooled under northern skies. Here are lofty
cliffs extending far as the eye can penetrate the misty atmosphere, their sides deeply festooned with vines and dense
verdure of all kinds from base to summit. Long arcades
and cavernous arbors are formed so deep that the vivid tints

TROPICAL GROWTHS.

of foliage and flowers are lost in shadows, which verge on
the darkness of night. In these green recesses I observed
one of those contrasts in which nature seems to delight.
Flocks of birds of a pure white plumage passed to and
fro in the dim light, as though they were blossoms of the

vines become animate, and in flight and twittering song sought companionship. Long stalactites of vivid green, around which flowers grew, hung from the roofs, the points emitting crystal streams of water, which were lost on carpets of moss and ferns. The lofty hills were clothed with broad-foliaged forest-trees so dense that the misty light of day was almost excluded, their tops covered with a surf of palms. Palmettoes, dracænas, ferns, lycopodiaceæ, and orchids were in charming harmonies and contrasts. Marvelous forms and colors crowded every spot, indeed bewildering the mind of the ignorant sailor, who only knew enough to feast on the beauty through which he tore his way. Leaping cascades of the purest water sprung from the cliffs, and fell hundreds of feet below, penciling their course in silver light, and wreathing the near growths in snowy foam.

But even in this fairy-land rude business intruded itself. We had to settle two quarrels which had occurred since we left the Galapagos, and which, according to the rules of the captain, were postponed until we reached shore. A ring being formed and fair play assured, a few minutes of down-right earnest effort buried all ugly grudges and heart-burnings in the beautiful sand, which the combatants had kissed in turn. Then we turned to more general enjoyments; all hands running races, wrestling, and skylarking on the shelving beach. Some waded off in the shallow water to gather the sea-stars, sea-eggs, shells, corals, and the marine plants which make the bottom of the bay almost a counterpart, in brilliancy of coloring, of the garden-land. Of this wondrous scene the gift of the artist and poet may relieve the sailor, in the following description:

> "Come down, come down from the tall ship's side;
>   What a marvelous sight is here!
> Look! purple rocks and crimsoned trees
>   Down in the deep so clear.

> "See where those shoals of dolphins go,
>   A glad and glorious band;
> Sporting amid the day-bright woods
>   Of a coral fairy-land.
>
> "See, on the violet sands beneath,
>   How the gorgeous shells do glide!
> O Sea! Old Sea! who yet knows half
>   Of thy wonders and thy pride?
>
> "Look how the sea-plants trembling float,
>   All, like a mermaid's locks,
> Waving in threads of ruby red,
>   Over these nether rocks.
>
> "Heaving and sinking, soft and fair,
>   Here hyacinthine, there green,
> With many a stem of golden growth
>   And silver-starred flowers between."

There is a tradition that the good Captain Cook planted a couple of hogs in this island to provide future visitors with stuff for sea-pies, and a portion of the crew organized a boar-hunt. Armed with a shortened whaling-lance, boat-hooks, and clubs, we clambered the steep hill back of the watering-place, and plashed noisily through the dripping bushes. We soon started a gay and festive boar, of grey-hound proportions and activity. With a grunt, a tail on end, and bristles and heels in the air, he dashed forward down the hill; we following, with yells, in his rear. Our outcries brought the rest of the crew up the narrow valley, when they brought the brute to bay. A lucky prod with the lance touched his life, and he soon went into his flurry, and turned on his beam-ends; but not before he had made several vicious charges on his surrounding foes, although, fortunately, none of the reckless boys were lacerated by his formidable tusks. Our visions of sea-pie vanished at once

CORALS AND MADREPORES.

as we regarded the victim. We had run down the mere frame-work of a veritable hog, with a hide loosely folded as a hound's, and as savage-visaged as a wolf. Slinging him over a pole, we toted him to the beach, and stripped off his hide without finding a trace of fat. Round, hard knots of muscular flesh formed what should have been ham, shoulder, and neck. But he was fully developed in teeth and bristles, and these formed the greater part of him. The entire flesh might have been eaten by our party at a meal. But we had our boar-hunt, and came home not empty-handed.

The significant point of our adventure was that, in the profusion of vegetable growth, the elements of nutrition were so scant that even a pig could not glean the material for his prerogative of fatness; and we read, in the brute's attenuated proportions, that the unfortunate wretch who should desert his ship might starve in this garden. In striking contrast with the absence of food in this most luxurious tropical growth is the profusion of sustenance afforded in the seeming desolation of the volcanic Galapagos. As represented in a former chapter, they are entirely igneous in their formation, vitreous scoria, pumice, and cindery ashes covering hills and plains; and these unpromising materials are so loosely arranged that the rains sink at once, and are entirely lost, but one known spring of water existing in the entire group. The cactuses, and a few thorny, gnarled, woody-leaved shrubs are the principal growths, and the small fruit of the prickly pear is the only vegetable edible by man. Yet on this most unpromising field nature has abundantly provided for the possible presence of the latter. In these low solitudes are found great numbers of small lizards, and the monster of the tribe, the great iguana. These great lizards were dainty feasts for the buccaneers of old, as they lay here in wait for the treasure-laden galleons of Spain, in passage from Lima to Panama, and when they returned from their hellish raids, laden with the plunder of desecrated churches and ravished homes. Here the English pirates found a congenial home. But the most remarkable provision for the peculiar needs of the sea-faring visitor is our old friend, the terrapin. At the end of several months' fast on the decks or in the hold of a ship, these creatures are found good for the table, with only a diminished store of fat and flesh.

As we traversed these seemingly recent formations, I was continually impressed with the thought that we were reading a first chapter in the book of Creation, wherein a soil was yet to be formed, and an order of life above the reptile to be introduced. And I was led to wonder at the strange order of nature that, in the arid desolation of the Galapagos, man may live in luxury, while the hog may almost starve among the fine vegetation of Cocos Island. This contrast extends even to the waters of the two localities. In the harbor of Cocos Island, as the seaman leans over the gunwale of his boat and gazes down into the intricate recesses of branching corals and waving plants, he sees vast numbers of highly-colored and brilliant parrot-fishes grazing upon the coral polyps which grow on the stony soil. In vain may he angle for a meal, for their ivory-toothed mouths are so small that they can not take in a large hook, and their jaws are so powerful that they will snap a small one. Our method of capturing the few we took was to anneal a small steel hook and render it tough, so that it might bend but not break short under the action of these strangely-formed fish.

At the Galapagos, the shallow basins of the shore swarm with great craw-fish, to be taken by the hand; and conger-eels, to be killed with a club. Half buried in the shallows are ray-fish, to be harpooned with a stick cut in a neighboring copse; black water-iguanas bask on the stones; enormous turtles slumber on the beaches, and their vast stores of eggs may be dug from the warm sands. Seals and sea-lions tamely lie on the rocky islets; the sombre pelican sits brooding on the ledges, so absorbed that the mischievous seaman may place a cautious hand under its contented tail, and tip it heels over head into the water below. Little land-birds alight upon your person absolutely unconscious of fear, and in the lagoons are beautiful fan-like mussels eighteen inches in length, and innumerable conch-shells. The deeper waters

SOME FISH.

abound in infinite numbers of fish, diversified in colors, forms, and qualities. Some of the larger of these are so easily taken, that you are well equipped for sport with a boat-hook and a square inch of red flannel. In four fathoms swarm schools of the excellent groupers, twenty or more pounds in weight. But beckon to them with the baited hook, and a half-score of scarlet beauties will answer the polite invitation by rising from the depths. Select your partner, drop your bait into the waiting mouth. He will close on it as a patriot will on a nomination, and he will hang on as a lover of his country and his kind will to place and power.

Were it possible to combine the life of these two groups of islands, what a garden of delights would we possess! But I suppose the elements of perfect bliss are generally separated by a space equal to the ten degrees which divide the Galapagos and Cocos. Before leaving the island, I employed a couple of hours in carving the name of the *Chelsea* among the hundreds already recorded on the rocks, and I also engraved the name of a young Pennsylvanian in whom I felt unsual interest.

On board ship we were now rich in fresh water, terrapin, potatoes, onions, and fruits; but our supply of fuel was short, and it was necessary to start for Selango, on the coast of Colombia, about eight hundred miles distant, to secure the needed supply. The wood of Cocos was succulent, and unfitted for fuel, except a rare kind. Glad to get into port, the sailor soon tires of uninhabited lands, and, "with a stamp and a go, a yo heave-oh," he runs the anchor to the bows, and cheerily sheets home his top-sails for a fresh cruise. Having cleared the land, the mast-heads were manned, and we stood south-south-east, shortening sail by night, as we were on good whaling-ground.

On the passage one of the boat-steerers approached me with a desire to enlist me in a scheme to desert with five others when the ship reached Selango, their intention being to take one of the boats, run down the coast to Panama, thence across the Isthmus, and find passage in some trader to an American port. I declined, but promised to preserve his secret, telling him that having shipped for better, for worse, in the old *Chelsea*, I meant to stick by her; and if things became unbearable, to lend a hand to right them rather than, by running away, let them go still worse. My mind was made up to return to America in the ship I left. No more was heard of the plan, and I hoped that it was dropped, for it involved some of the good men of the ship, and one of our best boat-steerers. On the passage south we took one small whale. A boat was capsized, but no further damage done.

As we approached the coast, a little north of Selango, we passed through a tract of many miles, in which the water was covered with branches of trees, some of considerable size, splintered and much broken, with great quantities of leaves, dead birds, and some dead monkeys. In the midst of the wreck were many small striped snakes. This was evidently the work of a whirlwind in the forests of the neighboring coast, and we considered ourselves fortunate in escaping its force. With a good breeze from the westward, we soon afterward made land on the larboard bow, and, without altering our course, steered directly into the noble bay of Selango.

CHAPTER X.

At about 3 P.M. we dropped anchor a short half-mile from the beach of white sand, which appeared to extend around the entire bay, broken in places by the encroachment of mangrove-bushes. Again we have before us a scene of tropical luxuriance and beauty. A few dusky spots beneath the shade of the grand trees mark the town, a place of no importance at present, save as a resort for an occasional whale-ship. As soon as all was made snug on board, the captain good-naturedly allowed us to go on shore, with injunctions to be moderate in eating the tempting but dangerous fruits of the country.

The two boats assigned to us were crowded, and we pulled off on our short holiday, mischievously rocking the boats and making the sombre old wood around ring with the jolly chorus of a rowing-song, so thoroughly determined were we to give a full notice to human and monkey natives that we were coming. The result of our boisterous play was a capsized boat and a moistened crew; those who were able swimming to the shore, and the remainder clinging to wreck or oars until picked up by the other boat. The principal part of the inhabitants, omitting the monkeys, were gathered on the beach to welcome us. The Spanish-Indian dialect was incomprehensible to most of us; yet we read in the people's faces that they were right glad to see us, and in their signs that fruit was plentiful, good, and cheap. They at once invited us to their houses to rest, and a few steps up the beach brought us to the dwellings, which we entered by climbing up short ladders and through a trap-door in the floor.

The houses are of the simplest construction, but are adapted to the climate and the habits of the people. They are detached, and built on a number of straight posts firmly planted in the earth, the cross-beams, sills, roof-plates, and rafters being made of bamboo, lashed neatly and with sailor-like precision by neatly-plaited sennit, or braided cords. The thatched roofs are admirably made out of a variety of the cabbage-palm. This plume-like foliage is composed of a stout midrib eight or ten feet long, with long, narrow leaflets, closely arranged in opposite pairs, and so sharply turned up at their edges that they form gutters, which discharge all the water falling on them from the pointed ends. The roof formed this way is open to the circulation of air, but impervious to the rain and the heat of a tropical sun. Siding and flooring boards are obtained by simply running a knife along one side of a bamboo and spreading it out flat; this process leaves a net-work of cracks, which afford ventilation and apertures through which all the dirt passes out. The floor so made is elevated about nine feet from the earth, the posts supporting the house being capped with rawhide, smeared on the under side with adhesive gums. Thus the houses are secure against the inroads of snakes, scorpions, centipedes, ants, spiders, and other creeping and crawling drawbacks to perfect enjoyment in the tropics.

The cracks in the sides furnish light as well as air; the overhanging thatch shuts off the sun; and the houses, upon the whole, look clean, cool, convenient, and not to be im proved upon. There are usually two rooms—one for storage, and one for residence. A pile of mats forms the bed. The people knit very ingeniously. Examine a fine Panama hat, and you may realize their skill in such work. The cord hammock forms their luxurious lounge. Gourds are put to the manifold uses of dish, vase, jug, and bottle, some of them being of immense size. The rooms are adorned with spears, broad-bladed *machetes*, or knives, and very excellent fishing-tackle, nets, etc.

In front of each house is a stage of poles, on which are suspended stores of bananas and plantains. To save these fruits from the depredations of the monkeys, they are cut while green and suspended in the sun, that they may mature in safety. The natives assured us that, should the banana be allowed to remain on the tree a single day beyond the time when it will properly ripen separated from the tree, the mischievous neighbors will organize a raid, and strip the orchard in a single night. The monkeys work strictly on the co-operative principle. The gray-headed elders stand sentry on trees near the dwellings, and keep sharp eye on the movements of their tailless cousins, while the young and active form a line from the fruit-trees to their hidden pantry or store-house. Good judges of fruit ascend the trees, and a stream of golden spoil flows steadily onward fast as the harvesters tear or bite it from the stem. If they are sur prised or alarmed by the signal of the watchman, every fellow scampers to the woods with such a load as he may happen to have in hand, and he will only relinquish his grasp to escape capture. Some assert that the mother will shake her baby from her back rather than relinquish the fruit, but I doubt this, in a place where bananas are so plentiful.

After partaking freely of the Guayaquil orange and the delicious fig-bananas, we found the cherimoya the most delicate, luscious, and ambrosial of all fruits. Under the temptations of the black-eyed, smiling Eves, we nibbled, and tasted, and ate, in utter forgetfulness of our captain's well-meant warning. But after eating a hatful of cherimoyas, we had to yield to even that most exquisite fruit. Satiated and used up, we then recalled the wise counsel of the captain, and determined to be prudent, abstinence being so easy a virtue when we had all we desired. To settle the good things eaten, however, and recover room for yet untasted sillwaula plums, papie, melons, etc., we walked a short distance into the woods to see the banana-orchards. I was surprised at the limited area in cultivation, which not only furnished twenty families with the staple of life, but left an abundance for ships visiting the bay.

Humboldt has told us that this plant surpasses all others in the production of food for man. It seemed credible to us as we stood beneath the broad foliage, and saw suspended from the twenty or thirty stems the great bunches in every stage of development short of ripeness. The orchards were fenced by bamboo rails lashed to posts or living trees, and were bordered with orange, and the cassava, or tapioca plant. The orange, guava, limes, pepper, and calabash trees were growing wild.

I believe it is an axiom in natural history that there are three misstatements in the vulgar description of the crab: "A fish, of a red color, that runs backward." When the naturalist visits Selango, he will nevertheless see the beach covered with crabs which are red, and which do run backward of necessity, as they would expose their defenseless tails if they retreated otherwise; whether fish or not, is a question. The Indians showed us numbers of pearls, some of goodly size, and, to our inexperienced eyes, of great purity and beauty. These are found in the oysters which abound in this bay. In the days of Spanish rule many pearls were obtained. Great heaps of large and exquisite mother-of-pearl shells were to be seen, and we selected a fair number of the choicest, intending to polish some into cream-skimmers for the dairies of home friends, and convert others into artificial flying-fishes, to capture the dolphin and albicore.

Having recovered our appetites, the women easily tempted us to renewed efforts on the fruits. Life is short, and the opportunity of eating cherimoyas confined to Peru. We improved the opportunity and ate a second hatful, before returning to our floating home by the soft light of a tropical twilight.

Three days of hard labor were passed in chopping, and conveying our wood on the backs of asses to the shore, and thence by boats to the ship. The favorite wood was the magnificent India-rubber tree, on account of its softness, ease of splitting, lightness, and richness. We also took pains to secure some of the beautiful ornamental wood, for canes and general whittling. The last day we intended to remain in port, two boats were sent to the north side of the bay to collect limes from the woods, and enough fruit was obtained to furnish us two barrels of pure-strained acid for use as an antiscorbutic in the long cruises before us. Up to this time we had not seen monkeys in the woods, although the natives assured us that they abounded; but as I sat under a branch, gazing idly into the dim cathedral light of the dense forest, and interested in the cackle, and scream, and bright colors of the parrots and macaws, my eye slowly settled on a knob in the crotch of a neighboring tree. By-and-by I could have sworn the knob was winking at me, and a moment later a broad grin transformed it into the head of a monkey, who was watching me from his lofty hiding-place. Holding a key to the situation, I looked into another and another fork, and in each was nestled a winking, grinning face. No stones were to be found; and arming myself with golden balls from a near orange-tree, I opened fire on the nearest heads. The mischievous imps, finding that they were discovered, came forth from their hiding-places, and every tree revealed one or more distant relations. Many had young ones on their backs, their necks being encircled by the baby arms, and the miniature winked, nodded, and chattered in concert with the mother. From this time out they took no pains to hide themselves, and came forth from all parts of the forest. The scattered crew engaged in gathering limes also found the forest suddenly alive with monkeys, and our progress was marked by the scolding of these audacious wood-sprites.

The shore-folk brought off a great store of bananas, oranges, and cassava roots, which were paid for in heavy unbleached muslins, two fathoms of cloth being the price for the largest bunch of bananas. When ready for sea, our ship was a toothsome sight. The bunches of bananas were suspended from the stays in every part of the ship, while the spars astern were fairly golden with the fine pumpkins of Peru. We were now in prime condition for a long cruise. A good stock of terrapin remained; water was fresh and abundant; wood filled every crevice in hold and 'tween-decks; and between the carlines, in nets, were oranges, onions, sweet-potatoes, cassavas, and limes. Every man had two or three quart-bottles filled with the little Chili or bird-peppers, gathered from the woods; and these, with vinegar, made pepper-sauce to season our salt pork. I enter into the details of good living on board to correct a common impression that a whaleman's fare is always poor:

> "Salt beef, salt beef, is our relief—
> * Salt beef, and a biscuit hard,"

as an old song wrongly has it.

On the night of July 25, in my anchor-watch, Jim and
Chipman, both boat-steerers, quietly inquired whether I had
changed my mind about remaining in the ship. I told
them that I thought the best chance to reach home was to
stick by her, and for my life I could see no reason for running away; that we had seen no ship in which there was
better treatment, and that our chances of a good voyage
were first-rate. I reminded them that the coast was exceedingly unhealthy for men exposed as they would be in an open
boat, and that, being penniless, they would have no chance
in Panama, where they were bound, save to ship on some
miserable coaster, hide-drogher, or merchantman. I strove
very earnestly to dissuade Chipman from the senseless undertaking. He was just the man to stand by the ship—
a healthy, brave, noble-hearted fellow; a first-rate sailor,
a good boat-steerer; a man we could ill afford to spare,
whether as fellow-laborer, or as companion on deck or on
shore. It was in vain. The foolish fellow had laid his
course, and it was not for a boy to argue away the fancied
wrongs on board which repelled, and the home visions
which attracted him from this safe ship. He grasped my
hand, said good-bye, and went below. This was the last I
ever saw or heard of Elisha Chipman, a model seaman in all
things save the damning weakness of the sailor for strong
drink. The runaways consisted of eight men: the two boat-
steerers, the steward, the capenter's mate, and four from the
forecastle. One of the latter we could well spare, and were
joyfully rid of. He had graduated on the Erie Canal, and
fairly earned the name of "Wicked Bill." Whether Major
Williams had got him by a general jail-delivery I can not
say, but this is certain: America's gain was our great harm
when he came on board the *Chelsea*. Too lazy to resist
sea-sickness, he was prostrated by it for four months, and
only recovered for duty when we had reached the calm lati-

tudes of the Pacific. He was despised by every soul on board, and shut himself from our sympathy in his sufferings by his obscenity and profanity—a gambler and cheat by profession, a ruffian by nature, lazy as a terrapin, and, to complete the ugly picture, a "sodger" every inch of him. As soon as the boys had left me, I slipped into the forecastle and stowed away beyond their finding my quadrant, paper, pens, and ink, simple drawing materials, and a small mariner's compass, lest their necessities might tempt them to despoil me.

CHAPTER XI.

The Boat lowered, and the Men leave the Ship.—Residuary Legatee, and Preparation of the Chests, with national Song.—Second Mate makes a Discovery, and discourseth thereon.—Muster-roll called, and armed Boat ordered away.—Give up Chase, and attack on Case-bottle.—Weigh Anchor for Payta.—Description of Balsa Rafts.—A Providence for maritime Men in the placing of Timber.—Shoal of swimming Crabs.—Black-fish Chase. — Arrive at Payta, and ship eight Men. — Introducing "Long Tom."—Jack and the Fairy in Broadway.—Jack's three Wishes.

LATER in the night, from my berth, a watchful ear caught the sound of the bow-boat in its descent from the davits, the cautious footsteps on deck, a low-hummed conversation, the dropping of the men, one by one, from the fore-chains into the boat, and then all was still. The forecastle was in darkness, for the runaways had extinguished every light on board. On calling, I found a number of the men had been awakened by the descending boat, but they had not suspected the cause. A light was struck, when the men were informed that the bow-boat had been taken and four of our shipmates were gone.

According to immemorial usage, the survivors proceeded to overhaul the chests of the departed, to secure any keepsakes they might have left to the mourning family, and to make sure that their "love-letters" should not fall into the hands of the captain, to the confusion of high-born dames at home. As in solemn duty bound, every thing was removed from the chests save an old deck of cards from "Wicked Bill's." These were of no use to honest folk, for they had the private marks of a knave in the dog-eared corners. They were accordingly left for cabin use. To soothe feelings aft, the words "TOO LATE" were inscribed in chalk on the lids, and we closed proceedings to the air of "God save the King," and the words,

> "One piece of beef for four of us,
> Not enough for two of us,
> Thank Neptune there's no more of us,
> God save the king."

Those of good conscience, at peace with the world, then turned in and slept the sleep of the just. Some time before daylight the second mate's pleasant hail awoke us, "Fo'c'sle there! whose watch is it?" when, discovering the absence of the bow-boat, he thundered away with a handspike on the deck, and yelled, "All hands turn out, every mother's son of you! tumble up naked, or I'll skin some of you!" The ebullition of his boiling blood led him to interlard his invitation to tumble up with divers maledictions on our eyes, our tarry top-lights, and our maternal progenitors, with some wholesale "cussing," sadly at variance with the pious intent of our good captain.

Thus violently aroused from our slumbers, we turned out leisurely, and tumbled up, inquiring of the irate mate, "What's the row on deck?" We found the captain very angry, of course; but a deeper feeling than anger was apparent when to the muster-roll two of the boat-steerers failed to answer, one of them his favorite harpooner. But it was no time for idle regrets. "Stir your stumps and get down a boat," was the order, soon as the extent of our loss was ascertained; but the order was not so easily obeyed, as the falls were lashed in several places, and plugs of soft wood forced into the davits so as to *jackson* them. After loosening these, it was found that some pins had been cut away. Thus nearly an hour was lost, while the impatient captain and mates fumed about the disabled boats. At last all was ready; six loaded muskets and sundry pistols were placed in the boat, with the most child-like confidence that we would shoot off the pesky things should we be brought to close quarters with our runaway shipmates. Maybe we would. Maybe we wouldn't.

Broad daylight saw us pulling around the north cape of the bay; but a vain pursuit of twelve or more miles and nothing in sight, convinced the captain that boat and crew had too much the start of us. He headed the boat into a little cove, where he opened his heart and a bottle of St. Croix, offering now to give us a *pull*. A long tug at the oar had so whetted our appetites that we added no water to our rum, and the fiery drink, with a snack of biscuit and pork, set us on our thwarts for the homeward pull.

The next morning we weighed anchor to beat up the coast for Payta, to make up our crew. On this passage we hugged the land at no time save at night. As best evidence of the pacific character of the sea immediately under the lee of the Cordilleras, we met large numbers of the singular craft termed *balsas* running with square sail before the steady south-east trade-winds. They are simply rafts of logs lashed together, with a raised platform for cargo, and a deep lee-board to give steerage. On this primitive arrangement the Peruvians make voyages of a thousand miles, and sometimes are met far off the shore. The *balsa* wood is perhaps the lightest, having a specific gravity about one-half that of cork, and is impenetrable to water when both ends are submerged. The tree attains considerable size, and it is well adapted to the purposes for which it is used.

As I regarded this provision I could but perceive another evidence of a careful Providence for the necessities of the sailor. Here we find the lightest and most impermeable timber in the world, growing in the immediate vicinity of the only sea on which raft navigation is fairly safe. Were the *balsa* wood placed on the shores of the stormy, change-able Atlantic, men would be tempted to perilous enterprise and frequent destruction. In place of this, the oak, the locust, and the pine are provided for the seas of Europe and America; the iron-like teak to endure the buffeting of the cyclones and typhoons of the Indian Ocean; the worm-proof mahogany for the heated seas of the West Indies, where marine worms will riddle a ship's bottom in a few months; the buoyant, leather-like birch bark for the shallow rapids of our Northern rivers; and the tubular bamboo, the antipathy of the crocodile, for the travel over the deep rivers of India.

We also met a vast shoal of crabs, several miles in breadth, moving to the northward; the water seemed alive with these active swimmers, and the entire surface was bright with the tints of their shells. They seemed to be on passage, and were exceedingly beautiful as the dense mass rippled through the calm waters.

Short-handed as we were, we took a whale on this passage, the only noteworthy incident being that the game was so close inshore that one might almost look for soundings; yet the water was blue, and must have been deep. We also saw great numbers of finbacks and humpbacks. The latter is a bone whale, but the bone is short and of little value; it affords considerable quantities of an inferior oil, however, and is pursued from shore fisheries, as it is liable to sink after death. In the bays or shoal coasts the dead whale is anchored and buoyed, so that it may be recovered on rising, which it does in a day or two, when the gases expand the body and give it the necessary buoyancy. We fell in with great numbers of black-fish, and spent several days in chasing them, finding much sport in their capture. These small whales are from sixteen to twenty-four feet in length, and furnish sometimes from three to five barrels of oil. There is little danger attending their capture, though they may sometimes capsize a boat, or stave in a plank or two. A simple chance of drowning, or of being taken in by a shark, is the only drawback. We took about forty barrels of this oil, to meet the necessary expenses of our forced visit to Payta. In the absence of the two runaway boat-steerers, the captain gave his bow-oar chances in striking these fish, as did the mate to the historian Posey; and as that auburn-haired hero saw beyond the tall hump of each monster the smile of the Nantucket syren, his harpoon was unerring as the barbed arrows of Cupid.

Rounding the bleak, sandy point of Cape Blanco, the extreme western land of the Western continent, we soon dropped anchor in the familiar waters of Payta. We here shipped eight men, two of whom professed to be boat-steerers. "Long Tom," who shipped for the captain's boat, was a specimen, New Bedford born and whaleman bred. Fire and wreck had cast him ashore at Monterey, Mexico, and fearing that a cruel fortune might cast him among the miserable hide-droghers of California, he worked his way to Payta for a chance of good society on board a whale-ship. Tom stood six feet two in his bare feet, for stockings he had not. He had a rough, good-natured, honest face, deep graven with lines of suffering, sorrow, and care, but not one of discontent and remorse. Thunder-scarred in brow, his heart was kind and soft, as Dibdin sings. The remaining seven were the rough drift of humanity continually cast up in these Spanish ports; the refuse, or waste, of hundreds of whalers, sealers, and merchantmen. Save that they appeared mainly very promising food for the whale fight, they were not notable.

New varieties of fruit having come in since our last visit, we tested them, but found nothing to wean us from the cherimoya. The ship was rich from the proceeds of our black-fish oil; and lest we might lack for vegetable diet, in our long-contemplated, oft-defeated cruise on the offshore, we replenished our stores of sweet-potatoes, yams, onions, pumpkins, etc. Sailors lack ingenuity in invention for the gratification of appetite, a limited number of good things, each abundant, satisfying their simple tastes. And here, gentle reader, I will thrust upon you two stories which are worth the telling, inasmuch as they prove how modest the wants of sailors are.

Honest Jack had just landed in New York, and was sauntering up the street of streets, when he saw a decrepit, poorly dressed woman standing wringing her hands on one side of Broadway's horsy life, and wishing to reach the other. Polite policemen overlooked the old and helpless one, to ferry over the painted craft that cruise in that sea. Poor Jack marked the old woman's despair; and, loving all womankind, in rough but effective politeness he gathered the poor palsied bundle of dry goods to his bosom, and forged his way, like a sea-steamer, through the current. When he reached the opposite side, he saw reposing in his strong arms, and nestling confidently to his loving heart, not the old woman, but the loveliest little rose-bud of femininity he had seen since the days of his childhood, when from a little cradle he had gazed on the face of his young mother. The fairy said to Jack—for the old lady was a fairy who came over with Henry Hudson, and had been wandering the streets of a great city for two centuries to find a heart that would do for age and deformity that which all will do for youth and grace—the fairy said to Jack, as the story goes, "You have restored me to my kingdom, and the three wishes of thy heart are thine. Wish with a bold heart, and be happy."

"Well," replied Jack; "faint heart never won, you know, so here goes for a kiss from your sweet lips."

That was a wise first wish, for the fairy would carry the compliment in her heart through eternity.

She continued: "Two more wishes remain to you; don't waste them."

"Ay, ay; but you may save them for poor folks," said Jack; "I want nothing more."

Poor, foolish Jack! With the world at his beck, Solomon chose wisdom, and all things were given to him. Jack asked for love, and was master of the world through its potent influence. His way from that day was smooth to the quarter-deck, and years after he told his grandchildren of the good fairy who totters down Broadway to test the hearts of the hurrying crowds.

Another sailor, not so wise as the hero of my last story, was put to the ordeal of the three wishes. First he wished that all the continents, and mountains, and islands, and little rocks, and coral reefs were tobacco; secondly, that all the oceans and seas, the lakes, rivers, little creeks, water-spouts, rains, and dews were grog. These two wishes were granted, and he tasted thereof and was glad; but the third wish bothered him. He cast about to see what more a jolly tar could desire, and decided that he had all he wanted.

So to our former store of potatoes and onions we added potatoes and onions; and, rich in all that heart could wish, we made ready for an early departure from this miserable place.

CHAPTER XII.

Leave Payta, and Long Tom's first Whale.—Bridled Whale.—Bow-oar hauling on.—Bill on Cephalopods.—Ben on the Squid.—Ben on Whale's Feeding.—Long Tom and Reef Squid.—Sandwich Islander on Polypus.—Troublesome Tenant.—First Mate's Story of Squid, and Drowning of Captain.

Aug. 10. We weighed anchor and stood out to sea, slanting to the southward, and intending to cruise on the off-shore ground as long as our water would allow. Within five hours from the time we broke our anchor from ground, we were in the boats, Long Tom steering ours. He had a *chirpy* way of keeping us to our work in a close chase, and some of his raillery, jerked out between the quick springing strokes, amused me much: "Now, Bill, it's for you and me to put the boat on that whale, but we won't do it if the starn keeps a-gaining on us. We must pull like thunder, I tell you, or the ' old man ' will carry the starn right over our heads. Pull, Bill, for good life; the boat's getting shorter every minute. He's shovin' the starn ahead like a spy-glass shutting up, and he'll spit that whale with the steerin'-oar." And he accompanied the aim of his two harpoons with, "Take that, and that, and may God have mercy on all our souls!" Cool as he was on the main-hatch, the old experienced harpooner meant every word in prayerful earnest. He recited adventures that would lead any thoughtful man to cry out, "God be merciful to me a sinner!" But we had little time for moralizing with our whale in tow. The creature gave his tail a quick upward fling, knocking the bow and tub oars out of our hands aloft. The next moment he apparently had an urgent call to windward, and hurried up to keep his engagement, we following him warily. A curious incident occurred in the chase. In turning, the whale ran across the line in such way as to bring it into his mouth; he closed on it, and held on until he turned "fin out."

Having him thus bridled, it was easy work to haul the boat well forward on his life; and thus, side by side, boat and whale almost touching, we had a splendid brush to windward, the captain busily prodding with the long lance for the brute's life. At length a side roll, intended to bring the massive jaw in play, laid bare the vital spot; in went the slender lance five feet deep, clean to the socket; and "churning" the weapon backward and forward without withdrawing it, the old man continued cutting desperately the vitals of the agonized monster. In vain the writhing! The great flukes went into the air; we were safely forward of them; and stab after stab fiercely followed, until the next spout, which, with a wild yell, we saw was thick blood—a fountain, twelve inches diameter, of bright red blood, "thick as tar," as the captain said. At one time the fellow's poor sightless nose crossed the boat, and with a deep, horrible gurgling, the sickened giant spouted across the boat, sending ruby spray over the naked heads and arms of the crew. Horrible! It poured scalding hot down my open breast, and, envenomed with rage, it seemed to blister and rasp the skin away in its lava-like course.

The manner of riding alongside a running whale is thus: having hauled as well forward as the position of the harpoon will admit, the boat-header reaches over the bows, and, taking hold of the line forward of the *chocks*, brings it around outside the boat, then giving it into the hands of the bow-oarsman, who has faced forward on his thwart. Now, as the man hauls on the line, the direction of strain is oblique, well back on the bow, and the course of the boat becomes parallel with that of the whale a few feet distance from him. The boat-header then has his chance to ply the lance with deadly effect. If the harpoon is well forward of the hump of the whale, the boat will run in comparative safety, as the strokes of the tail will be behind the boat, and the swing of the jaw in front. As long as the whale continues running in a straight course on the surface, the persistent boat will cling behind his fin as a bull-dog will to the nose of an ox. His only escape is to run deep, or, by suddenly *milling* or turning, to bring the boat in reach of jaw or flukes. The duty of the bow-oarsman is arduous when the whale is running fast, or there is a high sea. By his own strength he must keep the glancing boat in its position, though drenched with the flying spray from the bow. Should the strain wrench the wet line through his burned hands, the blessings of the excited boat-header are poured on his head with a vigor heard only in the rushing hiss of this " Nantucket sleigh-ride." But the position is also intensely interesting, as much of the time the oarsman rides face on, and has the best and closest point for observing the actions of a whale in his death fight. Generally it is the first class in the school, and the tyro learns the a, b, c of whale-catching, and he has but a step to the harpooner's place.

In the glowing sunset the great creature was peacefully anchored at the bow of our ship, and the *Chelsea*, with foretop-sail aback, drifted quietly in sight of Payta, under the shadow of the Cordilleras. Inspired by the incidents of the day, the calm beauty of the night, and our new companions, it is not to be wondered at that the earlier watches were spent in comparing experiences, and in the interchange of opinions concerning the mysteries of the life we were leading.

Of course we talked of whales and their ways. As we gathered in the forecastle, the plash of the waves on our prey, the slap of some hungry sharks' tails, and the rattle of the fluke-chain, naturally gave tone to the yarns of the evening. Whale-feed was the immediate subject, when Ben put in his oar: "Cephalopods be blowed! Just hocus the marines with them *Ciferen poddles!.* I tell you, sparm-whales feed on squid, and sometimes a blue shark is took in with the crumbs."

The bow-oarsman, myself, who had been talking, now continued: "With all respect for your extreme ugliness, my beloved Benjamin, I reiterate that the right-whale feeds on medusæ, and other minute forms of animal life; and the spermaceti feeds on octopods, cephalopods, and onycholenthus, the meaning of the same, in the vernacular, being the horrible polypus."

"Why didn't you stick to wormicular from the jump, and say *polly pusses* when you meant *polly pusses ?*" growled the old sea-bear, as he lay comfortably propped against the sleeping body of an old sow, which nightly served as a pillow to some luxurious sleeper in the watch on deck.

"If that lily-livered book-worm," Ben continued, "will permit a remark from an old fellow that was twice wrecked before he was kittened, I would venter to say that the yarns ashore about scuttle-fishes, and *uproriusses oxymuriaticusses* is all gammon and greens for the bringin' up of land-lubbers. You can remark, fellers, how the same works on Bill there. And they draw picters of 'em, too. Now that's ag'in natur', as far as the great squid is concerned; for I tell you, boys, one and all, no mortal man ever set eyes on it and come back to tell the story. The squid is the greatest mystery of the deep water. We don't know any thing about it, only that it lives, and that it nestles away deep, deep down about the roots and foundations of continents. And the wise Creator, before he launched the first sperm-whale, sheathed him with thick blubber, and cushioned his brain-pan with

EIGHT-ARMED CUTTLE-FISH (SEPIA OCTOPUS).—FRONT VIEW.

junk and case, so that he could follow the squid to its deepest home.

"A big bull-whale, you know, sounds down for an hour and a half, and he can go down three miles in twenty minutes, and he comes up with his hold filled with chunks of

squid bigger than the main-hatch. He hews off the arms,
or *tentackellums*, as Bill calls 'em, more 'n forty foot long.
Lord, how he just does go down, boys! He goes down like
a lump of lead, full ten-knots' speed, till he sinks so deep
that the squeeze of the water would mash in a mainmast;
so deep that water would drive through a cork; and so deep
that a thing must have life in it ever to get up ag'in. Why,
I heard Captain Swaim say that a whale must often bear a
pressure equal to three hundred thousand tons; but the same
I don't believe, of course, for the reason as I told you. Nobody comes back to tell what happens when the sperm-whale
and squid feed together. I am willin' to believe that the
whale gits purty close nippered, for I've seen him shoot out
of the sea jist as a water-melon seed slips from the finger
and thumb and shoots inter the face of our sweetheart,
God bless her! I jist believe—for there can be no knowing
—I just believe that the spermaceti squid is the very biggest living critter in the universe. There is nothing greater
than the squid, exceptin' our ignorance of it. They are both
without limit.

"Why, sirs, you and me have seen the lanced whale
snortin' thick blood, and heavin' up in his throat hogsheads
of squid. You may see broad flat pieces, of all shapes and
sizes, a-floatin' over the feedin'-grounds of whales, and you
never see a piece that gives you any idea of the shape or
size of the whole fish. You never see a piece as has a sel-
vage edge on to it. You never yet see an outside piece.
No, they are all chunks, cut ragged and jagged with the
teeth of the whales.

"I jist believe that the bottom of the bottomless sea is
only squid; it lays down there white as daylight, in the dark,
deep water; its great arms are coiled around the foundation-
pillars of the island, and its thousand other arms, bigger than
ships' masts, are gatherin' up dead whales, and drownded

sailors, and foundered ships; and it buries them all in its lower hold, and keeps the sea sweet and clean."

We applauded Ben's theory of the squid, and most of the old hands vouched for the facts on which it was based. Only one said he had seen a squid, but it was "Sighted from the mast-head with the cry of breakers ahead; and when the men came closer it was like an island of white coral sand, with white trunks of trees, shaped like corkscrews." The sea was breaking heavily on the low beach; and when the ship came within two miles it went down out of sight, so that we could run over the place without getting soundings. Our new boat-steerer, Long Tom, next told us of an adventure with the "reef squid."

"Once I was ashore in Lee Bay, Galapagos, and carried with me a seal club, as I wanted a lion for moccasins. I was wading round a low rocky point not half-knee deep, but deep just outside, when I saw a big 'reef squid' cutting along on top of water. He made considerable thrashing as he come along, like a whirligig water-wheel; his body part looked bigger than I am, and his arms two or three times as long. It headed into the little bay ahead of me, and when it got into about three foot water it dropped anchor, and begun to feel round with three or four of its arms. The upper side of the arms were brown-colored, like the rocks, with wrinkles and stiff bristles along the edge; the under side was white,. with suckers like saucers, in two rows. What I took to be the head had something like eyes, though I couldn't make 'em out plain. I didn't think of any danger as I waded to it, but it seemed to be watching me, for it squared around head on. I hit it a clip with my iron-bound seal club, when, quick as a thought, it took a turn around the stick and held on. I pulled my blessedest, but the critter was too much for me. Just then it showed its head; it shot out from the round knob in front—a brown and purple spotted head, and in a minute I felt its arms thrown around me; one arm touched my bare leg, and another my neck, and the suckers took hold like doctor's cups. It began to heave and haul on me. You may guess I pulled and hollered. I got out my knife and hacked at it, but I guess it would have mastered me if Captain Dagget hadn't come up in time and fired both barrels of his gun in its head. Then it let go, and slid backward into deep water. As good fortune, or something better, happened it, I was in shallow water, and so far off that only the ends of the arms reached me, or I am sure I would have been only as a little fly in the claws of a Selango spider. I fight shy of reef-squid ever since, and I wouldn't go in to swim in Selango Bay for the best sperm - whale afloat. I shouldn't wonder a bit if many men went under with this fish, when it has been thought they were attacked with the cramp."

I suggested sharks as a cause of supposed drowning also; Tom replied that the shark usually showed his back fin, but that "this cussed thing would just anchor on the bottom, and throw up one or two arms, and curl around your leg and yank you right out of sight."

One of the men shipped in Payta was a Sandwich Island Kanaka, named a new name, as is the custom on board whalers. His latest name was *Chock-a-block;* but he would answer to either, and sometimes to *Blockhead.* However, he was not so called from any deficiency, as he was shrewd enough, and had done good service in our boat. As he showed signs of knowing something about squids, we encouraged him to "loose his jawing-tackle and heave ahead."

Squid began: "Ouri mi ti petre" (bad fish); and in broken English, interpreted by Hinton, he went on to tell us the following story, from which I inferred that he had a polypus in his head rather than a squid or cuttle-fish. He described his fish as being like a glove, but large enough to catch and swallow sharks, etc., and very dangerous to men. The open end of the glove was the mouth, and the fingers represented long arms, which it could reach forward of the mouth to seize and hold its prey. It had but the one opening into the stomach; and when indigestible matter, as bones, etc., became inconvenient, it quietly reached two of its arms to the bottom of its stomach and brought away the superfluous matter. Leaving Chock-a-block for a moment, I will inform young and inquiring readers that the polypi are not particular as to diet—"All is fish that comes to the net;" and they have no aversion to eating near relatives. In a word, they will seize their kind, and stow the victims away in their capacious stomachs. According to the Kanaka, Greek meets Greek when polypus meets polypus. After a valiant tussle, one swallows but does not vanquish the other. On the con trary, the swallowed backs into some convenient recess of the swallower's stomach, and there puts forth his arms, foraging on surrounding territory, and unkindly eating all he can find, much to the loss and damage of the outsider. In due order, a second and smaller relative is taken in by No. 1, and No. 2 feels bound to dispose of every thing that comes down. He takes in the new lodger and a dinner at one gulp. Of course, this state of things can not continue long. No. 1 is getting hungry; he has been industrious, but it has been for others' benefit. He proceeds to investigate by swallowing the hooked end of four or more of his arms, and with these he overhauls cargo, and discovers the well-to-do eater of all his dinners. A writ of ejectment is issued, and summary process resorted to. But No. 2 has had such a good time in the oyster - cellar that he says Nay, and throwing around his arms, hooks, and suckers, he anchors fast to the wrinkled, emaciated stomach which he has so grievously wronged. Now comes the tug of war. No. 1 pulls for good life; No. 2 holds on only for a good dinner, so he is bound to come, and come he does. But he never lets go his grip, and turns the stomach of his antagonist inside out. This is to the eventual benefit of the revolutionized animal, who obtains a new stomach, and begins life anew, with a good digestion and resolves. Did you ever hear of a better cure for dyspepsia? Such was Kanaka's natural history of the polypi of the Polynesias.

Our mate, who not unfrequently lent a hand to an evening's entertainment in his more learned way, now joined in and told us that the Kanakas of all the islands have a well-founded dread of the shore-squid, for the strongest swimmer is powerless in its arms, aside from the paralyzing influences of the suckers.

An occurrence in the Mediterranean Sea was mentioned, as told by Sir Grenville Temple, in his "Excursions" over that sea. "A Sardinian captain bathing at Jerbeh felt one of his feet in the grasp of one of these animals. With his other foot he tried to disengage himself, but this limb was immediately seized by another of the monster's arms; he then, with his hands, tried to free himself, but these were also firmly grasped by the polypus, and the poor man was shortly after found drowned, with all his limbs bound together by the arms of the fish. And it is extraordinary that where this happened the water was scarcely four feet in depth."

Much to the satisfaction of the bow-oar, and to the distaste of old Ben, the learned mate continued his readings:

"The *Sepia octopas*, or sea-squid, sometimes reaches an enormous size. Mr. Henry Baker, F.R.S., states 'that it can, by spreading its arms abroad like a net, so fetter and entangle the prey they inclose when they are drawn together, as to render the victim incapable of exerting its strength; for, however feeble the octopas's branches, or arms, may be singly, their power united becomes surprising; and we are as-

MEMORIAL PICTURE.

Fac-simile of the Commemorative Painting in the Church of St. Maloe, France.

sured nature is so kind to these animals, that if, in their struggles, any of their arms are broken off, after some time they will grow again.'

"It is evident, from what has been said, that the sea-polypus must be terrible to the inhabitants of the water in proportion to its size. Pliny mentions one whose arms were forty feet long, and Dr. Schewediawer speaks of one whose limb measured twenty-seven feet in length, as it was found entangled in the jaw of a sperm-whale. One end of it was corroded in the whale's stomach, so that, in its natural state, it may have been greatly longer. 'When we consider,' says the doctor; 'the enormous bulk of the tentaculum here spoken of, we shall 'cease to wonder at the common saying of the fisherman that the squid is the largest fish in the ocean.' "

"He is right in that last observation," growled Ben; "but he had to guess at its size, without knowing whether it had ten or a thousand arms to swing about on the bottom of the sea."

The mate continued: "Here, you boy, bring a light from the binnacle, and I will show you the picture of a squid boarding a ship. It is a fac-simile of a commemorative picture in the Church of St. Maloe, France. Montfort gives the story of this painting on the authority of some of the crew of the vessel, to whom the adventure it represents happened. Their ship was on the West African coast; the men were heaving up the anchor, when a monstrous cuttle-fish appeared on the surface of the water and coiled its terrible arms about the masts of the ship; their tips reached to the mast-heads, and the weight of the cuttle dragged the ship over so that she lay on her beam-ends. The crew seized axes and knives, and cut away. at the arms of the monster, but, despairing of escape, called upon their patron saint, Thomas, to help them. Their prayers and knives finally succeeded in so alarming and wounding their enemy that it sank into the sea. The grateful crew, in commemoration of their miraculous deliverance from this hideous danger, marched in procession to the Chapel of St. Thomas, where they offered solemn thanksgiving, and had a painting made representing the conflict with the cuttle. This painting hung in the chapel when Montfort saw it."

Now the bard and nightingale of the ship sang:

> " His head he seeks 'mid coral rocks to hide,
> Nor e'er hath man his eye espied;
> Nor could its deadly glare abide.

> " Mussels and crabs, and all the shelly, race,
> In spacious banks still crowd for place,
> A gristly beard around his face.

> " When Medgard's worm his fetters strives to break,
> Riseth the sea, the mountains quake;
> The fiends in Nastroma merry make."

CHAPTER XIII.

The Sperm-whale as it appears to Whalemen.—As a game Animal.—Idle Life on board, and Prizes for raising Whale.—Pig Sacrifice.—Whaleman in the Boat.—The Perfection of Whale-boat.—Equipment of the Whale-boat.—Retrospection in Boat.

I HAVE been showing the board spread for the entertainment of the whale, and the master of the feast has not been described, complains a reader. That has been done in books innumerable, I answer. My business is rather with the ways of the whale, as he shows himself to us whalemen in incidents of the chase. I will not trouble myself with the anatomy of the whales or of the whalemen, but will show the ways of both as they come to us in the voyage before us. Forgetting mercenary considerations, one has but to look at this huge mammal with a sportsman's instinct, and the charm will be at once perceived which attracts the adventurous youth of New England to launch out on voyages lasting a large part of a lifetime on distant seas, and to encounter the icy rigors of the Arctic and Antarctic, and the burning heats of the tropics. If we regard the whale as a game animal, and his capture as a field-sport, then how regal our pursuit becomes in all its appointments! Our ship is one of a royal fleet of costly ships, amply provided; we are a squad only of an army of precious lives; we have flown on the wings of the wind over twenty-four thousand miles of this good world's surface, and have just fairly entered on the hunt; we have tracked to its haunts a game so huge that flocks of land animals measure less than he. We have means of attack and defense, in comparison with which those of the lion and tiger are infantine and trivial. We have had a slight foretaste of the exposure, privation, and danger, in comparison with which other field-sports are tame, safe, and effeminate. Name, if you can, another pursuit so courageous and grand!

Sept. 5. It is about three weeks since we took our last whale, and we have had the greatest trial which attend the whalemen. The dullness and tedium of life on board ship at such quiet times is almost unendurable. The uninterrupted fine weather, the steady trade-wind, the daily routine of make sail, man mast-heads, scrub decks; breakfast, dinner, supper; shorten sail, boat's-crew watch, and "turn in," give not a line for a journal. The men become morose and quarrelsome; we hate each other, and numerous scores are run up, and appointments made to fight them out in the first port we make. The violin fails to move, the song to enliven, and the yarn to interest us. According to custom, and as a diversion, a red flannel shirt has been offered as a prize to him who may *raise* the first whale captured, and a pair of duck trowsers have been added. Pounds of tobacco are offered by the mate, but the days pass uninterestingly. A bright gold doubloon is nailed to the mainmast, well out of reach, but in sight of all, as another reward to good eyes. Now there is more life at the mast-head. Not a white-cap can show, a porpoise jump, or finback spout, but that the alarm is given, in hope that it may lead to a capture, and so obtain for the discoverer the pretty piece of gold glittering on the white mast. In vain! All the whales seem to have gone to the bottom for a Rip Van Winkle nap. We all know they can do this, though it is contrary to the books, which tell us that they are warm-blooded mammals: even this is not the worst names the learned have given them. But whales are uneducated, don't take the papers, and without thought of irregularity, stay down to suit their convenience an hour or a week. Like the original Kentuckian, Nimrod Wildfire, we were spoiling for a. fight, when the captain ordered the sacrifice of a pig to propitiate our patron saints. The offering was accepted, for the protesting squeak of poor piggy was blended with the yell of "There she blows!" and "Sperm - whale, sir." "Where away?" roared the officers. And in answer was heard Hinton's sweetest song, "Four points on lee bow." We squared in the yards and kept off, and away we ran merrily. At two miles' distance from what seemed a good whale, the boats were lowered. The activity of the men, as they sprang barefooted into the boats and cast off the davit-tackles; the readiness with which they handled the long, heavy oar, and dropped them silently into the well-thrummed thole-mats, and the ease with which they fell into the stroke, were wonderful. Four boats were down and heading to leeward, their course divergent, so that at two miles from the ship we peaked our oars with a space of about one-third of a mile between the boats, thus commanding a reach of nearly two miles' front.

As the boats thus ride the long, rolling swell of the sea lightly and gracefully as an albatross (and I know nothing more graceful than that), let us glance at the whale-boat and its fittings. It is the fruit of a century's experience, and the sharpened sense and ingenuity of an inventive people, urged by the peril of the chase and the value of the prize. For lightness and form; for carrying capacity as compared with its weight and sea-going qualities; for speed and facility of movement at the word of command; for the placing of the men at the best advantage in the exercise of their power; by the nicest adaptation of the varying length of the oar to its position in the boat; and, lastly, for a simplicity of construction which renders repairs practicable on board the ship, the whale-boat is simply as perfect as the combined skill of the million men who have risked life and limb in service could make it. This paragon of a boat is twenty-eight feet long, sharp and clean cut as a dolphin, bow and stern swelling amidships to six feet, with a bottom round and buoyant. The gunwale amidships, twenty-two inches above the keel, rises with an accelerated curve to thirty-seven inches at each end, and this rise of bow and stern, with the clipper-like upper form, gives it a duck-like capacity to top the oncoming waves, so that it will dryly ride when ordinary boats would fill. The gunwales and keel, of the best timber, are her heaviest parts, and give stiffness to the whole; the timbers, sprung to shape, are a half-inch or three-quarters in depth, and the planking is half-inch white cedar. Her thwarts are inch pine, supported by knees of greater strength than the other timbers. The bow-oar thwart is pierced by a three-inch hole for the mast, and is double-kneed. Through the cuddy-board projects a silk hat-shaped loggerhead, for snubbing and managing the running line; the stem of the boat is deeply grooved on top, the bottom of the groove being bushed with a block of lead, or sometimes a bronze roller, and over this the line passes from the boat. Four feet of the length of the bow is covered in by a depressed box, in which the spare line, attached to harpoons, lies in carefully adjusted coils. Immediately back. of the box is a thick pine plank, in which the " clumsy cleet," or knee-brace, is cut. The gunwale is pierced at proper distances for thole-pins, of wood, and all sound of the working oars are muffled by well-thrummed mats, kept carefully greased, so that we can steal on our prey silent as the cavalry of the poor badgered Lear. The planking is carefully smoothed with sand-paper, and painted. Here we have a boat which two men may lift, and which will make ten miles an hour in dead chase by the oars alone.

The equipment of the boat consists of a line-tub, in which

are coiled three hundred fathoms of hemp line, with every possible precaution against kinking in the outrun; a mast and sprit-sail; five oars; the harpoon and after-oar, fourteen feet; the tub and bow-oar, sixteen feet; and the midship, eighteen feet long; so placed that the two shortest and one longest pull against the two sixteen-feet oars, which arrangement preserves the balance in the encounter when the boat is worked by four oars, the harpoon-oar being apeak. The boat is steered by an oar twenty-two feet long, which works through a grummet on the stern-post. The gear of the boat consists of two live harpoons, or those in use, and two or three span-irons, *i. e.*, harpoons secured to the side of the boat above the thwarts, and two or three lances, secured by cords in like position, the sharp heads of all these being guarded by well-fitted, soft-wood sheaths. The harpoon is a barbed, triangular iron, very sharp on the edges, or it is a long, narrow piece of iron, sharpened only on one end, and affixed on the shank by a rivet, so placed that before use the cutting edge is on a line with the shank, but after penetrating the whale, and, on being drawn back, the movable piece drops at right angles to the shank, and forms a square *toggle* about six inches across the narrow wound caused by its entrance. The porpoise iron is preferred among the Arctic whalemen, as, owing to the softness of their blubber, the fluked harpoon is apt to cut its way out. The upper end of a shank, thirty inches long, terminates in a socket, into which a heavy oak or hickory sapling pole six feet long is introduced. A short piece of whale line with an eye-splice at one end is then wrapped twice around the shank below the socket and close spliced. This line is stretched with great strain, and secured to the pole with a slight seizing of rope-yarn, intended to pay away and loose the pole in a long fight. The tub-line is secured to the eye of the short line after the boat is lowered. The lance is simply an oval-headed instrument, with a cutting edge, a shank five or six feet long, and a handle as long, with a light warp to recover it. A hatchet and a sharp knife are placed in the bow-box, convenient for cutting the line, and a water-keg, fire apparatus, candles, lantern, compass, and bandages for wounds, with waif flags on poles, a fluke-spade, a boat-hook, and a "drug," or dragging float, complete the equipment of a whale-boat. Among this crowd of dangerous lines and threatening cutting gear, are six pair of legs, belonging to six skilled boatmen. Such a whale-boat is ours as she floats two miles from the ship, each man in the crew watching under the blade of his peaked oar for the rising whale, and the captain and boat-steerer standing on the highest point, carefully sweeping the horizon with trained eye to catch the first spout, and secure the chance of "getting on."

At this moment of rest, when on the point of entering a contest in which the chances of mishap seem wonderfully provided for, I found that a green hand is apt to run back over his life with something of regret always, or forward, with a half-vow that from then and there, for ever and ever, he will be a better boy. The Frenchwoman found goodness possible when she was well dressed. I found evil hateful when I was near a sperm-whale. But how one wakes up from such moralizing as the captain lightly drops from his perch, runs out his steering-oar, and lays the boat around, with the words, "Take your oars, and spring; the whale's half a mile off!" That means that we are just four minutes from the whale, provided he is not running.

It would cheer a club man's heart to watch the movements of the crew, the splendid stroke and time, the perfect feather of the oars, their silent dip on entering the foaming whirl of the lifted water, the ashen shaft working silently in the oiled mat, the poise of the crew, as the five trained athletes urge their perfect structure through the waves. Long and careful training under danger breeds a unity in the men.

The five work as a single hand under the direction of him who is steering and throwing his whole standing force in the push on the after-oar. Every energy of my soul and body is centred in that bow-oar, and I do not differ from four others who share in the excitement. An occasional glance at my springing ash, the leaping little waves, and the resolute face of the captain, tell me to a fathom the position of the chase. His eyes are fixed on the rising and sinking whale; color has left his features; his pale lips are drawn tight as he sways back and forth to the stroke of the oar. He, too, is straining on, and jerks out words of command, exhortation, and promise, to urge our energies to fiercer effort.

We are coming up at killing pace. The captain, eloquent, unconscious of his words, yet with method in his frenzy, still urges us on. Now the puff of a spout joins the splash of the bow, and the old man's voice sinks to a fierce whisper as he promises all his tobacco, a share in his little farm at home, and his "lay" in the whale, as he adjures us to put him on. Human muscle can not stand the strain much longer; the boat seems as lead; boiling foam curls and bubbles around the boat's head. The old man glances almost as low as the head of the boat; a puff is heard just under the bows; my oar-blade dips in the eddying wake of the whale's last upward stroke, and right under its blade I see the broad half-moon of his flukes as we shoot across the corner of them. Now the odor of the whale, like a bank of seaweed, comes over us. "Stand up, Ben! Pull, pull for life! Good, good! Now again! Goody Lord, give it to him!" The backward start of the boat and the upward fling of the flukes tell the rest of that story. A stroke or two astern, and we pant for breath in safety.

But lest the reader might labor under the mistake that all our prizes are secured simply by the planting of the harpoon, I shall skip from the present whale, which gave us little trouble, to another.

CHAPTER XIV.

A Whale-chase.—Boat stove, and novel Rescue.—Spade to stop running Whale. — The good Captain savage. — Fast Line, and Captain cooled down.—Captain apologizes.— On Hand and Gun Harpoons.— Hand-lance and Bomb-lance.—Erroneous Figures of Whales.—Cuvier's Explanation. — Desmaret and Lesson. — Explanation of Illustration of Sperm-whale.—Sight of the Whale.—Description of Head.—Ben Russell's Pictures.—Professors Jameson and Murray.—A Harper's Whale. —Jardin and Beal's Figures.—How to see Whales jump clear of the Water, and to multiply their Tails.

Oct. 20. Lat. 5° 40′ S., long. 107° 37′ W. The watch was employed in breaking out to make stowage for one hundred and fifteen barrels of oil now on deck, the fruit of two whales taken on the 11th and 14th insts. While the decks were all a "clutter," we raised a school of sperm-whales. They were erratic in their movements, and it required several hours of manœuvre to get the ship in a position for lowering the boats. But once we were down, it was not long before the mate fastened to a large bull. This proved to be an ugly customer, cross-grained, and bent on mischief. He ran swiftly a short distance under water, and took out considerable line; then, turning in his course, he rose to the surface, and came down full speed, head far out of water, striking one boat partially with his jaw, staving in her broadside, and rolling her over. Our boat hurried to the rescue, and as we pulled up the scene was stirring to our nerves, be assured. The crew of the overturned boat were swimming, and all six heads could be counted, which was a relief. The whale lay a short distance from the boat, thrashing the water madly with his flukes, and before we got on he again attacked the wreck and struck it with his jaw, cutting off about one-third of her length. As we pulled past, two poor fellows, who were clinging to the bottom, begged for God's sake we would save them. The captain's quick eye saw that the swimming crew were well provided with means of support, and that the waist-boat was fast coming up; so he told them to hold on, and that he would coax the whale away. The poor devils had a right to be *gallied* just then, for the mad beast was coming down on them, his ugly fifteen-foot jaw at right angles with his body, and ivory gleaming about it. Watching a chance, Ben made a long dart and struck the bull before he reached the shattered boat. This seemed to astonish the creature, and with a grand flourish of flukes he put away to windward at a tremendous pace. Evidently, we had a desperate fellow to deal with. What with this continued speed, and the promiscuous manner in which he tossed his tail, it was impossible to haul line and range alongside. Resort was had to the spade. We hauled line until the head of the boat was a little astern of the spiteful flukes, and, watching his chances, the captain pitched the broad-edged tool over the flukes into the small, with the hope of severing the tendons of the tail, which here came near the surface. If this piece of surgery had proved successful, the whale must have heaved to on losing control of his propeller. But it was a difficult amputation to perform on a kicking, fighting whale. He ran with undiminished speed, often rolling as he went, so as to give his flukes a side-cutting power; with the amiable intent of smashing his little antagonist.

I have already described the method of sheering the boat to one side of the whale, and running parallel with him, by taking a bight of the line over the side of the boat. In this instance bow-oar had been tugging at the line for an hour, but was utterly unable to get the boat in advance of the flukes. A little line might be gained for a short time, but it would soon be torn through the clinging hands, almost taking the flesh with it. This was certainly aggravating to the excited captain. Captain B—— was a religious man, and under his own vine and fig-tree, with none to rile or make afraid, I guess he would average well in patience line. But with our troubles on this day, I believe he wished that there had been no sin in a ripping oath. He was a little hard on his bow-oarsman, and rather more than hinted at somebody's cowardice. This was too much for my hot Welsh blood, and with the aid of two others I brought the boat right up to the iron, and coolly passed a bight around the thwart and made all fast. This suggested that there would be a thundering row in the boat directly, if the whale was not killed.

The captain was delighted to be held so well up to his work, and he plied his lance, thrust after thrust; but the brute seemed to bear a charmed life. He would not spout blood, and the little jets of blood which spirt from a lance wound would not bleed a whale to death in a week. Our boat buried her nose in the waves, and the bloody spray leaped over her side as we swept right royally onward.

Now our majestic race-horse grew impatient of our prodding. He milled short across our course, and we ran plump against his head.

"Slack line!" roared the old man. "Starn all! Slack line and starn!"

He turned in his tracks to step aft of the bow-oar, fearing the up-cut of the jaw, when he saw that the line was fast about the thwart. "For God's sake, clear that line!" he shouted, as he sprung forward for the hatchet to cut; but the loosened bight went over the side, as the whale came up under the forward part of the boat, and carried the bow clear of the water as he rounded slowly forward.

At this moment the captain and old Ben occupied the stern of the boat, and in the perilous moment I was just mad enough to enjoy the expectant look with which the two old whalemen awaited the arrival of the oncoming flukes. Fortunately for us all, the blow was delayed a moment, and when the thundering concussion came, it cleared our boat by a few feet.

The other boats were out of sight, and the ship's hull was dimly seen to leeward. Yet for two hours more the whale ran and fought with redoubled energy. The captain got long darts with the lance, but to no good effect; the iron drew, and the victorious whale passed away from us. We were fagged and dead-beat; almost worn to death, and we did not reach the ship until long after night-fall. The other boats picked up the mate's crew, no one having been hurt.

On the following day the captain did handsomely by his bow-oar by remarking to me that an officer in the boat never meant half he said, and that such scolding was his habit. "But," he solemnly added, "never again, under any possible circumstances, make a line fast between the boat and a whale. Why, if that mad whale had gone down, the boat would have been a quarter of a mile under water in less than a minute, and half the crew might have been with it!" Bow-oar suggested that it was better to be under water than live under a charge of cowardice. The old man overlooked this impudence, and turned on his heel. Thus I have shown that the harpoon is to fasten to the whale, the line to keep communication with it, and the lance is the instrument by which it is killed, a spade being sometimes used to check a running whale.

I have heard of a modern invention to kill whales, in the form of a short gun, fired from the shoulder of the boat-header. The invention is known as the "bomb-lance." It consists of a tube of iron about eighteen inches long, sharp at the forward end, and provided with elastic wings at the back. These serve as the feather of an arrow. The cavity of the tube contains six ounces of powder, and a fuse which is fired in the discharge of the gun, and aimed at the most vital part of the whale. It is driven deep within the body, when it explodes, often killing the whale almost instantly. But our whalemen have never adopted the English and French "harpoon gun." It is regarded as clumsy, and uncertain in fastening. We throw the harpoon by hand, and experiment on the life of the whale after we are well fast with hand or bomb lances.

Judging by the illustrations of the sperm-whale, as given in the various natural histories which treat on it, there is great diversity of opinion regarding the form of both this species and of the right whale. Cuvier says:

"It is concerning very large animals that the greatest errors and confusion exist. This remark applies especially to the *cetacea*. They astonish every one by the immensity of their dimensions, and their capture has for ages given employment to unwearied efforts of activity and courage; but except under favorable circumstances, when rarely stranded near some intelligent naturalist, they have scarcely ever been described with accuracy, and still less minutely examined. Thousands of mariners have captured and cut up whales who have never accurately examined one of them; and yet it is upon their vague descriptions and figures that zoologists have endeavored to establish the natural history of these animals. This is the true cause why the history of the *cetacea* is so meagre, yet so full of contradiction and repetition."

Desmaret made the whale a special study, and wrote of sixty-three species; yet twenty which figure in his "Mammalogie" are doubtful, or not established. Lesson, learned and trained in observation, remarks, that of eighty-four spe-

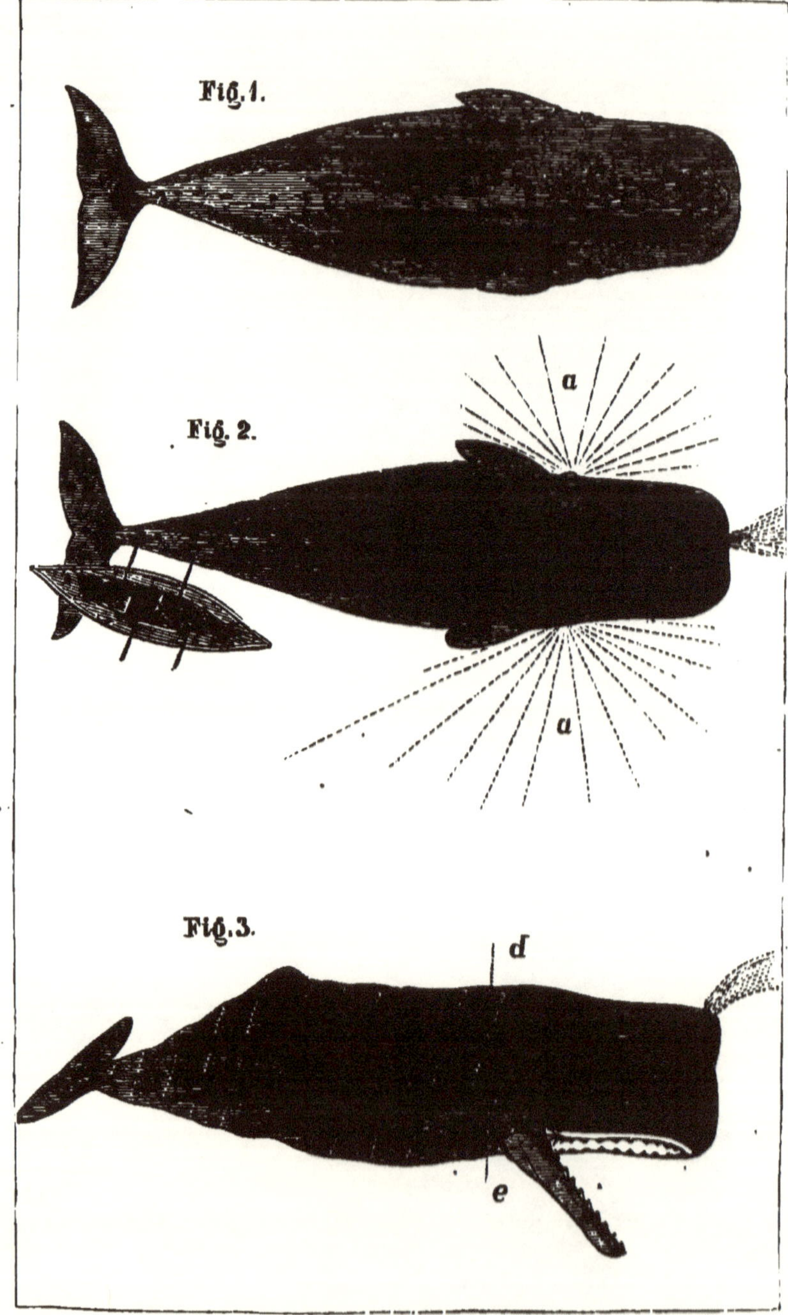

OUTLINES OF SPERM-WHALE.

cies he classified, he could vouch for the accuracy and existence of not more than fifty. And what whaleman would
venture to elect which has taken the widest departure from
reality in the delineation of the Greenland whale—the learned Frenchman, Lacepedas, or the experienced English whaleman, Scoresby? Lesson sounded deep in this fog-bank, and
in despair he wrote: "What an impenetrable veil covers our
knowledge of *cetacea!* Groping in the dark, we advance in
a field strewn with thorns." As a humble groper in this
thorny path, as one of the twenty "thousand mariners who"
to-day "capture and cut up whales," I present simple outlines of the form of the sperm-whale, remarking that the figures have been examined and approved by a number of our
old and experienced whaling captains—approved so far as a
representation of such immense dimensions could be rendered in so small a figure.

Fig. 1 and Fig. 2 give a view of the sperm-whale, as seen
with the belly and back uppermost respectively. Fig. 3 is
a side-view, and in such a position as the whale is generally
represented. It is this view which has conveyed the erroneous idea that the sperm-whale is a clumsy, illy-proportioned
animal, one obviously incapable of the feats of speed and activity which whalemen ascribe to it. Remember that the
motion of the whale's tail is up and down, and that it is the
upward blow which elevates the great head above the surface and impels his great bulk forward. And see how admirably adapted is his form for the most direct application
of his enormous power! A line drawn from the hump to
the root of the tail is the line on which his powerful muscles
act to give this upward blow. Then look at the clean-cut
run of these same parts, as shown in Figs. 1 and 2, with his
broad fins placed at the point of greatest width to balance,
guide, and aid him in turning or quickly rolling in the water.
In Fig. 2 the dotted lines converge to the position of the

eye, and show the visual angle. It is seen that a considerable space in front and a greater field behind is obscured. A boat is represented as crossing the corner of the flukes in act of going on to fasten. It is necessarily invisible to the whale, and remains so, until the stern is thrown around to bring the boat at a right angle with the whale (the position in which the harpoon is darted), and the order to back immediately given, so as to avoid the blow of the tail. The whale may now see the stern of the boat, but it is too late. The iron seldom fails to reach him, in spite of any movement he can make, except the most mysterious one of settling away, which will be described hereafter. In Fig. 1 the belly of the whale is shown, and the narrow under jaw, as closed into its close-fitting groove. The eye is just forward of the fins, which are a little beneath the greatest swell of the side, and almost on the belly. The two slits on either side of the genital organ represent the place of the dugs or teats, by which it nourishes its young. The anus is placed back of these. Fig. 2 also shows the back of the whale, and the square form of the forehead; the position of the spout-hole, a little to the left of the centre; the hump, and the smaller hump, which undulate the upper edge-line of the small, the position of the flukes, and a boat passing (*a*) within the visual ray. Fig. 3 shows the general outline of the whale as it floats in the water; the lower jaw is dropped as in feeding, or in attacking a boat. The teeth and the sockets are exaggerated in size necessarily. The dotted lines show the lines followed in dissection; *a* is the case; *b* the junk; *d e* the line of severing the head, the spiral line, and the line of the blanket-cuts.

There have been lately published by Benjamin Russell, of New Bedford, two illustrations representing both the sperm and right whale-fishing, which gives an accurate idea of the general features of the business, both in the boats and on board the ship. The illustrations show the positions of the boats in the contest, and of the ships, and in cutting-in, etc. Mr. Russell himself was a boat-steerer; and, guided by several years' experience, his artistic skill has embodied in the small space of two pictures the most correct idea of whaling which I have seen.

The upper head of the sperm-whale is disproportionately large, being nearly one-third the length and nearly one-half the weight of the entire animal. The lower jaw, in its external form, is cylindrical and narrow as compared with its length. It has from forty-seven to fifty-one teeth, there being always when the jaw is uninjured one tooth more on one side than on the other. These teeth are conical in shape, curved and hollowed at base in the growing whale, but losing the hooked form and solidifying at the root in the middle-aged. In the old they become much worn and rounded at the end. In the old bull these teeth are often found broken and shattered by desperate contests. The lower jaw, when shut closely, fits into a deep groove in the upper jaw, the teeth fitting into sockets. The head is nearly cylindrical where it joins the body, and just back of this point is the greatest girth of the body; from this forward the head flattens at the sides, and terminates in a forehead of a little less than the diameter of the body. The bottom of this ponderous head is under-cut somewhat as the stern or run of a ship.

I am not a great naturalist, but I know what a whale is not. What a whale is not, you will see in the figure given by the learned professors of British science, Jameson and Murray, so late as 1831. In this an irate monster is spouting in an impossible manner, and has a *chevaux-de-frise* bristling on his back, to impale the unhappy mariner who is returning from a skyward flight in the shattered boat. How could the British Government expect that any bounty or privilege could stimulate the whaling business while Fellows of the Royal Society and other savants were so frightfully illustrating its perils?   And see the whale that cruised off Joppa to pick up such Jonahs as might be cast overboard, and was caught by the Harpers to illustrate their fine edition of the Family Bible.   Such a representation has enough of the horrible in it to frighten every good little

WHALE "BREACHING."

boy from becoming a whaleman.   I particularly object to the circular saw which serrates the awful chasm from which the repentant prophet is so summarily ejected.

Jardin's whales, in his " Naturalist's Library," are more gay and festive.   The good-natured spermaceti are buoyant and smiling on the surface of the sea, but nine-tenths of their entire bulk are above the combing waves; in fact, they ride the crested foam light as an eider-duck. His right whales, spry as salmon, make clean leaps in the air over the heads of admiring boats' crews, and he actually found a captain of the Royal Navy to swear to such playful practice on the part of these lithe and active creatures. In connection with this habit of breaching, Mr. Bennet, F.R.C.S., remarks, in his narrative of a whaling voyage: "A large party of cachalots gamboling on the surface of the sea is one of the most curious and imposing spectacles a whaling-voyage affords; the huge size and uncouth agility of the monsters exhibiting a strange combination of the grand and ridiculous. On such occasions, it is not unusual to observe a whale of the *largest size* leap from the water with the *activity of the salmon*, display the entire of its gigantic form suspended several feet in the air, and again plunge into the sea with a helpless and tremendous fall."

And Mr. Beale, who gives by far the most correct drawing of the sperm-whale of any British author (yet incorrect in representing the small as very long and slender), also gives the figure of one descending head first, from a flight in the air, the end of the head being ten feet, and the tail sixty or seventy feet up. Now I am not willing to say that these gentlemen did not see just what is represented. I can only offer the negative testimony that, of the many American whaling-captains of greatest experience to whom the question has been put: "Did you ever see a whale thus leap clear of the water?" the answer has been "No."—"Do you believe they possess the power?" "No, excepting, perhaps, very young calves." From this I infer that such sights are seen from English ships, and are not seen from American vessels. I can only account for the discrepancy from the fact that our ships often sail without rum, and run on cold water. I have no idea of the look of a whale seen through a six - glassed magnifier, each glass containing a lump of sugar, with a spoon to stir the steaming contents. One of our old salts swears that an additional tail appears on the whale for every glass of grog after the third. He remembers once to have seen a whale (see Appendix A) that had a perfect fog of tails, and jaws clean down to the hump.

CHAPTER XV.

Enormous Supply of Blood in the Whale.—Sir John Hunter's Views.—
Whales' Spouts.—The Life.—Spouting thick Blood, dies of Suffocation.
—Flurry.—Fin out.—Telegraphing.—The "Glip," or Wake.—"Lob-
tailing."—"Breaching" and "Sounding."—Turning Flukes.—Regular-
ity in the Spouting, Time of Blowing, Submergence, and Speed of
Whales discussed.—Description of Spout.—Errors of Naturalists on the
Spout.—Skin of Whale.—Flesh and Blood.—Their Young.—Period of
Gestation.—Whale's Office in the Millennium.—Age of Whales measured
by the Teeth.—Sand-marks on the Teeth as affecting Question of Food.—
Settling of Whales.—Size of Whales and their Proportions.—My Views
indorsed by old Whalemen.—Jumper, and Captain Scott, R.N.—Captain
Basil Hall's return from Dinner ashore, and what he saw.—Power of
Whales to remain under Water at Will, and Captain West's Opinion.—
Opinions of Captains Gardener, Covill, and West.—No Blood in the
Whale's immense Case and Junk.—Queries suggested thereby on Cir-
culation and Animal Heat.—Offices of the Oil glanced at.—Cold Cur-
rents of the Pacific.—Sperm-whales frequent these.—What Ledyard
Brown did.

THE enormous quantity of blood which flows from a
wounded and dying whale is a constant subject of observation and remark. That the whales possess a quantity of
blood proportionately greater than that of land animals is
quite certain. The disposition and use of such a great store
was first explained by the learned Sir John Hunter somewhat as follows: To enable the whale to descend to great
depths, and to remain under water for long periods, it becomes necessary that it should have a supply of arterialized
blood to maintain the circulation. To this end, in all the
family there exists a reservoir, composed of congeries of
great arteries, which become charged with arterialized blood
during the time of breathing on the surface; and it is sup-

posed that, after the blood in the general circulation is vitiated by the prolonged sounding, the pure blood in this reservoir comes in play, and maintains the circulation until the whale again rises to the surface. Such is my remembrance of Hunter's views, and I believe they are accepted by later observers. The sperm-whale is required to descend to great depths to obtain its food, so the period of submergence is more prolonged than in any of the other species; consequently, it is supposed to be furnished with a reserved force in a greatly increased quantity of blood. The sperm-whale is also distinguished at a great distance by the number of its spouts. Fifty, sixty, and seventy spouts are not unusual; in fact, we pretend to mark the size of the whale by the number of spouts, allowing a barrel of oil for every blow made. Were it not for the prolonged rising, man would be unable to approach a sperm-whale with a boat, such is their roving disposition, and the distances traversed under water.

The blood reservoir, lying under the spine and in the vicinity of the lungs, constitutes what whalemen term the "life" of the whale. This is described as packed with arteries of great size, coiled in the greatest complexity, and containing in their folds an unknown volume of the vital fluid. This is the spot sought for with the keen lance. When rudely invaded, the bloody torrent pouring from the folds surcharges the lungs, and is expelled through the blow-hole. Suffocation becomes inevitable; all the air-passages are choked, and death follows, sometimes in a very few minutes after the blow is given. At other times, when the wound is not so deep, the dying beast will spout hogsheads of thick gore, and his agonies may be prolonged for a considerable period. The creature will lie on the surface, feebly propelling itself onward, and, with quick, repeated sobs, will pour out its blood, coloring the surrounding sea for a great distance. From this stupor it arouses to the last struggle.

The head rises and falls, and the flukes strike the surface in rapid succession. With great force it will rapidly swim in a large circle, sometimes passing two or three times around, and then closing the circuit by rolling on its side, dead. This is termed the "flurry," and the ending of the tragedy is "fin out." We never witnessed the death of a sperm-whale that was not immediately preceded by the "flurry," and such, I believe, is the general experience of whalemen.

I have a mass of additional testimony about the prolonged submergence of whales. The offshore ground of the Pacific is of limited extent, and during the season is often crowded with ships, not unfrequently two, three, or four being seen in a single day. This affords opportunity for the frequent comparison of notes. Now it is a noticeable fact that at certain periods, say at the full of the moon, whales abound all over the ground, and many are then taken. This busy season will be followed by a period of two weeks or more during which no whales are visible over the entire ground. Ships will be spoken from all points of the compass, and to the question, "Have you seen whales?" the answer will be, "Not for a week or ten days." The busy and dull seasons for whaling prevail uniformly over the entire feeding-ground, comprising an area of about six hundred miles north and south, by about nine hundred miles east and west. From his long experience in the "offshore" fishery, Captain West declares his belief that the sperm-whale can stay under water for two weeks. Captain Covill, while not agreeing to this theory, admits that off French Rock, New Zealand, the great bull whales appear as though they might have been reposing on muddy bottom. So stained and rough are they that they seem almost mossy; and not unfrequently the lower jaw will be fringed with the tubular barnacle, such as is found attached to floating timber at sea. He has seen at least a peck measure of these shell-fish fringing the jaw of an old bull sperm-whale. These are never observed, so far as I know, on the jaw of whales on other feeding-grounds; nor can I imagine that the shell could maintain its position on a member which is in such active employment during the feeding or fighting season.

In connection with this theory, I will submit certain facts which may have a bearing upon it. The sperm-whale is furnished with an immense receptacle of oil in the head peculiar to this species, and quite as remarkable as the vast arteries in which the excess of circulating blood is stored, as described by Sir John Hunter. At page 85 is a description of the proportions and formation of the junk and case of the sperm-whale; but at that point I neglected to consider a striking peculiarity, *i. e.*, the absence of blood in this immense structure. That the reader may be impressed as I was by this anomalous feature, I will recall the proportions of the mass under consideration. The case and junk of the largest spermaceti may attain a length of twenty-five feet, a depth of eleven, and a breadth of nine feet, or twelve hundred cubic feet; weight about sixty thousand pounds. Now in this animal matter there is not an artery or vein, or a single drop of blood. We find nothing which varies the peculiar color of the pale yellow oily portions, nor do we find evidences of any tubular structure, save the great breathing-pipe. Yet the animal heat is as great throughout the entire head as though the circulation of blood was perfect. How can we account for this? Is it true, as modern science asserts, that the soluble portions of food in the stomach are taken up in the blood, and, by means of its circulation—laden as it is with the products of digestion, the skin, the flesh, and every other part of the body—draws from it that which it wants? "The action of each of these organs, the performance of their various duties, involve in their operations a continued absorption of the matters necessary for their support from the blood, and a constant formation of waste products, which are returned to the blood, and conveyed by it to the lungs and the kidneys," etc., etc. Thus the blood is regarded as the common carrier of the animal economy, and the arteries and veins are the canals through which this strange commerce is carried on. I would ask, How can this hypothesis be applied to the case before us, in which such an enormous and most elaborate structure conducts the building and wasting processes twenty-five feet distance from the presence of blood, and in the absence of any visible tubes for the conduct of matter in form other than blood, from the stomach to the distant junk and case? And by what means is the temperature maintained uniform with the rest of the body, which is shown to be more highly charged with blood than the land animals?

The uses to the animal of this great reservoir of oil in the case, and of oily matter throughout the head, is entirely unknown. Most writers have been content to accept the hypothesis that the formation acts as a buoy to lift the nostril above the water, it being assumed that the light oily matter preponderates in the head. But the fact is, the head is much less buoyant than the body, owing to the great proportion of dense and heavy "white horse;" and while the whale itself, when dead, floats on its side, the head turns, the spout-hole down and the bony jaw upward, showing that the part containing the sack of oil is the heaviest, and unfitted to support the spout-hole above the water. May there not be a connection between this reservoir of fatty matter and the supposed power of the whale to sustain life for a prolonged period beneath the surface of the sea? May not the vital flame find sustenance from it during the whale's hibernation? You smile at the thought of hibernation in tropical seas. But the presence of cold currents flowing from the poles toward the equator have been demonstrated, and it is quite possible for the sperm-whale to descend to such depths within the limits of the great polar streams as to lie suspended in a temperature authorizing the term of hibernation. According to the observations of the United States Exploring Expedition, the water in the neighborhood of Cape Horn at four hundred fathoms fell to a temperature of 28° Fahrenheit, and they traced a powerful current of this cold water setting north, along the west coast of South America, until it reached the Galapagos, at which point the temperature of the water is so low as to prevent the formation of coral on the reefs and in the bays. These currents are supposed to waft the squid and other food of the sperm-whale from the frigid zones, and in them the whalemen look for their prey. Whales, in soundings, have carried out six hundred fathoms of line, and at such depths they would surely meet the icy influences of polar seas.

Sperm-whales have a means of communicating with each other at long distances — how long has never been determined; but certainly at distances as great as are commanded by the eye from the mast-head of a ship, or a radius of six or seven miles. The means are a mystery, but every whaleman has observed the fact, and has based his operations in the chase upon it. It has been suggested that, as water is so good a conductor of sound, it may be by sound; but the distances are too great for any sound which the whale is capable of making to penetrate; and it is observed that the telegraph is perfect as ever in high winds, when a thousand waves are breaking. Dart an iron into a bull whale, or *gallie* him by going on his eye, and almost simultaneously with his cutting flukes in the air the whole school will show alarm by running and cutting their flukes, or by disappearing from the surface, and coming up miles to windward and running head out. If it be a cow that is struck, the bulls are arrested in flight, and are apt to gather about her, and offer chances for more than a single whale. Again, when a school of cows and calves are running frightened to windward, and a calf be struck, the whole school will "bring to," and gather closely around the wounded young, sometimes so closely packed that the inclosed boat will not dare to use the lance; and they will thus remain as long as the calf is alive, or the iron holds. But should the iron draw or the calf die, the whole school will instantly scatter. Whaling-captains have taken pains to observe from the mast-head, when a boat was going on to a whale to leeward, the effect on schools miles to windward; and as soon as the eye could turn from one spot to the other, the alarm of the struck whale to leeward was communicated to those to windward. The fact, as I stated, is within the experience of all, although the manner of communication is not even guessed at by the oldest and wisest of our whalemen.

Another peculiarity of the whale is the "glip." When the sperm-whale is alarmed, or on the alert against pursuit, on going down for a run beneath the surface it emits a portion of oil, or its equivalent, which for a considerable period of time causes a smooth, bright surface on the water. This is termed the glip, or wake. The mystery of the glip is in a real or supposed communication between this smooth spot and the whale occasioning it. Should the boat-header incautiously pull his boat into this glip, or cross the line between the retreating whale and his glip, the effect will be to gallie the animal; and it, with all its relations and friends, will go tearing to windward, head and tail in the air. The unfortunate "greenie" who fired the train will be upbraided furiously by all hands and the cook. The tail, or, as it is universally known by our whalemen, the flukes, is the propeller of the huge mass. From its horizontal position and its vertical motion, it is admirably adapted, as I have said, to throw the nose above the surface of the water for the purpose of breathing, out of the reach of the wash of the sea. I am unable to give you the anatomical detail of the wonderful propeller, but can bear testimony to its beauty in curves, and its perfect mechanical form. It has a hardness almost of iron, with elasticity greater than steel; and urged by a thousand horse-power, it becomes the terror of the puny bipeds in their fragile boats.

The only evidence we possess of whales signaling by sound is in the practice often observed of "lobtailing." In doing this, the whale places itself perpendicularly in the water, head downward, and, with its enormous tail in the air, it will swing from side to side, sweeping a radius of thirty feet with awful violence, the cannon-like concussions of which may be heard for many miles, while the sea is churned into a mound of snowy foam, and the air is filled with a cloud of spray. Our observation did not lead to the belief, however, that this deep tolling of the ocean-bell was intended as a tocsin, but rather as mere frisky play, inasmuch as we could never notice that other whales paid any attention to the seeming signal. "Breaching" is common to all varieties of whales. The whale rises vertically from the water with such velocity that it will project about three-fourths of its length into the air, and, falling on its sides, will create a great pile of white water. This may be seen from the mast-head eight or ten miles in the case of sperm-whales.

When a sperm-whale "sounds," it first lifts the forward parts a few feet out of the water, giving a strong spout, and then dipping the nose, it rounds the back in a high arch, and revolves as on an axis. Rounding higher until the hump tops the arch, it lifts the flukes without any spray, and throws them aloft twenty-five feet, the next moment quietly disappearing in a perpendicular descent. In the act the sea is scarcely rippled, and the wake left scarcely exceeds the diameter of the body. When this performance is observed from the mast-head, it is announced by the cry of "There go flukes!" On our cruising-ground this is a certain indication of sperm-whale, as the finback does not turn flukes. The right whale is never found so far from shore and off soundings, and the humpback and sulphur-bottom whales are seldom seen on sperm-whale ground. The sperm-whale always descends in this manner when undisturbed by boats, whether in the act of feeding or on its passages. Speaking of the speed of the sperm-whale, and the extreme regularity of its movements, George N. Covill, an old whaling captain of New Bedford, says that he has followed a sperm-whale in a free wind with the yards squared in, and every thing set that would draw, the ship making eight to ten knots, without gaining on it for twelve hours of light. During this time it never varied its time of staying down a single minute, nor the number of spouts, and it did not vary from a straight course by the fraction of a point. I have it from other captains that, having ascertained the course and rate of speed of a whale in the afternoon's chase, they have followed on during the night, and raised him again on return of light. As a measure of speed, a boat of the *St. Lawrence*, Captain Edward M. Baker, fastened to a right whale that ran dead to leeward, towing the boat. The ship followed with a full top-sail breeze; yet in four hours the following ship was lost to sight, although the day was entirely clear. Finally the line was cut, and the whale allowed to go without a lance in.

When the sperm-whale first comes up, or when she blows with the nose a little submerged, as in rough weather, or whenever circumstances favor the entrance of a portion of water into the great respiratory canal, the spout is plainly visible in the form of a dense white mist, lighter in color than the surrounding water, as seen from the mast-head of the ship, but darker, and cloud-like, against a clear horizon, as seen from the boat or the deck of a vessel. When the whale is at rest in a calm sea, with the nose above water, the spout is invisible. Thus a ship may sometimes approach close to the whale without its being discovered from the mast-head, the exhibition of its flukes, as it sounds, being the first indication of it.

The breathing-pipe of a large sperm-whale is thirty feet long, and twelve inches in diameter, and the misty cloud of its spout enlarges from this size to four or five feet at its widest part, passing along the surface of the sea some eight or ten feet. When this spout is thrown into the boat and strikes the sailors, which is not seldom, it feels like spray, in density proportionate to the depth of the nose at the time of blowing. There is but a slight sound attending prolonged respiration when the whale is at rest ; but when frightened, or running, the whale makes a rushing sound, sometimes like a snort. I am of opinion that the inspiration does not occupy one-tenth the time required in the expiration; indeed, it is instantaneous in the running whale ; yet the shorter process is silent, and the longer noisy. How to account for this? Naturalists are greatly divided regarding the spout of the whales, and have exhausted ingenious theories to show that the spout is less an act of breathing than a means of getting rid of the superfluous water which enters the mouth with the food. "This water," they inform us, "is, by a most ingenious contrivance, forced into the nasal cavities while the animal performs the act of swallowing ; then the forcible contraction of the muscles surrounding the passage sends it out in a jet." Scholarly men contrive industriously for nature, and poets sing,

> " While spouting whales, projecting watery columns,
> That turned to arches at their height, and seemed
> The skeletons of crystal palaces
> Built on the blue expanse."

But no whaleman has witnessed a jet of water coming from the spout-hole of a whale—the very blood which clogs the lungs after the death-thrust is blown into the air as a fiery spray or mist. The nostril of the sperm-whale is a single opening on the extreme end of the nose, and the breathing-pipe passes the whole length of the case, parallel with the great oil-sack, and through the base of the skull, into the lungs, the length perhaps reaching thirty-two feet.

The skin of the whale is not naked, as is generally supposed; for beneath the external pellicle, or varnish, termed black skin, is a curdy deposit, which the day after the death of the animal is easily scraped away, and reveals a close fur about one-eighth of an inch long. This envelops the entire external surface, and is rooted in the true skin, or blubber. The flesh is a dark red, very firm, and of the texture of rope-yarns—tough as forecastle beef; not toothsome, but fit for food in a squeeze. The blood in heat reaches 104° Fahrenheit.

The whales in general bring forth their young alive, and suckle them by means of two abdominal mammæ. They are gregarious in habit, and occur in large schools, except the old males, which are often found alone. Their ordinary rate of travel is about five miles an hour; but this the sperm-whale can increase to ten and twelve miles, and in a short race perhaps more. The period of gestation in the right whale seems pretty well established at about nine or ten months, and we may suppose the same of the sperm-whale; yet every thing pertaining to this part of natural history of this whale must remain a mystery to us. The young have been taken from dead mothers, and observers represent them to be fourteen feet long. The milk of the whale is white, fat, and thick. How long the young remain with the mother is unknown, but it is observed that the herd seem to have a watchful care over them until they attain a considerable size.

Bold guessers allow the young twenty or twenty-five years to grow, and it is supposed whales live to a great age. In the old whale the teeth are blunt. In old bulls the teeth are sometimes worn down almost even with the jaw. Now consider that these teeth (especially those of the cow, which is not supposed to fight) have only to encounter the soft substance of the squid, and conceive the age necessary to wear down this hard ivory. Let us consider the signs engraved on the surface. When we regard the position of the eye of the sperm-whale, and its comparatively limited range of vision, and that the creature is without a hand to grasp and convey its food to an extremely narrow mouth, and then consider the activity of the fishes by which the whale is surrounded, we might naturally conclude that it could enjoy but a precarious existence at best. As we are led to inquire into the special provision made for the sustenance of an animal so huge, and yet so helpless, we are struck at once with the simplicity of one of the means by which it is enabled to entrap its prey. It is known that the squids or sepia, about which our readers have heard so many yarns already, are attracted by, and attach themselves to, a white or shining object. Fishermen take advantage of this by lowering hooked tin or other lures to attract and capture them. The jaw of the sperm-whale, the inner side of the mouth, and the tongue are of a silvery whiteness, and, some observers assert, are provided with a luminous or phosphorescent quality which is irresistible to the sepia, in the gloom of its home, the dark color of the whale's body being invisible in the deep water. Doubtless the smaller sepia such as we find abundantly in the stomach of the black-fish, are thus taken by the sperm-whale.

The great size of the deep-sea squid is within the whale's means of attack, and furnishes a rich feast. Remains of sharks and other large fishes are also disgorged by the wounded whales, however, especially in and about the Indian Ocean. But besides these recognized sources of subsistence, I am led to believe that they feed partly on other substances, for, on examining the worn surfaces of the whale's tooth, it will be observed that the ivory is marked with scratches, as though made with a coarse rasp. These are seen crossing the point in various directions, and obliquely down the sides of the tooth to the gum, showing that the tooth comes in frequent contact with matters harder than its own substance, and of minute and angular forms, such as corals, crushed shells, or sand. None of these things have been observed in the whale's stomach, however. I mention this unnoticed feature, that the future naturalist may take it into account in making up his chapter on the food of the whale.

The "settling" of the whale is so remarkable as to require a notice also. It is often a means of safety when the ordinary motions of diving or running are insufficient. From a position of entire rest, floating at length on the surface, and spouting at leisure, the whale has a power of sinking bodily with great rapidity, without altering its horizontal position, and without a motion of the tail or fins. As far as a person in the boat can determine, it often resorts to this means of escape when a boat comes suddenly within the range of vision, and so close at hand that the whale dare not round out to sound. I have seen the sperm-whale at rest suddenly seem a mass of lead, and sink from the head of the boat so rapidly that the harpoon was darted, but not delivered. Many whales escape thus; and nothing can exceed the mortification the occurrence causes the boat-steerer. He hauls in the still straight iron, and can scarcely credit his senses.

The sperm-whale attains a very great size. The measure of a whale, in whaling parlance, is indicated by the number of barrels of oil it will make. Ask any old whaling-captain of forty years' experience, how long is the longest sperm-whale, and he will strive to answer the question by estimating the known proportions of his ship. "Let me see. From just forrard of fore-swifter to the main-swifter, well, say forty-five feet, and you have his eye; allow one-third for the head, and you have seventy-two. Well, now, seventy-two feet is a long whale; but I never measured one." The largest whale we took made one hundred and seven barrels. Its length was 79 feet; from the nose to the bunch of the neck, 26 feet; thence to the hump, 29 feet; from hump to tail, 17 feet; length of tail, 7 feet; breadth of tail, 16 feet 6 inches; height at forehead, 11 feet; width, 9 feet 6 inches; girt at fin, 41 feet 6 inches; at junction of tail, 7 feet 9 inches; lower jaw, 16 feet long, and 41 inches in circumference at thick part. It had 51 teeth, the heaviest weighing 25 ounces. Blubber on back, 18 inches; on side, 12 to 15 inches; and belly, 9 to 10 inches. The hump was two feet above the level. The case made 19 barrels; body, 73½ barrels; junk, 14½ barrels. Captain Sullivan, of the *James Arnold*, of New Bedford, off New Zealand, took in one voyage eight whales that made over 100 barrels each, the largest yielding 137 barrels. The head of this made 52 barrels, and the case baled 27 barrels. It was 90 feet long; the flukes 18 feet, jaw 18 feet, case 22 feet, and forehead 13½ feet high. During the same season and on the same ground, Captain Vincent, ship *Oneida*, of New Bedford, took ten sperm-whales, which stowed 1140 barrels. Captain Norton, ship *Monka*, of New Bedford, took on the offshore ground a sperm-whale that stowed 145 barrels; the dimensions of this monster were not taken. The proportions of whales vary much with the sex and age. The young bulls and the cows are slender; the cows are about one-third the size of the bull, when measured by the oil they yield. Such is about the sum, embodied in rough and desultory notes, of what I saw and learned of the sperm-whale. I have striven to avoid guessing, and to note that which came to my simple, untrained senses. Most of these observations have met the approval of men of great experience; and if they should take a single thorn from the path of some future Lesson in his researches, it will not be in vain I have written.

In the waters of Japan there is sometimes seen a fish which, from its great size, is often supposed to be a whale. We know it by the name of the "jumper," from its habit of leaping entirely clear of the water, and falling with a great splash, like the sturgeon. So far as I can learn, nothing more is known of its form or habits than may be observed in its flying leaps. It appears to be of a slender make, and about as long as a ten-barrel sperm-whale. It does not come to the surface to breathe, but seems to inhabit the deep. We saw several during a few days. The crew all thought them to be whales, until Captain B—— informed us to the contrary. It may be this fish that Captain N. Scott, R.N., gives an account of in "Wood's Natural History." He says that he "has seen the whale spring to such a height out of water that the horizon could be seen under it, although the spectators were standing on the deck of a man-of-war. The whale was about three miles away from the ship when observed." I would ask what captain in the Royal Navy could distinguish this monster fish from the whale three miles away?

Once upon a time, under the shaded porch of the inn at Bridgehampton, Long Island, kept by John Hull, an old whaler, and a trustworthy boat-steerer, I heard Ledyard Brown, another boat-steerer, claim to have thrown his iron into a sperm-whale when it was bodily in the air above the level of his head. He steered Captain Rose, of Sag Harbor, and he is the only American I have met who claims to have seen a whale bodily in the air. Ledyard is brave, steady, and truthful, and I can only suppose that in the moment of striking a fighting whale he became a little bewildered with flukes, jaws, gleaming ivory, and roaring cataracts.

CHAPTER XVI.

Loss of Ship *Union* by a Whale.—Captain G——'s Experience with a
Sperm-whale.—Whaling favorable to Longevity.—Monument in Sag
Harbor to six young Captains proves the Contrary.—Loss of a whole
Boat's Crew.—Captain Henry Huntting and his good Fortune.—Captain
James Huntting carried down by a Whale, and cutting Line.—One of
his Crew recovered from the Line, and improvised Surgery.—Two Men
killed by the Line.

HERE I resume my neglected journal: Eight bells. Starboard watch on deck. A half-moon silvers the gentle, rippling sea. The ship rolls easily to the long swell, steadied by the reefed top-sails. One dozing fellow is at the wheel to keep the ship's head to the wind, and the remainder of the watch are gathered on the forehatch, calling upon Posey for a story of men famous in the ocean hunt. "Tell us of old Captain Gardiner, and his loss of the *Union*," we asked.

"You never saw that grand old man, did you? You should have that story from his own lips to appreciate it, but I will do my best. When twenty-two years of age, he sailed captain of the *Union*, of Nantucket, it being his first voyage as master. Twelve days out from Nantucket, the forward watch were alarmed at night by seeing a sperm-whale coming head on to the ship, which had such headway that the blow could not be avoided. In another moment the whale struck the ship a tremendous blow fair on the bow, which brought every body from their berths to the deck. It was apparent that the bows were stove in, and the ship was rapidly filling. Three boats were lowered, and a stock of water and provisions hastily placed in them.

Soon after the ship rolled over, and went down, leaving the crew adrift in mid-ocean in the fragile whale-boats, the nearest land being the Azores, distant about seven hundred miles. This was a trying situation for our young captain; but he was equal to it. Considering the danger of separation increased by his having the crew divided in three boats, he concluded to take all hands and the supplies into two, and abandon the third. Thus crowded, after eight days of perilous navigation and much suffering, he reached the Azores, without the loss of a man. His prudence and good conduct under such trying circumstances secured to him another ship as soon as he reached home. After this he sailed master for twenty years, and in all that long experience never had a man killed in his boat."

"Do you mean to tell us that he never met with any accidents after this first taste of the quality of old square-nose?" we demanded.

"No, he couldn't say that; for he is now a crippled man, eighty-eight years of age, but so hale and hearty that he will read manuscript without glasses. Once a sperm-whale threw its terrible jaw into his boat, and struck him on the head and shoulders, making a deep scalp-wound, breaking his jawbone, tearing out five teeth, breaking his shoulder-blade and arm, and crushing his left hand between the tooth and gunwale of the boat. When this broken man was carried on board, his young mates, hopeless of his recovery, were at loss what to do for him. He had to give directions for the preparation of the necessary splints and bandages, and instruct the men in the manner of reducing the fractures and bandaging them. After this, he ordered them into a port to which they were strangers, and, lying on deck at the point of death, he scanned the headlands, and piloted his ship into port. A Spanish surgeon visited him, and, after examination, advised him to send for a priest, for he was be-

yond surgical aid.   But this advice didn't chime in with his
Yankee idea that where there is life there is hope, and he sent
a messenger into the interior, some thirty miles, for a Ger-
man physician.   The good Samaritan hastened down to the
coast, dressed the captain's wounds, and giving him restoratives, brought him to bear transportation on an ambulance
slung between two mules, away from the unhealthy coast to
a healthy mountain home.   Here in six months the old man
recovered sufficiently to resume command of his ship, which
in the mean time had made a successful cruise on the offshore ground.   His left hand had healed into an unsightly
stump, with the two forefingers so contracted on the palm
that, when he afterward went in the boat, it was necessary
to wear a thick mitten to prevent the lance-warp from catching under them.   But the hand was still good to direct the
lance to the life of many a good whale.

"Such was the effect produced on his mind by this terrible encounter with the whale, that it became a favorite belief with the brave, good old man that he was a monument
of God's loving mercy, 'living on borrowed time;' and his experience of a protecting Providence, as especially extended
to those engaged in whaling, led him to remark that 'somehow men were wonderfully preserved who stuck close to the
business.'   In any other occupation he would say, 'A crew
of thirty-two men could not go out forty-eight months without some loss before the end, but he had seen them go safe
in whaling, voyage after voyage.   He told me of a family of
five brothers in Nantucket, all masters of whalers, now living at an average age of eighty-two years."

Hinton's rich mellow voice struck in here:

"The winds they blew a hurricane, the sea was mountains rollin',
  When Barny Buntlin turned his quid, and said to Billy Bowlin':
  'A strong sow-wester's blowing, Billy; don't you hear it roar now?
  How I pity all unhappy folks as lives upon the shore now!'"

Hinton (recitative:) "Old Captain Gardiner is one of the lucky ones; he has doubled the Cape of Good Hope for this life, with only one real squall that made him reef pretty close for a spell; but he has dipped up from the sea a pretty fortune, and he can, in his old days, sing with me:

> " 'In the downhill of life when I find I'm declining,
> May my fate no less fortunate be,
> Than a snug elbow-chair will afford for reclining,
> And a cot that o'erhangs the wide sea.'

"But, boys, I can tell you a different story from that which you have just heard," Hinton continued. "Away, away around the dark stormy cape, and up in the north, lies the quiet, shaded cemetery of Sag Harbor. Under the shelter of overarching elms is a beautiful marble monument, a broken ship's mast, around whose foot is coiled a broken and unstranded hawser. On the base is this inscription:

> " 'TO COMMEMORATE THAT NOBLE ENTERPRISE,
> THE WHALE-FISHERY;
> AND A TRIBUTE OF LASTING RESPECT
> TO THOSE BOLD AND ENTERPRISING SHIP-MASTERS,
> SONS OF SOUTHAMPTON,
> WHO PERILED THEIR LIVES IN A DARING PROFESSION,
> AND PERISHED IN ACTUAL ENCOUNTER
> WITH THE MONSTERS OF THE DEEP.
>
> ---
>
> ENTOMBED IN THE OCEAN, THEY LIVE IN OUR MEMORY.'

And six young heroes are named on another face of the base:

CHARLES W. PAYNE, Captain of the ship *Fanny,*   aged 30, killed in 1838.
STRATTON H. HARLOW,   "   "   "   "   *Daniel Webster,*   "   27,   "   " 1838.
ALFRED G. GLOVER,   "   "   "   "   *Acasta,*   "   29,   "   " 1836.
RICHARD S. TOPPING,   "   "   "   "   *Thorn,*   "   29,   "   " 1838.
WILLIAM H. PIERSON,   "   "   "   "   *America,*   "   30,   "   " 1840.
JOHN E. HOWELL,   "   "   "   "   *France,*   "   28,   "   " 1840.

And this records only part of the loss. Young Topping, of the *Thorn*, had his boat stove by the whale. He got into the mate's boat, and returned to the attack. Not one of that crew came out of the encounter alive. Captain, mate, and five men perished, just how no one witnessed; and none survived to tell the sad tale. This is a marble record that in ten years from this one port six masters perished, the oldest being thirty years. For them I could sing," Hinton went on,

> " 'Keep thy red gold and gems, thou stormy grave!
> Give back the true and brave;
> Give back the lost and lovely! those for whom
> The place was kept at board and hearth so long!'

"That is a black picture, Hinton," said Posey; "though I can't help holding, with the good Gardiner, that there's a 'sweet little cherub that sits up aloft, and looks out for the fate of poor Jack.' There is Captain Henry Huntting, a son of Southampton too, who ran the gauntlet, boy and man, boat-steerer, mate, and captain, and never had a man killed in his boat, and excepting one ugly knock on the knee from a whale's flukes, was never hurt in his long experience. And there's his brother, Captain Jim. If there ever was a man to believe that whalemen are wonderfully preserved, he is the man. Did any of you ever see Captain James Hunt-ting? No? Then just figure to yourselves a young giant, seventy-eight inches in his stocking-feet, two hundred and fifty pounds in weight, and not an ounce of fat to cut his wind—proportions of Hercules, and the face of man.

"When he was a boat-steerer, a sperm-whale stove his boat, and rolled it over on him. He came up under it all tangled in the line that was coiled in the stern-sheets of the boat. He fought like a giant to throw off the deadly coil. It was about his body, his arms, and his neck. It was for dear life that he was working, and he knew the odds were against him. He got rid of the line, as he thought, and had got a breath of the blessed air and a glance at God's sunlight, when he was jerked out of the sight of his horrified shipmates. A bight of the line, yet attached to the sounding whale, was around his ankle, and he bid good-bye to this world as he was plunging into the deep sea. Yet he was alert to take instant advantage of a slack in the speed of the whale. Drawing himself forward by the line, with his sheath-knife he severed the cord beyond the entangled foot, and rose to the surface, exhausted by the time he had been under and the lacerating wounds inflicted by the tight-strained line. The boats picked him up. No one on board knew any more of surgery than he did. So, with help from willing but unskilled hands, the broken ankle was patched up after a fashion, and kind Nature healed it, with the bones unshipped and out of place, leaving him nearly as good a man as he was before his awful plunge.

"Another instance of wonderful preservation from a cruel death by the line occurred in his experience many years after this, and goes to show how the whaleman is educated to perform, and inured to suffer in the stern vicissitudes of the chase. By some mishap the line kinked in the boat, and a man was caught and jerked from the boat by the running whale. After being drawn with frightful speed some one hundred and twenty-five fathoms from the boat, he was released by his limbs giving way to the strain. Thus freed, and almost unconscious, he rose to the surface and was picked up and carried on board the ship. On examination, it was found that a portion of the hand, including four fingers, had been torn away, and the foot sawed through at the ankle, leaving only the great tendon and the heel suspended to the lacerated stump. From the knee downward the muscular flesh had been rasped away by the line, leaving the protruding bone enveloped in a tangled mat of tendons and bleeding arteries. Saved from drowning, the man seemed likely to meet a more cruel death, unless some one had the nerve to perform the necessary amputation. At that time the New Bedford ships were the only ones that carried surgical instruments to meet such a case. But Captain Jim was not the man to allow any one to perish on slight provocation. He had his carving-knife, carpenter's saw, and a fish-hook. The injury was so frightful, and the poor fellow's groans and cries so touching, that several of the crew fainted in their endeavors to aid the captain in the operation, and others sickened and turned away from the sight. Unaided, the captain then lashed his screaming patient on the carpenter's bench, amputated the leg, and dressed the hand as best he could. Then, running to the Sandwich Islands, he placed the sailor in the hospital, where he recovered, returning to the United States, and for many years supporting himself by a little shop, and 'living on borrowed time,' 'another living monument of God's mercy,' as Captain Gardiner would say. In my opinion, Captain Jim suffered the most in that operation, because he couldn't scream to let off his feelings.

"See the portrait of my hero in the prime of life; see the same man at forty-six years of age, still hale and hearty, erect and powerful, with the rosy complexion

A NIMROD OF THE SEA.

of youth. There is not much change, considering the terrible wear and tear on as splendid a physique as ever trod deck on whaleboat. Chapters of story or song could not enlarge on the history recorded in the snowy hair and aged face of the second portrait.

"On another occasion," Posey resumed, "a sperm-whale stove one of the boats of his ship, and two men were lost. After the whale was killed, the men on the ship proceeded to haul in the line of the broken boat, when the two missing men were found entangled in several turns, and mangled almost out of the form of humanity by the action of the line and the swift towing through the water. Judge ye of the effect on the surviving crew, as one after the other of these poor wrecks were towed up from the grave in which they had been so suddenly and deeply buried."

"This is growing too serious, boys," cried Hinton; and he piped up:

> " ' What argufies pride and ambition?
> Soon or late death will take us in tow;
> Each bullet has got its commission,
> And when our time's come we must go.'

"Now strike eight bells, call the larboard watch, turn in, and dream of spermaceti."

Sept. 14. With the lofty land of Albemarle, Galapagos, in sight, we were spoken by the *Science*, of Portland, Captain Whippie, eighteen months out, four hundred barrels. We hailed ten months, and four hundred and fifty barrels. Such are the items of interest to two whalers as they cross each other's path on the fishing-ground. An "All well" ends the interview, and with a sweep of the trumpet the order is given, "Brace forward mainyard." So we part strangers, as we met.

CHAPTER XVII.

A Quarrel, and Knife drawn.—Portuguese flogged, and Reflections thereon.
—Sunday on Board, and Library.—Religion on Board.—Pythagoras on
Board.—The Providence for Sailors.—Books in Demand, and Kind.—
Chips and his Journal.—Chips in the Battle of Plattsburg.—His Views
of the Sabbath.—Right-whale Porpoise taken.—Five hours' Chase un-
successful.—Another Chase successful.—Rock of Dunda mistaken for a
Ship.—Fishing off Abington Island.—Second Visit to Cocos Island.—
Hector, of New Bedford.—Hunt for wild Hogs.—Beautiful Parrot-fish.
—Growths in the Bay, and Sea-porcupine.—Boat lost.

Sept. 16. A quarrel between two of the men resulted in
Antonio, a Portuguese, drawing a knife on his shipmate.
The weapon was knocked from his hand,

> " With a God d—, those syllables intense !
> Nucleus of England's native eloquence."

A regular breeze was the consequence. The second mate
reported the row to the supreme authority, and the fiery
Antonio was summoned to the quarter-deck to answer. His
offense was serious; it was shown that he meant mischief,
and we could not seriously demur when we saw him lashed
to the weather main-rigging, and his yellow back exposed to
the rope's-end. But, however much we condemned Antonio's
act, when we saw and heard the rope's-end cut the writhing
flesh, and heard the man's moaning supplication to " Santa
Marie" and "Jesu Christo," we forgot it. Very serious
thoughts occupied my mind as I looked on the cruel scene;
and for the first time in the voyage the life became horrible
and hateful to me. The sentiment of obedience to authority
must be instinctive in human hearts, or how could a few offi-

cers hold men in thrall to such humiliation? It is not a mere question of the power. The distinction of the quarter-deck and the forecastle disappear at such a moment, and officer and sailor face the occasion as men governed by one law.

Sept. 20 (*Sunday*). According to rules, we abstain from all labor on Sunday, save the necessary handling of the ship and the pursuit of whales, if any are seen; and of course we keep the try-works going, should we have blubber on board. In these warm, calm, and bright latitudes we spend the day very quietly; a few men write or·draw; some *scrimshone*, or carve keepsakes for friends from bone of the whale's jaw, the ivory of the teeth, or the rich woods and mother-of-pearl found on the islands; some read; and some sleep. We have on board a scant ship's library of uninteresting religious books, provided by some Seaman's Friend Society with kindly intent, and an inexhaustible store of tracts entirely too childish for men famishing for intellectual food. We turn unsatisfied from these dying experiences of some good souls as they descend to the dark stream of death, as we live habitually so close to the brink of the sombre river that we are not impressed by them. Pardon me for speaking plainly, but the picture of our life would be incomplete if I withheld expression of the thoughts of the forecastle on such subjects. The comments of the men on these tracts, if heard by the givers, would not encourage their distribution. Seamen see so little difference between the partial and capricious Deity pictured by the dyspeptic fancies of presumptuous writers and their own officers, that they mix up in a disrespectful jumble captain, gods, and mates. Half mutinously they answer "Ay, ay, sir," alike to the order to "scrape top-masts" from the one, and "Stand by to keep·the Sabbath-day holy" from the other. Now I pray you, good hearts who really wish to elevate these rough children of the sea, not to jump to the conclusion that my shipmates reject all religion. I

read to them to-day the following words, ascribed to the old
heathen Pythagoras, and they listened understandingly to
his teaching:

"The Divine mind and universal spirit that pervades and diffuseth itself
     over all nature.

"All things receive their life from Him.   There is but One only God,
  Not seated above the world, and beyond the orb of the universe;
  But being himself all in all, he sees all things that fill his immensity.

"The only principle, the light of heaven, the Father of all,
  He produces every thing; he orders and disposes every thing;
  He is the reason, the life, and the motive of all things."

And this reading seemed to satisfy their sense of the relation between themselves and their Author.   They may not
have. known, but I think they felt, that the power of this
Deity found expression in the beautiful and wonderful works
among which we live.

Poor Jack! he has few ports or havens of rest and safety
provided for him! He meets with little kindness or consideration at the hands of his superiors; he feels that he is exposed to danger on the sea, and more deadly perils on shore.
No one extends the helpful hand.   All he hopes is that there
is a better future in store for him.   Dibdin's "Sweet little
cherub" becomes a hymn of faith, and he believes in it as
a gospel. If you would reach him, show that this Providence is not only aloft, but that it cares for him on earth;
that it planted the succulent cactus, and created the water-
bearing terrapin on the scoria of the Galapagos, that man
might not perish.   Teach him that where rains are not, the
great God provides the dew-imbibing pitcher-plant and the
refreshing melon, that man might know his goodness; that
it is he who places the oil-bearing nuts and animals to feed
the lamp of life in the frigid zones, and the cooling acids
and sugary fruits to quench fevers in the torrid heats; that

A LAND SHARK.

the fur-bearing animals, the resinous woods, and the vast coal-fields are his provision against the rigors of one; and the broad umbrella foliage and dense growths his screens against the blistering sun in the other. Show to these children that their Father so loves them that he has surely provided for all their needs.

I am quite sure that the landsman's idea of the sailor

would be modified could they have witnessed scenes in our forecastle in the calm nights on our cruising-ground, when the watch gathered about the windlass or main-hatch. Under the starry sky hard, worn faces were upturned, as a young comrade recited the stories, stranger than fiction, about science. Let me say that a copy of St. Pierre's "Studies of Nature" was to us a book of religion; two old volumes of the "New England Farmer" were a popular fund of instruction; works on natural history, especially those illustrated, were in great demand; so were "Delano's Voyages," and all works, not forgetting the Bible, which shed positive light on the path of life. The biographies of strong, self-made men had a great attraction, and the best novels were appreciated. Such works as these should fill seamen's libraries.

At 1 P.M. we raised a large breach to leeward, and we ran off for it; but as we came up the tall spout revealed the finback. We then resumed our course south-west, with a stiff breeze, and at sundown shortened sail and stood on the wind.

Sept. 23. The last two days the "C was ruf," as old Chips, the carpenter, has it. He is the only one on board besides myself who keeps a journal, and he is writing for the amusement of his "old woman." He says she delights in the beauties of his spelling and language, and he swears that my way lacks originality, as I always spell the same words the same way, while he never spells it twice alike. Chips is a remnant of the last war, having been in the very early part of the battle of Plattsburg, but he retired soon after firing commenced, badly wounded — in his feelings. He had his trained eye placed on the back-sight of a battery gun, aiming at one of the British ships, when a shot from another struck somewhere on the breech of his gun, within, he says, "an inch of my nose, and, you see, the crash sounded as if the heavens and earth were coming together; and when I come to and got the infernal hum out of my ears I was settin' on a bench in a cabin at the foot of one of the Adirondacks, about thirty-five mile back of Plattsburg, and they told me the fight was over, and we had licked the Britishers. I jumped right on end and hooraed for dear life, for I know'd we could lick 'em."

Chips has a habit on Sunday mornings of combing his hair and mounting a pair of green spectacles, so as to distinguish the Sabbath from other days, and he would not give a " continental cuss," as he expresses it, for the chances of a man who holds that the maintop-sail is white on this day. Barring these weaknesses, Chips is a good workman, and can repair a *chawed* boat neatly and expeditiously.

During this rough weather we have had many porpoises under the bows. One of the boat-steerers standing on the martingale pitched the porpoise-iron into one, and with much noise and confusion it was hauled on deck. It was a beautiful right whale porpoise, distinguished by a broad stripe of pure white running from the tip of the snout to the end of its flukes, and contrasting perfectly with the polished jet of the rest of its body. We stripped the thin blubber from the body, and let the cook try it out for the forecastle lamp, thus saving two gallons of sperm-oil. From the body we took some dark meat which, with onions, made a savory fry. This was the beef that Major Williams promised us, granting that we might eat all we could catch. It is a frequent dish, for we neglect no chance to banish salt-beef from our table by the capture of this beautiful little whale. The lower jaw is closely set with polished, curved, and sharp teeth, which make no bad substitute for a comb, having the necessary strength to straighten unkempt locks, and to bring away such tangles as gather in a week's repose. In the base, or pan, of the lower jaw is a marrowy fat, which yields a thin limpid oil, in great request by watch-makers, gunsmiths, etc., and we neglect no opportunity to collect it. A good jaw will yield several ounces, by exposing the fat to the full heat of the sun.

At meridian I got out my almost forgotten quadrant, and made an attempt at "shooting the sun" (as taking the sun's altitude is termed) with my complicated instrument. I took a pretty good aim, and brought down a latitude the first shot, and made our position to be 4° 54' S., quite proud that I had kept south of the equator in a first attempt. Soon after eight bells, the song came, "There she blows, blows! hump all out. Sperm-whale close aboard on the lee beam!" Four boats were lowered at once, and we pulled our best stroke by spells for five long hours, with never a chance to dart. Mournfully we skulked back to the ship, tired, wet, and crusty enough to cover a sea-pie. The whales were in great.numbers, and unusually large for school-whales, being estimated at eighty-barrelers.

.Sept. 27 (*Sunday*). The wind has been high for the past two days; and to-day, while running under single-reefed fore and main top-sails, we raised a sperm-whale on the lee bow. We lowered two boats, and Mr. F—— went on; but the whale settled, and avoided the darted iron. After a two hours' chase to windward against a heavy combing sea, which kept the afteroarsman bailing, our boat gave up the chase, and we pulled for the ship. Our boat was scarcely on the cranes, when the man at the mast-head shouted out that the mate's boat was fast. Before we could reach the scene, the whale was spouting thick blood, and now a seventy-barrel whale is floating alongside, and we are laying head-yards aback, with a considerable sea running. Lat. 5° 40', long. 107° 37' W.

Nov. 4. This morning we raised Albemarle Island, and soon after the singular volcanic Rondonda, or Rock of Dunda. This formation rises to a considerable height, almost perpendicularly, from the water's edge. Blue water beats against it. At a distance it resembles a huge tower, isolated by many miles from other islands. Tradition hath it that it is sometimes mistaken for a ship, and that a tipsy skipper once ran under its stern, and hailed: "Whence, and whither bound?" and the rock-bound coast echoed, "whither bound?" Now we squared away for Cocos Island, to take in water.

The following morning we ran close under Abington Island, and sent in two boats to obtain a mess of fish. Anchoring in five fathoms' water, we found an abundance of a fish called the grouper, some of which might weigh thirty pounds. A number of the curious and unsuspecting relatives would often follow a captured fish to the surface, and were killed with a sharpened waif-pole. We took nearly a ton weight of this fine fish. The sport was much enjoyed by all, as was the cookery of the "Doctor" when we returned on board. We now are on our course for Cocos Island.

Nov. 6. Twelve months from New London! We have six hundred and fifty barrels of oil, and ought not to complain, considering our erratic course, and the work of many ships we have heard from.

Nov. 9. Second year. Came to anchor in the harbor of Cocos Island, and stowed two hundred barrels of water. In the afternoon the *Hector*, of New Bedford, Captain Norton, ten months out, six hundred barrels of oil, anchored beside us, also to water.

Nov. 11. Finished watering last night. All hands had liberty on shore. A party started on a hunt for wild hogs. The weather was less wet than on our previous visit. Men on the beach reported a gleam of sunshine, a notable fact in this pluvius spot. After a scrambling chase, a tall, bristling boar was pulled down. He showed fight with his ugly tusks, but a blow with the heavy seal-club brought him to earth. Being in for a joyous time, we worked up material to the best advantage, and decorated ourselves with vines, the flowers of air-plants, and passion-vine. Then, with our prize slung over a pole, we marched to the beach, chorusing,

> " Though it rains, it hails, it snows, it blows,
>   Yet this day a boar must die."

We came in jolly and thirsty, and infinitely more steady than the barons of old from their royal boar-hunts. In our hog we found material for a sea-pie. The rock bearing our ship's name was almost buried in the sand, and all hands united in rolling it up out of the reach of the waves. A solitary grave was pointed out as being that of a poor fellow who was drowned in attempting to swim ashore and desert to this land of continuous shower-baths. With slender, barbed spears we took several varieties of the beautiful parrot-fish, which abound in the coral groves in the bottom of the bay. These fishes are of beautiful metallic colors—red, green, and purple, finely contrasted in belts and spots, and in blending clouds. The head, plated in an armor of broad, thick scales of the greatest brilliancy, is fitted for browsing on the zoophytes which dwell in the sharp cells of the branching corals and madrepores. In these growths, and amidst the waving tangle of many-colored marine plants, these fish, with multitudes of other strange and beautiful creatures, are seen in great numbers. From caves great cray-fish protrude their fringed heads and azure feelers; and the loathsome toad-fish creeps from bunch to bunch of the grasses. Flapping over the tops of the marine forest we also see the brown devil-fish, and the echinus, or sea-eggs. Tempted to reach for some sea-flowers, and wading the shallow, I touched a sea-egg with my bare foot, and ran to the shore in agony. The thing is like a porcupine, and the sole

of my foot was penetrated by its black spines, which broke
off short, leaving many points envenomed and rankling in
the wounds, each like the fiery sting of a hornet. My pleasure for the day was destroyed. We strove in vain to remove the shelly barbs, but they would only come away in
little disks. A piece of salt-pork rind was applied to draw
the poison, and after some hours the pain subsided, but
each puncture became surrounded with a dark blue ring.
The captain took two boats and pulled to the windward side
to get cocoa-nuts, which there abound. In the evening his
party returned, the two crews in a single boat. The other
boat was caught in the surf in landing, and dashed on the
rocks. The crew escaped to the shore, and walked some
distance to a point, when they were taken in the other boat.
The double crew loaded the boat so deeply that they could
not bring nuts in the face of an ugly chopping sea.

CHAPTER XVIII.

Race with the *Hector.*—Alternate Success.—Our final Triumph.—Bone-shark.—Anchored at Charles Island.—No Water, no Woman, and took to Fishing.—*Elmira*, Captain Marchant, and Preparations for a Fandango.—Governor Villamill comes on Board, and Captain gives all Hands a Drink by Proxy.—Details on Defense, and how the Yankees did it.—Hunt a Bull.—Hunted in Turn.—Bull killed, and a Row.—The Ship to be taken.—The Row settled.—Story of the Lava Cave.

Nov. 12. Got under way, in company with the *Hector*, on a race, as agreed upon. Both captains prided themselves on the sailing qualities of their ships, and determined to test them. At sundown we were ahead about five miles, having a stiff breeze, under top-gallant sails, and running sharp on a wind. We were more than surprised at daylight the next morning to find the *Hector* full eight miles ahead of us on the weather-bow. She was under top-sails. We had furled top-gallant sails during the night. We immediately set maintop-gallant sail, but in twenty minutes it blew out of the bolt-ropes; and we then stood along under top-sails after our saucy antagonist. We trimmed our yards, and only the best men went to the helm. As we were a little down by the head, we brought from the forehatch ten casks of water, and rolled them aft. After this the ship steered better, and we gradually overhauled the chasé, and at sunset were up with her, about a quarter mile to leeward. The wind having moderated, we set fore and main top-gallant sails and flying-jib, and in the morning watch got on the royals. At day-light, "Hurra for the *Chelsea*" from the watch brought all hands on deck, and we found the *Hector* ten miles on the lee quarter. We continued dropping her, until the setting sun showed her from the mast-head nearly top-sails down. We then shortened sail, and she came up with us during the night. The next day we ran side by side, and interchanged boats' crews through the entire day. At evening we parted with our pleasant company, and sighted the carcass of a whale stripped of its blubber.

Nov. 16. A large bone-shark was seen alongside the ship. He was near the surface, and we judged his size to be about thirty feet in length, although we could not make out his form accurately. We wished to lower a boat and attempt capture with the harpoon, but the captain said that as the shark was a gilled fish, and would not rise to the surface to allow a chance for the lance, and was far too powerful to be restrained in its running, it would be useless. This fish is believed by sailors to have a mouth furnished with bone, like the right whale, though much shorter; hence the name of bone-shark; and if seamen's accounts be true, the creature is unknown to naturalists.

Nov. 23. Seeing no whales in the vicinity of Cocos, we squared away before a light breeze, and ran for Charles Island, Galapagos. At 2 P.M. to-day we came to anchor in nine fathoms' water in an open roadstead, affording good holding-ground. This is the nearest safe anchorage to the landing-place of a small colony of Peruvianos, seven miles distant. The colony is established about three miles inland, near the only fresh water found on the entire group. In front of our anchorage is a beach of sand, and the low-ground back of it is pretty well clothed with low bushes, while on the hills the cactus is seen, and a few trees. Throwing our lines over the side, we took enough fish for supper, and, by-the-bye, fishing about these islands affords constant surprises. Each fish one catches is odder in shape, and different in size and color from its predecessor. The varieties are so great that they seem inexhaustible.

Nov. 24. The object of our visit is not apparent to us, but we are not curious. We take the good the gods provide without question, and, with the careless improvidence of the sailor, "eat, drink, and be merry, for to-morrow" we may die. If it suits the captain and the owners that the good ship should ride at anchor in Charles Island, well and good, provided we have liberty on shore to stretch our sea-legs, and time to bury them under the warm sand of the beaches, to draw the treacherous scurvy taint from the bones and tissues—assuming that sailors have tissues. Thus far we have had liberty on shore, opposite the ship, every other day, while the watch on duty has been transporting to the ship a few barrels of sweet-potatoes and pumpkins from the distant settlement. We have had our longest vacation on a small island where there is not even drink to intoxicate the brain, or a woman to stir the heart:

> "Some eyes they are so holy,
>   They seem but given, they seem but given,
>   As splendid beacons solely,
>   To lead to heaven, to lead to heaven.

> "While others—men believe them—
>   With tempting ray, with tempting ray,
>   Would lead us, heaven forgive them!
>   The other way, the other way."

We are here safe from the sirens, holy or otherwise, heavenward-bound or otherward; and we roam at large under conditions which made the Garden of Eden intolerable to the first gentleman of his time. We philosophically take to fishing, and industriously add to previously known varieties, without waiting to classify, but roasting and eating our varied catch.

A little Yankee fishing-smack with its "live well" would make a fortune in supplying the coast markets with fish from these islands. In the evening the *Elmira*, of Edkinton, Captain Marchant, twenty-four months out, fourteen hundred barrels of oil, dropped anchor close beside us. We pulled on board, and gave them a store of fresh fish of varying sizes, forms, and colors, and for the same they had valiant stomachs. The evening we spent on board the stranger, with song and yarn, music and dancing, until ten P.M., when, at peace with all men, we bunked and slept.

Nov. 27. The Yankee and the Spaniard having exhausted each other's resources in trade, the courtesies of the vikings were then extended to the ruler of the land which held our anchor. We "snugged up" the ship, screened the unsightly try-works with shrubbery from shore, and dressed her with all the red, white, and blue which we had and could borrow. Every thing was made gay and festive to welcome Governor Villamill and lady, with a party of grandees, who had accepted our invitation. At 2 P.M. the dignitaries of the shore, and the captain, officers, and most of the crew of the *Elmira*, came on board. The señor was accompanied by Señora Villamill, a pretty, pleasant-faced woman, strikingly in contrast with her husband. They and their party came in two whale-boats manned with crews of ragged convicts—this being a penal settlement. These latter beauties were not permitted to come on board, lest they might appropriate the spare anchor or the good name of some of the crew. Jollity was the order of the day. Captain B—— warmed up for the occasion, and determined to give his crew a regular blow-out for once at least. He ordered the steward to bring up his comfortable case-bottle of Santa Cruz, and, pouring out a stiff horn, sent it forward with an order for music to the "Doctor," who sat atop a cask tuning his violin. The benign old darkey imbibed; the drop was alone needed to bring the fiddle to tune, and in lively measure he struck up our favorite jig, the "Chelsea's Crew," a composition of his own. The captain considered all hands as treated, by proxy, in that single glass of rum, and we thanked him for his thoughtfulness. He allowed the Spanish dons to fire their blood, and Captain M—— to soak himself with the remainder of the square bottle. Fortunately we were inured to temperance, and heartily took to dancing. Señor and don, Pedro and Emanuelo, danced fandango and cachucha, and Jack took kindly to the reel, breakdown, and hornpipe. A chowder interrupted the "light fantastic," etc., and our crowded deck was soon turned into a banquet-hall. After the dinner dancing was resumed until midnight, when we sought comfort in old rye—straw.

Nov. 29 (*Sunday*). Starboard watch on shore. A mischievous freak of part of our watch nearly led to serious results, and the adventure is worth a place in the journal. I am aware that such details may prove wearisome to the President and his secretaries when they seek history in my journal, and I suspect that others might prefer a disquisition on the igneous play which enabled these islands to hold their heads above water. But I put to you, gentle reader: How are you to realize the adventurous life of the boys who have completely mastered the proud situation of the American whaleman, if I suppress our mischief and fun? How could you understand the race, which has proved an overmatch for one of the most matchless races the world has known, the boys who met John Bull on his favorite tramping-ground, the sea, and in "fir-built frigates" and hulking whale-ship backed him square down? How could you realize how the hollow-chested Yankees drove from the seven hundred and fifty million square miles of Pacific hunting-ground, the bluff, hearty Britons, if I did not give the points which show the character, good and bad, of the fellows who did it? I do not think it could be done.

The party on shore were intent on the pursuit of seals, but we soon marked the tracks of cattle in the sand, and so far away from the settlement that we held the animals legitimate objects of the chase; so we started on the trail. After a short search we found a young bull, hidden in a thicket of mangroves. He was so wild that he seemed a foeman worthy of our clubs. After some threatening demonstrations, he started on the run for the interior. As ill luck, my length of leg, or training on the hills of Pennsylvania would have it, I outran my shipmates, and soon the bull and I had the fun to ourselves. Suddenly he turned, and stood for a moment measuring his foe. He then lowered his horns and made for me. I at once appreciated the change of the situation, and the difference between a frightened bull's tail receding and a mad bull's horns advancing. The game was now changed, and I ordered a retreat, but found that he was too fast for me. I was at bay, and a well-directed blow of the iron-clad seal-club brought him to his knees. He soon recovered, and with an ugly bellow came at me twice, and twice more I baffled him. It now occurred to me that yelling for help was in order, and this soon brought my companions to the scene of action. They overmastered my antagonist, and he lay panting on his back, with his horns tucked well under the neck and stuck deeply in the soil, a prisoner. A council of war was held. The majority were reasonable, and voted to report him to the Spaniards, to whom he would be valuable. But a few of the men secretly resolved to have fresh-beef supplies, and they followed the released bull to the beach, where they killed him, foolishly, in the sight of the *Elmira.* Some Spaniards on board that ship reported at once to Captain B——, who, much angered, pulled ashore and brought beef and butchers on board.

Although late in the day, the captain proceeded at once

to town to settle the unfortunate affair with Governor Villamill. The señor was exceeding wroth at the misadventure, and Spanish-like magnified the offense to an attack on his dignity, etc., etc., demanding the immediate surrender of the offenders. This, of course, Captain B—— peremptorily refused. The señor replied, "I will send thirty-five soldiers, and take them from the ship." The captain informed him that several times that force would be necessary for the job. The governor then threatened to hold Captain B—— until he surrendered the men, and to this the captain replied :

"Señor, let us cease bantering. My men did very wrong in killing the bull, and I am sorry for it. I will pay you seventy-five dollars in cash, or one hundred in black-fish oil, we keeping the beef. As for detaining me, I have provided for that. My boat has returned on board, and if I am not on the landing to meet it on its return, the second mate will be here to look into the cause. We can count on the *Elmira*, and, my dear governor, there will be a sure row, if sixty Yankees get a loose foot in this town of yours."

On such representations the worthy man accepted the seventy-five dollars and pocketed the affront. Thus happily ended this tempest in a tea-pot. I may remark that Mr. F—— got the ship in a very pretty state of defense, on the captain's prudent hint. Captain Marchant offered aid if it came to blows. I have an idea that the town was in peril last night; but the captain's return made all smooth again.

Posey and myself, with a very intelligent young fellow named Carson, belonging to the *Elmira*, proceeded back from the beach to examine the lava bubbles, which are occasionally found in these islands. Their name indicates their formation. They sometimes are so thin as to form treacherous footing to the incautious traveler. Whenever we met the rounded outline indicating a bubble, we tested its safety with a heavy stone, even though it was not directly in our path. Sometimes the roof would fall in with clinking sounds, revealing a deep, dark cavern. Having thus broken into one cell of considerable size, which proved easy of entrance, we crawled in for shelter from the intense heat of the sun's rays. Our conversation, naturally directed by the strange surrounding, led Carson into the narrative of an adventure in a lava tunnel and cave which made a deep impression on my imagination. I will strive to tell his story, preserving rather the spirit than the language. The exhibition, as he described it, is seen in a small way, in the crystallizations of sulphur and cooling metals, and in the dark tubes of certain optical instruments.

"In a sharp, deep valley of Albemarle we had broken in the roof of such a bubble ; but the cavern was much deeper than this, and as we looked in we saw that we had opened the way into a tunnel about fifteen feet in width, and extending either way as far as we could see from our position. By the light which entered from above we made out the floor as about twenty feet beneath us, and that the walls were curiously marked with columnar forms. Brown, my companion, who had dabbled in the sciences, proposed that we should take an under-ground view of volcanic action and appearances.

"So, on the following day, provided with a couple of lamps, a coil of knotted line, and a couple of waist-lines and iron poles for staves, we proceeded on our exploration. We descended with the knotted rope around our bodies, and stuck our feet in the rough side, lighted in our way by a single lamp. We carefully watched for any side openings which might confuse us or lead us astray in returning, but we saw none, and felt safe. It soon became evident that the tunnel had not been formed by a rent of the mass after cooling, but rather by the molten lava's having drained away, after a crust had formed upon it. This may account for the

singular and beautiful formations by which we found ourselves surrounded. After proceeding some distance through
a passage with a pretty uniform width of from fifteen to
twenty feet, and about an equal height, we paused to examine the formation of the cavern. The dim light of our lamps
illuminated the pilastered walls, and a roof raftered and groin-
ed with straight and curved beams of crystalline structure,
many feet in length. Some of these were of a reddish appearance, and others had a vitreous lustre, resembling immense crystals, in places broken into the semblance of foliage, which reflected an olive-green light. The gloomy splen-
dor of this solemn architecture was relieved by the gold or
amber reflections of crystals of sulphur, which, like mari-
gold or sunflower, gleamed in the arches of the passage.

"The broad bases of the pilasters were enriched with
counterfeits of fern, palms, and growths intricate and delicate as the pencilings of the frost-spirit's pictures. But
these metallic pictures, under the limning of the fire-fiend,
had been inlaid with the brilliant facets of igneous minerals
green and brown in tint. Tempted onward by the increasing beauty of the scene, our lamp revealed new objects of interest in the increasing lustre of the arched ceiling and the
carved and painted walls. Our lamp was multiplied by the
sparkle from the faces of unknown minerals. In places the
passage was divided by central columns of basalt crystals,
which terminated in curves, and were in form and tracery
varied beyond man's power. The rude Goth for his cathedral, the Moslem for his mosque, the Celestial for his pago-
da, might have drawn inspiration from this solemn portal to
Nature's vast workshop.

"As we advanced farther into the recesses of the mountain, the character of the cave changed. The angular crystalline forms which indicated the sudden withdrawal of the
molten matter, or the deposit of elements sublimed by in-

tense heat, yielded to smooth and rounded structures, like the worn rocks of the river-side, giving the impression that the walls had served as a sluice to fiery torrents pouring from the volcano. A few steps farther showed us the singular curtain-like foldings ·of a substance resembling lamp-black. Absolutely without lustre, and absorbent of every ray of light, it was present, as it were, only to the touch. With certain misgivings under this curtain of gloom, we entered a cavern, the form or extent of which could be known only by touch of hand, for no possible brilliancy of light would command an answering reflection from the absorbent surface. Broken as was the surface to the touch, to the eye it was without form. The floor was invisible, and we were only guided in our steps by our staves. It was like stepping into primal chaos, before light and form had birth. A profound chasm seemed to yawn at our feet, yet the rocky floor rang to the blow of the staff; and with cautious tread we proceeded. The flame of the lamp met no responsive glow, save from the two intruders, who stood awe-stricken in this strange emptiness: it stood, in the still blackness unflickering, like a solid. Feeling the broken walls, the hand was met by an oily softness; the eye was useless, and even the touch now failed to guide us. Solid walls were not to the eye; rocky barriers seemed simply impenetrable darkness to the hand.

"From repeated contact with the sooty walls, we became covered also with this strange light-absorbing powder, until we were enveloped in an invisible mantle, and also passed from each other's sight. Eye alone answered to eye in their reflections of the light. Too deeply impressed for conversation, we stood still with outstretched hands. Brown asked at length, 'May it not be even so in the Valley of the Shadow of Death?' And we looked for strength in each other's eyes, and linked our arms that we might have the companionship of touch. We were now thoroughly frightened, and turned to retrace our steps; but which way? We stood in a sea of nothingness—locked in the foundations of the mountain. The walls were lost to the sight, and were nothing to the touch. We stooped to the deep dust of the floor, and held the flame to read our foot-prints; but this soil of carbon absorbed the light, as the sand of the desert does the rain-drops. We reached forward, and the hand failed to meet the wall; we reached downward, and there, too, was but empty space. The light failed to show the defining edge between the solid rock and the void. We swung the lamp over the brink on which we lay; it revealed nothing. We dropped a heavy stone into the chasm, and listened for the rebound. No sound was returned as it sank into the profound. We cast another stone across to test the width, but this, too, was lost to the senses. Silently they passed away, as the mist-wreath on the hill-side. And then we knew we had been preserved from death. A careless step, and we had found a grave in the depths of the world's foundations. We realized that we were lying in trembling safety on the threshold of the extinct volcano, and lifting our useless eyes from the impenetrable blackness, the awful whisper 'Lost!' passed between us. We were afraid to move, but the wasting oil of our lamp warned us that time must not be lost. Presently our ears caught the beat of the surf on the rocks as the tide came in, and, following this direction, we finally reached the entrance, almost fainting from joy when we stood beyond this chamber of gloom. Once more we stood under the wondrous tracery and reflections of the outer gates of the inter-world of mysteries.

> " 'There is a dungeon, in whose dim, drear light—
>   What do I gaze upon? Nothing. Look again!
>   Two forms are dimly shadowed on my sight,
>   Two insulated shadows of the brain.' "

Such is a weak version of Carson's story, and he added: "Since this adventure in dreams, I have hung suspended from, or slid helplessly down, that awful brink into that silent black space; and when I have awakened in terror, I have realized again the nightmare which oppressed me during the moments I lay peering into the volcano."

CHAPTER XIX.

Post-office of the Galapagos.—Señora Villamill's Monkey.—Farewell to
the Galapagos.—An unfortunate and mutinous Ship.—The wide Range
of Whalemen.—Burke's Eulogy on American Whalemen.—The Mutiny.
—Bingham's Row with Second Mate.—Council of War in Forecastle.—
The difficult Decision.—Man tied up.—Hans returns Good for Evil, and
strikes back, and Row generally.—The Captain slashes round.

A CURIOUS feature of the Galapagos is the novel post-office,
established there by Commodore Porter, during the last war
with England, while the *Essex* harbored in the island which
bears the name of her worthy captain. He placed a large
terrapin shell on a conspicuous point of Black-lava Rock. As
round and white as a huge skull, it is a prominent landmark
to vessels coasting among the islands. The enormous shell
forms the roof of the letter-box, and it is the custom of ships
to send a boat ashore and overhaul the mail for any letters
that may have been left there for them, and to deposit any
letters they may have directed to ships long out which may
touch at the islands.

The evening before we sailed, Señora Villamill presented
the captain with a monkey, and the governor sent on board a
splendid red-hackled Spanish game-cock—whether as tokens
of the estimation in which they held the good man or not,
I can not say. The monkey was christened "Ichabod;" the
game-cock, "Commodore Porter." The *Elmira* got under
way at the same time with us. Captain Marchant is one of
Nature's noblemen, and consequently has a good crew, capable of putting captain and ship through a tight place when
needs be. May every success attend them!

Dec. 2. We have lost sight of the islands. Whether they

are to be again visited is hidden from us, but very pleasant memories remain of them. May every poor sea-worn mariner, once in his life at least, enjoy, as I have done, a visit to these desolate but blessed islands. The wind is fresh, and we are dashing merrily on our course to the S.W. Our night watches are rendered pleasant by a brilliant moon, and the doctor's fiddle, with the dance and Hinton's tuneful voice, enliven the early watch. A light-hearted, happy race are old Ocean's sons, when they have half a chance. For some time now I have been blessed with a spirit of contentment, and have taken great satisfaction in merely living. I can say, with Izaak Walton, " Every misery I miss is a new mercy, so let us be of a thankful spirit." This spirit is in striking contrast with the spirit of unrest which spoiled greater external means of enjoyment in the tame safety of a Pennsylvania farm.

Dec. 9. Two sails in sight. One of these we spoke. She was the *A*——, of Hudson, Captain F——, out twenty-five months, with but eight hundred barrels of oil. She has been most unfortunate. Her story is the old one of an unreasonable captain, and a stubborn crew. It has not been with them, as it must be for success—

> " A long pull, a strong pull, and a pull altogether,
> As sailors say at sea."

But while the captain sailed his end of the ship, the crew anchored theirs; and the *A*—— has but two or three of her original crew. The men were in a desperately mutinous condition when the anchor was dropped in Payta, and they refused even to furl the sails, as the crew represent the case. The consul came to the rescue with a number of Spanish soldiers (such poor creatures as put us in the guard-house !). Yankee blood was up, and seizing irons, lances, and handspikes, the sailors drove the Peruvianos pell-mell overboard.

The captain was badly wounded in the head, and had his arm broken. The foremast hands left the ship in a body, leaving the sails hanging in the brails. There being no man-of-war in port, the authorities of the place had not force sufficient to overcome the mutineers, as all the sailors in port, American and English, sided with the latter. A new crew was shipped, among them one of the men who ran away from us in Selango. Poor fellow, he had suffered much since he left us, being broken down by the coast fever, and the worse dissipations of Spanish sea-ports. He told us that the boat had been overhauled by the Peruvian armed vessel *Congresso;* that the boat had been appropriated, and the entire crew·pressed into the service. Bad food and brutal treatment prevailed, and all pay was denied them. They deserted as opportunity offered, and became scattered one from the other. What became of our old favorite, Elisha Chipman, he could not tell; but he said, hopelessly, "I don't believe one of them can be alive to-day."

Captain F——, of the *A*——, profited by his dearly-bought experience. The old-time customs of "hazing" and "working up" have passed away, and his present crew, to a man, honor and respect him. All hands are working hard to retrieve past hard fortune.

Our approach to the "offshore ground" is apparent from the number of sail in sight almost every day—occasionally three or four are in view at one time; yet, how many other hunting-grounds are in like manner overcrowded by the eager hunters of oil! Besides the fleet now cruising on this ground, others scour the equatorial seas, away west among the coral islands, on the savage coast of New Zealand, and about the unfriendly shores of Van Diemen's Land and New Holland; also on the coast of Chili; ten thousand miles due west on the east coast of Africa; in the Channel of Mozambique; away north-east on the shores of Alaska, and its opposite, the Okhotsk Sea; in the extreme polar regions; far up in Behring Strait; on the banks of Brazil; across the whole South Atlantic, and about the waters of Japan! Almost every sea is plowed by the keel of our whalers, and the glorious Stars and Stripes flutter in every gale. In the infancy of our national enterprise, Burke was inspired to eulogize the American whalers in terms so exalted that no more praise need be spoken. We can only quote his glowing language as applied to the early enterprise of our fathers. He said, in the British Parliament, in 1774:

"Look at the manner in which the New England people carry on the whale-fishery. While we follow them among the tumbling mountains of ice, and behold them penetrating into the deepest frozen recesses of Hudson Bay and Davis Strait; while we are looking for them beneath the Arctic circle, we hear that they have pierced into the opposite region of polar cold; that they are at the antipodes, and engaged under the frozen serpent of the south. Falkland Island, which seemed too remote and too romantic an object for the grasp of national ambition, is but the stage and resting-place for their victorious industry. Nor is the equinoctial heat more discouraging than the accumulated winter of both the Poles. We learn that while some of them draw the line or strike the harpoon on the coast of Africa, others run the longitude and pursue their gigantic game on the coast of Brazil."

The imagination of this eloquent statesman was thus stirred in contemplation of the short flights of our whalers in the well-known waters of the North and South Atlantic. Could he, were he alive to-day, with all his wealth of language, find words to express his admiration of the enterprise which now grasps the waters of the world, and " runs the line and strikes the harpoon " under every latitude? Since he spoke so eloquently we have advanced marvelously.

Dec. 13 (*Sunday*). "Now is the winter of our discontent." For some time a grudge has been working between Mr. S—— and a stout green-hand, Bingham, who hails from Kentucky. Bingham has been worked up energetically at all unseasonable hours. When the ship was pitching her worst, poor Kentuck was ordered, slush-pot in hand, to grease down topmasts, and when the roll was added to the pitch he was ordered to wipe off said grease because it was too thick. The next rough spell, he was required to again grease the topmasts, much to the disgust of the cook, whose perquisite the "slush" is. Bingham must work, rust off the chain, and tar down inaccessible stays. In fact, an undue share of the most disagreeable duties of the ship fell to Bingham. He submitted with, perhaps, ill grace, and the grudge passed from bad to worse, until last night, in the middle watch, we who were below were aroused by Kentuck's coming down the forecastle scuttle on the run, followed by the blacksmith's tongs, and a rasping blessing from his angry officer. Of course, such a storm brought us on end at once. Bingham was too much excited to post us as to the row, and he had not time to overhaul his log, for in a few minutes, in stormy quarter-deck slang, the captain ordered the poor fellow on deck. He obeyed, and we indignantly heard the thwacks of some heavy thing on the person of our unfortunate shipmate, and his pleading that, "Indeed he had not been to blame, and that he acted only in self-defense." Good clean paper should never be soiled with the Billingsgate of a mad captain and a mate. In a few minutes the deck watch came below, and a council of war was held.

We then learned that Mr. S—— came suddenly from abaft the try-works to Bingham, who was sitting on the end of the windlass. Catching the greenhorn by the collar, the mate charged him with sleeping in his watch on deck. This

Bingham denied somewhat roughly, saying that he had just sat down. The men on the forehatch confirmed his statement, when the mate ordered them "to shut up, and not put their oar in this muss." Blows soon followed high words, and the mate assaulted the bulky Bingham with the tongs aforesaid, and chased him, with oath and blow, into the forecastle. And one deponent added: "In course there'll be the devil to pay. The officer of the deck has had his head punched, and been jammed down in the deck-pot. He didn't get satisfaction out of Bingham's head with old Blowhard's tongs, so of course there'll be a werry nice little muss." The case was before the court.

> "Jack was embarrassed—never hero more,
> And as he knew not what to say, he swore,
> Nor swore in vain: the long congenial sound
> Revived Ben Bunting from his pipe profound;
> He drew it from his mouth, and looked full wise,
> But merely added to the oath 'his eyes;'
> Thus rendering the imperfect phrase complete."

The bow-oarsman got out his "Bowditch's Navigator," and opened it at the well-thumbed digest of the United States marine laws. The scene afforded a striking picture. In the confines of the ship's forecastle the foremast-hands were crowded. Some were lying in their bunks that the others might sit on the sea-chests. Old Tom, with wisdom written in every line of his aged face—a face profound as Jack Bunsby's—was sitting on a bread-kit, holding the flickering, smoky, forecastle lamp over the open book, to enable the improvised lawyer to find safe moorings. The men waited silently for their sailing or fighting orders, as might be decided upon. The moment was trying to one who was yet fresh from the peaceful influences of that friendly sect which teaches "that ye resist not evil," and that "whosoever shall smite thee upon one cheek, turn to him the other also." It

was with a troubled spirit that the young sailor turned the
pages, not so much to read the words, which were graven on
his memory through much study, as to impress on the good
fellows about him the consequences of any error of judgment. The thought came distinctly to him: In resisting
your officers, you break a law; if you resist with violence, it
becomes mutiny; and if violence is let loose, who may restrain it? To succeed you become pirates, and stand outside the pale of human protection. How can we, then, save
Bingham from the lash (that of course was a settled thing)
without getting the whole ship's crew into greater trouble?
Such was the burden of my great concern. To do this
it must be made to appear that we restrain the captain
within the law, and use only such force as may be needful
to prevent his committing an illegal act of violence upon
one of the men; and that, rendering cheerful obedience to
lawful orders, we would resist unlawful assaults on our persons. "Well, my boy, what do you make of it?" asked old
Tom, as the boy closed the book and looked around the
company. The men were very quiet; not a word had been
spoken; and he read in the eyes of all a settled resolve to
fight the thing to the bitter end, if need be. So he wasted
no words, but replying to the question, said:

"Mates, there is nothing in the law that authorizes the
captain of a whale-ship to seize up and flog one of the crew.
The lash is repealed on men-of-war, and is not permitted on
whale-ships. He may iron, imprison, and carry an offender
into port, to be tried for his offense; that is all. And I believe we may rightfully restrain the captain from illegal violence on our shipmate."

"That's right law, and straight to the point," said Tom,
enthusiastically. "And so far as in me lies, by the Lord
above us! a shipmate shall not be flogged." And a solemn
amen ratified his resolution.

A general resolution was then arrived at: no unnecessary words, no altercation, no scolding were to be allowed in the men, and no laying on of hands or violence, save in the very last extremity of self-defense. One of the crew was appointed spokesman, and all communications from the crew were to pass through him. This settled, we turned in to uneasy sleep, until the call of the watch brought all hands on deck.

Then the crew gathered in the starboard waist. Before us stood Bingham, lashed by the upraised wrists to the main-shrouds, his shirt stripped off, and his white, unspotted, un-scarred Kentucky back bared to the eyes of his shipmates. His helpless look and pleading eye stirred all the manhood in our natures to stand by our resolution. He gathered something from the aspect of the crew which blew grit into his heart; his head went up, and a hope lit his eye. He looked away seaward, and left his case in safe hands. The captain also read the same signs as Bingham, and in a rough, excited tone ordered us "forward of the windlass." A few of the crew, from old habit, walked forward; but the major-ity stood their ground. This was the first act of disobedi-ence, and greatly enraged the captain. He seized the end of the fore-brace and struck Hans, one of our men, to the deck. Hans was Dutch, of the New York kind, and the flatter you knocked him the higher rose his blood. He sprang up in an instant, and pitched into the captain's hair, tooth and toe-nail. Thus our peaceful programme was spoiled.

The third mate, with the predisposition of Mexican blood to be in hot water, tackled Hans, and pulled him from the captain, who ran to the cabin, doubtless for arms. The third mate was having a good Spanish time of it, with Hans under his knee. One hand was busy tangling poor Dutchy's hair while the other was laying dark shades about his eyes. This was clearly opposed to our treaty, and an onslaught was made in Hans's favor which sent Mr. B—— below, whence he did not return. Mr. S——, the cause of all the trouble, evidently saw that there was a rod in pickle for him if he came to close quarters, and very wisely he held the lee quarter-deck. Mr. F——, with a terrribly pained expression, was walking the weather-quarter, evidently having washed his hands of the affair. The four boat-steerers stood on the main-hatchway, neutrals. The frightened cook clattered his pans in the galley, about the door of which the war raged. The cooper and carpenter leaned over the larboard waist, looking into deep water. The men concluded that Bingham was safe for the time being, and as the captain doubtless would re-appear armed, it was best that further proceedings should be taken in our own quarters. We therefore walked forward of the windlass, and clustered on the roomy forecastle-deck. We had scarcely taken this vantage ground, when the captain, blind and blazing with fury, came at us, with a heavy ivory-tipped club elevated over his head. The weapon fell, as it happened— for I am sure he did not see who he struck—on the head of a little boy named Sam, from Philadelphia, and the child fell senseless to the deck, the blood flowing profusely from an ugly scalp-wound. Before the madman could again strike, the club was wrested from his hand and thrown overboard. The baffled man then stood facing the silent, observant crew, pouring out his rage in threats and abuse. The calm voice of Mr. F—— was now heard, pleading for peace, and the mate came forward and led the captain aft.

CHAPTER XX.

The Captain's Law.—Man cut down.—Ship adrift with Yards aback.—
Men refuse Duty, and still drifting.—The "Round Robin."—Make sail
for Sandwich Islands.—The Treaty, and a Peace-offering.—Remarkable
Tenacity of Life in Sperm-whale.—Finback.—Gam with *Adeline Gibbs*,
Captain West. — Greenwich and Mean Time compared. — Fighting
Sperm-whale of the Galapagos.—A Yankee Trick on a Whale.—How
Whalemen are made: Cabin-boy at ten, Master at twenty-two.—Love
of the Profession. —The Sailor dreams he is Captain, and goes on a
Whale.—Shyness of Whales rather than diminished Numbers length-
ens Voyages.—Balloon suggested to take Whales.—Water-spouts dis-
cussed.— Mowee raised, and anchored at Honolulu.—Sad History of
the *Washonk.* —Slaughter of the Crew, and recovery of the Ship.—
Smuggling Rum on Board.—Pig-headed Perversity.—Offenders taken
on Shore.

AFTER a time the captain ordered us into the waist again.
We found him standing at the carpenter's bench, by the
companion-way, bare-headed, more calm, and evidently determined as to his course. At his hand lay a pair of pistols,
the roll of fate (the ship's articles), and a volume in law-
binding. We stood in line, under the range of this formidable battery, and were allowed to gaze, while our antagonist
arranged his weapons. This began to tell on the men; for,
while the pistols had no terror for them, the great white
roll, which mysteriously held them bound, body and soul,
and the thundering big book, at least twice as large as our
"Bowditch," had an awful threatening aspect. We were
getting a little shaky, when the captain drew from his hat
a "colt," and the sight of the hated rope's-end closed up our
fluttering rank. The captain opened fire by reading from
the "Articles" how we had clearly forfeited our "lays" by

disobedience and mutinous conduct, and he informed us that we were wretched outcasts, beyond the pale of human society and law; penniless, and of no account. Amen, we thought; we can lose no more, and so we held our course.

Our spokesman was now pushed forward to ask him "to read the law which authorized the punishment of the lash, without even the form of trial." For a short time the captain turned the leaves of the book, but he failed to find the law he sought. Then, with a threatening glance down our line, he took up both pistols, ready cocked, and said, "This is the law by which I will flog this man." He added to this a remarkable expression, characteristic of the whaling-captain: "On the other side of the land I have my masters, the owners, and *One above;* but on this side of the cape I am master on board this ship." And stepping forward a pace or two, with pistol in one hand, and "colt" in the other, he continued, "I will flog that man, or any other of you, who may give occasion, and I give you fair warning that I will send a bullet through any man who interferes!"

Now came the crisis; and very quietly was it met! The crew filed across the deck in double line between the after-hatch and the rail, between the captain and Bingham. Resolute old Tom then turned, and with his sheath-knife severed the yarns which held the captive's wrists, and told him to "cut his lucky" and go forward. It was too plain a case. The captain saw in the faces of the men that the death of one would not deter them, and there was a crouch preparatory to the spring apparent in their bodies which showed that short shrift might be his if he fired. No single man on earth could have faced down the quiet resolution of that band, I am certain.

Now all was quiet on the drifting ship. The cook failed to appear with breakfast, and a committee waited on him to remind him of the fact. It was surprising how soon he corrected his oversight. In half an hour more the steward came forward with an order for Frank to go aft (it was he who took the club from the captain's hand). Frank went; then Hans and the boy Sam were sent for, and they obeyed. Another was called, but we saw through the captain's game, and returned word that when the three men were returned to us any other would go aft, but not before. Again the ship drifted, under short sail and mainyard aback. No man was at the mast-head; a boat-steerer was at the helm; every body was mad and snappish as a wolf. No bells were called, no watches stood. Loose and lawless our little ship drifted in mid-ocean, a speck of hell on earth. The men absolutely refused to touch line or sail until some terms were reached.

Dec. 14. Threats of the darkest kind were made by the crew, who kept a strong watch on deck during the night, to prevent surprise, and this morning they united in the demand that the men decoyed aft should be liberated, or the ship put away to some consular port. Meantime the ship drifts at the mercy.of wind and wave another day.

Dec. 15. The captain resorted to various means to entrap or intimidate the men. A threat to starve us out, by closing the bread and meat casks, was met so promptly and energetically that it was not persisted in. During all this time the men have abstained from noisy demonstrations. All communications have passed through the spokesman; and Mr. F——'s utmost influence (and it is very great) has failed to move the men from their steadfast purpose to refuse all duty until their shipmates are set at liberty.

Dec. 16. This morning we all signed a "round robin," setting forth our "willingness to return to duty on the liberation of the three men." Our names are written in radiating lines, like the spokes of a wheel, so that there is no leading name to the list. Query: Is it from this custom of signing dangerous papers that the term "ringleader" was derived?

No immediate notice was taken of the "robin," but after a time the mate brought us word that the captain had determined to run to the Sandwich Islands, and there deliver the ship into the hands of the American consul. To this we had no objections, and, provided no time was lost in cruising, we consented to work the ship into port. Accordingly we shook out the reefs, sheeted home the courses, squared in the yards, and set light sails and sternsails, and went bowling along under a cloud of canvas. Mr. F——— now called us about him on the forecastle, and asked us to go in the boats after whale, with the understanding that as soon as any grease was had we should continue our course. To this we assented, as we should have done to almost any thing he could have asked of us, as he had both the confidence, respect, and hearty good-will of the crew.

The test soon came, and the "sweet little cherub" offered a chance for us to retrieve our voyage. The mast head had been scarcely manned when a whale was raised close aboard, the creature having ventured too much on our demoralized condition, evidently. The captain came from the cabin at the cry, and, looking anxiously forward, hesitated to issue the usual orders. The mate, in bluff, cheery voice, broke in, "Come, boys, hand sternsails." "Ay, ay, sir," and with old-time alacrity we took in light sails, braced the yards, and brought the ship to the wind. A bright gleam of something more than satisfaction lighted the careworn features of the "old man" as he busied himself in overhauling gear in his quarter-boat. The ship came to, with mainyard aback, within half a mile of the unconscious whale. At the next rising we went on, our boat fastened, and in twenty minutes our prey lay fin out. When we were pulling on board, the captain perceived a chance to heal the old wound. This fine whale was a peace-offering. The captain was in good humor, and said that if we would promise to behave ourselves he would let the men go, and we should continue the cruise on offshore ground. All this sounded very pleasant to us, but after coming on board, he found some technical difficulty, and refused to free them. Thus our last chance was lost, and it appeared that we must lose the season, and perhaps our voyage. Again we were in the dumps; our mates were in irons, and confined in a dark, suffocating hole in the hold. The whale alongside promised fifty barrels.

In striking contrast with the shortness of time, and the seemingly slight means employed in the capture of this whale, I will present the experience of Captain Maloy, of the bark *Osceola.* The account from his journal is much as follows: "Lat. 19° S., long. 25° 30' W. Saw. large whales; lowered and struck with waist-boat. Soon after starboard boat struck same whale, and got stove; the waist-boat then fired a bomb-lance into him, upon which he stove her, knocking the bottom entirely out of her. After picking up the crews of the stoven boats, kept the ship for the whale. On seeing the vessel he rushed at her, struck us on the bows, knocking off the cut-water with his head, and at the same time tearing the copper and sheathing from the bow with his jaw. Got into position and ran for the whale; ranged alongside and fired two bomb and two whale lances into him, but these failed to kill him. He remained on the surface, and in the vicinity of the stoven boats; lowered a boat, and without fastening fired two bomb-lances into him without sensible effect. As it was near night, I called the boat aboard, and made sail to hold our position during the night. The whale was occasionally heard fighting the fragments of the boats, oars, etc. Thus through the night he held his ground, although he had two lines (six hundred fathoms) towing on to the harpoons, five bombs exploded in him, and other wounds from lances. At 7 A.M. lowered two boats to renew the attack with bomb-lances; fired thirty-one into him before he yielded. He stowed down one hundred and fifteen barrels of oil, one-half of which was head matter."

What a fearful disarrangement of internal economy must have arisen from such a bombardment, remembering that each bomb is driven deep into the creature's vitals and explodes nearly half a pound of powder and iron tubing! Yet I suppose none touched " the life," or the lungs would have been suffused with blood, and suffocation ensued. Here we have very strong evidence that it is only by touching one vital point that the monstrous power of the whale is speedily overcome.

Jan. 6. It must be an ingenious man of a strongly inventive mind who can keep an interesting daily journal of a passage in the trade-winds. Four bells succeed eight bells; watch relieves watch; mast-head divides our duties with the helm; no whales are seen; no fighting occurs; and a man must go into the " head " to swear, if a fit comes on irresistibly. The grub is regular, the water unstinted, and we have had a steady north - west course since our trouble. Some days since a noble finback whale exhibited himself in perfect safety to those who were so anxiously seeking his distant relative, the spermaceti. The finback ran parallel with our course for a considerable period, and often rose to spout within one hundred feet of the ship. I improved the opportunity to go aloft and observe the movements of the huge but graceful swimmer. We were making fully ten knots; yet he kept beside us with little effort, and rose and sank leisurely, with a slow, regular sweep of his vast propeller. We estimated his length at ninety feet. It is asserted that two whales of this species have been measured—one, one hundred and five feet long; and Sir A. de Capell Brooks states that a finback is occasionally seen one hundred and twenty

feet long. The thinness of its blubber and the shortness of
its whalebone render it of far less value than others of its
species, while its extreme swiftness and strength make its
capture very hazardous. It is rarely struck with a harpoon,
a favorite expression of our whalemen being that it "will
run the nails out of the bottom of a boat." Scoresby
struck one, and says that it sounded and ran out four hundred and eighty fathoms of line in a minute, or at the rate
of thirty-two miles in an hour. Singularly enough, this
whale, so seldom taken, is more correctly figured in natural
histories than either the sperm or right whales.

Our meeting with a friendly ship afforded us some diversion that we would not otherwise have had. "What ship's
that?" we hailed, as we passed almost under her stern.
"*Adeline Gibbs*, of New Bedford, Captain West, seventeen
months out, nine hundred barrels of oil. Come to, and I'll
send a boat on board." We complied, and Mr. F——, with
a boat's crew, went on the *Gibbs*, while Captain West visited us. We braced forward and stood on the wind, and our
companion ship lay under our lee. Of course I was exceedingly anxious to gather all I could of the rich experiences
which would doubtless pass between the two captains, and
I had an opportunity as I stood at the helm. The two old
seamen retired to the cabin for a short time, to compare
chronometers, I suppose; for their bronzed faces were a
flush redder when they came on deck again, and a brighter
gleam in their keen eyes expressed satisfaction at the comparison. Greenwich time from a case-bottle, as compared
with mean time from the "scuttle-butt," has a wonderful influence on "jawing tackle." · As they came up the companion-way, my ear caught from Captain West, "Galapagos—
old bull—regular sodger—spouting blood;" and when they
took seats near the binnacle, Captain West lighted his cigar,
and went on with his story:

"The rest of the school worked off to leeward, and the three loose boats followed them. My boat was pretty busy with the job in hand, and didn't take much notice of the rest, for our whale began to show the ugly. He milled round, and brought his nose right on to the broadside, and blew thick blood right across the boat. I laid the boat around and pulled ahead to clear his jaw; he was snapping his spout-hole close alongside with a force which would have mashed a hand. The crew kept cool, however, and worked like clock-work. They were the same good fellows that came on board with me.

"Directly he settled away out of sight in the bloody water, and came up on a half-breach right amidships of the boat and sent us kiting. The boat came down keel up, with a tangle of the line about the stern and loggerhead. I got on the bottom and found she wasn't badly stove, so I called to the men to come alongside and help right her; but our ugly neighbor was ranged alongside, and the boys preferred to hug their oars. The next moment the whale started slowly to leeward after the school, and the boat followed stern first about ten yards beyond his flukes, with me still clinging to the keel. Then I felt real bad; there were my poor fellows holding on to the oars; the sea was pretty rough, and considerable white-caps were running. I could count only four heads, and I knew one had gone down. Away to leeward was the ship, and the other boats were out of sight from where I lay. I shouted to them to keep good heart, and Brown, the boat-steerer, cheerily answered, 'Ay, ay, sir,' as I slowly passed away from them, the whale sobbing thick blood just ahead of me, and staining the wake deep red.

"Then I felt that the line must be cut, sure. I crept to the stern, and could see the tangle hanging in bights about the stretched line; but it was three feet under water, and I couldn't reach it. I had only a short-bladed pocket-knife—

sharp, however, and I hoped to be able to cut. Watching twenchance, when the whale slacked a little, I dived for the line, missed it, caught a bight, and got on the boat again. I looked back, and could see the heads of my crew as they were raised on the sea. They soon would pass from sight, and I felt sick at their peril. After several efforts I succeeded in righting the boat, but it came over on top of me. I clutched at the smooth bottom in a vain effort to secure a hold. It glided over and away from me. When I came to the surface she was three or four feet from me, and going faster than before. I almost gave up; I was almost tuckered out. Just then a line touched my hip; it made me almost leap from the water as I thought of being tangled in the line. But on seizing it, I found it was the boat-warp, and with its aid I drew up to the bow, and after considerable effort was able to get into the boat, and creep forward and cut the line with the boat-hatchet. Then I was done for. I lay back against the cuddy-board, and shut my eyes to catch a minute's rest; but what could I do, in my waterlogged boat without oar or sail, for the poor fellows to windward? Captain B——, I an't ashamed to own it, but I don't believe that it was all sea-water that flooded my eyes in that moment of helplessness. God save them, thought I, for they seem past human help. Just then the voice of the mate came over the sea, 'Hold on, Captain West; I am at hand!' I was as much surprised as though my prayer had been answered, and the Lord's angels had come from heaven to save us, for when I had last swept the horizon there was nothing in sight except the distant ship. The mate pulled up, and took me on board; I then found that the cook had been lost, and the after-oarsman was lying insensible on the thwarts. I ordered the boat directly to the ship for restoratives for the exhausted man, and sent back for the stove boat. The second and third mates meantime had got a good

"The to leeward.. Thus we were saved by the first mate having pulled promptly to windward when signal of 'stove boat' was made from the ship. A little time lost would have cost the lives of as good a boat's crew as ever went on a sperm-whale."

"Why don't you keep her steady? She's three points off the wind," said Captain B—— to the interested helmsman.

"Steady she is, sir," said I, as I put the helm down and brought the ship again close to the wind.

The cigars were out, and the captains retired to the cabin again to wind up the chronometer. I suppose that is a duty never to be neglected, lest you lose your reckoning on the deep water. I guessed it worked hard, as their faces were a little redder than ever when they returned.

Then Captain B—— told of another fighting whale, which fought nearly all day, staving three boats with his jaw, and cutting every thing which caught his eye, whether mast, sails, boats, or water-kegs. But this behavior made Yankee just as mad as old Spermaceti, who was now fated to be scalped. Accordingly, the captain took advantage of the whale's bad humor, and towed down a ninety-gallon cask for the brute to practice on, and while the whale was discussing this nimble float, he probed industriously with the keen lance. Thick blood and the flurry followed, and eighty barrels of oil repaid for the lost boats, leaving a handsome balance also.

In reply to a question, Captain West said:

"I went to sea as cabin-boy at ten years of age; at fourteen, I steered a boat and struck my first whale; at sixteen, I was second mate. Our first mate didn't much like a whale; a wife and children hung on his lance-arm, and made its aim uncertain. They freighted his boat down, and I could always beat him in the chase. I was a boy who meant to be captain or to go under, and didn't mean to go under if

I could help it. At twenty-two I was master, and in twenty voyages have followed the right whale from ground to ground, from the banks of the South Atlantic, around the East Cape to the Pacific, through Mozambique to Delgado Bay, East Africa; most everywhere a whale could be found, in fact. Once I passed Behring Strait into the Arctic Seas, when the ice began to swing in on us, on the 5th of September. Away up there we met the bow-heads, or true Greenland whales, old fellows that would turn up two hundred and fifty barrels of oil, and give three thousand pounds of bone, single slabs of which would run to fourteen and fifteen feet in length. There we might turn up one thousand barrels of oil without letting the fire down in the trý-works, and in that day our oil might be worth from seventeen to twenty-five cents per gallon; bone would bring seven cents. The latter wasn't worth hoisting in. Don't you think a man must have loved whaling to go for that? I tell you I did love it. I might not be bailing a fortune in the sea, but I had the tallest kind of hunting, and we always picked up some sperm-whales in our passages, which always paid."

The spirit of the enthusiastic captain touched an answering chord in the heart of the young dreamer, who leaned against the idle wheel; and he stood no longer the slouching, half-clad sailor, at the beck and call of every superior, but was master of a ship, beautiful as the one he steered. I had a good boat under me, with a crew who could trust in me, and in whom I could trust. A good whale had just risen a short half-mile ahead of me; three minutes of time; ten capping seas lay between the harpoon's point and leviathan. I would change places with no king, for no royal huntsman from the days of Nimrod was ever so equipped or had such regal game to tempt to the chase! I have girdled the world that I might be here; I have swept a planet to run this race. With five brave fellows, trained in many a contest, until my life is their life, and my will is their will, I am all in all. The very boat is part of me. I talk to myself, and five souls respond in the quick stroke of the oar. The cloven, bubbling sea flits beneath me. The fleeing whale rises and sinks. My eye alone drinks in the grand sight and diffuses the excitement to my men. Foot by foot we draw on our game, and my energy bends the supple oar like the bow of the archer. Two silver crowns yet lay between us; the music of the spout comes through the light rush of the boat, and the wild scent of a strange breath touches our dilating nostrils. The blood is on fire with the madness of the moment. The whale will spout but a few times, and we shall lose him forever. Now, my merry men, for him! We spring all; we leap from the crest to the valley; we fly in a milky way through the boiling eddies of his monstrous effort. Now the corner of his waving flukes gleam azure beneath the boat. Another mighty effort; the whale glides beneath us. Stand up, and take him as he rises! pull for dear life! steady! Now give it to him! With hissing plunge, the keen iron pierces the rising game; an instant the breath is held for the cut of the flukes. Amidst spray and foam the boat is backed from the danger, and an eighty-foot whale whirls the line from the tub, until the loggerhead is lost in the smoke of burning wood.

This is royal sport which a wild democracy may love. In this supreme moment the hunter is uppermost, and few men then count the value of the oil, be it measured in pennies or human lives. My teeth are deep set in the huge flank of our gigantic prey, and we will not calculate the dollars until blood returns to a level with arithmetic. Only a dream yet! Only a dream, interrupted by the captain's voice which awakened me to the conversation.

Captain West seemed to think that voyages were lengthened by the wildness of whales, rather than by their scarcity!

"You see whales enough, but how to get on them is the question. In my last voyage on the False Banks, South Atlantic, I saw right whale laying flukes 'and fins. We ran the ship well to windward and lowered, dropping one end of the boat first to prevent the swash. We ran down with sails, putting only the tip of the steering-oar in the water, and no man spoke above a whisper. Thus we ran down silent as a bird's flight; but, at about a quarter of a mile, the nearest rounded out his flukes and went down; then another, and another, slowly and solemnly, without white water, until all were gone. Then we rounded to, so as not to run into their wake, when wooshoo! like an exhaust steam-pipe, sounded the blow of a great fellow half a mile away. And wooshoo! here they were again lazily basking on the surface, all on the alert and keeping exact run of the boats. Do my cunning best, I didn't get nearer that day to a school which would have filled my ship ten times over. It was like chasing the rainbow. Now, what are you going to do in such a case?"

"I do not know," answered Captain B——, "unless we tow out a small balloon from the boats and drop a bomb-lance with lighted fuse, and blow up their insides. I guess an ingenious man might arrange that in light weather among school-whales. It is evident that the fear of the whale-boat has been transmitted until it has become instinctive, and we must attack them from the air. When Pennsylvania's oil-wells give out we will try this trick on."

As we had seen water-spouts during the early morning, this phenomenon now became a subject of discourse. Captain West described one which passed so near the *Adeline Gibbs*, that with his glass he could distinguish the flying-fish glancing out of the foaming base of the cone, and falling outside the influence of the vortex. In this he was confirmed by seeing a number of gonées flying around the foaming col-

umn, and darting upon the exposed fishes.   While he was
watching their motions, one of the birds got within influence
of the whirl, and with only time for a loud squeak it disappeared, whether upward or downward the captain could not

WATER-SPOUT.

affirm, but that it was thus suddenly caught he could not
doubt.   The bird was plain in sight when caught, and so
near that its cry could be heard.

"But," he continued, "the mystery of the water-spout is

in its power to render the water fresh—that is, if it takes the water upward. I have observed this interesting phenomenon off Panama Bay, where the spouts abound in the rainy season; also on the Line, in the Gulf Stream, and in the Indian Ocean. I have seen thirty, perhaps, of varying sizes, in a single day; but I never knew it to rain salt-water, nor have I heard of any one else doing so."

The visit was at an end; Captain West went to his own ship, and our mate's boat returned, with some interesting books, secured in exchange for those which we had exhausted. The *Gibbs* squared her yards and stood away to leeward, and she and her pleasant captain and crew passed away.

On the evening of the 6th we raised the high mountain peaks of Maui, as they loomed sharply in the western sky, above a heavy ledge of clouds which obscured the setting sun. So far I realize visions created by reading the charming accounts in Cook's voyages of these favorite islands, on one of which he lost his life.

Jan. 7. Passing near the islands Rhani and Morotoi, toward evening we ran in for Diamond Head, and dropped anchor outside the coral reef between the head and the narrow entrance into the harbor of Honolulu. On account of heavy gusts which swept from the mountain gorges, we sent down the light spars, and made every thing snug alow and aloft, with both anchors down. The captain ordered his boat on shore. The wind was strong and dead ahead, and we had a hard and wet pull. As we approached the pier, I was surprised at the number and size of the houses built in the American style. The pier was well built out of hewn coral. The fort to the right seemed of considerable strength; the guns were small, but commanded the harbor and its approach.

The captain left the boat at the pier, with orders that the crew should remain by her, and not wander into the town so we had no opportunity to test the new civilization of the islands. Time would have hung heavily enough on our hands, if a boat-steerer and two of the crew of the *Washonk*, of Falmouth, had not come down on the pier and recounted their terrible experience while cruising off some of the savage islands of the Line. The incidents were so remarkable that our officers took pains to verify the account, and the following is, as near as I can remember, the substance:

On the morning of the 18th proximo the *Washonk* found herself partially becalmed in the vicinity of the Mulgrave Islands. A large number of the natives came off in canoes, and, pretending to want to trade, were allowed to climb aboard the ship. One of the older seamen had, in a former voyage, suffered from an attack by these treacherous people, and he warned the captain against the danger of allowing so many on board; but the master felt secure, and paid no attention to the warning. The natives occupied much of the deck, and mixed freely with the men, trading shells and fruit for hoops and other articles of iron. They had, without exciting suspicion, gathered at points favorable for their murderous purpose, and the first warning the crew had of their danger was an attack by the natives, armed with the sharp spades they had found in the spade-rack under the spare boats.

The captain was the first victim. He was beheaded by a blow of the broad-edged spade; the poor fellow at the helm fell about the same moment. The first mate was killed as he leaped down the forehatch; and several others were killed or grievously wounded as they retreated to the forecastle. The second mate ran out on the jib-boom, where he was struck with a stone or spear, and, falling, was clubbed to death. The natives had now possession of the deck, and they proceeded to fasten the hatches and companion-way, so as to cut off the egress of the crew. One in command now went to the wheel, and headed the ship toward the shore. The boat-steerer, who was on the lookout at the mast-head, and a man at the fore, were horrified spectators of the slaughter on deck, and feeling that their only safety was in getting the yards aback, they ran down the rigging and cut such of the braces as they could reach without getting in range of the spears and stones of the yelling savages. The effect was to allow the yards to swing freely, and the ship lost steerage-way, and drifted before the light wind, fortunately toward open water. The chief at the wheel, as soon as he saw this movement, gave vent to his rage in a round of English oaths, thus revealing the fact that a white man was leader in the murderous attack.

While these events were occurring above decks, there was a storm brewing under the hatches which these devils little suspected. Under the third mate, there were gathered in the dark, narrow forecastle the remnant of the crew, all told, nineteen men. Two were at the mast-head, and they had reason to suppose the rest had been killed. Of those in the forecastle six were more or less gashed by the terrible spades, but there were thirteen able-bodied men awaiting the grating of the keel on the coral-reef. They supposed that it was only a question of time; yet these brave hearts cast about for means to renew the fight. The third mate leading them, they wormed their way over and through the casks between decks, and reached the cabin, which they rejoiced to find unoccupied. The thirteen determined men gathered around the arms-chest in the cabin; such weapons as they found were loaded and distributed, and, as fully prepared as possible for a desperate sortie, they passed to the companion-way, only to find the door securely fastened on the outside. Now they were thoroughly alarmed, and they returned to the cabin, where, in fearful suspense, they await-ed the shock of the ship striking; but the mate's eye caught the movements of the tell-tale compass in the cabin, and this awakened a new hope.

At this moment the deck sky-light became obscured. On looking up, the men discovered a face peering through the glass. "That's for you!" exclaimed the mate, as he fired his musket through the light, and a fall on the deck told that the white man had drawn first blood in this prolonged contest. The smell of the powder-smoke inspired the crew with a new idea of escape. The mate quietly ordered them to open the "run," and get up a keg of powder. They placed a quantity of the explosive contents on the upper step of the companion-way, and laid a train of oakum and powder to the cabin. The mate prepared to fire the train, while the men stood ready for a rush. He told them not to wait for him if any harm came to him, but to dash through the smoke and take the savages in their first fright. On the word he fired the train, and in a moment the explosion took place with a fearful crashing of timbers, followed by the screams of the burned and torn savages who were gathered about the companion-door. Bursting through the pall of smoke, the crew sprung on the now terror-stricken brutes, who offered very little resistance, and, leaping from the ship, sought safety in their canoes. A large canoe filled with them was broken by an anvil dropped into it, and not a man escaped the shots from the deck. The retreating canoes were followed by the vengeful bullets as long as they remained in range. Then, repairing the braces and getting steerage-way, the well men bandaged the fearful wounds of their shipmates who were left bleeding in the forecastle. The bodies of the slain had been thrown overboard by the savages. Thirteen of the latter were found dead, and several mangled by the effect of the explosion. The men at the mast-head reported a number blown overboard, and described the effect of this volcanic mode of warfare as decisive in the extreme. Several of the wounded savages were thrown into a canoe and set adrift to be recovered by their countrymen.

On the passage to Honolulu, the wounded men suffered greatly from the effect, on such broad and deep flesh-wounds, of the hot climate. They burned the wounds with a hot iron, as the best thing they could do. After a tedious voyage, they arrived at Honolulu late in December, expecting to go directly home.

Such is the fearful story of the *Washonk*, as recounted to us by one of the actors in the tragedy, adding another to the list of perils which beset the path of the whaleman. It is finely characteristic of the courage and self-reliance in emergencies of the men who make up the whaling service.

The captain returned from the town silent and morose, and we pulled him on board the ship without taking with us fruit or refreshments, save certain fluids contained in bladders partly filled, so as to stow conveniently and secretly about the person. These pigs' bladders are in great demand in ports frequented by whale-ships, as by them liquor may be smuggled on board in spite of the vigilance of the officer. No evidence of its presence is manifest while it remains outside the man, and when it is inside, a good stomach-pump, vigorously applied, can only cheat Jack out of his stolen gratification. I think such an instrument is a needful part of a whaler's outfit.

Jan. 8. To-day the powers that be again perversely ran counter to our fortune, and added to the hardships of our life. Early in the morning the captain's boat was ordered away with a selected crew. These were the men shipped in Payta, excepting the boat-steerer. Hans and poor little Sam were brought from confinement, both pale and sick, and placed in the boat. The regular crew of the boat wondered somewhat at their being left on board the ship, but no one suspected the scheme of the captain; and so the poor fellows pulled away from us to a prison without even a farewell from their comrades.

CHAPTER XXI.

Angling for Sharks.—Shark in Stays.—Carpenter of the *Jolly Ananias* and unfortunate Shark.—Land-sharks dealing with our Crew.—Consular Brutality and Injustice.—Six Months in an Indian Fort awarded.—A surly Crew at the Windlass.—Captain's Speech, and Comments.—Our Kanaka Crew.—Speed of Whales argued.—The Run described.—Coughs and Colds.—General Wretchedness.—Tropical Rains and Water-spouts.—Want of Faith in Science avowed.—Job on Rain and bad Weather.

WE on board killed a hog, and dressed it for an immediate sea-pie; and while the "Doctor" was cooking the body, some of the crew tied the entrails to a line, and fastened them to the spars projecting over the stern. The motion of the ship alternately lifted and dipped them into the water, and in a short time we were surrounded by a crowd of sharks, who worried themselves badly about the unsavory morsel. Meanwhile we prepared a more substantial meal for the voracious monsters. Baiting a chain-guarded shark-hook, we awaited sport. A great fellow turned deftly on his side, seized the tempting lure, and dashed for the depths; but our good gear was too much for his strength, and with the most vigorous protestations he was brought head out of water alongside. A running bow-line inclosing the line was passed over his head and below the great fins, and hauled taut. So he was hauled over the rail on to the deck. The sharks were large and numerous here, and we adopted the most expeditious methods of disposing of them. In the opinion of sailors, cruelty to the shark is fairly beyond human contrivance, and in this spirit we played a practical joke on a gray-headed patriarch of the family. According to usage, when the crew are not of a blood-thirsty mood, they simply put the shark in "corsets" and let it go, the "corset" being inside the "varmint." We thrust an old iron pole down our friend's ample throat, leaving still room for a little savage, or large pair of boots; and after taking care that one end of the iron projected, that he might exercise his teeth and ill temper, we tossed him overboard. As the rigid pole held him to a course, he made a straight wake on the surface, much to the entertainment of the boys, whose possible coffin the brute was. One shark, fifteen feet in length, I dissected to the extent of his leathery jaw, which was garnished with half a dozen concave circular saws. I intended to carry this trophy home to show the Radnor people.

It is said among sailors that the hard digestion of a hungry shark has brought the dead to life. As the yarn goes:

The carpenter of the *Jolly Ananias*, of Nantucket, Captain Marcy, died off Zanzibar. He was stitched up in canvas, and a pet grindstone was lashed to his feet to anchor the body. An affectionate chip of the poor old block, standing by the gangway-plank, reached over, with tearful eyes, to catch a last glimpse of his father, when his foot slipped, and he fell in almost at the same time as the dead man. Just then a great white shark swept around from the bows, and, very naturally, the poor boy and his father were out of sight in an instant. The shark leisurely swept under the quarter, shaking red flannel from his saw-teeth, and casting up his hungry eye for any more boys there were to spare. Captain Marcy was a cool-headed, friendly man, who struck twice before he spoke at all. He was about launching an iron at the brute, when young Coffin, the mate, suggested that he might hurt the boy. The captain said he hadn't thought of that, and a baited hook was dropped. Quick as a flash the bait was taken, and in as little time the monster was lashing the quarter-deck. A blow on the head settled him, when, to the amazement of the crew, a cutting sound

came from within, and the dead carpenter's voice was heard
addressing his son: "Now push ahead, my boy, and hail
the first craft you see." Out came the half-naked boy, followed first by the grindstone, and next by the revived carpenter, not much the worse for wear. His story was that
in his watch below, as he thought his funeral, he awoke
dreaming that he was going through a threshing-machine,
and found that something had torn his hammock, and was
digging into his back. He knew this was an awful moment
for him, and that he would be dissolved in no time if he did
not present a "counter irritant," so he offered the grindstone to the shark, as he found his assailant to be, and took
off the keen edge of his appetite. He then felt comparatively comfortable; and presently, to their mutual surprise,
father and son met. The boy now held the stone to the
cutting edges of the shark's digestion, while his father put
an edge on the boy's sheath-knife, to fight their way out by
a short cut. They felt the bump on deck, and cut at once.
"He who would be free, himself must strike the blow."

While we sailors were thus tenderly dealing with the
sea-shark, the land-sharks were more summarily devouring
our poor shipmates on shore.

In the evening the captain returned from the shore, bringing with him but one of the old crew and ten Kanakas.
The remaining crew were terribly enraged at this; they felt
that he had acted unfairly by them. By word and action,
at the time of taking the last whale, he had allowed the idea,
that he came to this port *pro forma,* to satisfy a legal tech-
nicality. He had almost said to us, "I must report to the
first American consul, and then we will turn to and retrieve
lost time." The thought of going to sea with such a hea-
thenish crew as now darkened our forecastle was intolerable.
When we learned the treatment and fate of our shipmates
on shore, our resentment knew no bounds. Stimulated by

the rum brought on board yesterday, our excitement became so intense that, thoughtless of consequences, some of the men were in danger of committing a monstrous crime, and pulling to the shore during the night by the light of our burning ship. The captain and the second mate wisely kept their cabins, and allowed our old favorite, F——, to face the storm. All the great-hearted man could do was to look sorry. There were no tears in his eyes, of course; but we knew they were in his heart, and we heard them in his voice, as he kindly advised us to be patient under our supposed wrongs. This saved the ship. A single harsh word or threat would have fired a train which would have consigned most of us deservedly to share the fate of our poor mates.

The action of the consul, as it appeared to us by the report of the returned man, was brutal and tyrannical. On the appearance of the crew before him, he addressed them thus:

"You infernal rascals, you have been guilty of mutiny, have you?"

One of the men replied: "We suppose we have been brought before an American consul to have that question settled by a fair trial."

Such an idea seemed to amuse him and restore good-humor. He laughed as though the fellow had perpetrated a capital joke; but the man spoiled the fun by continuing:

"As American citizens, I and my shipmates demand a trial, with opportunity to call witnesses, now on board the ship, and prevented from appearing by our accuser."

The consul angrily replied: "You impudent scoundrel! do you think I haven't the facts of the case before me? The captain has posted me, and I won't have any more of your jaw."

In vain the men pleaded that Mr. F——, the boat-steerers, and carpenter might be heard as witnesses; but this simply aroused the devil in this petty representative of a great nation, and he abused the poor fellows in words of stinging and blasphemous insult. "Had I been Captain B——," he concluded, "I would have flogged every man of you before the mast."

This was too much for one of the poor fellows, who had stood silent up to this time. Stepping forward, he shook his great fist in the face of the consul, and said: "It an't in you; for we would have passed you to the sharks before you had touched even that poor sick boy!" pointing to little Sam, who, pale and emaciated from long confinement, and his unhealed wound, sat looking with wondering, tearful eyes on the scene.

Thus ended the trial; the men were hurried away to the fort, sentenced to six months' imprisonment and hard labor under Kanaka task-masters. The man who returned had carried his official Protection papers "as an American citizen," and the brutal dispenser of injustice did not dare to trample these underfoot.

Jan. 9. The captain, taking a crew of Kanakas, and steering himself, went on shore and staid until afternoon. When he returned, he ordered the anchor up. The crew were dogged and sullen, only awaiting provocation to be worse. Slowly the windlass went round; the usual heaving-songs and chorus were hushed; the slow clank of the chain was the only sound; and daylight passed into night before the first anchor was to the bows. Before supper the captain mounted the windlass and spoke to us. He said: "I have noticed, and been grieved at your conduct. My mind was to end this unfortunate trouble differently, but I found it necessary to place the ship in the consul's hands, and have acted under his advice. I am going to sea for a three-months' cruise, and then will return to recruit for Japan. Then you shall have full liberty on shore. Now eat your supper, and let us have a better face in the morning."

We made free use of the sailor's ancient prerogatives, growling and grumbling, and various were the comments on the captain's speech as we cut heartily into the unctuous pork and briny beef. Posey, in his reasonable way, chimed in, "Well, boys, you must allow the captain did the handsome thing in apologizing, instead of damning your eyes, as he had a legal right to do."

"That's so," answered an old salt, more briny than the beef he was munching; "that's so; but it's my opinion if the captain would cuss more and pray less, our mates wouldn't be in that fort, and we could trust him more. It don't seem natural to hear these mushmolly, softly-go-easy ways in a tussle with the sea. The captain 'll do for a soapy landsman, but he don't fit to the quarter-deck."

Jan. 10 (*Sunday*). With the crew slightly improved in temper, we hove the second anchor to the bows, the wind being light and the weather pleasant. Our Kanakas have all seen service on whale-ships. They appear to be a cheerful, inoffensive people, and they regard with amazement the angry, quarrelsome race they have come among. With the characteristic justice of the Anglo-Saxon in dealing with a "man and brother of a darker hue," we have treated the recruits as though they were answerable for the confounded row of the past few days. The Kanaka names are long, unpronounceable, and unfitted for the quick orders of a ship's deck. Therefore the islanders are always re-named when they enter the service. The nautical name seems to please them, and they always report and answer to it: "Spun-yarn," "Maintop," "Jack of Maui," "Jack of Oahu," are examples of their new christening. I intend to pick up the lingo of our brown mates. Hawaiian will serve in polite society to hold my own against traveled friends who patter French and Latin. It may show that I, too, am a traveled man, who has learned the difference between a lion, a bear, and a turtle-dove. "Hookee nui, mi ti, ourrie hana pah," may prove an excellent diversion in company. The sound of the islanders' talk is low and pleasant, full of vowels and soft sounds, without an *s* or *izzard.*

Jan. 15. Since my last we have lowered once for whales. In the early morning we put off, and with sail and oar chased them thirty miles dead to leeward; but they gained on us, and we gave up the chase. I am now satisfied that the speed of the sperm-whale in traveling is much greater than is allowed by most writers. To-day we had a good breeze, sprit-sail set, and five pairs of arms to urge forward the fastest sea-going boat the world knows, but still the whales gained several miles on us. Nevertheless, they were not *gallied* or making unusual exertions, so far as we could judge, and I should not like to say that ten miles an hour is the greatest speed this whale attains when aroused to fullest exercise of its power. Brothers of the lance and harpoon, recall old memories, and bear me out in saying that the speed of a young, fifty-barrel bull whale, under the spur of a harpoon, and the provocation of a single boat, is the maximum of water-travel—short of steam-power; and, further, that railroad travel is tame compared to the sensation of a four-mile dash to windward, close behind the playful flukes of a whale. Ye who doubt, ascertain for yourselves. Experienced watermen quote the behavior of a boat towing behind a steamer, as evidence that a whale-boat would capsize at a speed of twelve miles an hour. An empty boat would, to be sure; but it is not an empty boat behind a whale, and that makes all the difference. The racing-boat has on her thwarts six trained men, whose lithe bodies sway to her motions as the rope-dancer does to his unsteady footing. The order of the officer in such a boat is, "Steady, men—trim boat—don't shift your tobacco;" and the boat is thus preserved in a run in which an empty boat would be instantly capsized.

I verily believe that a fast whale, for fifteen or twenty minutes, can run at the rate of fifteen or twenty miles an hour, and I would rather add two than take one mile from the estimate. As I think I have before explained, the dash of a whale is known as a "Nantucket sleigh-ride;" and 'tis perhaps the most killing ride the world wots of. I am aware that very many experienced whalemen hold the speed of the whale at a lower estimate; and Captain Sullivan, of New Bedford, warned me against falling into the usual over-estimate. He stated that ten or twelve miles is the whale's greatest speed; that in passage the creatures do not travel more than five miles; and that we misjudge the speed of the boat because the eye is so close to the water. At any rate, to-day our whales beat us out, and I guess we got our boat through the water at more than five miles an hour.

As we advance southward, the weather becomes squally and wet, and all hands suffer more or less from severe colds. The hoarse, barking coughs we hear in the nightwatches are an unpleasant reminder of Northern climes. The first time in my long life—and I am almost of age—that I have had to study up pulmonics has been while I have been standing barefooted on the wet deck, saturated with sea-spray, · and baying at the moon in a midnight watch, between the tropics of Cancer and Capricorn — an admirable position, surely, for practical knowledge of the enduring capacity of the human lungs. The cause of sickness on board is the constant wet from deluging rains and spraying seas leaping over the bows of our beautiful craft. At 9 P.M. to-day the gaff-topsail was blown into ribbons. We double-reefed fore and maintop sail, and ran our course.

Jan. 16. In the third watch we were visited by one of the

deluges of rain which tropical wanderers strive to describe. In the darkness we could not see its approach, but the distant sound was as of a storm of wind through a forest's foliage. The men were stationed at halyards, clew-lines, and reef-tackles, to "let run and clew up" at the word. The roaring torrent came on us with little wind, however; it almost becalmed the little gale which preceded it, and it struck us like the break of a combing sea. It may have fallen in drops, but such drops! I am persuaded that Noah's neighbors would have been disposed of in less than forty days of such a shower. We felt actually beaten to the deck by the down-pour, and we fled to the protection of the up-turned spare boats and the slight poop-deck. Here, in the roaring darkness, we crouched, surrounded by a noisy river, which swept the rolling decks gunwale deep. The scuppers gave no relief, and the surging water dashed against and over the low bulwarks of the waist, as the laboring ship rolled under the deluge. From this time and forever, I hold my assent from savants who attempt to explain their knowledge of the "treasures of the snow and the treasures of the hail;" and of the "way the light is parted which scattereth the east wind upon the earth;" and of Him "who hath divided a water-course for the overflowing of the waters, or a way for the lightning of the thunder;" and who explain away "the causes of the rain where no man is; on the wilderness, wherein there is no man, to satisfy the desolate and waste ground, and to cause the tender herb to spring forth." Learned and experienced teachers of men, gird up your loins, and answer ye me: "Hath the rain a father? or who hath begotten the drops of the dew? out of whose womb came the ice? and the hoar-frost of heaven, who hath made it?" Your theories of evaporation and condensation are insufficient to explain or belittle the phenomena of a tropical deluge from a seemingly limited cloud, and gravitation is at fault in the suspension in light air of the millions of tons which descend from apparent mist.

The clouds fairly weep over our presumptuous sciences; and under the pelting of their tears I strove to possess my soul with patience regarding the mystery of the rain, and, with the truly wise and learned Job, to put my hand reverently on my mouth before the power of Almighty God, and still ask, with the inspired writer, "Hath the rain a father? or who hath begotten the drops of the dew?" I almost believe that our sciences are sufficient for the phenomena of Nature in her gentler moods; but they fail to explain when the tornado overturns temples and rends armadas; when the imponderable electricity thunders in the clouds, and shatters to dust the rocks and man's proudest monuments; when the influences of creative power in the earthquake play at town-ball with continents, and bowl the isles of the sea as a child's marble. At such displays of power, we fall from our learning upon an "inscrutable Providence," or say, "exceptional phenomena in no way affect the fixed laws of science," etc. Gravitation brought the rain to the deck, I admit; but what sustained the enormous flood against gravitation! The captain concluded that the torrent was the breaking of a water-spout; but this, again, was taking refuge in a name explanatory of nothing. Pray what is a water-spout?

CHAPTER XXII.

Water-spout described.—Query: Effect on Newton's Theory.—Kanaka
Hymns.—Stupor and Gloom.—The old Woman's Curse.—Flying-fish.—
Dolphin.—Albicore a sign of Whales.—Angling for Albicore.—Poison-
ous Fish.—Influence of the Moon on Fish and Men.—A benevolent
Enemy.—Scrimshoning and Pigs.—The Pig as a Pillow.—Man-of-war
Hawk.—Strange Companionship at Mast-head.

Gosse, in his "Wonders of the Great Deep," says:

"These are perhaps the most majestic of all those 'works
of the Lord and his wonders of the deep' which they behold
'who go down to the sea in ships!' They frequently appear
as perpendicular columns of many hundred feet in height,
and three feet or more in diameter, reaching from the surface of the sea to the clouds. The edge of the pillar is perfectly clear and well-defined, and the effect has been compared to a column of frosted glass. A series of spiral lines
run around it, and the whole has a rapid spiral motion, which
is very apparent, though it is not easy to determine whether
it is an ascending or a descending line. Generally the body
of the clouds above descend below the common level, join-
ing the pillar in the form of a funnel. Much more constant
is the presence of the visible foot, the sea being raised in a
great heap with a bubbling and whirling motion, the upper
part of which is lost in the mass of spray and foam which is
driven rapidly round. The column or columns, for there are
frequently more than one, move slowly forward with a state-
ly and majestic step, sometimes inclining from the perpendicular, now becoming curved, and now taking a twisted
form."

This is about the sum of our knowledge of water-spouts.
Let us suppose that Newton had seen columns of sea-water,
as spirals of glass three feet in diameter, ascending to the
clouds, instead of that noted apple falling from a tree. Query: Might not his reflective and ingenious mind have worked
out a different theory of gravitation? And would not the
schools have been just as well satisfied? Much of science
might be different had that gifted Englishman, instead of sitting in his orchard, observed nature in a mast-head watch
on some South Sea whaler.

Jan. 17. Until yesterday the weather continued wet, disagreeable, and squally, quite contrary to the idea that the
Pacific is pacific. But this morning is calm, sunny, and beautiful in the extreme. From the forecastle-deck the voices
of the Kanakas are heard in hymns of praise and thanksgiving, in airs familiar to my ear. Their voices are not remarkable, but their time is admirable. I account for this in the
fact that it is in recitative and chorus that their histories
and traditions are preserved and handed down. By the aid
of an interpreter, we have added much Hawaiian lore to the
old-fashioned yarns of our forecastle. I might almost say
that their chant has replaced the rollicking fun and instruct-
ive discourses which prevailed before our unfortunate visit
to the islands. In consequence of uncongenial surroundings,
I feel very lonely and restive. Only three foremast hands
in our watch speak English, and but one with whom I can
speak on subjects other than those of our passing life: The
yarn, the song, and the skylark are seldom heard charming
the hours and banishing the drowse of the nightwatch as of
old. The books of our library are of such a class as only to
increase the gloom and melancholy. A few books of worth
would serve much to brighten the dark, long, lone path
which opens before us. But cast on my own resources, I
may be weeding tares from my garden, and growing truer to

my own nature. Who knows? A whale-chase to stir us from this deadly stupor would be a Godsend.

Jan. 20. Once upon a time there was a sailor, and his name was Jack, and Jack was beloved and loved. Yet Jack, with the inconsistency of the winds, and the fickleness of the sea—for it is the sea and the winds that form the sailor—changed his love and went to sea. Then his Polly *raised a wail*, and fell back on her mother for comfort. Her little heart was to the full of bitterness, and she said, "May Jack and his ship sail always in a gale of wind!" But her knowing old mother said: "Nay, my daughter, under such luck Jack would get all snug under close reef, and lay at his lazy length under the lee of the long-boat, and spin yarns about the gals ashore. Wish him variable, light winds, with constant rain, and keep him box-hauling the yards in a wet jacket." Some old lady's curse is close after some inconstant heart aboard this ship, for such is our weather. Rain every night, is the order of the day, as an Irishman would say, and we bless all old women in return for their maledictions.

In these seas, as the ship plows her way, flying-fish in great shoals rise from under the bows, and sail away to windward, in flights of fifty or more fathoms. The broad spread of their silvery fins, with their blue bodies glittering in the sunlight, present a spectacle beautiful as singular, even to the accustomed eye. Perhaps no fish excite more interest in the mind of the voyager than these little sparkling gems of the deep water. They are an almost constant presence before the moving ship. The dullest sailor and the least observant passenger will pause in their occupation to watch their flight, and will await with interest their coming on board, as they are eagerly pursued by dolphin, albicore, or skip-jack. When thus chased, they sometimes fly over the lee bulwarks and fall on the ship's deck, sometimes striking as high as the fore or main sail. Naturalists are not agreed as to whether this is a prolonged leap or a flight. I should call it a flight, for the reason that the distance covered is so great that no possible velocity acquired in the water could carry them through the air without additional impulse from the broad wing-like fins. Again, the flight is to windward when the fish is free to choose, that is, against the greatest resistance; and it is not in a straight line, but curves very considerably, especially toward the end of the flight. A leap, we would suppose, would continue in a straight line, as in the case of the long-leaping dolphin and other leaping fish. It is observed that the flying-fish touches the surface merely long enough to moisten the wings, and its motion through the air is certainly attended by a vibratory motion of the fins, if we may judge by their glitter in the sunlight. The general opinion with us is, that the flight continues so long as the fins remain moist and tractable, for the flight is especially prolonged in cloudy or rainy weather. The formation of the tail is such as to preclude the idea of its giving an impulse sufficient to carry the fish three or four hundred feet through the air, and to attain the altitude of the hammock nettings of a frigate. Moreover, the great fins, however closely folded to the body, must prove a serious impediment to motion in the water; and for this and other reasons we believe they actually fly, and are in reality as well as name flying-fishes.

The dolphin, or coryphene, is the most active and deadly of its marine enemies. It pursues the flying-fish by immense, and rapidly repeated leaps in the air, and its darting motion furnishes a fine contrast with the waving, uncertain flight of its timid prey. The pursuing fish streams through the water like a streak of azure light; so rapid is its motion that the form of the fish is lost to the eye, and it launches in the air, in a high, arching, exceedingly graceful bound of thirty or forty feet. Then, dropping into the sea for an instant, it again shoots into the sunlight after the palpitating sparkles which flit before it. Thus the distance shortens, and as the exhausted flying-fish drops into the waves this beautiful sea-tiger seizes them.

In observing the motions of these and other fishes from the mast-head, whence the eye is enabled to penetrate to considerable depths in the water, it seemed to me that the motion of the flying-fish alone provoked the pursuit of the dolphin and albicore; for we have noticed that in calms, or when the ship has had little headway, the shoals of albicore would swim lazily about the ship, or lie almost motionless directly under the flying-fishes, without noticing them. The latter apparently escaped attention by lying motionless with the wings partially extended, as though dead. Doubtless, one of the causes of the albicore's flocking about vessels in such great numbers is that their motion through the water alarms their prey, and causes it to betray its presence by flight. These fish accompany the whale for like reasons, and their presence is considered a good sign of whales on cruising-ground. The pilot-fish precedes the shark or a running vessel. The albicore also seek the presence of the ship as a protection against their most deadly enemy, the sword-fish. The habit of sea-fishes, of congregating frequently in immense numbers about ships, is the source of a welcome supply of food to the crews.

The capture of these magnificent fish, thus herded and driven to our hands by the wolfish sword-fish, afforded a fine field for the exercise of my angling propensity. For tackle I had a hundred yards of three-stranded line, carefully twisted and laid by my own fingers; a large cod-hook, the shank mounted with a revolving plate of mother-of-pearl, and wings of white muslin, which made a very pretty flying-fish. Time, whenever the ship had a good breeze, and on a wind, so that the line would be carried well out to leeward; position, the head of the jib-boom; method, pay out as much line as the wind would waft, say fifty or sixty yards, and with skillful play skip the shining lure in long flights from wave to wave, as the ship dashes on her course. Now, with a thousand or more albicore, some forty or fifty pounds in weight, gleaming in a sea rivaling the blue of the sky, we await a rise; the fly skips twenty feet at a flight; a great albicore breaks for it, and with splendid leap falls a few feet short of the hook. As you hope for a supper, don't be tempted to humor his disappointment and slack your motion to wait for him! if you do, he will turn from the passive fly; but, rather, by a vigorous jerk, send the hook ten feet in the sunlight, and fifty feet forward, and your sure prize will fall a few inches short of taking it in the air. Do your prettiest to keep the bait in swiftest motion and away from him, with splash, dash, and a flying leap. He will be under it when it just tips a lifting wave, and the hook will be deep buried in his throat. And what a strike it is! The ship is speeding onward through the crested waves, carrying a "bone of foam in her teeth." You are swaying on the spar, thirty feet above the swift current, and your prize, with the strength and vim, and triple the leap of salmon, at the full run of your line, is tugging, and glancing in and out of the water, and giving you full-handed play for the next half-hour. With hands armored in horn, case-hardened by oar and rope-haul, you may hang on without the running-lines cutting to the bone. Fathom by fathom you gain line; yard by yard you lose. Hope and fear, hard work and royal sport, until, amidst the shouts of the excited lookers-on, you toss a gleaming mass of blue and silver on the deck weighing, perhaps, sixty-four pounds. And all hands and the cook may help themselves to the dry, chippy flesh you have taken. The breast is passable, but the rest is generally thrown to the sharks. This is a portrait.

I present to you also an attempt to portray the dolphin, an attempt to render graceful form and radiant colors in lines of miserable white and black. The picture is the shadow only of a creature so beautiful, that no art can convey to you the reality as it basks in tropic seas, or sweeps in arching leap under a brilliant sun. To-day we took one on hook; it was nearly four feet in length, of much depth, but scarcely thicker than my hand. It was pronounced unfit to eat, as a piece of silver was tarnished by the flesh when cooking. This test is applied to these fish whenever cooked, as instances have occurred of crews being poisoned by them. A belief prevails among seamen, by-the-bye, that all fish are rendered poisonous by exposure to the moon's rays, and that their flesh becomes phosphorescent in a short time when thus exposed. The moonlight is said to have a still more malign influence on man, and it is also asserted that to sleep with the face exposed may cause a permanent distortion of the features. No seaman, therefore, sees one of his mates sleeping in the light of the queen of the night without kindly kicking him in the ribs, or pulling him by the heels into the shadow. A hard old salt was once observed to lay a monkey-jacket over the phiz of a bitter enemy, benevolently remarking as he did so, " I owe you a licking, you 'tarnal critter, when I git ashore, and I want to know you when I ketch you."

Jan. 23. The sky is clear, with fresh winds. We are now regularly cruising, with not enough to do to keep a man off a growl. As this habit only cankers the soul, I prefer to scrimshone. Odd minutes are now employed in the rigging of a little brig. She is carved from a piece of the beautiful California cedar, hollowed out neatly, and sheathed in planks of black whalebone, the port streak being of white bone from the sperm-whale's jaw. The masts and spars are of the same material. The blocks are of pearl-shell, carefully ground and polished, and it is my intention, as time is nothing, to give her every appointment of a brig above deck. Her shrouds are now neatly ratlined up to the top-gallant head, and some of her yards are across. In scrimshoning, we carve and work much in the ivory of whales' teeth, and by inlaying with pearl, some beautiful objects are wrought. Handsome canes are made of the white bone from the broad pan of the jaw of younger sperm-whales; also from plates of black whale-bone, heated and twisted.

Heretofore the pig has been described by me as only the source of sea-pie, but it has another claim on our attention. The pig is naturally a big-hearted, affectionate creature, and by no means lacking in intelligence. He is easily attached by kindness, and clean enough on board ship, where there is no mud to wallow in. We have two pigs that are quite petted by the hands. We don't understand all they say, but they talk away to us in every imaginable variation of chuckle, grunt, and squeal, and I imagine their vocabulary is almost as copious as the Kanaka. But after sea-pie, the chief comfort we take in these good-natured porkers, is to convert them into pillows for a snooze on deck, and for this occupation they are admirably adapted in consistence, form, and disposition. It is wonderful how complaisant they become under the influence of a well-applied scratch from the horny nails of their human deckmates. By a vigorous rasping along the bristles of their backs their confidence is secured; by a tickling behind the ear and a gentle push we lead them to a secluded nook beside the bowsprit-bitts; and a little more scratching thrills their very hearts, and with a grunt of satisfaction they will place their soft, warm sides in a most convenient position for the head. So piggy and Jack pass to the land of dreams.

Jan. 24. A person of observing mind is thrown much on his own resources in the tedium of the idle cruise, and is led to watch and weigh every object that appears. I have been much interested in a constant attendant on the ship in our offshore cruisings—the man-of-war hawk, or frigate-bird. This beautiful creature is one of the common but most remarkable birds which frequent the tropical seas, at points most distant from the land. Its plumage is of the densest black, relieved by a bright red patch of naked skin on the side of the neck. Its length is about thirty inches, with a spread of wing about six feet. It has a strong hooked beak, much longer than the eagle's, and its feet are devoid of the usual web of water-fowls. We never observed it alight or dive in the sea. It frequents desolate shores and islands during the breeding season, but during a great part of the year we believe it is constantly on the wing. I may remark of this inhabitant of the air, that no other bird offers such favorable opportunity for close study of their habit of flight. In the many hours which the bird and I have spent, one swinging and the other soaring a hundred and fifty feet in the air, diverse and strange questions were suggested. The flight of my feathered attendant is exceedingly easy and graceful; at times it may be seen balanced in mid-air, its head alone betraying life by its motion; again, with outstretched wings, soaring kite-like over and around the mast-head, approaching and receding, sometimes just outside of the arm's reach. It is fearless and will sweep in graceful circles, without the apparent motion of a feather. At such moments it is evident, however, that there is a vibration of the quills, as a distinct rustling whisper is heard, as of the folds of silk in a lady's dress. It has been observed that its bones, in common with other long-flighted sea-fowl, are large in diameter, thin and light in structure, as compared with the bones of land-birds, and are hollow, instead of being filled with marrow— simply cylindrical air-chambers, in fact—light in weight, but strong.

CHAPTER XXIII.

New Theory of the Flight of Birds.—The Bird a Balloon.—Adventure with a Shark, and a Man in Danger.—Questioning Darwinian Theory.—Grinding Crow-bars to Sail-needles.—A Gam of Whales, and five killed.—A Ten-barrel Whale and Boat stove.—Death boards us.—A sad and suffering Death-bed.—Lowered for Whales.—A dead Shipmate, and Respect for a dead Body.—Funeral at Sea, Sperm-whales attending.—In a Region of small Whales.—Pets of the Ship, Cats; Monkey, and his Love of Eggs.

THE hawk and I talked this matter over at the mast-head; and these are some of the suggestions it made: If the enlarged bones be filled with air, then the buoyancy of the body is not increased, for the air-filled space simply displaces an element of equal density. The buoyancy of a fish is made greater by a bladder of air, in which a lighter displaces a heavier element. The caverns in the bones have a purpose, however, as have the cellular structure of the shafts and the plumelets, and the great cavities of the body. At length a thought came in explanation of the wonderful power of suspension. As fish are endowed with a power to supply their sound-bladders with air from the water, may not my companion be able to command an element much less in specific gravity than the air it displaces? Such an element is hydrogen, an element found in its food, as air is found in water for the purposes of the fish. And it is not a whit more surprising if the bird has power to assimilate the one, than it is that the fish has power to procure the other. Considering this bird as a balloon filled with hydrogen, with muscular powers of dilation and compression, the phenomenon of its soaring flight is less a mystery; for then its specific gravity might bear such relation to the atmosphere as does the body of the fish to the water. None who has seen the man-of-war hawk swoop from its lofty flight on to its flying prey, can have failed to observe its instant diminution in bulk by the close packing of its feathers, and the seeming contraction of its body, with the wings half shut to its sides. It descends with an arrow-like rapidity, utterly different from its buoyant flight of the preceding instant, and both motions are performed without a movement of the wings. When it has seized the flying-fish in its talons, it again ascends into the air to devour its prey.

At the fastest speed of a ship this bird will for hours sail around the man at the mast-head, with a rare stroke of the wings. At other times sweeping great spirals, it will soar until it is lost to the eye of the observer. Sailors aver that it is, sleeping and waking, on the wing for nine months of the year. It can not alight on the water, or rise from it if it should happen to fall. Here I leave it, with the remark that books in the libraries will show you what savants think on the points I have touched. I only write of what the sailor sees, thinks, and believes. I may add, however, the following description of the bird's power of inflation, given by Captain Wilkes, in his visit to one of the Coral Islands: "The number of birds was incredible, and they were so tame as to require to be pushed from their nests to get their eggs. The most conspicuous among them was the frigate-bird; many of the trees were covered with their nests, constructed of a few sticks. The old birds were seen, as they flew off, inflating their blood-red pouches to the size of a child's head, and looking as if a large bladder were attached to their necks."

Jan. 31 (*Sunday*). Something in the air and the calm beauty of this day led many to remark upon it as the most delicious since we left home. Toward evening the little wind died away, and the ship lay becalmed. A party of swimmers went overboard for practice, and the result was that my poor name was nearly stricken from the roll of the *Chelsea.* Our Kanakas were paddling, duck and porpoise like, about the ship, but I, foolishly, to show off my skill, went well outside the crowd, rolling, diving, and sporting in the calm sea. To my astonishment I saw the lookout at the mast-head motioning violently to attract my attention, and to come on board. Thinking he saw a whale or a breeze coming, I struck out leisurely for the ship, observing that the men were scrambling up the sides in an unusually lively manner. At the same time it struck my imagination that I heard the word " shark " from the mast-head, and I cast a furtive glance backward to see whether such an enemy was in my rear. But meeting no sign, I thought they were playing a cruel hoax on me, and felt mad rather than frightened. I struck out strongly, making my length—a full fathom, and an inch added—at a stroke, and it was not until nearing the ship that I saw the captain take a lance in the quarter-boat, and beckon me to that point. Then my heart misgave me. Again I glanced over my shoulder, and still failed to see a dark fin furrowing the smooth surface. I was now so near the ship that I could notice the captain's eye fixed on a point slightly beyond me. Not a word was spoken; the officers and my shipmates were standing watching the rapid approach of the lone swimmer, stroke by stroke, the best art of swimming in full play. My eye was on the captain's, as he stood, lance in hand, to cover my approach. I could now trace the motion of the pursuer by the slow turning of the watchers' heads. I came in a direct line between the old man's eye and the object it was directed to; yet I felt that it did not see me. I held my breath at that moment, as I awaited the flashing break of the water beside me, and the appearance of a wide, ravenous mouth. Gathering courage,

I cried to myself, "Don't think, but swim—swim for dear life, for those who love you, for the future, so beautiful, so hopeful; strike out, and don't let the leaden heart sink you." Three strokes more — two strokes — and I was under the boat. The keen lance was now gleaming just overhead, and I felt safe under the sure aim of that trained hand. A bowline was thrown by glad hands, and in a moment I stood panting, almost fainting, in the chains; below me, in the blue water, the shark. "All right; thank you, boys," I murmured. "I only want breath." And all hands resumed duty, my adventure having added a drop to the tide of events in the *Chelsea's* cruise.

The Kanakas seem to be in their native element in the sea. I was told that some of them leaped from the rail to-day, and passed under the keel, coming up on the opposite side. "Jack of Maui," with serious face, tells us that bad Kanakas dive and steal their neighbor's fish-hooks, when fishing in deep water. Now, a pearl hook is the result of much patient labor, and such a prize might tempt a lazy angler to take to deep water to obtain one. A favorite story of Mr. F——'s humorously illustrates the patience of these people:

An old Kanaka, trading with some ship, had set his heart on a sail-needle; but the supply having run short, he was denied. He saw a crow-bar, however, and went to the captain, and made trade for this, as the nearest fulfillment of his want. After a cruise the vessel returned, and the crew found the old fellow patiently grinding away his bar with a piece of pumice-stone, in the hope of ultimately working the coveted needle out of it. But his heart was worried by his inability to get an eye into it, after all. Mr. F—— said that the production of one of their beautiful pearl hooks, with their simple appliances, required a degree of patience well illustrated in the grinding of a crow-bar to a sail-needle with pumice-stone.

LANDING.

Feb. 9. At 2 p.m. we raised a school of small whales; at 3 we lowered waist-boat, went on and fastened to a cow. The rest of the school brought-to around her, and in a short time each boat was fast to its own whale. The captain put a lance into the life of a loose whale, and she went into her flurry before the others were killed. For a time the scene was truly exciting. The whales kept close together, and at times, one or more of the boats were beset by the bewilder-ed creatures. They seemed to have lost their wits, and lay about, heads and points, not often using their flukes. Five were killed, and three hauled alongside by dark. The other two were lost during the night. All were small cows. The only peculiar incident of the day was the thorough bringing-to of the school. A great number might have been killed had we got among them earlier in the day.

Feb. 10. The whales caught yesterday are so small that it seemed almost like working around black-fish in cutting them in. At noon the bodies were stripped, and the heads hoisted in on deck. They will not make more than fifteen barrels each—much less than is sometimes bailed from the case of one good whale. While we were heaving in the last head whales were raised close aboard. The mate's boat was badly broken by a little fellow, afterward killed by the third mate. Our boat picked up the swimming crew and brought them on board. As we had the cutting-tackle rove, we cut in to-day's whale before supper, and hoisted the head on deck beside the three others. It would be a fine chance for a student of comparative anatomy to determine questions of great interest in the structure of these great masses. After supper we lighted the try-works on very thin blubber, and will cut the heads to-morrow. One of our men, named Beers, is very ill. He came from America with us, and has been acting steward since the Selango desertion. He has been off duty since we came into this trying climate.

Feb. 12.

> "Shadows to-night
> Have struck more terror to the soul of Richard
> Than can the substance of ten thousand soldiers
> Armed in proof."

It fell to me to watch the bed of our sick man. He was stowed on a narrow shelf in the pantry, scarcely wider than his body, with a rough board ledge to prevent him from rolling off. So narrow were the quarters, indeed, that his dying face and mine were only separated by a few hand-breadths. It could not have been known that he was so ill, for he has been unattended, until unable to help himself. I was sent, with my utter want of experience, to smooth the way for the poor fellow. He was delirious seemingly, but unable to speak, and his parched, swollen tongue protruded from his mouth. His emaciated face presented a sad spectacle. At a guess I mixed a lime-juice drink, and moistened his tongue and mouth, and bathed his head with vinegar and water. This seemed so grateful to him that I also bathed his body and limbs: presently he drank, and seemed refreshed, and became easier. I thought of calling the captain, but remembering from experience the scope of our medicine-chest and treatment, I considered poor Beers past such brutality. After a time he recognized my face, so near his own, and gasped, "O God! Bill, you don't know how hard it is to die, as I am dying, so far from home and kindness." The little I could say, I said, and I ventured words of hope of a home and kindness nearer than he thought. Soon he went off in a delirious dream, and kept repeating the words, "How lonely! how lonely!" And the thought of being cast overboard in the unfrequented sea pressed on his mind continually. Reviving a little, he murmured, "How lonely to go down into this sea where no man has been buried! And if, as the sailors say, the sea has no bottom, I'll sink, and sink forever. Oh, how lonesome I will be here! If it was on the offshore, I'd find the company of a thousand who have gone before. But no ships ever come here."

Thus for hours the poor boy raved, and I sat helpless, trying to soothe and aid him. All I could do was to hold him from rolling from his narrow bed; and as I sat and ministered according to my means, in that dark, noisome closet, I almost cursed the inhumanity which could consign a man to such a sick-bed. It was the same coarse tow-cloth bag filled with rye-straw in New London fifteen months ago. The air we breathed was laden with the effluvia of the dying man, and the stench of bilge-water, tarred cordage, and refuse food. A tin plate holding an untempting, untasted meal, and a quart cup from which the patient was drinking, completed the hard, cruel picture. As I looked into the poor boy's eyes a feeling of savage, unutterable hardness came over me. I thought that in all animated nature a pervading fellow-feeling leads to sympathy and concern for the suffering. Man alone seemed indifferent outside his own little class. At times in the lone night a fearful impulse stirred me, and I wondered if it would not be merciful to take the poor suffering boy in my arms. and restore him to peace by dropping him, from the filth of his surroundings, into the pure, healthful sea. In his place, I should have prayed for such release. But such an act would be misunderstood. Hours passed until the dim light, when the solitude and the surroundings became more than I could bear; I hailed the deck and demanded relief. It came, and I devoutly thanked God for his pure air, as I went to the bows and sat in the sweet wind. From this time out death in the whale-boat will be endurable.

At 2 P.M. we raised whales on the weather bow; lowered the boats, and after a very hard pull, found that the school were as distant as when we lowered. Much disappointed, we gave in and returned to the ship. We had been on deck but a few minutes, when the captain, in an agitated voice, called for a couple of men to come below. Garvin and myself ran below, and found Beers with his head hanging over the edge of his narrow berth, apparently dead. On lifting him into the cabin, he breathed a moment, and was at peace.

Now comes the strange part of my sorrowful story, showing the inconsistency of the queer mixture we are made of. The captain stood by that soiled, ragged remnant of humanity, and wept, not a silent tear, but with child-like anguish. I can never know what that old man saw in this poor dead sailor. I could not read the memories of other dead which this may have recalled, but I respected the officer the more who could be thus moved by the sight of the poor boy. And we, his rough shipmates, yet wet from a chase, in which we might have wrestled with death tearlessly, we gathered up the sheaf in Death's harvest, and carried him to the quarter-deck, where we spread the ship's colors over him, backed the mainyard, and left him to sleep. We had been informed that while the boats were off, he came unaided to the deck and in his old voice hailed the mast-head watch to know where the boats were, and whether any were fast. When answered, he went below, and all alone, perhaps, he "babbled of green fields," and died.

The next morning, with the dead weighing down the good ship and the spirits of her crew, a school of sperm-whales came close aboard, strange but fitting attendants at the funeral of their enemy. The event struck us all as very remarkable, and appealed strongly to the natural superstition of the credulous sailor. At no time during the voyage had whales approached thus close to the ship, or manifested such indifference to her presence. "Respect for the dead," the captain said, " forbids the thought of lowering the boats."

And we leaned our arms on the rail, and wondered at the tameness of our usually wild game.

Strange inconsistency! Consideration for the living would not for an instant have restrained the captain; probably not to save the life of Beers would he have allowed the boats to remain on the cranes with whales so near. He had been habituated to risk his own and other lives almost daily, and can and will thrust five souls, with himself at the head, into the valley of the shadow. But when the divine spirit has fled with the breath of life, leaving nothing but an unsightly casket, he stands reverentially before it, almost afraid of the slightest sound. At 8 A.M., lat. 1° 13′ S., long. 145° 32′ W., we placed our shipmate in the blue water, the captain reading the funeral service from the Episcopal ritual. As the white canvas form passed from sight in a broad undulation of light, his words of the nightwatch came to my mind: "How lonely, so far from home and kindness!" Yet I know that such thoughts do not now concern him. Assuredly he is in better company than he left.

We then braced forward; the mast-heads were manned, and a sharp lookout kept for the whales that tempted us in the early morning; but they were lost to us.

Feb. 15. We stowed down the oil of the last four whales. They made but sixty-five barrels, which brings the voyage up to seven hundred and fifty barrels. We are evidently in the region of small whales, and the herds of this sea are almost entirely composed of cow whales and their calves. We have not seen a bull whale lately. Is it possible that we are intruding on their lying-in hospital and nursery? May it be that it is among the Coral Islands of these seas that the females retire to bring forth their young? Captain Covill thinks that the Philippine Islands are such a resort, as he has there seen calves so young that their flukes seemed scarcely unfolded. Thirty degrees east of this, or in long.

110° W., we find bull whales again, frequently whole schools of young bulls without a cow among them. Still farther east, or in long. 90° W., we find schools of cows, accompanied by the bull whales. Near Japan, and off New Zealand, very large whales abound.

As I have bestowed some attention on the pigs of the ship, it is proper that mention should be made of other animals who share our wandering life. We have two cats of the species called Tom. The one rules the cabin and the other the forecastle mice; while 'tween decks is the dark and bloody ground where both join in nightly brawls and caterwauls. The fine sense of smell in the cat is well shown by their detecting the presence of flying-fish in the chains. Almost immediately after these fish strike the side or deck of the ship the cat will come from below, and, by its motions, persuade us to climb over the rail and get the stunned fish for a meal, it being understood that the flying-fish that come on board are the cat's perquisites. Except in fine sunny weather, when there is no spray to wet the deck, our mousers rarely venture on deck, and below they have rather a miserable time, between the oil and the tar.

Señora Villamill's monkey is the mischief-maker of the ship. He delights in tormenting the cats, and spends much time in watching the nesting of our two game-hens. His idea of supreme bliss seems to be to bury his comical face in the broken end of an egg, and we find amusement in observing his calculated movements to gratify this taste. He has closely studied fowl nature, and knows to a minute the time and place of the precious deposit; and in spite of the watchfulness of the steward, captain, and chanticleer, every now and again he may be seen running up a stay, with an egg deftly carried under one arm, to be deliberately emptied of its contents in some inaccessible part of the rigging. It has been a favorite game of the tailless monkeys against the tailed one, to hide an egg in the tar-pot, under the eye of the interested watcher. At the first opportunity the little brute would abstract the prize and run aloft with it. Of course, by the time he had eaten it he was in a pitchy mess ; and as the tar dried in the air, his long slender fingers adhered to the rigging, and his matted hair stood on end like quills on the fretful porcupine. The only cure was to dip him in oil to soften the tar, and allow his miserable monkeyship to gradually recover his original shape and appearance.

CHAPTER XXIV.

Game-cock as a Time-keeper.—Cockroaches in an Economical Point of
View.—Medical Practice adapted to Working-men.—Fancies, and Sick-
ness on Board.—Cure for Scurvy.—Captain Mathew's Story of Boiled
Eggs.—Extravagant Use of Butter and Sugar.—Etiquette of Meals.—
Want of the Same on the Forecastle.—Grub, and Manner of Serving.—
Coral Island seen.—Small Whale, and Stove Boat.—Wash-day.—An-
tonio as Washer-woman, and Chemical Experiments on him.—Grand In-
cantation and Appearance of Satanus.—We make Sail for the Islands.—
Trade-winds.

THE Spanish game-cock is a time-keeping phenomenon.
The usage of his kind, from the time of Peter the Great,
has been to crow at or about eight bells, or 4 A.M.—an easy
thing at any fixed point, but it becomes an affair of adjust-
ment in a ship running east or west, and changing her meridian constantly.   Remember, that for every degree of longitude a ship runs, her time is changed four minutes.   Now,
we took the cock on board at the Galapagos, long. 90° W.,
and carried him to the Sandwich Islands, in long. 160° W.,
a difference of seventy degrees, or a time difference of four
hours.   Some days we made four degrees of longitude, and
set forward the watch sixteen minutes; yet the cock would
keep the time, and crow at or about eight bells, or 4 A.M.,
at the western, as he had at the eastern islands.   Doubtless, one might circumnavigate the globe with one of these
birds, and his "shrill clarion" would wake the morn at his
accustomed hour, making or losing an entire day with the
ship.   This is not accountable to the appearances of the
coming day; for the time will be kept in the high latitudes

where the nights are so short that four o'clock comes after the rising of the sun.

Feb. 27. Is it true that conscience makes cowards of us all? The men are still under a nightmare fashioned since the death of Beers. The "doctor" insists that he has seen a pale lambent light hovering over the chest of one of the men. The man himself is very ill, and takes it into his head that he is dying of Beers's disease; but as he did not see the·case, he is at a loss to describe the symptoms. I find it good medicine, when he complains to me, to say, "That's not at all the way Beers felt;" and he will be better until he goes off on another tack. But symptoms don't count in our simple practice. Upon "all the ills that flesh is heir to" we open our attack with a dose of glauber, or horse salts, which takes such a strong hold on the patient that he is bound to confess that we are doing something for him. It may happen that the patient grows worse, and a dose of castor-oil, to work off the salts, is the next resource. He takes hope in the moving evidences of the medicine; and the more he endures the more he hopes. Should oil fail us, the ulterior of our modern healing art is to administer a rousing dose of calomel, with the intention that this shall work off salts, oil, and itself. In severe cases we repeat the entire course, and either kill or cure.

Our second mate is also sick, and has not stood his watch for several days. It may be imagined, then, that we are not at present a cheerful crew. I am loath to think that it is a fear of death that demoralizes our men. I rather think it is a shrinking from the unnatural prolongation of suffering, and the gloomy attendants of a death-bed, since we do not shrink from death in the boat. It may be that the terrible depression that has settled upon us arises from scurvy taints. The captain seems to think so, for he called us aft this morning, and made us tuck under our flannel a glass of glauber salts, and an equal measure of pure lime-juice. This dose was to "work off" scurvy: it seemed like swallowing a saw.

Speaking of eggs, and captain, monkey, and man greedily watching at the nest for them (as I did a few pages back) recalls a yarn spun by Captain Mathews, of New Bedford. When he sailed as boat steerer with Captain Blank, the steward placed three eggs by the old man's plate at breakfast one day. The superior looked at them a while, with the corners of his nose turned up suspiciously. "Halloo, steward!" he growled, "didn't I tell you to boil some eggs?" "Them's eggs, sir." "Them's eggs, sir!" mockingly said the irate chief, "I'll egg you, you scoundrel! Call three eggs eggs, do you?" "Eggs for the captain—you—sir!" "And where is eggs for the men? None, eh? Well now, just you tell me what mean cuss you have been sailing with?" "Captain Lucius, sir." "Captain Lucius! Well, you are worthy of him. He'll reach Fiddler's Green through a Galapagos terrapin; but just you don't forget that when you boil eggs, or any thing else for the cabin table, boil for all hands, and place in the middle of the table. If I don't get my fair share, it's because I don't want it. Now clear out, and boil some eggs."

This story of Captain Mathews's grew out of a discussion as to the different qualities of fare provided in the cabins of various whalers, and the old man went on to say, "It's not that captains are always hard and mean by nature, but they have been brought up with such men as Captain Lucius, and really believe that the way is to be stingy on deep water."

"Why, Captain Mathews," said one, "you don't let the boat-steerers come to your table just as you leave it, do you?"

"And why not?" he asked.

"Well, it's extravagant, to say the least, to leave butter

and sugar, when molasses will serve for both. I always tell the steward to put molasses in place of them."

Said Saint Mathew, "Such an order would ache me worse than rheumatism, and my butter would breed dyspepsia."

" Look here, Captain Mathews, that kind of talk's all very pretty; but, your owners will bring you up with a round turn some of these days, for pampering your men with butter and sugar, and such *menavelins*."

" I'll take care of that, sir, as I am an owner myself; and the others have the sense to feel safer in the venture because I don't shift grub on my table."

This anecdote illustrates some of the different views that are held about the proper kind of food for sailors.

The etiquette of meals on board ship is very amusing to Jack at the helm. The order of procedure for dinner is somewhat in this wise: The sun's altitude has been taken, and eight bells struck. The captain is pacing the weather and the mate the lee quarter deck. The second mate is somewhere or other, but surely to windward of the third mate. All hands are as hungry as wolves. The steward comes up the companion-way, and touching his greasy Scotch cap, announces, " Captain B——, dinner is on." "All right;" and the captain takes a turn by the binnacle, if we are running a course, and peeps at the compass. Then in the companion-way, on his way down he stops, takes a long look at the sails, and, as it were, a last farewell of the light of heaven. "Mr. F——, dinner is on." " Ay, ay, sir," says the mate, as he strolls to weather-deck. Now Mr. F—— takes a shorter peep at the compass, and, pausing in the companion, he, too, takes his upward survey. The two other mates go through precisely the same performance, only according to their respective ranks they take yet shorter peeps at the compass and glance heavenward. They then arrive simul-taneously at the table, to find the captain and Mr. F—— leisurely in their second plateful. Now, the misery of the arrangement is in this: the officers must come up in reversed order—third, second, first mate, and lastly the captain. A third mate has thus only about seven and a half moments to dispose of his grub. The old man last of all appears on deck, picking his satisfied teeth in the most tantalizing manner, and the four boat-steerers next make a dash for the table, and make clean sweep of the remnants.

With the men there is less formality—in fact, no formality at all. A tub, called the meat-kit, is provided; one for each watch. Into this is dumped the boiled pork and beef, and into another similar tub, the unpeeled potatoes, rice, beans, and whatever dessert there is. With fingers for forks and a belt sheath-knife, each fellow pitches in, mauls, turns, picks, and cuts for the choicest bit, transfers the mess to his tin plate, and sitting on hatch, windlass, terrapin's back, or bread-kit, proceeds to discuss his grub, ungratefully swearing all the while at owner, captain, and cook. The coffee in the morning, and the tea at night is served in buckets, and a quart cup is a usual allowance, unless the man be thirsty, when a half-gallon is not denied. The difference between the tea and coffee is less discernible by the taste, than by the difference in the texture of the grounds. I always thought that the tea most resembled a weak vegetable-soup, floating grease being somewhat more apparent on it than on the coffee. But both decoctions are dished boiling hot, and this is their chief recommendation, inasmuch as the heat is pretty sure to dislodge any of the white bread-worms, say an inch long, which may lurk in the soaking biscuit. Its after-warmth, moreover, softens the bread, so as to save teeth in the eating. After meals each fellow slips his plate into the netting over his berth, and the cockroaches see to it that his crockery is clean for next meal.

We are keeping a sharp lookout for land, as a small low

coral structure, called Hero Island, is located on our charts near our present position.

Feb. 28. At 2 P.M. "Land ho!" from the mast-head told us that we had reached Hero Island. Although but six miles away it was not visible from the deck, but by evening we were nearly up to it. It appeared a low, flat spit of sand:

> "A coral island, stretching east and west;
> In God's own language to its parent saying,
> 'Thus far, no farther shalt thou go; and here
> Shall thy proud waves be stayed.'"

Such growing islands as this, right athwart our track, add much to the dangers of the devious, drifting cruise of the whalers. Can one conceive the horrors of wreck on such a spot, out of the way of possible aid and rescue? We have not seen a ship in these seas. The grave responsibilities streak the hair of officers with early frost. For instance, there is Mr. F——, who was married just before we sailed. Young and brown-haired then, he promises to return to complete his honey-moon a gray-haired man.

March 2. After two unsuccessful chases this day, in a third we took a miserable little ten-barrel whale, and that at the expense of a broken boat. Mr. Burroughs went on and had the side of his boat laid open by the flukes. The second mate came up and killed the whale. Mr. F—— failed to fasten. Two small whales rose under his boat, and lifted it clear of the water. He cried to the men, "Hold your irons!" but when the boat touched water again things were so mixed on board that the whales were out of reach before the irons were recovered. Therefore, we must grease up for two small casks of oil.

March 5. This is washing and mending day. The oily clothes which have been soaking in a solution made of the alkaline cinders of the try-works, are first well tramped on

deck with our bare feet, and then attached to a line and
towed overboard in the wake of the ship. Thus the dissolved oil is worked out; after which, by a judicious exposure to six hours' flapping in the wind, much of the other

A STOVE BOAT.

dirt is also disposed of. A clean beast is defined as one
that cheweth cud and has a cloven hoof. I chew the *quid*,
but have not the cloven hoof, and in consequence may be
called an unclean beast. I certainly abominate washing-
day; but by a wise use of part of my store of tobacco, I

have secured the services of Antonio, the Portuguese, to keep me clean.

Antonio recently took advantage of his importance, however, and became somewhat extortionate in his demands. He raised his price two "nigger-heads" of tobacco a week, and I decided to show him the superiority of mind over brute force, with the aid of Posey, and Ichabod, our monkey. Antonio comes from Cape Verd, and is a zealous Catholic and a firm believer in the devil. In reply to some of his pious twittings, about a "heritico," I suggested that we should raise the old boy, and see who could best stand his assaults. He assented, and I went to work. My materials were calculated to produce something like the witch scene in "Macbeth," although they consisted simply of a bottle of phosphoresced sweet-oil and the monkey. The words of the incantation were to be recited from the tragedy. I counted largely, however, on the effect of the latter gentleman's illuminated tail. The Kanakas and Antonio were interested spectators, when all preparations were complete, although they lost much of the beauty of Shakspeare through ignorance of his language. The night was a little rough, and the darkness of the forecastle, with the creaking of timbers, the gurgling of the well water, and the deep-drawn sighs of my hidden confederates—the two cats tied tail to tail in the hold—produced a very theatrical effect. In the weirdest voice I could control, I mumbled,

> "Double, double, toil and trouble,
> Fire burn and caldron bubble.
> Weary seven nights, nine times nine,
> Shall Antonio peak and pine;
> Though this bark can not be lost,
> Yet it shall be tempest-tossed."

Now the wizard's face glowed with a pale flickering flame, and the mysterious monkey was thrust forward, with his little tail gleaming hell-fires. The rattling of a chain by Posey, and a few brimstone matches, came in appropriately at the same time, while I continued:

> "Double, double, toil and trouble,
> Fire burn and caldron bubble.
> For a charm of powerful trouble,
> Like a hell-broth, boil and bubble;
> Double, double, toil and trouble,
> Antonio burn, Kanakas bubble."

By this time I was almost as ready as the frightened audience to see "Auld Clootie himsel'" peering through the darkness between decks; and all hands scampered up the ladder to escape the sulphurous fumes which Posey was industriously generating, clanking his chain at intervals mean while. He said afterward that the effect was splendid, seen through the opening into the hold, through which he thrust the phosphorized monkey. The peace of mind of poor Antonio was destroyed. Formerly he only believed in his satanic majesty; now he knows of him. I must in mercy initiate him into the virtues of a horse-shoe to avert the malign influences of bogies, spooks, and other evil beings.

March 6. The repairs of the stoven boat have been the main work, and knotting yarns and picking oakum the recreations of the watch on deck. The captain has been trying his hand on a rawhide rope, or rather whip-cord plait, for a wheel-rope. The sailor is no match for the farmer's boy in working rawhide; the little I had learned stood me in good stead to-day in helping the captain to a neatly-plaited rope. To-day we are in lat. 2° 24' S., long. 156° W., only one degree east of Hawaii. The current here is so strong to the westward that we have made but one degree eastward, after steadily beating for two months, the drift of the night under short sail setting us back all we made by day. It is in these ocean rivers, where the food of the sperm-whale is gathered,

that these animals collect to pasture. By the establishment
of the regular watch to-night, and our putting on top-gallant
sails, we are informed that the present cruise is over, and
that we are bound for the islands to recruit. It is full time,
for the old crew are in a worn condition, and incapable of
the best service in the boats; and pains in the bones, loss of
color and elasticity in the muscular flesh, and ugly blue spots
on the legs are evidences of scurvy among them.

March 7. The weather in the morning was mild, calm,
and showery. Great numbers of porpoises were playing under the bows, and we darted the iron into one; but the weapon drew, and the injured creature fell back among its companions, who make short work of relieving the suffering.
Such, at least, is the belief among sailors.

At about 11 P.M. we entered the north-east trade-winds by
a well-defined line. South of lat. 5° 40′ N. we experienced
calms, alternated with squalls and sudden puffs, accompanied
by a great depression of our spirits and lassitude of body.
It is a hopeless, doleful region, where whales are very small
and hard to get. We thanked God audibly when the clean,
bracing north-east wind struck our sails and laid us almost
on our beam-ends—so sudden was it. We handed top-gallant and gaff-top sails, and hauled close to the wind, but we
could not lay a course for the Islands by three points, and
must work a traverse to gain the weather-gauge. It is
guessed that we may make the Sandwich Islands in about
twenty days.

13

CHAPTER XXV.

"St. Elmo's Fires," close Examination of; Superstitions on. —Longfellow and Shakspeare Versions.—Phosphorescence of the Sea.—Riding
the Gale aloft, and ravishing Sights.—Second-mate Sick, and Reconciliation.—Killer Whales, and Modes of Attack: unsuccessful Chase for
One.—Boat-mending, and Flying Squid.—Plenty of Fish, and Jib carried away.—Approaching Land, and Smell of the Land.—Land Dead
Ahead, and the Mystery thereof.—The Reason of Man proved equal to
the Instinct of the Bird.—Hawaii in Sight.

In the middle watch of last night, in the murky damp of
this climate, the "ampizant" was seen on the boom-irons of
the main and maintop sail-yards. These are globular lights,
about the size of a man's head, with well-defined outline, and,
as seen from the deck, gleaming with a peculiar and supernatural light. This phenomenon is known in the books as
"St. Elmo's fires;" but the common term on board is the
"ampizant," or composants. The fires continued so long, and
burned so steadily, as to excite speculation and the superstitions of the men. Antonio remembered the fearful incantation scene, and had no hesitation in holding that there was
some connection between the two mysterious lights alow
and aloft. Being curious to observe these lights from a
nearer point, and willing to keep up the character of the necromancer, I went aloft and crawled out on the mainyard-arm,
somewhat cautiously I confess. When I reached the fire
and my eye was brought close to it, the appearance changed,
and the edge only of the iron was luminous, as though rubbed with phosphorus. The halo was lost to me, although
the men on deck said it remained unchanged to them. On
touching the spot with the hand, cautiously, I thought that

became luminous also, but I was not conscious of any sensation other than that caused by the natural coolness of the iron. Those on deck said the ends of the fingers presented luminous points while the hand was on the iron. A superstition prevails that the ampizant is the visible presence of sailors who have died on the ship; and with this theory in my mind, I thought of Beers, and his lonesome grave, from which we were creeping. As I placed my hand in the light, I acknowledge that my flesh crept a little. My shipmates explained the impunity with which I had shaken hands with a ghost to the care I had taken of the dying man. If their idea is right, it only goes to show that nothing is lost in merciful actions. But Antonio says that no good can come to me from touching a bogie.

It is also a common belief that the fires indicate the approach of bad weather; but our barometer has suffered no change during the existence of the phenomena.

Longfellow says:

> "Last night I saw St. Elmo's stars,
>   With their glimmering lanterns, all at play
> On the tops of the masts, and the tips of the spars,
>   And I knew we should have foul weather to-day.
>   Cheerily, my hearties! yo heave-ho!
>   Brail up the mainsail and let her go,
>   As the winds will, and St. Antonio."

Shakspeare leans more to our opinion of the spirituality of the fires, as will be seen in this passage from the "Tempest:"

> "*Prospero.*   Hast thou, spirit,
>   Performed, to point the tempest that I bade thee?
>
> "*Ariel.*   To every article.
>   I boarded the king's ship; now on the beak,
>   Now in the waist, the deck, in every cabin,
>   I flam'd amazement; sometimes I'd divide,
>   And burn in many places; on the topmast,
>   The yards, and bowsprit, would I flame distinctly,
>   Then meet, and join."

While the seas and skies have their frowns and portents, they have also their smiles. One of the most beautiful phenomenon attending a passage in these latitudes is the phosphorescence of the water. To attempt a description of this must be more or less futile, for many words of brightest meaning fall still short of the sparkle of a star. Many times the wake of the ship is a broad belt of pale yellow light, far as the eye can follow it. The whirling eddies are almost aflame, and they fade in the darkening distance into a nebulous light. The infinite sea surrounding is a fit setting to the brilliant coruscations. The combing break of the waves flashes like sheet-lightning on a summer's night; and as the cresting flame of the head-sea is scattered by the bows, its spray falls in drops of fire on the watch, and the scuppers gleam with stars run wild. Deck, sea, and sky are illumined with myriad points of light, of rivaling brilliancy.

On one occasion, after hauling out a weather ear-ring for a close reef in the foretop-sail, I paused as long as other duties would permit, to drink in the ravishing sight which, with torrent speed, was rushing beneath me. The whole sea was wild with broad sheets of light under the tossing of the gale; the spray from the wave-caps was as a shower of fireworks, and the bows and head-gear of the ship were illumined from the watery light under the forefoot. Two hundred feet to windward, and holding a course parallel with ours, was a magnificent finback whale, the minutest outlines of its great form defined in light, as though it was of burnished gold. His spout, given in a tumultuous sea, sent a stream of fire half-mainyard high. And I saw how grand and resplendent whales may be in each other's eyes as they disport in the phosphorescent seas of the tropics. At last I felt compensated for the innumerable heart-sinkings and cold sweats of apprehension I had endured, and I drank into my inmost memory the lesson of the power and grandeur of a gale of wind as seen from the swinging yard of a tossed ship at sea.

The lights are revelations of the teeming life which crowds every foot of this vast ocean surface; but that is all I know. In the absence of knowledge, I am content and happy to look on and admire, while something whispers in my ear, " Such are God's ways on deep water."

March 16. Since my last writing we have had the trade-winds, strong and steady, and we have had to keep close-hauled all the time. The steady pitch of the ship becomes tiresome; and one begins to mistrust, lest fastenings yield, and starting planks let in the hungry sea. Our true oak and iron hold yet, however, and the faithful fibre of the hemp tugs and strains. The leagues and degrees are left behind, and the curious atoms in command eat and drink, work and sleep, and in patience take the buffets of outrageous fortune, without varying from the aim which launched them in their undertaking.

The continued illness of Mr. S—— may still farther add to our misfortune, and the fear is growing that he may be unable to accompany us on the Japan cruise. Mr. S—— is an excellent boat-header, and since the unfortunate mutiny he has been all that could be desired, treating the miserable remnants of a splendid crew with every kindness and consideration. Had he left America in the same temper that he bears to-day, we might have continued our offshore cruise, and carried to Japan twelve hundred barrels of oil. This would have brought us home within the three years for which we shipped; but now a fear prevails that a year may be added to the contract time. But I apprehend that good to some future crew will come of it; for when Mr. S—— sails as master, he will not lightly incur the pains and penalties of mutiny on whaling ground.

Nine shivering grunters have been added to our swinish

family, and so we have pillows galore, with prospects of countless sea-pies.

March 18. For two days the weather has been stormy, with occasionally vivid lightning and distant thunder. Much of the time we ran under close-reefed top-sails, and had all we could stagger under. A sharp lookout is kept for the high peaks of Hawaii; and to-day the wind is lighter, and we run under full top-sails. Heavy banks of clouds to the west shut off the distance. This morning we saw a school of the small whales called "Killers," which some writers affirm kill both the sperm and right whales. I should suppose that the sperm-whale is invulnerable to the attacks of this creature, and is abundantly provided for defense in its active jaw, aside from its provision for deep sounding, which would carry it far beyond the reach of its so-called enemy. But the right whale may be exposed to its attacks. Right-whale men assert that it has been observed to thrust its head into the mouth of a dead whale towed by boats, and tear out great pieces of the tongue; and they assure me that the tongue of the living whale is the part vulnerable to the attack of the killer. It is declared that when the right whale is swimming with its great lips opened as in feeding, the head of the enemy is inserted into the mouth and fastens upon the tongue. One can imagine that if this fierce animal once fastened its sharp teeth in the great oily tongue of the right whale, the latter might be as powerless to shake off its antagonist, as an ox with a bull-dog fastened to its throat. In vain might it close the elastic bone of the jaw on the smooth armor of its enemy; in vain cut its formidable flukes to strike its inaccessible assailant; and breeching would be impossible, with tons of weight pendent from the mouth. Moreover, the killer would be equally at home beneath the surface; and if sounding were possible, the assailed whale could not thus shake off its antagonist. The contest is said to end in the death of the greater whale, and its enormous tongue becomes the food of the victor. It is also affirmed, that when the buoyant tongue is removed, the right whale sinks through the weight of the bone in the head. I inquired from my informants whether they had ever found the wounds or scars of conflict on the tongue of the right whale, and they had not. And, rather than give up their pet theory, they insist that every whale thus attacked is killed, and every whale thus killed sinks, never to rise again.

The captain lowered his boat, and gave chase; but the roughness of the sea, the erratic movements of the killers, and their short risings, prevented our getting on. They manifested no fear of the boat, as they rose and rolled about it, giving us a good chance to observe them at some distance, but evading closer examination. The killer is considered the most beautiful of the medium-sized whales. Their form is slender, and they are agile and graceful in their movements. They are of a jet black, as polished and lustrous as satin. Near each eye is an oval spot of pure white, large enough to form a marked contrast with the general color. A cimeter - like fin on the back projects above the water, and is a conspicuous object as the graceful creature glides about.

Captain B——, to his other accomplishments, adds that of boat - builder, and he is now engaged in mending and painting a battered boat, to put on the Hawaii market in exchange for refreshments. Such craft are in great demand at the Islands, and from past tinkerings this one has become too heavy for our purposes. From repeated accidents, all our boats are somewhat dilapidated, in fact; but it is wonderful to see the restoration of a shattered boat under the hand of a skillful workman. If the keel and gunwales be not broken, the splintered wreck will be right and tight in a few days. For this purpose a store of light cedar-boards, and ready - bent timbers are carried in the ship; and the boats are of such simple construction that they are easily repaired.

During the late stormy weather, numbers of the beautiful flying squid came on board, leaping fairly over the weather rail, or striking the outside, and falling stunned in the channel. Vast flocks of them were seen, darting from the water, and making long leaps from wave to wave, with a motion swifter and more arrow-like than that of the flying-fish, but with much shorter flights. Those that came on board were six or seven inches in length, with eight arms, provided with suckers along their length, and two tentaculæ. The prevailing color was a glassy white and azure, with a bright emerald green over each eye.

The flying-squid are considered a dainty bit by the albicore and skip.-jacks; following these we see more swordfish than we have heretofore met. Great flocks of boobies and gannets also hover in the air, and share the feast of squid with the swarming fish. Our Kanakas were wild with excitement at this exhibition of their favorite food, and exclaimed enthusiastically, "*Pehe nui nui, miti*"—plenty of fish, very good.

March 20. A squall struck us yesterday and burst the jib. We reefed top-sails and kept a sharp lookout for land; which we raised directly ahead to-day—a dim outline away up in the sky, soon melting and lost in the haze of the horizon.

The glad cry of "Land ho!" came sweetly enough from the mast-head to us tired wanderers of the blue waste. You who dwell on the firm land and see the verdure of the earth every day, can never read the full significance of the joyful sound. Its interpretation to us is liberty, health, enjoyment, and the companionship of our kind. You who have never been long separated from the good-giving ground, can never know the smell of the land, the fine aroma that greets the sense of the sailor on his return from the open sea—the perfume exhaled from the mosses and ferns, the grasses, the flowering shrubs, and the shading forests. It strikes the senses of the hungry children of the sea, as the fragrance of the mother's milk strikes the little baby. The rugged, storm-beaten man, with softened feelings, welcomes the familiar influences under which he was born; but the thrice welcome airs of the distant continent, grateful as they are, yet make him faint and sick with thoughts of home and kindred.

The odor guides us to our haven, as the scent of the water attracts the camel in the desert. But other senses than that of smell are cognizant of the far-reaching influence; for to the scurvy-stricken mariner it comes as the curse of Prospero:

> "I'll rack thee with old cramps;
> Fill all thy bones with aches; make thee roar,
> That beasts shall tremble at thy din."

A crisis in this disease being induced by this mysterious land essence, is soon followed by recovery or death.

To the question from the deck, "Where away lies the land?" "Dead ahead" is the answer.

Again let the sailor question you—you who lose your way on fenced roads, and rush along iron tracks which clamp you in the ·path you should go. Let me ask, can you realize the full significance of the answer "Dead ahead," after months of drifting on trackless seas? Of course the sought land will be "dead ahead" on the course of the frigate-bird, for it is piloted by that God-given-compass guide, an unerring instinct; but how happens it that yonder speck of land is dead ahead to the weather-stained waif of the sea whose wanderings you have followed in these pages? Our white-winged lady sails, endowed with the wonderful inventions of men's minds. With the magnetized finger of steel to point the course; with the faithful chronometer to preserve the time of Greenwich; with the nautical almanac to give the positions of named stars for years in advance; with the quadrant and the sextant to measure altitudes and take meridians; with the mysteries of the logarithm to resolve the calculations; and with the chart of the earth's surface before him, the sailor to-day, as the shepherds of old, may find his way to a haven of sure rest by following the motions of a star in the east. Though seeming lost on the trackless ocean, by observing the meridian of the sun, our rough old captain has stuck a pin in his cunningly-lined chart, and given us a course—"North-by-west-half-west, and steady at that." And, although months have intervened since we saw a plain or a mountain peak, and although thousands of leagues have been traversed, we to-day have learned that that reason the good God has endowed us with is more than equal to the instincts of my mast-head companion, the frigate-bird. Yet I have met those who, in the safety of home, have said to me, "A chance rules;" "There is no God." Poor souls! What power not of God could plant that something which guides alike the bird and the man in the darkness and storm, through the immeasurable loneliness of the seas, to the land and home?"

At sunset the cloudy outline had taken definite form; the grand volcanic dome of Mauna Kea stood out against a glowing sky, and as the last rays of evening light lingered, the snow and ice of that lofty mountain gleamed in the heavens as a beacon, fourteen thousand feet above our heads. As I sat in the bows and drank in this glorious scene, I felt the presence of infinite power and majesty.

I doubt whether there is another spot on earth so grandly calculated to inspire the artist with a sense of magnitude, as the entrance to the straits which divide the island of Hawaii from Maui. This passage is about twenty miles

wide. On the right tower the heights of Haleakala, rising
precipitously ten thousand six hundred feet, and topped by
an extinct crater five miles across. On the left, by a series
of terraces, is the volcanic Mauna Kea, fourteen thousand
feet high, and crowned by an active crater of twelve miles'
extent. In most mountains the spectator must rise far
above the level of the sea, from which their altitude is measured, before he sees the peak; but here you stand on the
sea level, and look right up the whole ascent. And from
the grand old fire-points again you may look straight downward and over the level sea. No other spot have I seen in
which creative power is exhibited in such overwhelming
proportions.

CHAPTER XXVI.

Coasting the north Side.—Natives fishing from flying Canoe.—Native Trade.—Native Songs, and Tradition of Love of Pele for Kamehameha.—Conflict between the Chiefs of Hawaii and Maui, and *Fête* of Swimming.—Kealakeakua Bay the Scene of Cook's Death.—Our Anchorage.—Three- beautiful Boys, and my Hycamee.—A profitable Investment.—A naked Kanaka civilized from the Breech upward.—Liberty on Shore, and a Feast.—Cooking described.—Place of Burial.—Taboo, and the peaceable Dispositions of the Children.—The Mothers diving for Shells, and Emulation.—Inability to take Shore Exercise.—Surf-board, and wonderful Skill of the Natives in Swimming.

March 22. As we ran along the north side of the island of Hawaii, its appearance was very rugged and uninviting. Immense fields of black lava flanked the base of Mauna Kea, without a spot of verdure. In places this lava seemed to have poured over the precipitous rocks some hundreds of feet into the sea. Three or four miles from the shore, there were some trees and bushes, and the mountain heights seemed covered with forests. Above all, towered the great dome, with snow visible in large fields on its side. Great numbers of streams of water fell from the high cliffs into the sea, making white lines against the dark lava. As we ran through the straits, we reached the western, or lee side. This was more fertile, judging by the greater growth of trees and bushes, and the land was more level. On the western flank of Mauna Kea are extensive table-lands, on which, the Kanakas say, herds of wild cattle find pasturage. These belong to the king, and their sale adds to the very limited royal revenues. In some parts of the island the trees must be of great size, as a double canoe swept past us to-day, in which there were forty paddlers, although the craft seemed made from a single log. As we were now under the lee of the land, the winds became light and baffling. Opposite Kirua we observed several double canoes fishing. They were moved swiftly by a large number of naked Kanakas, who timed the quick stroke of the paddles with a chant and chorus. All we could see of their tackle was a swinging pole, seemingly worked by guy-ropes. This arrangement seemed to work with ease and certainty, for we saw them swing numbers of large fish to the platform between the canoes. Shortly after, a number of the natives came off in their outrigger canoes, bringing bananas, bread-fruit, pine-apples, nuts, cane, shells, etc., to trade for iron hoop, knives, needles, hooks, and tobacco. We were somewhat immoderate in our indulgence, as it had been months since we had eaten of fruits or fresh vegetables, and the craving for them was irresistible.

At the set of the sun the shore natives were warned off, and the cook made us a nice supper of fish and fresh vegetables, the captain having procured onions and sweet-potatoes for his half-sick crew. When the night settled on the deck, Jack of Hawaii was inspired by his island home, and, surrounded by the Kanakas of the watch, he sang of the glories of Kamehameha, the great war chief of Hawaii. The history of this chief is known to most English readers, and it is not for me to touch upon it; but the chanted traditions of the common people are not so well known. I caught such scraps of the chant, through the interpretations of Waheleheli, as led me to regret that I could not understand the whole. The bard sat on the bowsprit-bitts, surrounded by his comrades squatting on their heels, and accompanying the recitative with a modulated "ha-ha-he-ha," and a curious waving of the spread hands, at times bringing the palms together with a clap. Voice and motions were in absolute accord, as our tall, dark-featured Hawaiian went on with his story:

"Kamehameha, the solitary chief, the strong man, the dweller on the side of Mauna Kea: he was loved by Pelé, the goddess of the flaming mountain, the dweller in the heart of Mauna Loa: twin mountains of fire, Mauna Kea at the rising of the sun, Mauna Loa at the going down of the day. On Kea lived the lone man; on Loa, the lone woman. He was a stranger to his own great heart until he read of it in the eyes of Pele, who loved him for his power. And Pele whispered to Kamehameha, 'It is I who bring the mountain islands from the heart of the world; my hand brings the sacred fire through the waters, and the fiery lava through the deep seas, and makes homes for my people. At our feet is rebellious Maui, and Lanai, and Molokai, with Oahu, the land of sweet taro; and beyond all is fiery-hearted Kauai. I will make of these a throne for my loved one. Will he seat himself in it, and rule my children with a strong hand? Will he guide them wisely, that war may not stain my lava red with the blood of my children, red as it ran from my fiery home.' And Kamehameha said, 'I am one man; with the love of Pele I may melt the mountains, and turn the hearts of the people from blood. If she will guide me, I will wash the stain from the throne which she brought in flame through the deep waters.'"

Such was the cause that led Kamehameha from his mountain fastnesses, first to conquer the great island of Hawaii, and afterward, through a fierce war, to bring all the remaining islands under his rule. And the bard sang of how the terrible warrior of Hawaii met single-handed the great war chief of Haleakala, armored in his cocoa shield, and with the knotted war-club in his hand; how Kamehameha, standing naked, with folded arms, in the prow of his war canoe, ordered his rowers to advance on his armed opponent, standing in the shoal waters of the shore; and how, with the love of Pele in his heart, Kamehameha slew the war chief of Haleakala, and conquered the island of Maui. He sang also of a time when the war went against Kamehameha, and the sons of Haleakala burned his war canoes, and he was cut off from the help of the people of Hawaii, and driven to the mountain which overhangs the narrow sea. He could look down into his home, but his people could not hear his voice, and they knew not the peril of their chief. Then two chiefs came to Kamehameha, and said, "The darkness of the night is on the deep water, and the storm-winds have driven the canoes of Maui from the straits. We will swim to that near land, and bring thee help." And through the darkness of the storm, lighted by the broad torch of the volcano which flamed fourteen thousand feet above them, they were guided the twenty miles which separates the islands; and their chief was saved by this act of devotion.

Such were the noble themes we listened to beneath the lofty mountain peaks of the Pacific, and under the broad glow of Pele's torch.

It was not until the afternoon of the 23d that we dropped anchor in Kealakeakua Bay, the scene of Cook's death. After furling sail, and getting the decks cleared of rigging, the trading Kanakas were allowed to come on board, with fruits, shells, tapa cloth, etc., which were offered in exchange for articles of iron. These people are sharp enough at a bargain, and the equals of our sailors in taking care of their end of a trade. The chief advantage we had was that our iron would keep while their stuff was perishable. A curious mistake was made soon after we came to anchor, which caused considerable merriment among the men. In a canoe floating a short distance from the ship sat three Kanakas, of great beauty, carefully covered with folds of ornamented tapa, and their long hair decorated with feathers and flowers of brilliant colors. I took it for granted that I was looking on those ideals of female loveliness portrayed in the descriptions of early voyagers. Knowing that a wise law forbade women to visit ships at anchor in any of the Hawaiian ports, I beckoned them to come alongside, as I meant to drop them a fish-hook, as an offering to their graces. I was simply prompted by an innate love of the beautiful, for "I love all that is lovely, love all that I can." The canoe shot alongside, when, dropping their tapa mantles, to my intense disgust three splendidly formed young fellows, with the agility of monkeys, scrambled up the side and stood beside me. All of them exhibited muscles that might have wrung my neck on provocation; and I would have kicked them, had it not been for my Welsh veneration for three as against one. So I reluctantly gave them the three hooks I had exhibited.

About an hour before sundown, when the deck must be cleared of strangers, a giant, one-eyed Kanaka, laden with fruit, approached me, and said something in Hawaiian, his single eye beaming with jolly good-will meanwhile. Waheleheli said, in explanation, "He verry much good Kanaka; he hycamee friend you; you hycamee friend him; he give name you; you give name him; you takee pig, fruit, house, eberry ting; he takee shirt, white shirt. All good; old way here." Mr. F—— told me that a friend would be of use on shore, and that Waheleheli had interpreted truly the custom implying exchange of names and possessions for the time being. The white man's name, and a white shirt or two, in brief, would be accepted as a full equivalent for the use of all the Kanaka's possessions during the few days I should have ashore. I struck hands with Kakilolo on this bargain. I became Kakilolo, and he Davikhee; he gave me all his fruits, and I gave him my white shirt. He had to place at my sole disposal all his worldly possessions, personal service included, in further consideration of another shirt, or its equivalent, before the ship sailed. As I was to get much, and he little, naturally for a white man and a brother, I said *"Miti"* —good. So Davikhee drew the linen over his ugly mug; and to complete the picture I gathered the fluttering garment around the waist with a bright red bandana handkerchief— a remnant of my shore toggery. The effect was ludicrous in the extreme. My giant Kanaka in his native nakedness was sublime, in this fluttering rag he was ridiculous. As I afterward noticed this flag of truce fluttering in the evening breeze, I hugged myself with the thought that I had advanced a brother one step in the scale of civilization, that *my* Kanaka would never again feel decent with less than a cravat about his neck.

These people greatly prize articles of American dress, and wear with pride such articles as they can obtain, regardless of fit or fitness. It is told that a chief headed a wedding procession dressed in a naval lieutenant's blue swallow-tail coat, gilt buttons and all. This was not out of the way, perhaps, but except the mare, or breech-cloth, and a wreath of feathers about his manly brow, it was his only garment.

Similar negotiations to mine had been going on in forecastle and steerage, and the crew went to their bunks to dream of the good things in store.

March 24. Starboard watch had liberty on shore. To provide against contingencies, I drew a couple of fathoms of bright figured calico from the slop-chest, and placed a few sail-needles and fish-hooks in my pocket. The larboard watch landed us on the south shore of the bay, in front of a cluster of grass huts, sheltered beneath cocoa-nut trees. A number of the natives awaited us. Among them was a pair of naked legs, surmounted by a fluttering white shirt, which combination claimed me at once as all his own. The friends of Chipps and Posey had clubbed with Davikhee to make the expected feast at the house of one of the trio, and we now went to inspect the preparations for the entertainment. In a hole in the ground, in front of *my* house, was a brisk fire, which had been burning for some time. A mass of living embers was on the bottom, and in the midst was a heap of lava. This was the oven. A couple of small pigs, nicely cleaned of hair, a turkey, a large fish, and a liberal supply of potatoes and yams, were the contributions of our hosts. Very deftly, with a crooked stick, the hot stones were withdrawn from the embers, and the dust blown from them. They were then placed inside of the pig and fowl, and a savory steam soon issued forth. The meat was next rapidly wrapped in broad leaves, and placed in the oven, which had been cleaned of most of the coals. The vegetables were next arranged, and the whole covered with the hot stones, embers, and leaves, a small quantity of water being poured over all. A sweet smell of wholesome food arose, and held us hungry sailors to the spot; but " the watched pot never boils;" and, to facilitate the cooking, we tore ourselves away, and proceeded to inspect the town.

Many of the grass houses were in small garden inclosures, surrounded by loosely-piled lava walls. Within we observed patches of sweet-potatoes and yams, melons and pumpkins, with pine-apples, and plants which were new to me. Overhead was the cocoa-nut and a few bananas. The black lava soil seemed rich and productive. On the bluff fronting the bay, and separating the two towns, numbers of goats were seen, and pigs abounded, though we saw no horses or cows. Wild cattle are said to abound on the table-lands, however. In the face of the bluff, and at a considerable elevation, were numbers of small excavations. These, we were told, were once the burial-places of the people. The dead lowered from above were pushed into the caves, and left to the disposition of Pele, who dwelt in the neighboring volcano. In front of a hut we observed pieces of tapa tied around some cocoa-nut and other fruit trees. This we were informed constituted a "taboo" of the trees; the effect of which was that no one save the family who placed the taboo were allowed to touch the fruit. It appeared that the owner of the neighboring hut was sick, and unable to provide for himself, and this simple means was resorted to, that he might not suffer from want. The religious observance of the taboo has been described by almost every visitor to the island, and it is not necessary for me to enlarge on the singular and interesting feature of society, farther than to say that the taboo is a sacred restraint, rarely broken. I have heard of streams tabooed that ships might water from them, and the sacred word would pass up to the sources by word of mouth, and no natives would wash their hands even in the running water. But I fear much that modern civilization will preach this simple restraint out of existence, and replace it with the less effective machinery of patent locks, courts, and penitentiaries.

We were particularly charmed by a large company of small children, who were playing, naked as when born, on a shelving beach of sand, on which the gentle swell was breaking in miniature surf. The little brown beauties were from six months to six years of age. All were fearlessly playing in the water, at depths proportioned to their years; dabbling as naturally as young ducks, the elder having a watchful eye on the younger ones. With great glee this guardian would roll a sprawling, choking youngster upon the sand, and by patting his shining back, enable him to cough and sneeze out the effect of a momentary submergence. I judged that all over fifteen months were able to swim, and take such care of themselves as was necessary in this shallow water. Those younger were making fair efforts in the same accomplishment under the encouragement and direction of their elder playmates. A very noticeable feature in the merry group, was the absence of all loud, discordant cries, angry exclamations, and evidences of a quarrelsome disposition. I am told that such is very rare; and it rarely happens that the hand of one is raised in anger against another. The same peaceful disposition was wonderfully manifest in the ten Kanakas of our crew. In the three months they have been on board, there has certainly not been a quarrel among them; nor can I recall a harsh word between the poor heathen. But of us white and black Christians the same can not be said. The happy mothers of our little savages were swimming in the deep water of the bay, and diving for shell-fish, each having a long gourd anchored in her vicinity, into which she might drop such shells as she secured.

We laid ourselves upon the lava ledges which overhung the beautiful scene, and the swimmers observing us, they with great shouting and splashing attracted our attention. A friendly competition then arose, in the exhibition of their skill as divers. A black-haired, black-eyed mermaid, more beautiful than the syrens of old, I'll be sworn, stood erect in the bright water, and clapping a pair of pretty hands gracefully over her head, with musical cries strove to secure our special attention. Then, turning and undulating as a wave, her twinkling feet for a moment shot in the air, and the vision disappeared long enough to cause us to hold our breath in sympathy. Arising at length, the pretty head, with long black locks all afloat, was again turned in our direction to see that we recognized her; and with clapping hands we cheered her and the other competitors. To show that their efforts were not in vain, they would exhibit the shells brought up, and, swimming to the gourds, deposit their prizes.

After our long absence from the land, it is remarkable

how little exertion we are capable of. As I ran up and down our lofty spars a few days ago, I thought over the probability of getting permission to penetrate the interior of the island, to scale Mauna Loa, fourteen thousand feet, and descend into its heart thousands of feet; to take a lava bath with Pele, and write a history of volcanoes in general, with a concise theory of earthquakes appended, and a top view of thunder-clouds. All this seemed as a good, honest day's work; heights and depths counted as nothing to my aroused imagination. Only put me ashore, I thought, and to scale the heavens or descend to hell will be but boys' play. But on shore, behold me! Before my dinner is cooked, my poor scurvy-tainted limbs are sore and aching under me; I am sitting, resting my prematurely old bones, on the rocks, singing " Well done !" to the poor shell-divers.

When rested, we were attracted by the shouts of natives, and we sauntered to a point of rocks on which a magnificent surf was breaking. Here we witnessed an exhibition of skill in swimming, in striking contrast with that of the women we had just left, and one perhaps to be witnessed nowhere else. Here we found a large number of the natives enjoying themselves on the surf-board. It was a new sight to us to see men and women playing in a surf such as we would scarcely expect the natives of the water to live in, such as it is questionable whether the seal and the otter could have contended against; and it was with some terror that we watched them riding, with head inclined, on the crest of a foaming wave, with the speed of a bird. They came shooting forward, almost on to the terrible rocks, against which a preceding wave had broken in a deafening roar; but just as they seemed fated to strike the deadly barrier, just as they were on the very boiling suds of foam, the happy, shouting performers would disappear beneath the surface; a moment more, and they would be seen buffeting the incoming roller, and diving to allow it to pass over them, bearing on its crests some of their playmates, and soon again they regained the outside of the breakers, pushing their board with them.   Here they would mount the board again, to career once more over the frightful course; and thus they played by the hour, far happier than beaux and belles in the ball-room.   The wilder the surf, the more intense their enjoyment of it.   The surf-board seemed about five feet long, and a foot wide, turned up a little in front.   It was placed lengthwise under the breast as they rode on the crest of the wave.

CHAPTER XXVII.

RETURNING from this wild and fearfully exciting scene, we noticed a young fisherman practicing the gentle art, but not with hackle or May-fly, or with the supple ten-ounce angle. Our naked Adonis stood on a projecting point, at some ten feet elevation, with a stout bamboo or reed of twenty-five feet, the butt supported in his crotch, and played with the right hand, while the left manœuvred the fish. From the outer end of the rod was a stout line equaling it in length, and baited with a dummy fish, made of a roll of tapa, about twenty inches in length. This practice is to acquire dexterity in landing the fish. It consisted of swinging out the fish to the extreme reach of the rod and line, and allowing it to rest a moment on the water; then, with a dexterous backward surge of the rod, swinging the fish clear of the water, and bringing it directly under the left elbow, at the same moment passing the thumb of the left hand into the gill, and thus securing the fish.

We sat on the rocks admiring the precision with which the fish was brought forty feet distance, and securely planted under the grasping arm of the angler. It was, in its way, as fine an exhibition of skill as the fly-fisher casting his feathered lure the same distance into the circle of wavelets left by a rising trout. When we examined the beautiful hooks of these islanders, we found they were not finely pointed, and the barb was ill fitted to hold a fish securely; so they could not allow their game to play and exhaust itself before it was landed. The practice of our angler was simply to convert the rush by which the hook was taken into a leap of forty feet, directly from the water to the hand of the fisherman. The people are so expert that few fish are lost that once take the hook. Indeed, they are considered very skillful fishermen, whether with the rod, the deep-sea troll from the canoe, or with the nets. Fish is a favorite dish with all classes, either cooked or raw, the latter being preferred.

Tired with our interesting ramble, and fairly wolfish in appetite, we returned to the town. At the outskirts we found our hosts awaiting the party. They conducted us to the oven, which was now uncovered; the still warm stones were carefully removed, and the potatoes and yams were placed in a deep calabash and covered with fine grass, to keep in the heat. The outer wrappings of the animals were charred and brittle. These were removed until the inner leaves were reached, and the latter were next placed in broad, flat gourds, surrounded by some of the hot stones from the bottom of the oven, and covered closely with grass. A gourd filled with the milk of cocoa-nuts, and an acid drink of limes or lemons, completed the preparation. It had been determined that we should all dine at the house of Chips's host, that being the largest and most commodious. Our friends, with the assistance of some attendant Kanakas, therefore mounted the dishes on their heads, and proceeded in single file to the appointed place, each of the guests following next to his special entertainer. And as we filed through the streets, our hosts, in recitative, in part unintelligible to us, recounted our wonderful prowess in chasing and killing the big fish of the sea, and our great possessions in "Amelica." On the way we were joined by some of our Kanaka crew, and we bade them join in, as we felt sure that we six could not eat two hogs, the turkey, a big fish, and much over half a bushel of roasted roots. Nothing loath they consented, and joined in a chorus about the greatness and goodness of white men, paying special tribute of praise to Poehee, Chippee, and Davikhee.

Reaching our destination through an admiring and, judging by their longing eyes, a hungry crowd, the feast was spread on a clean mat of plaited flags on the floor of a large room. Around this we arranged ourselves in a classical attitude, while opposite to us squatted our happy hosts. Minus knife and fork, the carving was effected by dexterous twists and jerks, detaching head, leg, or wing, and bringing all connected muscles in convenient form for biting at. The stone stuffing rattled out, still steaming from heat; and with the hind leg of a hog in one hand, and a great potato in the other, with occasional nips at turkey, or fish, we sea-dogs reveled in the abundant rations before us. As I reluctantly abandoned the idea of scaling Mauna Loa, I attacked my second quarter of pork, and at length had to admit that my eating tackle was exhausted, much to the disappointment of My White Shirt who kept urging me to the encounter. All I could do was to sit contentedly watching the Kanakas polishing off the last bones. The pipe then passed from mouth to mouth, and we took the hearts of Our White Shirts by storm when we distributed the calico for their women, and the needles and hooks for themselves. The setting sun found us ready to take canoes, and our friends paddled us to our home.

March 26. Yesterday following our carousal was our day on duty aboard, and the watch was busy getting off wood, sweet-potatoes, yams, pigs, and goats. The decks were filled with Kanakas trading with us for needles, hoop-iron, etc., giving in exchange the pretty shells, tapa, etc., etc.

At 1 P.M. Governor Adams, called the head chief of the island, came off in a large double canoe on a visit of ceremony to Captain B——. He was enormously fat, and to bring him on board, we rigged a tackle from the mainyard, and slung it over his great chair (which he had brought with him). When seated therein, we ran him up with a "yo, heave-oh," and a merry chorus, evidently to the satisfaction of his excellency, and the enjoyment of his staff and followers, who expressed pleasantries and approval of our elevator. His excessive flesh prevented his going into the cabin, and his entertainment was under an awning decorated with the ship's colors. As he slowly walked about the deck, two attendants followed with his chair, that he might seat himself while observing the ship or conversing with the captain or officers. He spoke English easily and well. All the accompanying chiefs were large and remarkably fine-looking men. I was much impressed with the marked superiority of the chiefs over the common people with whom we have daily intercourse. Of course there was an object in this formal visit, but this we were not allowed to learn. A whisper got abroad, however, that it was in some degree connected with the culture and working of cotton, which Governor Adams had much at heart. He left a present of fruit for the men forward, and we bade him adieu with three hearty cheers, which he gracefully acknowledged.

To-day it was our watch on shore. I have in some degree got my land-legs aboard again, and find I can prolong my walks without the intolerable "toothache" in every bone of my body. I had made arrangements with My White Shirt to fish for the bonita, and while he was arranging the canoes, Chips, Posey, and I strolled into an open thatched shed, prettily shaded, where some twenty-five women were beating out tapa. This substance forms the principal clothing of the natives. It is of the consistence of a thick, soft paper, and is made of the inner bark of the paper-mulberry-tree. The borders are prettily ornamented with simple figures, printed in colors, red and black predominating. All the women engaged in this work were young, and some of them were good-looking. Gentleness and good humor are the prevailing expressions of all the women of the island. They welcomed the advent of the three white men with smiles, and what we took for compliments. One invited me to seat myself beside her, and without hesitancy I squatted on the ground and watched with interest the curious process of spreading the closely interlaced fibres of the bark into thin sheets of a uniform thickness, about eight to ten inches square. After this had been done, the edges were united by whittling and beating with a light wooden tool with a notched face, and the small pieces were felted together, until sheets of twelve feet square were made. The broad sheet is folded very prettily about the body, and is sufficient protection for this climate. The pleasant-eyed "nut-brown maid" explained as best she could the processes going on, and I gravely nodded approval.

She then placed her hand on the head of her white companion, and took delight in running her taper fingers through the long curling locks which I took special pride in cultivating. But as she lifted and arranged the curls she murmured, "*Miti, miti*"—good, very good—and gently drew my head into her lap, thrusting her fingers deep down about the roots. It gradually occurred to me that this beauty was on a hunt for very objectionable ideas which she would not be likely to find, and she pushed the empty head from her lap, now exclaiming "*Oury miti*"—no good. I was quite ready to tear myself away after this, and start on my fishing trip.

We were now on the north side of the bay, near the spot

where Captain Cook met his death, in 1778. It was with the usual arrogance of the English breed of white men that he underrated the character of these people for bravery, and their haughty indisposition to submit to the strangers' tyranny. The loss of this great explorer is to be deplored, but no unprejudiced jury, even on the English account, could render verdict other than " served him right." A small pile of stones long marked the spot near which he fell, but the hand of the spoiler was fast removing this trace, when an English man-of-war placed a small sheet of copper, bearing an inscription, on the trunk of the nearest cocoa-nut-tree. The trunk of the tree was subsequently conveyed to England and placed in the British Museum—a very cheap monument to England's greatest navigator and explorer. An old chief who professed to remember the unfortunate occurrence, pointed out the flat table of lava on which Cook was beaten down, and with pantomimic action he endeavored to portray the incidents, now running to and fro, now personating the marines, with " boom, boom," and "*ourymiti;*" and now showing how his countrymen ran to the water and dipped their cocoa-mat armor, thinking that the moisture would extinguish the bolt of flame which they saw issue from the deadly gun. They supposed that the flame inflicted the deep wound, and reasoned that a wetted mat might arrest the death-dealing fire. Finding that this expedient failed, the great dread possessed them that the white man was armed with the sacred fire with which Pele had overcome the sea-god, and brought their island home up through the great deeps. This thought intimidated them more than the slaughter of their companions. But it must be admitted that they manifested a cool courage and a ready presence of mind.

Our entertainers announced that all was in readiness, and we embarked in a double canoe. This structure was composed, as its name implies, of two canoes placed parallel with each other, about eight feet apart, and secured together by two arched ties. On these connecting ties or beams was erected a light staging, on which the freight was placed, leaving the long narrow canoes unencumbered for the paddlers. A large double canoe will require perhaps thirty or forty men at the paddles, and they are very swift. The men regulate their stroke by a chant or chorus, in which all join, and the effect on the water is very fine. The old war-canoes were beautiful specimens of workmanship. Our carpenter was an excellent workman in his craft, yet he remarked on examining the governor's canoe, that with the advantage he possessed in perfect tools, he would not dare to touch it with the idea of improving the finish; he might add ornamentation, but not finish. Our canoe was manned by eight paddlers, two steersmen, and three to manage the rod; adding the three white men, all told, sixteen men. From the back part of the stage projected a stout bamboo-rod about thirty feet in length, secured in a recess formed in the stage, with two stays, or guys, leading over a short mast in the bow of either canoe. By drawing on these, the pole could be elevated, so as to swing the captured fish on to the stage. From the outer end of the rod depended a line of equal length, and attached to this was the white bone hook, and a pair of the wings of the flying-fish. The method of fishing was simply to paddle the canoe with such speed as would cause the lure to skip from wave to wave, in semblance of the motions of the flying-fish, and the bonita would greedily seize it. The instant the fish struck, the two men at the guy would elevate the rod, and the fish was swung to the man on the stage. We were out about three hours, and took about eight hundred pounds of fish. Our entertainers said that the sea was much too smooth, or we should have taken a greater quantity. Much pleased with the novelty of the sport and the completeness of the arrangement, we returned to the ship, each bearing a couple of fine fish for the mess.

March 27 (*Sunday*). Mr. Baldwin, of Pennsylvania, a missionary stationed near this place, preached to us to-day. The entire crew formed his small but attentive and interested audience. The service recalled the Sabbaths of home, the first I have experienced for seventeen months. The good word spoken was chiefly of value, as it evidently came from a loving heart, sympathizing with us in our exposures, temptations, and peculiar hardships, and encouraging us to keep our faces to the right, though gales of temptation might drive us from the true course; though we might live far from goodness, said the preacher, still to keep up the love of good. Never say to evil, be thou my good; never excuse the evil of your course, or love the evil in others; hate evil, though you may not do right to-day; hate evil, and the hope remains that you will, in the fullness of God's mercy, live to cease from wickedness. After all, I felt that it was not from ignorance that I was so wide of the true path. After dinner he distributed some tracts, which I fear failed to reach the witness within, and he invited the crew to call at the mission for Bibles.

On the 29th of March we hove up anchor, bound for Honolulu, but the wind failing us, we had to let go again to save the ship from drifting on a ledge of rocks at the southern entrance of the harbor. We lay easy until the following morning, when we got up the anchor, and by towing with the four boats made an offing from under the lee of the bluff, when a fresh breeze filled our sails, and we dashed merrily on our course for Oahu. As we ran along to the south of Maui we had a beautiful view of the volcanic peak of Haleakala, "the house of the sun," so named because the morning sun rose over its lofty summit to the populated portions of the island. It is ten thousand six hundred feet in height, and its summit is excavated by a great sandy crater some three miles in extent, and of vast depth.

CHAPTER XXVIII.

Jack of Owyhee sings the Song of Haleakala, and the Wars of Fire, Water, Air, and the Sands.—Admirable Qualities of the Kanakas.—Sunday at Honolulu.—Outer Anchorage.—Fitting Ship for long Cruise.—Mr. Deil, Seaman's Chaplain.—Drunkenness on Shore.—Meeting Daniel Wheeler, and we disagree.—Good News of our imprisoned Shipmates.—The Power of the United States interposed, and they are liberated. — Weigh Anchor for Japan.—A Woman swims thirty Hours.—Mr. S—— left at the Islands.—Reach Japan, and Bill is promoted.

In this night's watch Jack of Hawaii, our Kanaka bard, chanted to us the song of the Haleakala: " The goddess Pele, with the sacred fire, had contended with the water-god for long ages, and had brought the island up out of the deep sea, and made herself a soft resting-place in the great lake of fire on the bosom of Haleakala, away out of the reach of the water-god. Then the spirits of the Blue Sea sought the spirits of the Beaches and the spirits of the Air, to aid in driving Pele from her home in the high mountain. Now, the Shore remembered how Pele had buried its sands and beautiful shells beneath the burning lava, and the winds moaned over the black smoke and the sulphurous odors with which Pele had polluted their sweet breaths. Then the sea lifted its treasures of sand to the shore, and the great North Wind lifted the sand in mighty whirlwinds and poured it into the crater of Haleakala. Pele fought against the sand, she laughed at the little stone splinters, and threw them into the clouds; but the winds held their breath, and the sand returned from the sky, and fell again in the face of the goddess. Thus for ages the fountains of the sand played into the air, and returned again to the contest, until the little grains which restrain the power of the sea, were victorious over the volcanic rage of Pele. The sand ran back and back forever, giving no rest to Pele. It filled her eyes that she might not see, it filled her throat that she could not breathe. Then she shook the land with earthquakes, and the affrighted people fled to their canoes, lest the land should sink in the sea; but the God of the Waters brought great armies of little worms to prop the land with coral rocks. Thus the sand and the worm restrained the earthquake and volcano. Then Pele fled to Hawaii, and built up Mauna Kea and Mauna Loa out of the solid lava rocks, and carried her walls into the kingdom of the ice-king, where the feathered snow caught the sand and carried it over the waterfalls into the ocean, whence it came, so that no longer do the winds lift the beaches to war against Pele in Hawaii.

The peculiarity of the crater of Haleakala at the present time is the presence of vast beds and banks of sand and gravel, which doubtless gave rise to this legend of the war of the elements.

The more I see of the Kanakas of the Sandwich Islands, the more am I drawn to them. In my poor estimation, they rise infinitely above the populations we sailors meet on the main-land. The thriftlessness, dirt, indolence, superstition, cowardice, and treachery which one meets in the mixed breeds of the Spanish Main contrast badly with the unselfishness, the unfailing good-nature, the poetic temperament, and the courage to back us, in boat or on the yard-arm, which characterize the brown-visaged children of the isles.

April 3 (*Sunday*). At daylight we were close in to the outer harbor of Honolulu, and by the rising sun we dropped anchor outside the coral reefs. The people are such rigid Sabbatarians, under missionary influence, that no pilot is permitted to point the way to the coming mariner on this day, and we are left in an open roadstead, exposed to the wind and sea. In the afternoon, on throwing the offal of a goat overboard, it attracted several large sharks about the ship, and under the persuasive influence of a harpoon we enticed one of them to the deck. It measured fourteen feet ten inches. Soon after, the *Howlin*, of Nantucket, Captain Worth, anchored near us; six months out, with three hundred barrels of oil. The captain had a disturbance on his ship, and was obliged to put into Payta in distress.

April 26. For twenty days we have been moored in this pleasant resting-place. It is not for me to shed ink in the descriptions of towns, or to travel on roads made dusty by previous travelers. For descriptions of the city of Honolulu and its surroundings, I refer to almost any modern book of travel on the Pacific, and to the records of missionary enterprise in the Islands. Commodore Wilkes, for instance, is very interesting in his description of this place, and of the manners and customs of its remarkable people.

We have been busily refitting ship for the long cruise to Japan which lies before us. On alternate days the watchers have had liberty on shore, but much of the time has hung wearily on my hands. Except the reading-room provided by the Seaman's Friend Society, there is no resort inviting to the sailor who is not attracted by the sensual indulgences which are usually prepared for him. Mr. Deil, the seamen's chaplain, has been active, however, in making the better ways of life attractive to our poor fellows, and we are all indebted to him for moments of rational enjoyment. At this season of the congregation of the whaling-fleets on the passage to Japan, Honolulu is very dissipated. In spite of the strenuous efforts of the Government to discourage the traffic in spirits, much drunkenness prevails, and many poor wrecks of white humanity drift about the streets, a scandal to the boasted civilization with which we would supplant heathen customs. The traders find profit in vice, and they stand constantly opposed to the efforts of the missionary to check an evil which threatens the very existence of the people. In a low hole I saw a man acting as fiddler and master of ceremonies to a dancing squad of half-drunken sailors. Once he considered himself a gentleman, and had sailed master of a large East Indiaman.

Late one night I went down to the pier to take a canoe for the ship, and there I found an old man in the familiar garb of the Quaker, striving to send his unaccustomed voice across the waters in hailing an English schooner which lay far beyond. My younger lungs were placed at his disposal, and in a few minutes his boat was on its way ashore to take him off. This was Daniel Wheeler, sent out, I believe, by the Yearly Meeting of Friends in London, to examine and report upon the missionary labors on the islands of the Pacific. The good old man was evidently surprised at hearing the plain language of Friends from the rough sailor at his side; and on learning that I actually " belonged to meeting," and hailed from Philadelphia, he cautiously beat about the bush to learn to which persuasion I belonged. A manifest frigidity stole over his manner when he learned that I hailed from the camp of Elias Hicks, and I wondered a little that the devil of sectarianism should reach so far as the Sandwich Islands, and come between two lone men on that silent night on the coral pier of Honolulu. Daniel did not know that in his withdrawal of interest and sympathy he had in a degree performed an *auto-da-fe*. I found that he was laboring under the prevailing error that the American whaling sailor is entirely beyond the pale of God's mercy, and, as he expressed it, is " God-defying, Heaven-abandoned." I

strove to show to him that society was in no small degree
answerable for Jack's faults, and I pointedly inquired whether he had of his abundance spared for the enlargement of the
field of usefulness of Mr. Deil.   I also told him plainly that,
besides the reading-room, there was not a decent roof on the
shores of the broad Pacific where the sailor could lay his
head.   Before his boat arrived, he thawed to the extent of
offering to supply us with reading matter of a profitable
form.   The next day I went on board his vessel and received
a number of books; but I fear much they were not peculiarly
adapted to the wants of our boys.

On inquiring for the men who were thrown into the fort
three months ago, we learned that the sloop-of-war *Peacock*
had released them after about six weeks' detention, Captain
Kennedy holding that they were improperly confined.   Such
as claimed protection as American citizens were taken on
board the *Peacock;* the remainder shipped on other vessels.
I may anticipate here, for the sake of sequence, that many
months after this date we met the men on board the *Peacock,*
in the port of Callao, and it seemed that there had been much
trouble on account of the manner of their trial.   We understood that Captain Kennedy held that our captain was liable
for false imprisonment, and that subsequently the men recovered wages in the courts of the United States.   Mention of
this is made as evidence that the legal adviser of the men in
our mutiny kept them clearly within the law.

We bade adieu to Honolulu with little regret, our opportunities for enjoyment having been extremely limited, and
we received orders to heave the anchor for an eight months'
cruise with satisfaction.   On the morning of the 26th of
April we weighed anchor, and stood along the shore three
miles outside of the coral reef.   We were accompanied by
some twenty men and women, relatives of our Kanaka sailors.   They staid on board until afternoon, when, with much

good cheer, the entire party plunged into the water and struck out for the shore.

> "Fearlessly they skim along:
> Their hopes are high, their limbs are strong;
> They spread their arms like the swallow's wing,
> And they throw their feet with a frog-like fling."

Their friends on board showed no concern whatever; yet we must have been more than two miles outside of the reef, with a heavy surf breaking. Doubtless it was a slight effort to these splendid swimmers. The following incident, taken from Wilkes, shows what these people are capable of in the water: "All swim, and have little fear of loss of life by drowning. They appear quite as much at home on the water as on land, and many of them more so. Many remarkable instances of their patience under this kind of fatigue were mentioned to me. One of them, which happened the year of our arrival, is well authenticated, and will also tend to show very great attachment and endurance in their females. As the Hawaiian schooner *Kiola*, commanded by an American named Thompson, married to Kaiha, a female chief, was going to Hawaii, having on board many passengers, the vessel ran ashore on getting into the straits between Maui and Hawaii, and all on board, forty-five in number, were obliged to take to swimming for safety. Thompson could swim but little, but his wife was quite expert in the art. She promptly came to his aid, placed him on an oar, and swam for the shore. The accident occurred on Sunday about noon, when she, with many others, began to swim for the nearest land, which was Kahoolawe. She continued to support her husband until Monday morning, when he died from exhaustion, and she did not reach the shore until that afternoon. She clung to him to the last, at the imminent risk of her own life, and was thirty hours in the water."

We left behind us Mr. S——, the second mate, and one man, both being too sick for the cruise before us; and one of the boat-steerers was discharged for inefficiency. We shipped three Kanakas, making thirteen in all, who, with three blacks and fourteen white men, compose our entire crew. At this time I was promoted to steer the captain's boat; and whether I can stand the test or not remains to be seen.

June 11, lat. 31° 28′ N., long. 178° 10′ E. After a passage of forty-five days, we have reached the eastern verge of the cruising-ground of Japan. We have accordingly established boat-crew's watches, and for the first time our young boat-steerer has headed his watch, and put on airs accordingly, pacing the weather quarter-deck, and taking a new interest in the ship's course. "How does she head?" he asked, with unnecessary frequency, as we forged slowly along under reefed top-sails and furled courses. A vigilant eye was also kept for the impossible dangers of this unknown sea. The most decided change for the better which I have experienced is that my meals are eaten in the cabin at a table, instead of on the forehatch, and our dishes are washed by the cabin-boy, and not scavengered by the horrible cockroaches of the forecastle.

CHAPTER XXIX.

Cockroaches as Hunters of the wicked Flea, and as Scavengers.—Swarming Schools of Albicore.—First Japan Whale raised.—Tame Whales.—
Darkness approaching.—Lost Whale.—A Gale of Wind, and Trouble
in holding Whale.—Slaughter of Sharks.—Sharks suggested for the Amphitheatre.—Cutting-in under Difficulties.—Animal Life surrounding us.
—Sword-fish and Albicore.—Taking the Sword-fish.—Whales lost and
taken.—Active Work in the Boats.—Whales every Day.—Bill's first
Chance.—An exciting Approach, and one hit.—Gam with the *Caroline*,
of London.—Musical Inharmony, and a Row.—We are ordered in to the
Boat, where the Song is finished.—Fourth of July Celebration.

A WONDERFUL institution, fearfully made, is the cockroach
of the tropics.   His chief recommendation is his insane pursuit of the flea.   At times, in Spanish ports, a man succeeds
in capturing a host of the latter insects, and the first night
thereafter the roaches make a happy hunting-ground of his
person.   The unfortunate flea is allowed no rest until he
takes refuge in some crack too small for his pursuer to enter.   At the entrance the roach will keep watch until the
flea is compelled by hunger to venture forth, when it is
seized and destroyed.   But it is a horrible experience to
awaken at night, in a climate so warm that a finger-ring is
the utmost cover you can endure, with the wretched sensation of an army of cockroaches climbing up both legs in
chase of some Spanish unfortunate!   It reminds me of how
many times I have placed my tin plate in the overhead nettings of the forecastle, with a liberal lump of duff reserved
from dinner, and on taking it down at supper, have found it
scraped clean by the same guerillas.   They leave no food
alone, and have a nasty odor, which hot water will scarcely

remove. But one becomes philosophic at sea in matters of food. When butter has twice crossed the line, and has reached the age of two years, no stomach can accept it as butter; but as cheese, it seems quite mild. About this time the epicures on board hesitate to bite the ship-bread in the dark, and the custom is to tap each piece on the table as you break it off, to dislodge the large worms which breed in it.

To commemorate the day, we killed the old sow which we brought from America, and as sea-pie she came to a natural conclusion. But her death brought good luck; for in the evening the ship was surrounded by swarming shoals of albicore, the first we had seen since leaving the Islands. From this indication we look with confidence for sperm-whale.

A peculiarity of the waters that we are now in is that in the night the fish have a lambent, greenish flame, without the usual phosphorescent trail. As thousands of them dart about, their forms are sharply defined in light. We are puzzled to account for this, as there is no light from above to be reflected from their bodies, and the cresting foam of the waves does not indicate a phosphorescent condition.

June 12 (*Sunday*). This morning we observed quantities of broken squid floating about the ship—the best sign possible, as they are evidently the remains of some sperm-whale's feast. And hurra! there they are! Sperm-whale off the weather beam, six miles away, coming to leeward. At about 4 P.M. we lowered three boats. The mate soon fastened; but the whale behaved ugly, and the captain lowered his boat, and assisted in killing the brute. Thence we ran down to aid the waist-boat, away to leeward, in securing a whale it had caught. We were in the midst of a great school of seventy-barrel bulls; and they were so tame that we might have taken as many as we needed, but darkness was fast settling around us. The boat got fast to a running whale, from which it had to cut, and we went on board, leaving two boats slowly towing the dead whale to windward.

It was a remarkable sight, seen only in the earlier days of whaling. The great beasts were lying thick about us, taking no notice of the boats. Captain B—— restrained his hand several times from sending the lance into the great hulks, as they rolled and spouted around us, because it was so late in the day, and, as he said, we were so distant from the ship that we could not have been benefited had we slain. Furthermore, he observed, "It would be a waste of precious gifts to do so under the circumstances." I prayed for a chance, but he put me off, saying, "Be patient, and resolve to make sure work when I ask you to stand up to it."

June 13. The two boats we left with the dead whale came on board at midnight. The wind had increased to a gale, and the seas ran high. We double-wafted the whale, but the carcass strained alongside so violently that it snapped the heavy fluke-chain, and we should have lost it but for the activity of the officer of the deck, who bent a line on to an iron in the starboard boat, and planted it in the body as it slowly drifted past the weather quarter. The entire line was paid out, and the sag and spring of the long line kept it in tow until daylight. With much difficulty, we then succeeded in getting a fluke-rope about the dead whale's small, only to see it parted by the heave and roll of the tipsy ship. Two large hawsers still served to keep our prize alongside.

The sharks collected in great numbers about the dead whale, and soon the white, bowl-shaped excavations about the small of the body revealed to us the perfection of the surgical instruments .they are provided with. At each mouthful a quart of sperm-oil was lost to us, and we went to work with lances and spades to stop the leak. My arm became weary of the slaughter. Standing in the chains, with a guard-belt about the waist, and over the rail, we transfixed the ugly brutes until they actually were educated to a sense of the danger, and hovered, frightened, at a distance. At times the ferocity of their hunger was frightful. On more than one occasion, when a blow of the spade left the bowels of one protruding, the others would seize on the bait, and tear and drag it through the water. The sailors may not have been close observers, perhaps, but they asserted that they saw what led them to believe that sharks thus disemboweled returned to the tempting feast. At all events it is certain that, with back and sides gashed with wounds, insensible to pain, they would tear the dead whale or each other. All their feeling seems centred in the broad, thin nose which projects far over the crescent mouth; for, whenever we succeeded in striking that part with the sharp weapons, the wounded fish would dart away at full speed, and return no more. One great fellow was transfixed through this tender part by a lance, which, penetrating deep into the body of the whale, pinned him there, and held him close prisoner. As the waves receded and exposed his full length to view, his struggles were terrific, and his tail thrashed the smooth blubber with cracks like the fire of musketry. The whole exhibition was one to fill a midsummer night's dream with the horrors of a nightmare.

How came it, we wonder, that none of the fiends in human shape who have tortured poor humanity never thought of having an arena of ravenous sharks to rend, slay, and bury their victims? What a fine sensation it would have furnished on a Roman holiday! and what an exquisite adjunct to clerical machinery for the punishment of heretics!

The gale continued the entire day (13th), but the morning of the 14th opened with somewhat moderated, but still rough weather. The whale alongside had so swollen that much of its huge bulk rose above the water, and it was monstrous to behold. A great portion of the blubber, and much of the muscular flesh from the hump to the tail had been eaten away by the sharks during the night. Bitter fortune of whalemen! Such columns of figures as the following, you may see in almost every whaleman's journal:

> No 1. Whales killed and saved.
> No 2. Killed and lost.
> No 3. Struck and escaped.
> No 4. Boats lowered for whale without getting on.

We succeeded in cutting-in during the day; and when the stripped carcass floated away, the sharks held high carnival. A flock of mollemokes also attended at the feast.

June 21. Since taking the last whale, we have been surrounded by many albicore, and occasionally the beautiful dolphin has been seen. Flying-fish in thousands have glittered in the bright sunlight, and flocks of various birds have hovered over their flight to pick them out of the very mouths of their other pursuers. At the mast-head I had an opportunity of observing the motions of the sword-fish in pursuit of the albicores. The sea was smooth, there being only wind enough to give a gentle headway to the ship. I had observed that the vast school of the albicores had collected close about the hull, swimming in dense ranks, now on one side, now on the other; sometimes about the bow, and then again around the stern, all evidently alarmed and seeking protection. After a time I saw the cause in a sword-fish swimming deeply beneath the affrighted multitude. It was apparent that he feared to make his upward dart against the bright copper bottom of the strange monster floating above. The manœuvres continued for some time, the sword-fish gradually coming into plainer sight as he rose from the depths. At length he disappeared from my view directly under the ship; that he was still rising was apparent from the increas-

CARCASS ADRIFT.

ing agitation of the albicores, however. They huddled as closely as they could, and coursed round and round the ship, and in a short time more, as by a common impulse, the dense array started away at fullest speed. But it was in vain. Their pursuer, now so close to the surface that his back-fin and part of his tail could be seen, was almost instantly in the midst of the flying throng, and with cut and thrust of his sword, too rapid for the eye to follow, he killed several instantly. Then he gave up the chase, and the now scattered school returned directly to the ship. The captain, who had been watching his opportunity, ordered the boat to be cleared and lowered, and approaching cautiously with paddles, he succeeded in harpooning the tyrannous sword-fish and bringing it on board. A fine feast for several days it will be, as it is the most toothsome of all the deep-water fish. The sword was finely edged and pointed—nearly three feet long. As I observed his motions, I saw an explanation why the sword-fish occasionally strikes the bottom of a vessel and drives his formidable weapon through the planks. It is simply done in his overeagerness to catch his prey.

At 10 A.M. we raised sperm-whale to leeward. After a chase of two hours, the third mate had a chance; he darted, missed, and gallied the whales beyond all chance of pursuit. So we came on board mad, and blessed the unfortunate boat-steerer in a left-handed fashion. The boats were scarcely hoisted, and the decks cleared, when a whale rose within a few hundred yards of the ship. The mate called for an instant crew. I jumped for the bow-oar, quite forgetting my new-fledged dignity, and in five minutes we formed an attachment, close and lasting. Not in the least appreciative, the whale sounded out nearly all our line, and remained down one hour and ten minutes. When he came up he was thoroughly exhausted, and lay quiet while the mate set on him with the lance. He was in his death-flurry within a quarter of a mile of the place where he first rose to our sight, and we voted him a seventy-five-barrel whale. As we returned on board, with good humor restored, we at once rigged the cutting-fall, and by set of sun had his blanket in the blubber-room, the head remaining overboard.

June 22. Bright and early we hove in the junk, and were bailing the case, when we saw whales coming to windward head out, and evidently flying from the pursuit of a ship, which we saw manœuvring to leeward. All four boats were lowered, but a hard chase resulted in their escaping us. About 3 P.M. we raised another school. The third mate, after an hour's close chase, succeeded in fastening and killing a forty-barrel bull, which we hove in next day. Our blubber-room pretty well filled, we now started the try-works on the two whales.

June 24. Raised whales; lowered three boats. The second and third mates had two darts at them and missed.

June 25. About 11 A.M., lowered three boats in chase of whales to leeward of the ship. The first and third mates had chances to fasten, but their boat-steerers missed and gallied the whales. Captain B—— was aroused. "Now your time has come, Bill," he said to me. "Clear away the boat, and let's get after them." It would be untrue to claim that my nerves didn't flutter as I cleared the irons and placed them in the crotch, but ten minutes' tugging at the oars settled me. We were now directly to windward of the coming whales, when we hove up, set the sail, and bore down directly for them. We had a spanking breeze, and the boat made splendid headway. When I turned from setting the sail, I saw two great bulls coming for us, noses on a square line, rising to spout, and pitching under in exact unison. The space between them was so narrow that their sides must have touched under water. The moment was grand, beyond my poor powers of description. Their heads were high above the surface, and the white foam was combing from their square fronts. On they came, dashing for us at twelve knots. Our boat danced on the cresting waves and sprang toward them at fully ten knots. Thus we were coming together at race-horse speed. With the right knee firmly braced in the close-fitting cleet, the left braced on the starboard timber of the thwart, I was welded to the swaying, rushing boat; and with the pole of barbed iron well poised in the left hand, and the right laden with spare coils of the line, grasping the after-end of the iron pole, the boat-steerer stood to take his chance.

One short sea off, the grand old heads were out, beating back the waves, as breakers off a black rock. The steam of the spout almost reached the boat. Heading squarely between them, the captain exclaimed, "Take that fellow on the larboard bow, and jump overboard if you miss him!" "Ay, ay, sir." And the two black walls on either hand rose at the bow, half filling the boat with the surf, and blinding the men with the acrid spray of the spout. The ear was dinned with the rushing roar of many waters. There was little time for thought, passing each other at the rate of twenty-two miles an hour, or the whale's length in one and a half seconds. The great hump rounded out not ten feet from the eye, and irresistibly attracted the keen-edged harpoon. At that moment all energy was concentrated in the blow, and the iron was buried to its socket. No hand could be quick enough to have caught the second iron, as the boat, arrow-like, shot ahead. Two thundering flaps of the immense flukes astern of the steering-oar telegraphed the news to the distant school that an accident had befallen one of the family. The boat was thrown around, and the fight commenced with a running sperm-whale.

But I say to you readers who sit cozy in the snug comforts of home, a man takes a long breath after he has passed through that "raging canawl."

Captain B—— did his part very well, and the whale was soon riding at ease alongside the ship, a sixty-five-barrel bull by estimate. Now time ran along to June 30th, when we spoke the *Caroline*, of London, England, with whom we exchanged courtesies in a way so characteristic of the two peoples interested, that I shall venture to describe it. A boat's crew was chosen to pull the captain on board the *Caroline*, consisting of Hinton, the nightingale; Posey, of Vermont; Bingham, of Kentucky; Garvin, of Old England; and Bill, of Pennsylvania. As the fact has a bearing on the events which follow, I may mention that Bill, who stood six feet one inch in his stockings, was the light weight of the crew; and I may further mention that our mate, a good boxer, had somewhat trained us in the use of our "daddlers," to meet the emergencies of shore cruises. About the set of sun the old man was landed in the cabin of the *Caroline*, to discuss "London particular," while we boys went to the forecastle to discuss a jorum of grog, which, English fashion, was set before us. Good-fellowship prevailed. The joke and yarn in their turn amused us. Of course the song must come in, and as we took pride in the voice and execution of the Nightingale, "Blue-eyed Mary," "Cease, Rude Boreas," etc., etc., wiled the fleeting hours. In an unfortunate moment, however, the Dibdin of the *Caroline* gave us the naval ditty, "When the Galliant Jarvis sailed." Now the difficulty of our position was just this: Dibdin might sing all night of the rows between Johnnies Crapaud and Bull, without touching our corns; but we had no musical reminiscences of naval warfare which might not breed a sudden storm in our peaceful circle. Song for song had been the order of the exercises, and theme for theme. Expecting a row, we gathered about Hinton, as he trolled out the modest "Constitution and Guerrière," beginning:

> " It ofttimes has been told
>   That the British sailors bold
>   Could whip the tars of France so neat and handy, oh !
>   But they surely found their match
>   When the Yankees did them catch,
>   For the Yankee boys at fighting proved right handy, oh !"

Our hosts looked glum, but bore it right manfully. Soon as Hinton ceased singing, however, Dibdin struck up with the fight between the " Chesapeake and the Shannon," the words of which I did not take to heart, as no true American takes any interest in that fight. But the song was an unnecessary affront, as they could have sung all night of the glories of England's prowess on the sea, and we would have shared in their just pride. There was no help for it now; and Hinton next sang:

> " You Parliments of Engeland, and House of Commons, too ;
>   You'd better mind what you're about, and what you're going to do ;
>   You are now at war with Yankees, and I'm sure you'll rue the day
>   You roused the Sons of Liberty in North A-meri-ca.

> " First you sent your *Boxer* to box us all about,
>   But we had an *Enterprising* brig that beat your *Boxer* out ;
>   She boxed her up to Portland, and moored her off the town,
>   To show the Sons of Liberty your *Boxer* of renown.

> " Next you sent your *Macedonian*, no finer ship could swim,
>   Decatur knocked her gilt work off, and then he took her in," etc., etc.

The list was piled up until forbearance ceased to be a virtue, and a grizzly old tar cut it short by shying the bread-kit · at Hinton's head. A long arm stretched that " heart of oak " at his length between the chests, and the row was firmly established. We backed into a corner, when only about our own number could face us, and we managed to hold our own pretty well. Our weight and training stood us in right good stead, until the two captains sprang down the scuttle and interrupted our musical exercises. Captain B—— ordered us into the boat and paid out the line astern; but Hinton finished his song, as he felt our friends were entitled to it, and I can aver that he never was in finer voice, or sang better; all of which led us to an increased love for the "blasted Hinglish," you may be sure. The *Caroline* hailed, "Twenty-one months out, with five hundred barrels of oil."

July 4. No whales to aid us in celebrating our nation's birthday. We did our best in having a good time. Our two rusty old guns were sealed in a salute of one gun for each hundred barrels of oil we had in the hold—ten in all. Our banquet consisted of a Hawaiian pig in sea-pie, yams, onions, the everlasting pumpkin-pie, and a mince-pie, made of goat's meat, dried apples, and raisins, enlivened with lime-juice, and flavored with New England rum. Our Kanakas thought Fourth of July "belly miti," and inquired how often it came in the year. Toasts were drank in the usual order. The cook had won our hearts with his mince-pie, and the captain secured our votes at next election by sending forward a can of grog for each and every man of us. We could not afford a libation to the gods; but we divided the "swig" into two equal portions, one to the toast "Our Country," and the other to "Captain B——'s good health, and early return home with a full ship." A patriotic speech, which captain and mates cheered, wound up the ceremonies; but I felt sad to think that only nine Americans were left on board to "celebrate the day."

CHAPTER XXX.

The shaded Side of the Picture: a heartless Captain, and unhappy Crew.—
We take an Englishman from her: a Waif of the *Alliance.*—Two small
Whales taken.—Three Whales struck, one taken.—"Shall I pick you
up?" "No; kill that Whale."—A butting Whale killed under the
Counter of an English Ship.—He is Unlucky.—Cruelty to the Islanders.
—Whales getting wild; several lost.

July 5. We spoke the *E——*, Captain W—— (I withhold
the names, as neither should live). She is nineteen months
out, with six hundred barrels of oil. As I am drawing a
picture of American whaling, the sketch would be incomplete if such dark shades as are furnished by this ship's history were omitted. We met her entering the harbor, as we
were coming out of Payta, about twelve months ago. Since
then she has not let go her anchor, and has taken but a scant
supply of vegetables or fruit—only twice, by sending in a
boat. Captain W—— came on board our ship, but sent his
boat immediately back, without allowing his crew to come
on board. This surprised us, and we voted him a crusty
curmudgeon, not suspecting him as worse; but when we afterward accompanied Captain B—— to his ship, we learned
his character by what we saw and heard. I saw there the
worn skeleton of a black man, seemingly far gone in con-
sumption, a man bearing the most dejected, hopeless expression I ever saw. We learned that when he was taken sick,
the captain swore he would have no "sodgers" on board his
ship to eat the bread of idleness, and he applied appropriate
medicine, by rope's-ending the poor fellow until he fainted
under the cruel blows. He was only revived by the mates
running a bowline over his legs and ducking him into the

water.   As he became too weak to perform the duties of the ship, he was secured by his hands to the handle of the grindstone, and compelled by blows to turn and turn the stone, whether in use or not.   And he has not been allowed to go below to sleep now for months.   When the poor wretch told the captain that he was a dying man, the heartless reply was, " Why don't you hurry up, and get us rid of you?" Such is a small part of the sickening details of the treatment of this poor creature, who, if our religion be true, was a temple of the living God.   Angels of mercy could alone have traced the semblance in the wreck I saw.

The mates and men seemed to live in constant fear of the captain, and a dark brooding spirit pervaded the very .atmosphere of her decks.   As soon as our captain had accomplished the purpose of his visit, he squared yards and ran away from the vicinity, and expressed regret that he had exchanged courtesies with the wretched being.

Our boat brought with us from the *E——*, as a passenger, an Englishman, who gave the name of Norville.   His story is that he came out in the *Alliance*, of Newburyport, about seven years ago, and while cruising near the Navigator Islands, a boat was sent with him on shore.   The natives attacked it, and, after a hard fight, he was captured.   As time passed, he rose to be of some consequence among them. An length an opportunity of escape offered in the *E——*. He agreed with Captain W—— to furnish two and a half tons of hogs, a boat-load of taro, and a boat-load of yams, in payment for his passage to some port frequented by English vessels.   The captain was to give him forty dollars in money. After getting to sea, very. curiously, a point of religion created a difference between them, which naturally, with such a tyrant as Captain W——, soon ended in an open rupture. When Captain B—— heard his story, he offered to give him the passage, and he induced Captain W—— to stand to. his bargain, and give the man the forty dollars agreed upon. Mr. Norville seemed quite happy at escaping from the *E*—— with his life, and says that he would rather trust to the tender mercies of the cannibals than to Captain W——. He seems to be an educated man, and expresses himself well for one so much out of the practice of his native language. Lat. 31° 12′ N., long. 173° 45′ E.

July 12. While washing deck, sperm-whales were raised at 7 A.M. We lowered, and took two, of about twenty barrels each—very small for the Japan ground. We hove them in before dark.

Aug. 3. In the early morning we lowered and fastened to three whales; but the two mates lost theirs—the iron drawing in one, and the line parting in the other. Our whale lifted us twice with his flukes without disabling us, and strove to breach into the boat, but a quick movement of the boat brought his fall alongside. Nobody hurt.

Just before sunset we raised another school of spermwhales; lowered, but night broke up the chase. We were spoken by the *Emily Morgan*, of New Bedford, Captain Wray, thirty-seven months out, with eleven hundred and fifty barrels of oil. We hailed eleven hundred barrels. To-day's whale is placed at thirty barrels.

Aug. 6. Weather somewhat squally; saw a sail to leeward of us. At 1 P.M. noticed that two sails to windward of us had squared away, and were coming down before the wind. Suspecting that they were following whales, we tacked ship and beat up, keeping a sharp lookout. We soon raised whales coming to leeward; lowered two boats, and pulled up to take our chance with six boats coming down under sail. The whales went down, however, and passed under our boats. We then lowered two more boats. The captain's boat went on, and we got two irons in well under the hump of one. The third mate joined us, and also fastened. As he was going on to lance, a quick cut of the flukes stove in his broadside, knocking mate and boat-steerer overboard. Captain B—— asked, "Shall I pick you up, Burroughs?" "No, sir; we're all right. You kill that blamed whale, though," he stuttered. So we left them hugging ash and white cedar. But we came mighty near the same predicament. Three different times we thought we were gone: once from a rattler with his flukes, and twice he butted us with his head. But the steering-oar brought the blows glancing, and saved us. He was the most active whale of the size that we had yet tackled. He ran us to windward, and, with three wild cheers, we hazed through the fleet of six boats, which were pulling sullenly back to their ships; thence, at full speed, with the whale carrying the "pirate's red flag" at the fore, we glanced under the stern of the *Eliza*, of London. The usual flurry ended the contest, and the whale rolled fin out, with head to the sun, within a half-mile of our transatlantic relative. We placed him at seventy-five barrels.

Aug. 9. At 3 P.M. cooled down the try-works, cindered the decks, and washed down, scouring every thing bright as a new pin. There was no other evidence of grease on board than one hundred and ninety barrels of oil, the product of the three last whales, ranged and lashed to the bulwarks. We were hailed by the *Eliza*, of London, ten months out, with one hundred barrels of oil. Captain L—— came on board, and spent four hours with us. He was a burly specimen of the British sea-dog, and had been unfortunate as a whaleman, but I judged you might count on him for sure backing in a fight. They have had no albicore around their ship since they came on the Japan ground, while with us the school has been constant and undiminished in numbers since it first joined us in the early part of June last. And, what added to the superstition of our men, the great school left us while the *Eliza* floated near us.

Our visitors have three Marquesas Kanakas on board. They were carried off against their will, to replace three of the crew who deserted on one of the group. The captain demanded of the chief to return the deserters under reprisal. The chief refused, and the captain double-shotted his nine-pound guns, sent a round into the crowded grass huts of the village, and carried off the three natives. We Christians must not be unduly shocked when we hear of retaliation by the savages on the next ship's crew that falls into their power. The surgeon of the *Eliza* came on board to administer to four of our men who were on the sick-list; and in return for this kindness, on the following morning we sent our neighbors a present of fish.

Aug. 31. Since the 9th we have had much squally weather and rain, with some lightning and thunder. The season of typhoons is coming round, and it is time that we were east of the meridian. To-day we set regular watches, and ran during the night—the first omission of reefing and furling close for three months. We were spoken by the *Charles Frederick*, of New Bedford, Captain Young, eight months out, eight hundred barrels of oil. She is the most fortunate ship we have met. Whales are getting very wild, and difficult of approach.

Sept. 3. We are working our way to the eastward; have had several very hard chases. Once we lowered soon after sunrise, and chased to the end of the day without success. To make this day's mishaps the harder to bear, we had three first-rate chances on large whales. Two were fairly missed: the boat-steerers seemed gallied; the third iron twisted off near the head. The second mate's boat-steerer was broken, and Posey appointed in his place. Now is the lover's chance. None who know of the bright hopes which hang on this opportunity can doubt his success; and could true love have its way on the next whale, he would throw his iron clean

through it.   Ah me ! we might have·had two hundred barrels of oil alongside.

Sept. 4. Lowered for whales, but they fought shy. The
second mate had to caution his new boat-steerer against
breaking his oar, in his frantic efforts to lift the boat from
sea to sea.   But his time had not come yet.

CHAPTER XXXI.

Posey's first Whale, and lost Whale; we struck him, he struck back.—The Boat crushed by his Jaw, but Whale saved.—Boat cut in two by a Whale, and Hinton a Shade whiter.—The Portuguese Man-of-war, or Sea-nettle.—Passage from Japan.—Pets all consumed.—Grub does not improve with Age.—Minutes longer by Day and shorter at Night.—Bully Sprague, and Jonah's Whale.—Well-spun Yarns a Necessity.—Captain Covill, and fighting Whale.—Boat bit in two.—Tried to butt the Ship.

Sept. 6. To-day Posey won his spurs. Early in the morning we raised sperm-whale. They were traveling slowly to windward. At 2 P.M. we lowered away, and after about two hours' chase, the second mate's boat went on. I saw Posey stand up, and the next minute white water showed that he had dropped a thought of his sweetheart into that whale. He had won his Nantucket love by that good blow. The whale, spouting thin blood, sounded out all their line. Our crew were to windward, and took the game as he came up, and, between the lances of the two boats, he was soon considered a dead whale. Again he sounded, and remained down nearly an hour. The second mate had returned to the ship for a new line, and we were carelessly reposing on our oars, when we were aroused by the rasp of the whale's teeth against the boat as he rose, with open mouth, the boat fairly in it. He caught the boat between the tub and after-oar, and closed on it. The dropping of the long end of the boat brought the stern-sheets square with his great square snout. The men leaped into the sea; and the shortest way to safety for the boat-steerer was right across the enormous junk. I stepped on to the head, and thence plunged clear of immediate danger, though shortly after I had to dive deeply, to allow the whale to glide over me. It may be a low habit, but certainly it is very human to moralize in intervals of overwhelming dangers. Thus, on rising from the sea, the resolve was graven on my mind to be worthy of the great deliverance, as in the past I had surely been unworthy of it.

The old fellow showed a great disposition to fling his ugly jaw at every floating object, and it became prudent in our boat-steerer to remove his curly locks from his range of vision. After butting the boat from side to side, to the manifest disgust of those who were riding her bottom, the whale decorously retired a short distance, and went into his flurry. The mate's boat picked us up, and the whale, which will make about fifty barrels, was saved. The only injury we suffered was a man's hand jammed by the whale's tooth.

Sept. 13. The mate went on to a sperm, and had his boat cut entirely in two by the whale. Hinton got an ugly tap on the head. We supposed it would have killed a white man, but it only straightened Harry out for half an hour, when he woke up, not much the worse of the wear. We were very anxious, for we could ill spare his musical voice.

"Did you get the whale?" was his first inquiry.

"Yes."

"All right." And the subject was dismissed. But I thought Harry was a shade whiter after the accident—as he had a right to be, owing to the white blood in him.

We must not leave these waters without allusion to the beautiful mollusk, the sea-nettle, or Portuguese man-of-war, which is sometimes seen in great numbers. The colors displayed by it when floating on a calm sea are attractive to the rudest observer. Varying shades of blue, pink, and yellow mark the body, which has a fringe of strongly contrasted colors, the outer filaments being crimson, and the inner a dark purple. The naked swimmer, on coming in contact with them, experiences a stinging sensation resembling that of nettles; hence the name. We are now standing to the eastward on a passage, meeting the varying incidents of storm and calm, which go to make up the journal of the mariner who merely journeys over this waste of waters.

DREAM-LIFE.

"The staghounds, weary with the chase,
Lay stretched upon the rushy floor,
And urged in dreams the forest race
From Teviot stone to Eskdale moor."

Were the visions of the night which inspired and refreshed the soul of the weary sailor of no more significance than the dreams which came to the soulless brute? The tedium of a long cruise, and the absence of incident in our waking hours, seemed to incite the imagination to a greater activity in our sleep. At times the dream-life was so connected, that a question arose as to which was the reality—the toilsome, wearisome bondage by day, or the bright, happy freedom of the night. Dreaming of home became habitual, and somewhat under control. When I closed my eyes in sleep with the thought "I will go home," then the spirit of dreams set me gently in the walks of boyhood, and the faces of friends welcomed me. But in all my dreams I was with, or of, the ship, and ever conscious that I was dreaming. The old craft formed part of the phantoms of the night. Once we anchored her in the shallow stream abreast the old saw-mill in which I graduated as a mechanic; and she rode securely moored in waters so shallow that it might be waded to grapple the suckers and mullet from under the stones. And we happy fellows clustered like bees about the well-remembered cider-press, to suck through straws the luscious juice of new-pressed apples, a good father standing by with welcoming face to bid us make the most of the chance.   In Moscow I had a favorite dream resort.   A quaint, unusual structure, with arched brick gate-ways and paved courts, was visited so often that the face of mine host grew familiar to me, and the arched doors swung open at my bidding.

But there was one dream which rose to the dignity of an inspired vision, and which imperatively shaped an after happy life.   This air-drawn picture I will sketch, and, with its sequel, leave to the philosopher, doubter, or dreamer to reconcile the strange coincidences.   It occurred at a period in our voyage when thoughts were somewhat homeward-bound, and anxious forecastings of the future occupied waking moments at mast-head, the helm, and the nightwatch. Reviewing the past, the dangers and temptations which beset our careless lives, the impression grew that, alone and unaided, I might yield and fall by the wayside; that safety lay in the pledge of love and honor to some one worthy of my love; that, unmarried, I must not again tread the path before me.   Then a great despair settled as a cloud, and obscured my way of life.   For who, among the women I could cherish, would accept the hand of the wanderer?   What would I ask of her?   Weeks only of wedded life, with years of bondaged widowhood—not a tempting boon to lay at the feet of true womanhood.   Yet none but the truest might hope to hold the errant sailor to the path of rectitude.   Such was my unrest, when the spirit of dreams came to my aid, and brought peace on its wings.

In the visions of the night I stood in an unremembered room, and with me was a woman, the seeming of my future partner in life.   The consciousness of the time which must elapse before we could meet was perfect, and the dreamer asked, " By what token may I know you ?"   Then she wrote on a paper, and threw it to me, saying, " By this shalt thou surely know me !"   And the vision faded.   When I awoke,

the vision of the writing remained, but I had no memory at
that moment of the words nor of the person, save that she
was young and of pleasing presence. But a new peace possessed my whole being. The long-repeated questioning was
answered, and gradually the vision slumbered in my memory. It might have remained in oblivion, as an idle fancy,
but for the sequel which elevates it into a real interview of
stranger spirits living on opposite sides of the earth.

Two years from the time of the dream, and months after
the returned sailor had resumed the staid, orderly habits of
home-life, his mother, who was a zealous worker for the
emancipation of the Southern slave, received a letter from
the treasurer of a woman's antislavery society, requesting
the collection of certain pledges of money made by neighboring friends of the cause. The letter was passed to the
son, with the desire that he should collect the funds and
transmit them to the writer. When his eyes rested on the
writing, the long-forgotten vision of the Pacific rose vividly
before the mind's eye; the well-known characters of the mys-
tic card were before him, and the words, " By this shalt thou
surely know me," were recalled. Here was his affinity, and
in what guise? A treasurer of an antislavery society; a
woman abolitionist; a female intermeddler in other people's
business; a strong-minded creature; a "blue;" a bore, of
course; and probably old. Such were the terrible fancies
which grew out of the now familiar handwriting. An in-
voluntary farewell to home, and the acceptance of an awaiting berth for a second voyage, flits through the mind of the
reader. You must know that the barbarian of the waters
was strongly imbued with the patriotic and peculiarly American idea, that an abolitionist embodied all that was to be
despised by every true lover of his country and kind. A
mother and brother engaged in it alone saved the cause from
his utter condemnation. So with a fervent " Get thou be-

hind me, Satan!" the money was gleaned, and inclosed in a courteous letter to the dreaded woman treasurer.

But no word of inquiry respecting her passed the sailor's lips. He feared to know who or what she was; for had she been "all his fancy painted her," then welcome the stormy main, and the perils of ship, boat, or shore. Months, however, passed in safety, and the impending fate passed into forgetfulness, and the danger was pooh-poohed as the baseless fabric of a dream. Again the good mother pressed her unwilling son into antislavery service, as her escort to a conventicle of the agitators at a Quaker meeting-house in a neighboring county. Under the stress of filial duty, the service was rendered; but had it not been childish, the reprobate would have sat with the horses outside, rather than lend his presence to mischief in the holy place.

However, taking the backmost seat of the back bench, with disapproving glance he observed the earnest faces of the assembly. The idle, indifferent gaze was presently arrested by a pair of great, deer-like eyes, which looked from the shadow of a plain beaver bonnet on the sulking unbeliever. He recognized, with a thrill of heavenly contentment, that this beautiful creature was the author of the begging letter which had so disturbed him, and the writer of the dream-token that had so consoled him; and in her lustrous eyes he felt the spirit which had spanned the globe to meet him in the old vision of the sea. From this time out he felt that he had a sure anchor by which he could ride out the storms and temptations of a somewhat checkered life. And that antislavery angel now laughs at the gray-beard as he spins his whaling yarns for the entertainment of their children.

Oct. 15. Our long cruise on Japan seas is accomplished. Land-sick, we are running into our old tramping-ground, the Galapagos, for terrapin. We have eaten all our pets. The last pig was buried in pie-crust long since, and my poor milk-goat passed into a menavelin stew. Our water, nearly eight months in the cask, has become horrible, but the bread is more tender as time passes. Industrious worms, an inch in length, have bored and cut it so thoroughly that it is no longer necessary to soak it in our hot coffee in order to adapt it to our teeth; but still fastidious eaters do so to scald the creepers out of the holes, and then skim them from the cup "which cheers but not inebriates." The butter is more like cheese than ever, and the beef is daily more oak-like to the eye and more briny to the palate; choice bits susceptible of a high polish serve as cane-heads, and the beef has this to recommend it, it keeps the grinding appa-ratus of the stomach in full play. Three things alone seem to be permanent—the pork, molasses, and watch on deck. I am inclined to believe that the last has increased materially in length. I still hold that there are but twenty-four hours in the day, and sixty minutes in each of the four hours of the watch; yet the minutes, like dullest music long drawn out, seem to run to treble their ordinary length. You un-derstand, then, how tiresome the watch is. Posey suggests that the order of nature is always balanced, and that the long minute on watch is made up by the rapid flight of time in the watch below.

In this state of affairs the song and yarn are necessarily somewhat spicy and strong to pry the heavy portals of the eyes, and the "Arabian Nights" and "Tom Moore" fail to stir the sluggish blood. In such a mood to-night the cry arose for "Bully" Sprague's yarn about Jonah's whale; and though it had often been told before, we hoped that it would tide us over the yawning gulf until eight bells. The yarn was in these words:

"You have all heard of Bully Sprague, who steered Cap-tain Sartori so many years on a second mate's lay; but you have never heard why the captain fell in love with him. This I'll tell you first, that you may know your man. During the last voyage of the *Anaconda*, of Ipswich, the captain laid Bully on to a sperm-whale, and Bully darted his iron real mad; for they had had a hard chase. The next minute the captain saw the iron pole bobbing end out, ten feet the other side of the whale.

"'Thunder! You missed him!' he said to Bully.

"'Missed your granny!' rejoined the harpooner; 'that iron went through him.'

"Sure enough, when they killed him they found the tow-line rove through below the hump, and the iron acting toggle on the other side. Sartori swore that he never would have any other boat-steerer while Bully lived; and so Bully sailed on a second mate's lay until he quit and took to farming back of Ipswich.

"But he came near losing his number in the mess on the second voyage after this, and he tells his own story in this way: 'Down off Timor, Captain Sartori laid me on to an all-fired big bull-whale. Soon as I stood up I knew it was Timor Tom I was on. He was grizzly and white; his hide scarred an' furrowed, and old irons stood out of his white hump like stubs in a corn-field in snow-time. I was gallied some when I saw his white back, but I couldn't help hitting him, you know, from long habit; so I added two irons to the score in his back.

"'Just as quick as winkin', his old jaw came up and cut the bow right off at the bow-thwart, an' we two (that is, the bow and me) went a-kiting, I tell you! When I turned to come down, there was the whale end up, mouth wide open, waitin' for me; his throat looked like a whitewashed cellar door, but I saw his teeth were smooth with the gum, an' I took some comfort in that. When I struck his throat, he snapped for me, but I had good headway on, and was splash-ed against the soft bottom of his stomach, when I heard his old jaws come together with a noise like the flap of a main-top-sail in a gale before the ear-ring is hauled out. I was pretty much tuckered out for want of breath for a little while, an' I sot down on the sou'-east corner of his liver, and swung my legs York fashion, while I got my wits aboard. It wasn't at all dark down there, for there was ten thousand of them little shining sea - jellies, stickin' all around in the wrinkles of his stomach, and there was plenty of room, too. Bymeby I got easier, an' kind o' accepted the situation, when I saw a black patch on the starboard side of the stomach well forrard, and I walked over to see what it might mean. I picked out a jelly-fish bright enough to light a pipe a'most, and held it up, and I saw pricked in Injey-ink, in great big printin' letters, "JONAH. B.C. 1683." Then I knew just where I was, and began to feel real bad. I remembered how my old mother used to read that story to me when I was a babby, to turn me agin' whalin', and how I used to tell her that harpoons weren't invented in them days. I kind o' felt as if a judgment had come on me, and I took a fresh quid for consolation sake. I saw at once that Timor Tom warn't used to tobacco, for a kind o' turnin' of the stomach began. So I picked up a jackknife I saw layin' on the floor, and hacked a big plug all into little bits, and slipped 'em into hundreds of little poutin' mouths in the stomach, that I saw a-gapin' at me.

"'The physic worked to a charm. The whale began heavin' an' squirmin' real awful, when, all at once, the stomach turned clean over with a flop like an earthquake, and I was shot out with about a cart-load of chawed squid that laid around the floor. The mate's boat was then pickin' up Captain Sartori and the crew, and they took me in too. When I told them about the printin', they laughed right out; but when I showed them the horn-handled jackknife, and they saw Jonah's initial on one side and a picter of the American eagle on the other, why, they believed my story. Just then I heard some one yell down the companion-way, "Watch ahoy! turn out; eight bells." Then I knowed I'd been a-dreamin' an all-fired lie of about forty nightmare power.' And that's Bully Sprague's story of Jonah's whale."

"I am sorry he dreamed, for I should like to have proof of that story of Jonah, which I feel in duty bound to believe," said the big Kentuckian, Bingham.

And allow me to say just here, that the object of the yarn and song at sea is to keep the watch awake. If the reader will recall what has been already written of the overmastering drowsiness which assails us in our night watches, he will make allowance for the exaggeration and high spice which is thrown into the recitals. It requires stirring incident to banish sleep from the eyes of a man who would scarcely waken under the shower-bath of a sea leaping the bulwarks. And if I banished the yarn from my story, you would have a weak picture of the real life aboard a whale-ship.

A page may well be devoted also to our meeting with the *Mount Vernon*, of New Bedford, Captain Covill. His son, George Covill, had sailed as cabin-boy, man before the mast, boat-steerer, and now ranked as second mate in this ship (and I may add that he afterward, as first mate, and for two voyages as master, continued in her). As second mate, he was steered by a man named Brooks, and gave us the following story, which I repeat for the sake of the information it contains relative to a sperm-whale:

"A whale was coming to windward at a tremendous rate, and his course lay directly across the head of our boat. I told the men to heave up and lie still, but to keep their oars in their hands, and I ordered Brooks to stand up. It looked for a minute as though the whale was going clean through us; but with a 'Steady, boys! keep cool, and watch your chance, Brooks,' I laid the boat round on his course, to save the surge when the box-line was out. His old, scarred head shot out just under the blade of the bow-oar, and he spouted and pitched like a flash. Brooks had only time to get in one iron, that just behind the eye; but the next spout was thin blood. 'Well done, Brooks! That iron was a settler.' The whale shot two or three lengths ahead, and stopped short. Brooks came aft· and took the steering-oar; I took the bow, loosened my lance, and ordered the men to pull ahead, that I might put in the second iron.

"But the whale had his eye on us; for as soon as we dropped the oars, he milled short round, and came down on us. I had the iron in my hand, and when his snout came in fair dart, I let drive. You might as well have darted against a cotton-bale. The iron was thrown right back; he brought his jaw up with a sharp snap, and just nicked the bow, putting a hole through the garboard-streak. 'Why, Brooks,' I said, 'it looks as though the whale meant that for us!' 'It did look like it, sir,' said he. Then the brute straightened out, sagging on the surface, spouting thin blood, and snapping his spout-hole.

· "'Do you hear that, men?' I exclaimed. 'You keep cool, and move together. Now pull me on.'

"He met me again square, head on, and pushed the boat astern. We knew he would use his jaw if he ranged his nose beside the boat; but when he offered his life I put my lance in, and he answered by spouting thick blood. From this out he was ugly enough. He did not count much on his flukes, but meant mischief with his jaw. So we sparred for a time, when he rose under the stern, belly up, with his lower jaw standing at right angles with his body. He brought it down like the quick snap of a hound, cutting the boat in two, except on one gunwale. I just caught a glimpse of Welsh, the tub-oarsman, as he was squeezed in the clamping jaw; and the after-oarsman had his leg from the instep squeezed clean off.

. "The line fouled in the wreck, and the boat was carried right down, leaving only the oars to float us. One couldn't swim, and the wounded man was in a bad way. We got them on the oars, when, to my great relief, the bow, or big end of the boat, rose close to us, and we were able to cling to it. The whale rose again, however, and commenced nosing round the wreck, pushing it from side to side, and rolling the frightened men into the water as fast as they climbed on.

"The old man saw our trouble now, and ran down with the ship to pick us up. As he came to just to windward of us, the whale made straight for the ship, and feebly butted her. Backing off, he returned and butted her again, rubbing his great head up and down her sides, with the best will for mischief. Loss of blood told, however, and finally he went into his flurry, and we were picked up by the mate's boat."

CHAPTER XXXII.

Captain Huntting, and fighting Whale off the Rio de la Plata.—Bomb-lance failed to kill.—Four Boats lost, and their Gear.—The Whale holds the Field.—A demoralized Crew allowed to desert.—Two Years out, and we double back: a running Sketch of Month's voyaging.—The *Washington*, of Nantucket: two Men killed.—Her third Mate caught in the Jaw, and bitten.—The *Ocean*, of Nantucket: Mate killed.—Weigh Anchor in Valparaiso Harbor, and sail for Right-whale Grounds. — Boar *versus* Skunk; or, Theory *versus* Fact.—Approach the Right Whale with misgivings.

BEFORE bidding adieu to the sperm-whale, and passing to an account of the southern right whale, I will relate the experience of Captain Huntting, off the Rio de la Plata.

Some sage has remarked, by-the-way, that hunting tigers may be fine sport, but that when the tigers take to hunting the hunters, the sport has a different aspect. The aspect of whaling is not improved, certainly, when a ninety-barrel bull whale hunts on his own account in deep water. Such a one was met by Captain Huntting. When the monster was struck, he did not attempt to escape, but turned at once on the boat with his jaw, cut her in two, and continued thrashing the wreck until it was completely broken up. One of the loose boats picked up the swimmers, and took them to the ship. The other two boats went on, and each planted two irons in the irate animal. This aroused him, and he turned his full fury on them, crushing in their bottoms with the jaw, and not leaving them while a promising mouthful held together. Twelve demoralized men were in the water, anxious observers of his majestic anger. Two men who could not swim had, in their terror, climbed on his back and seated themselves astride forward of the hump, as perhaps the safest place from that terrible ivory-mounted war club which he had brandished with such awful effect. At one time another man was clinging to the hump with his hands. The boat which had gone to the ship with the crew of the first stove boat now returned, and took the swimmers on board.

The whale had now six harpoons in him, and to these were attached three tow-lines of three hundred fathoms each. He manifested no disposition to escape, but sought to reduce still further the wreck about him. Boats, masts, and sails were entangled in his teeth; and if an oar or any thing touched him, he madly struck at it with his jaw. This was entirely satisfactory to Captain Huntting, who was preparing other boats to renew the fight. At length two spare boats were rigged, and these, with the saved boat, put off again. The captain pulled on; but the whale saw the boat, and tried his old trick of sweeping his jaw through the bottom of it. She was thrown around out of his sweep, however, and the captain fired a bomb-lance, charged with six ounces of powder, which entered behind the fin and exploded in his vitals. Before the crew could get out of his way, "he tore right through my boat, like a hurricane, scattering all hands right and left." So said Captain Huntting. Now four boats were utterly lost, some twelve hundred fathoms of line, and all the gear. The remaining two boats were hastily and poorly provided, the men were gallied, the sun was going down, and the captain, when he was fished out, consented to give up the day and cry beat.

All hands went to work to fit other boats. Through the night, under shortened sail, the ship lay near the scene of conflict; and while the weather was calm it was possible to keep track of the whale as he occasionally beat around. But the breaking day brought rough weather, and the captain proceeded to Buenos Ayres, as much to allow his men, who were mostly green, to run away, as for the purpose of refitting, as he knew they would be useless thereafter. In this design he was not thwarted. Most of them promptly deserted, having had enough of wrestling with the fighting whale of the La Plata.

Two years from home, and we are again swinging around the old orbit. As history repeats itself, so we double back on our old track; to the Galapagos for terrapin, and a renewal of the old delights in Nature's desolations; to the Cocos Islands for water, and refreshment of the soul in the fertility and beauty of Nature's garden; to the Galapagos once more, where four men desert in a boat; to Payta, with its filth, drunkenness, and prostitution, until on April 4, of the third year out, we are in lat. 23° 10′ S., long. 118° 27′ W., running south-west. We have been picking up whales now and again, and adding to our experience, without meeting incidents which would bear repetition. We were disappointed in not touching at Easter Island, which we passed to the leeward. Took two more whales, and stood for Callao, to recruit.

May 28. We gladly came to anchor in the fine harbor of Callao. Hungry for the land, while I was furling sails my eyes wandered up the beautiful valley, through which runs the Rimac River, to the famed city of Lima, situated some three leagues inland, and I felt keenly that, with the opportunity and desire to see so much of exceeding interest to me, my short liberty on shore and my very limited means, would preclude all hope of visiting a place of such historic interest. But I am only a whaleman, not a traveler; my business is to fasten only to such events as may rise within dart of my boat. Farewell, then, to the turbulent city of the Pizarros, once a gem in the crown of Spain.

Inside of us lay anchored the *North Carolina*, the *Peacock*, sloop of war, the United States schooner *Enterprise*, the British frigate *Actæon*, the French frigate *Venus*, two armed brigs, one whaler besides ourselves, and a number of merchantmen. These, with many native coasting-vessels, and numerous boats pulling or sailing in various directions, gave a life and importance to the port which we had not before witnessed on this side of the land. The brightness of the scene was enhanced by a state visit of the President to the *North Carolina*, and the British and French men-of-war. The yards were manned—the first time I had witnessed the ceremony, and certainly, when done on a ship so grand in her proportions as the *North Carolina*, it is majestic, and a fitting honor rendered by one nation to the chief of another. At the sound of the first gun of a national salute, seven hundred men—previously clustered about the masts—ran out on the yards, and standing erect, each with a hand on his neighbor's shoulder, presented the beautiful sight of a pyramid of men, reaching from the lower yards to the skysail of each mast, their snow-white garments fluttering in the wind. Thus they stood, while the smoke of the great guns clouded the surface of the water, and the deep booms echoed in the neighboring hills.

The boat containing the President lay quietly on the water; but as the last gun sounded, it moved toward the *Actæon*, when the magnificent spectacle was repeated on a smaller scale. Here the French frigate took up the music, and her guns awakened the echoes, and the mariners of France fluttered, white as her lilies, against the ever-cloudless sky of Peru. Thus we were welcomed from our long cruise to the port of Callao, and I hereby tender my grateful acknowledgments of the deserved honor, which three great nations united in rendering us. May they all grow in sense and honesty, and may their powder always mingle fraternally as it did on this glorious May day!

After a few days spent in refitting ship, and getting off a

supply of water and vegetables, we were allowed liberty on shore. We landed on a well-built pier, which also served as a breakwater, surmounted on the sea-face by a neat iron railing. At the top of the landing-stairs and along the pier were stationed armed sentries, dirty and shabby beyond comparison with the most sea-stained whalemen. Could I say more? Near the pier we saw a small market, and soon after, seated on an old gun, a couple of sailors might have been seen munching apples, which we here first met with on the west side of the Cape. And we stuck to the apples, allowing the tempting oranges, bananas, etc., to rest in peace. The houses we saw were one story high, flat-roofed, and from the harbor looked like a mud town in ruins. I visited what is called the lower fort, and was treated courteously, and shown every thing of interest, by an officer who could blend sufficient of English with his Spanish to make himself intelligible. He was a patriotic little fellow, and commented on the ruinous, unarmed condition of the fort, which was the more surprising as the people were at war with Chili, and expecting an invasion. But my surprise was increased as the same officer showed me through the castle, an enormous fortification, built in massive masonry, and requiring ten thousand men to garrison it. On its extended ramparts and bastions not a single gun was mounted. A few were seen barbed on the two enormous towers which centre the works, and these, with a water battery, completed the armament of perhaps the largest and strongest fort on the American continent. Many of the guns have been removed to arm war-vessels, three of which were in the harbor when we were there, the largest being the *St. Francisco.* On board this vessel we found Philip Hyde, our old-time cooper's mate, who ran away from us in Selango, over two years ago. For some time he worked at his trade as carpenter in the city of Lima, when he easily made from eighty to one hundred dollars per month; but his old enemy rum ate it all, and finally he lost his employment. He shipped on board the *Brandywine*, again deserted, and then brought up on board this Peruvian man-of-war. We found him heart and home sick; he had a wife and children in America, and wanted to get back to them. At his request we laid his case before Captain B——, and soon enlisted his good feeling for the poor fellow. With his usual energy, the good man went on board the *North Carolina*, acquainted Commodore Ballard with the case, and claimed Hyde as a deserter from his vessel. The claim was made, and the authorities on shore promptly granted an order for his release. The lieutenant of the *Carolina* proceeded in his boat to the *St. Francisco*, but received the information that Hyde had deserted the previous night. There was no redress; but the lieutenant was confident that the man had been spirited away, as he was a valuable man as carpenter of the ship.

We have reason to believe that it is a regular system of the Peruvian naval service to tempt seamen to desert from their ships, and then, by means fair or foul, to get them on board their own vessels. The war with Chili made them doubly anxious to fill up their complement of men, as the Chilians were not a whit behind them in like practices. It is sad to think that in case of a naval engagement it will be mainly English and American blood which will flow in their senseless quarrel. While we lay here, six of our Kanakas were enticed away, leaving their clothes and "lay." The captain offered a reward of one hundred dollars for each man. Some of our men soon afterward saw two of the deserters in the calaboose, partially intoxicated, and the captain proceeded to the prison to recover them; but they were then gone, the officer on guard denying, with protestations, any knowledge of them. The captain felt that the cards were stocked; so he withdrew the reward, and shipped five men, three being Spaniards. Thus we are more short-handed than ever, and lower in the scale of civilization.

We had brought the ship to a presentable shape, when Captain Kennedy, of the *Peacock,* and Commodore Ballard, of the *North Carolina,* honored us with a visit. The former gentleman had never before been on board a whale-ship, and, meaning no disrespect, I will say that he was in a degree verdant. It must have been "off-duty day" with them, for they took a leisurely survey fore and aft. The commodore was pleased to observe that the whale-ship was the best school for seamen that the world had known. I asked myself if it was not true that if our midshipmen took primary lessons on board such ships, and graduated as boat-steerers before being transferred to the men-of-war, they would be more effective in storm or battle. One or two grand rows with fighting whales would make the boarding of a frigate's deck seem a holiday pastime.

The *Peacock* has been to Oahu, where she took out of the fort all the American and English seamen confined there, three of our old crew among the rest. They are now on board that vessel. The consul was not on hand, as I understand he habitually has business on the north-west coast whenever our men-of-war visit his post.

Of course, our opportunities are extremely limited to learn any thing about the social or political condition of the people we are visiting; but enough reaches us to satisfy us of the wretchedness of the country, arising from the struggles of military chieftains for the control of affairs. The present ruler, Santa Cruz, we are told, instituted war with Chili to give employment to the soldiery, and to remove the military element from mischievous idleness, holding that a war was less expensive and hurtful than peace. Revolution is the order of the day, and pronunciamentos the common literature of the country. Oppression and extortion prevail, and every thing, life included, is held on an uncertain tenure. A horrible story is told of the last capture of Callao. The garrison had been marched by tens near to the burial-pits just south of the fort, and then fusiladed by the savage conquerors. The dead bodies were left to the dogs, hogs, and vultures. We were invited to visit the horrid scene, where evidences of the butchery still existed, but we declined.

That such a disgusting exhibition should be tolerated is less surprising when we consider the usual method of disposing of the dead of this brutal people. Commodore Wilkes, who visited the burial-ground, thus describes it:

"Outside the walls of the fortress are several large vaults, filled with the dead, in all stages of decay, and on which the vultures were gorging themselves. This was a revolting spectacle. Many were thrown in naked, and covered with a few inches of sand. Great numbers of skeletons are still seen with pieces of clothing hanging to them. Dogs and vultures in great numbers were everywhere feeding upon the dead, or standing aloof fairly gorged with their disgusting repast."

Is it a wonder that, after three weeks' sojourn in such a community, we hailed with joy the order to weigh anchor and put to sea? Death in a whale-boat, and a clean funeral in the sea was more to our American taste than association with these miserable Peruvians.

Cruising leisurely up the coast of Peru, now standing well out to sea, now running in, and seeing the magnificent sun rise over the jagged wall of the Cordilleras, we spent our third Fourth of July as best we might. Our largest hog patriotically stepped into a crusty pie, to help us through the day, and such of the dried-apples as the worms had left us, combined with pumpkins, salt beef, and chopped figs, made a mince-pie. Posey wanted to add onions for a flavor, but he was overruled. These luxuries, with the national bever-

age of switchel—molasses, water, and vinegar—and a quiet
conscience and good-natured spirits, tided us over the nation's holiday. Having taken one small whale, we proceeded
to Payta, and anchored for the fourth time in this pandemonium, with the object of replacing the men who had left us
in Callao. Then cruising a while in Lee Bay, we spoke the
Washington, of Nantucket, thirteen months out, with four
hundred barrels of oil. She had two men killed by whales,
and her third mate was very severely injured, having been
caught across the thighs in a whale's mouth, and nearly
drowned by the whale's repeated dipping beneath the surface while he held the poor wretch in that awful grip. The
man escaped without broken bones, but the laceration of his
flesh was awful, looking much as though two or three fence
rails had been shot through the fleshy part of the thighs.
He seemed content, as he exhibited his wounds, that they
were no worse. We also spoke the *Ocean*, of Nantucket,
eleven months out, with six hundred barrels of oil. Her
mate had been killed by a whale—just how, we did not
learn.

Aug. 20. We left Lee Bay, and bade a final adieu to the
black volcanic peaks of the Galapagos; cruised for a short
time on the offshore; again ran in sight of Easter Island;
ran into 33° S., and soon after made the islands of Massa-
fuera and Juan Fernandez, for the story of which overhaul
your "Robinson Crusoe." When found, make a note that
it is now a penal settlement of the Government of Chili.
Thence we went to Valparaiso, which would be worthy of
more space than the line I employ, were I a voyager or traveler; but as we stopped only to recruit our wings for new
flights in stranger seas, I have only time to get my fruits
and stores aboard, before flying southward to acquaint myself with the forms, manners, and customs of the baleen,
or right whale. Having enjoyed ourselves in Valparaiso

very much more than in any other Spanish port, we hove up our anchor, and bore away for right-whale feeding-grounds, among the islands which skirt the western coast of Patagonia.

It must be admitted that we approached this new experience with some trepidation, as officers and men were totally inexperienced in this fishery. The boys encouraged themselves, however, with the general theory that the right whale, as compared with the spermaceti, is a clumsy, simple-witted, and altogether harmless creature. An amusing incident of my boyhood led me to distrust the theory, and stamped on my youthful mind a profound reverence for simple facts. It happened somewhat in this wise: When quite a little fellow, with unbounded confidence in the hunting qualities of a wheezy old terrier. who accompanied me, I made many venturesome expeditions in the neighboring woods and hills. On one occasion Carlo came to a very decided stand in front of a hole in the rocks which my hat would have covered. His cautious movement and nervous backward starts indicated the formidable nature of the animal we had holed, and my sharp eyes detected long and black hairs adhering to the rock. I got a forked stick, and twisting it about the bottom of the cave, I brought away some more long and coarse black hair. All the circumstances flashed the thought of " bear " through my young head. The wildness of the secluded spot rendered bear possible; the sharp bark of Carlo, who, hair on end, was dancing around, announced bear as probable; and the wish being father to the thought, made bear positive. A suspicious odor from the end of the stick suggested skunk. The size of the hole was certainly against bear. But a young bear and a small hole could be reconciled, and moreover, I had never smelled bear. So reasoning, I thrust in the well-sharpened fork, and twisted vigorously against a soft yielding mass, until a good hold was assured. Then I cautiously withdrew the rod, evidently bringing the tenant of the cave with it. Presently I was sure it was a black bear unwilling to come to the light; but suddenly an awful stench drove me back from the hole, and a skunk, in all its native ugliness, stood revealed. As I was fairly in for it, and the "varmint" had done his worst, I killed him on the spot.

MORAL: Whenever theory places a large animal in a small hole, reject the bear, and suspect the skunk.

In accordance with this, I accepted the theory of the inoffensive character of the right whale with allowance, especially as we were sperm-whalemen, who had been accustomed to haul close and run broadside on, or, as the man-of-war's men would express it, "engage yard-arm and yard-arm." I adopt the naval lingo, that landsmen may better take my meaning.

CHAPTER XXXIII.

Head of the Right Whale.—Description of Drawings of Whale's Head.—
Contrasts between the Right and Sperm Whales.—Different Manœuvres
of Boats necessary in attacking the two.—Dispositions of these Whales.
—Natural History of the Right Whale better understood.—The Sperm-
whale a Mystery.—The weak Point in the Right Whale, not mentioned
by Scoresby.—Instant Arrest of forward Motion.—Pricking the Nose to
direct the Course of the Whale.—Immediate Consequences of touching
the Small.—Fastening to Right Whale.—Winrows of Brit, and Whaling-
ground off Chiloe Island; go on Whale.—Struck Blubber, and Iron
failed to enter.—An Iron in Blow-hole, and Effect illustrated.—Large
Right Whales.—Dimensions in Detail of Right Whale.—The upper Jaw
considered as a Dining-room.—Tongue equals ten Oxen.—Mode of working its sifting Apparatus.—Dimensions continued.

In the baleen, or bone whales, there are no teeth; instead
of which, the mouth is provided with five or six hundred
plates of a horn-like consistency (known as whalebone), attached by a deep gum to the upper jaw, and extending from
the throat to the end of the narrow roof. These plates run
parallel on either side, transversely with the sides, and are
about one-fourth of an inch apart. The inner edge of the
slab terminates in a hairy fringe, which, interlacing, forms
an admirable sieve to retain the small mollusks, medusa, and
jellies which form the food of the gigantic creatures. The
gullet is very small, and said to be too contracted to admit
even a herring; but this may be fairly questioned, when we
consider the mass of water and minute food which must be
taken in at a swallow. The cavity of the mouth, when the
lips are closed, exclusive of the tongue, is equal in capacity
to three hundred barrels, and the mass of the tongue may
occupy two hundred and fifty barrels, leaving about fifty

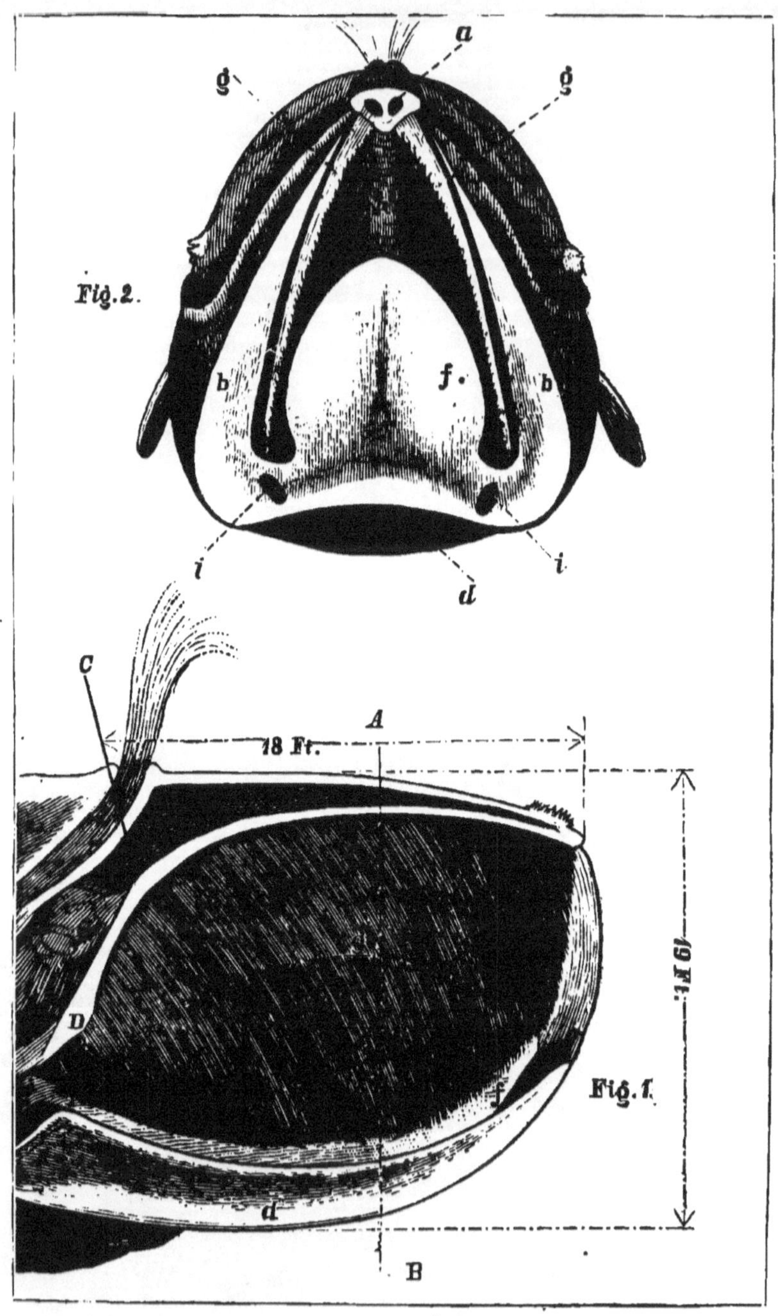

SECTION OF RIGHT WHALE'S HEAD (MOUTH SHUT).

barrels charged with some eighty million animated forms to compose a mighty mouthful. Now a pipe three inches in diameter would be inadequate to pass such a volume, in the time the whale devotes to swallowing. However, I must forego this line of statement, as our business was with the blubber and oil-bearing parts of the dead, and with the action in chase and battle of the living whale. I had little opportunity to study the general anatomy of the gigantic forms we so frequently carved; and this is not a matter of especial regret, as they have been described very minutely in various histories of the whale. Nevertheless, the pictorial representations of the head of the right whale have failed to convey to my mind a correct idea of the wonderful mechanism, the monstrous proportions, and the admirable adaptation of the parts. As in the course of our labors we shall dissect the head, and cut and hoist it piecemeal, I shall attempt, with such poor art as I may possess, to convey a machinist's view of the wonderful contrivance. And if successful in a degree, I may excite in other minds some of the wonder and admiration which impressed me when heaving at the ponderous windlass moving the fragments.

I shall strive to preserve the proportions, forms, and positions of the parts so as to convey a correct mechanical idea of the structure of the whale's head and mouth.

Fig. 1 is a longitudinal section of the head of the right whale, with the lips closed; the line C D, drawn through the spout-holes, is the line along which the upper jaw is severed from the head to secure the bone. The line A B is a line of intersection, by which Fig. 2 is drawn.

Fig. 2 is a sectional drawing of the whale's head, showing the interior of the mouth, looking toward the opening of the gullet: *a* is the upper jaw; *b b*, the lips; *d*, the throat; *f*, the tongue; *g g*, the bone-plates; *h*, the hairy sieve; *i i*, the bone supporting the lower jaw. The dotted part in the tongue and lips exhibits the 'fatty matter penetrated by coarse-fibred muscular flesh, and is known as "plum-pudding."

Fig. 3 shows the same, with the lower jaw depressed, and the lips thrown apart, as in the act of feeding.

The right whale is the opposite of the sperm - whale in many important features.

The sperm-whale is an habitue of the deep water, seldom found on soundings, and feeding on creatures of great size in the profoundest depths of the ocean. The right whale frequents the bays and shoal waters of the coasts; it feeds on minute shrimps and mollusks, which float upon the surface of the sea or at moderate depths.

In the sperm-whale the male is much larger than the female. In the right whale the female attains the greatest bulk.

In the sperm-whale the upper jaw, case, and junk form the great portion of the head, the under jaw being furnished with ivory teeth. In the right whale, the lower jaw, with its great lips and tongue, is greatly disproportioned to the slender upper jaw, which is furnished with the elastic slabs of whalebone.

In the sperm - whale the great respiratory canal is elongated, and terminates in a single spout-hole a little to one side, on the extreme end of the head. In the right whale this canal branches into two channels, which terminates in two spout-holes about eighteen feet back from the nose.

The head of the sperm-whale is impenetrable to the harpoon, and insensible to hurts. In the right whale the great lips and throat offer fair target and good holding to the whaleman's irons, while the extreme tip of its upper jaw is so sensitive that a prick of the lance or harpoon upon this spot will instantly arrest and deflect the motion of the whale. Of this I will speak more fully when we meet him in the boat.

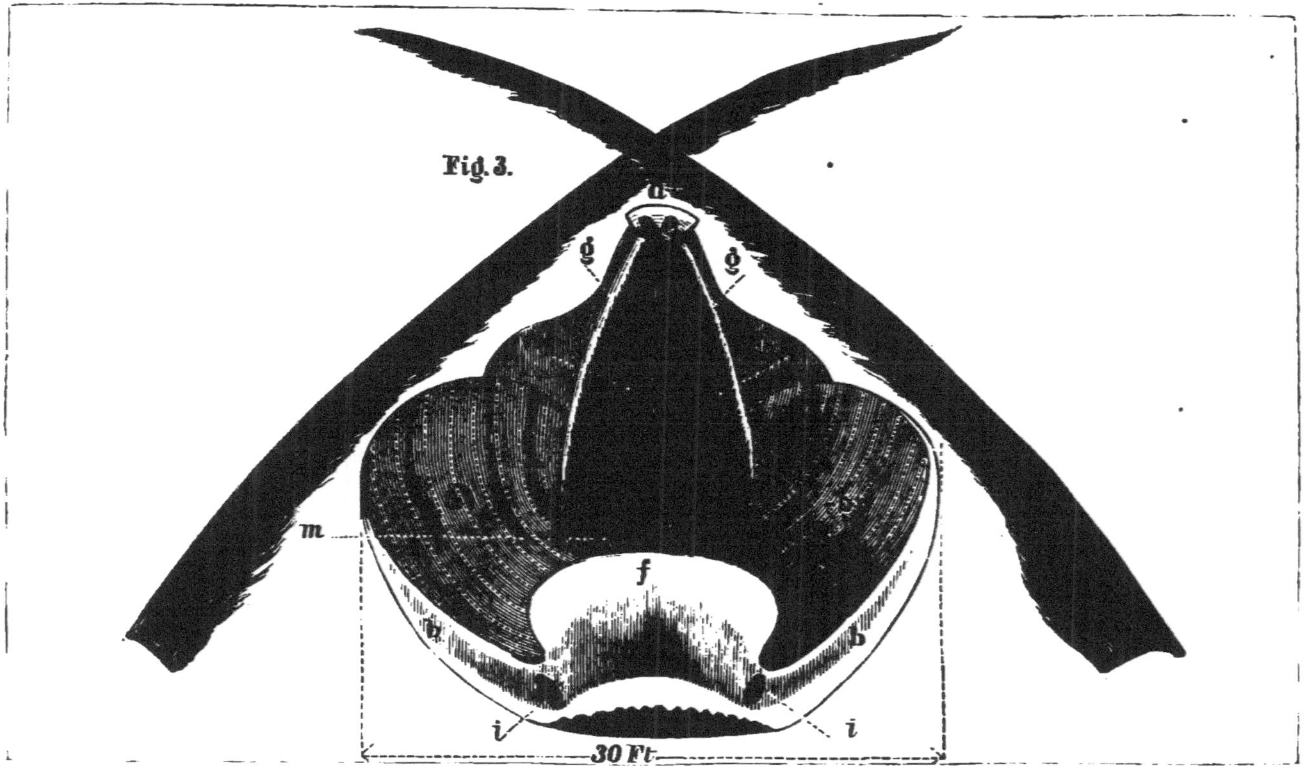

SECTION ACROSS RIGHT WHALE'S HEAD (MOUTH OPEN).

The sperm-whale is dangerous at either end; but the motions of its flukes are limited, as compared with the right whale. Its blows are delivered vertically; and when it strikes right or left the blow is performed by a rolling of the body. To compensate for this rigidity of the flukes, it is possessed of admirable skill in fencing with the jaw. The most fatal accidents in boats arise from this weapon. The motion of the jaw is quick, and its sweep tremendous. In a large whale rolling, with the jaw distended, the sweep may include a circle of forty.feet, and woe be to the boat whose bottom receives the upward cut, while certain death follows the reception of the downward blow! Thus it is possible for two boats placed forty feet apart to be broken by the same blow from the jaw of a rolling sperm-whale. The right whale, on the contrary, is comparatively harmless with the head, but is possessed of great lateral reach with the flukes, sweeping, as whalemen express it, from eye to eye.

To judge from external evidence, the sperm-whale is much the more combative of the two. No large bull whale of this species is taken whose great square head is not scarred and furrowed with marks of the teeth of rival bulls; and often the shattered teeth, and broken or distorted jaws, attest the fierceness of their combats. The right whale, however, is incapable of more than severely paddling its enemy with its tail.

The sperm-whale, of the two, is more regular and much longer in its periods of spouting, and of remaining under water. It will spout sixty or seventy times, and remain under water an hour or more—even when not pursued. The right whale spouts twelve or fifteen times, perhaps and then descends for a short period. Both turn flukes as lift the tail perpendicularly in the air, when they go down. The oil of the one is rich in spermaceti; the other furnishes the lower-priced train-oil.

The natural history of the right whale is comparatively well understood, from its coming more within the range of our observation; and the time of gestation, the manner of bringing forth their young and nursing them, and the manner of their feeding, are accurately described. But the natural history of the sperm-whale is yet as much a mystery as when the first dead whale floated ashore to furnish precious medicine to the ills of man. Its history is as obscure as that of the earthquake, the aurora borealis, and the nebulous light of the comet; and every wise man feels entitled to have his guess on the subject.

Had the right whale the habit of "jawing back," as the sperm-whale has, it would be next to impossible to secure him by the present weapons and methods of our whalemen. But, as we are told, the wind is tempered to the shorn lamb; so the blow of the whale is tempered to the hunter's powers. Read Scoresby, Jardin, and Beale, the fathers of whaling literature, and they will not reveal the secret of the weakness of the right whale. Whalemen and naturalists, they have failed to record the important fact, that on the tip of the upper jaw there is a spot of very limited extent, seemingly as sensitive in feeling as the antennæ of an insect; as keenly alive to the prick of lance or harpoon as a gentleman's nose is to the tweak of finger and thumb. However swiftly a right whale may be advancing on the boat, a slight prick on this point will arrest his forward motion at once. I think it safe to say that he will not advance a single yard after the prick is given. He will either pitch his head, and round down like a great wheel turning on a fixed axis, or he will turn shortly to the right or left, according to the part of the nose which is pricked. Sometimes he will throw his enormous head straight in the air, and settle backward tail first, by this motion exposing his whole throat to the thrust of the harpoon or lance: he may take any course, save the one directly forward. It seems almost as though this sensibility to touch was a guard against the collision of parts so important to existence with other objects, and which are beyond the line of vision. And it is also endowed with a backing power which is simply marvelous, when we consider the enormous weight moving forward with great speed.

This very marked peculiarity of the right whale is constantly taken advantage of by the whaleman, who, working about its head completely out of the reach of its active flukes, parries the charge of the enraged monster as deftly as the fencer glances the thrust of his antagonist's sword. If an advancing whale glides under the boat, and the back, or "small," touches the keel, then, quick as the lightning flash, the responsive flukes will whip up, and send boat and crew into the air, amidst a perilous tangle of kinking line, sharp harpoons, lances, spades, hatchets, knives, and boat-gear generally. An accursed attribute of such sharp company is to travel point or edge first, and form closer acquaintance than is agreeable.

Knowing this trick of the right whale's flukes, and experienced only in the dangers of the spermaceti's ugly, insensible head, it required my very best nerve to stand unmoved at the head of our dancing cockle-shell, measuring the cadences of the rise and fall of our first right whale. His blowing formed the measure of my breathing as I awaited the decisive moment. The great snout glided within a yard of the prow, and then, with steady hand, I directed the point of my iron against the little centre of sensation. Successfully pricked, the great hulk, without losing speed, changed its direction as by magic, and rounded down without touching the boat, exposing his great back, on which fifteen feet breadth of "black skin" tore the harpoon from my hand. Following this there was a cloud of foam, a roar of broken waves, and the whirl of the line through the "chocks," which gave a sequel to my story of the right whale.

In the early spring of the Southern seas, the latter part of September, we reached our cruising-ground off Chiloe Island. The first indication that we were on whaling-ground were the red winrows of right-whale feed, or "brit," which in long clouds reddened the surface. We were not long in waiting before several whales were seen feeding on the rich, red pasture-field spread about us. The boats were lowered at once; and as we pulled on to a large whale feeding, with its great basket elevated to the spout-hole, and slowly plowing its way across our bows, the captain laid us on just abaft the head. My old habit of avoiding the head of the sperm-whale led to the mistake of heaving the harpoon at his submerged body on the opposite side of the boat. On feeling the prick, the whale settled away, and my iron came back doubled up. It had struck him fairly, but had not entered. We were at a loss to account for the mishap; but further experience taught us that when the whale is doubled into a bow in any direction, there is formed in the concave " slack blubber." This is impenetrable to the best-thrown harpoon. Ignorantly my iron had been hurled against slack blubber, and we lost that whale.

Mr. F—— did better. He pulled on much in our manner, and his iron was planted just behind the blow-hole. The illustration appended shows the whale as it appeared to the astonished whaleman the moment after it was struck.

"Why," said Hinton, afterward, "I could have sworn in court that it had a dozen tails, and they were all going quick, too."

We had little trouble in killing it: we worked about the head, pricking the nose whenever it came down on the boat, and causing it to mill, or turn short in its course, and afford us good chances at the life. It ran less than was usual with

the sperm-whale, and manifested no intention to fight. In
cutting-in, we were also struck with the great depth of the
blubber, and its softness and oiliness, as compared with that
of the sperm-whale, and the greater viscidity, or stickiness,
of the oil. The upper jaw was a curiosity to us. The bone

GOING ON RIGHT WHALE.

was about nine feet long—very much less than is often tak-
en; but I suppose a fair average size. How much oil this
whale made was undetermined, as we piled fresh blubber in
the room before it was tried out. Long after this event,
Captain Isaiah West, of New Bedford, informed me that he

had taken a right whale on the False Banks which made two hundred and fifty barrels of oil, and whales of even larger size have been taken. Of the bow-head, or Greenland whale, such as is found in the Sea of Okhotsk and Behring Strait, our modern whalemen have taken cows which stowed three hundred barrels of oil, and three thousand pounds of bone, single slabs of which measured seventeen feet in length. Captain Sullivan and Captain Taber, both of New Bedford, speak of bone of the bow-head which measured seventeen feet.

I should like to convey to the reader some idea of the dimensions of the creature from which such bone is taken. To do so is only possible by entering into the details of the various parts, with their sizes, and by comparison with objects familiar to the mind. The blubber, or "blanket," of such a whale would carpet a room twenty-two yards long, and nine yards wide, averaging half a yard in thickness. You good, loving housewives, think of such a blanket-piece for the dark, cold nights of winter! And you farmer boys, set up a saw-log, two feet in diameter and twenty feet in length, for the ridge-pole of the room we propose to build. Then raise it in the air fifteen feet, and support it with pieces of timber seventeen feet long, spread, say nine feet. This will make a room nine feet wide at the bottom, two feet wide at the peak, and twenty feet long, and will convey an idea of the upper jaw as shown in the longitudinal and transverse sections of the head in the illustrations, pp. 370, 373; *h* will represent the complete room, *a* being the saw-log, and *g g* the slanting supports composed of bone, which in a large whale will weigh three thousand pounds. Now refer to the illustrations again, and you will perceive that the wall of bone is clasped by the white blubbery lips, *b b*, which at the bottom are four feet thick, tapering to a blunt edge, where they fit into a rebate sunk in the upper jaw. The throat, *d,* is four feet thick, and is mainly blubber interpenetrated by fibrous, muscular flesh.

The lips and throat of a two-hundred-and-fifty-barrel whale should yield sixty barrels of oil, and, with the supporting jaw-bones, *i i*, will weigh as much as twenty-five oxen of one thousand pounds each. Attached to the throat by a broad base is the enormous tongue, the size of which can be better conceived by the fact that twenty-five barrels of oil have been taken from one. Such a tongue would equal in weight ten oxen. The spread of lips, as the whale plows through the fields of "brit," is about thirty feet. Sometimes in feeding the whale turns on its side, so as to lay the longer axis of the cavity of the mouth horizontally. Keeping the lower lip closed, and the upper one thrown off, and standing perpendicularly, it scoops along just under the surface where the "brit" is always most densely packed. After thus sifting a track of the sea fifteen feet wide and a quarter of a mile in length, the water foaming through the slatted bone, and packing the mollusks upon the hair-sieve, the whale raises the lower jaw; but still keeping the lips apart, it forces the spongy tongue into the cavity of the sieve, driving the water with great force through the spaces between the bone. Then, closing the lips, it disposes of the catch, and repeats the operation until satiated.

By these details I have striven to convey an idea of the completeness and the immensity of the apparatus by which this largest of animals is enabled to glean a plentiful harvest of the smallest creatures of the sea.

The tail of such a whale is about twenty-five feet broad and six feet deep, and considerably more forked than that of the spermaceti. The point of junction with the body is about four feet in diameter, the vertebra about fifteen inches; the remainder of the small being packed with rope-like tendons from the size of a finger to that of a man's leg. The great rounded joint at the base of the skull gleams like an ivory sphere, nearly as large round as a carriage-wheel. Through the greatest blood-vessels, more than a foot in diameter, surges, at each pulsation of a heart as large as a hogshead, a torrent of barrels of blood heated to 104°.   The respiratory canal is over twelve inches in diameter, through which the rush of air is as noisy as the exhaust pipe of a thousand horse-power steam-engine; and when the fatal wound is given, torrents of clotted blood are sputtered into the air or over the nauseated hunters.   In conclusion, the right whale has an eye scarcely larger than a cow's, and an ear that would scarcely admit a knitting-needle.

CHAPTER XXXIV.

Try-works overboard.—Dreaming.—Adventure of Captain I—— H——
with a fighting Right Whale.—Two Men lost, and fearful Peril of the
Captain.—A Fight of Three-quarters of an Hour. — Ship fails to part
the Combatants; Captain saved by Mate's Boat.—Why Right Whales
sink.—Greenland Whales, or Bow-head.—First Bow-head taken by Captain Covill.—Entrance of Whalemen to Behring Strait.—Edible parts
of the Whale.—Sad Picture of the Ship and Crew.—In Talcahuana.—
Weigh Anchor for Home.—Doubling Cape Horn.—Touch at Pernambuco, and meet Gale off Bermuda.—Cold and Fog off Long Island.—
Land in New London.—Hospitality.—Profit and Loss Account.—Arrive in Philadelphia, and Finis.

OUR experience with the right whale was so limited that
I can not venture to dwell at length on it; but after recount-
ing somewhat at length interesting incidents in the experiences of others, I will proceed on the homeward voyage.
We remained on the ground about two months, and took
eleven whales, which made six hundred and fifty barrels.
The bone was cleaned from the gum, and tied into bundles.
Now the ship was declared full, having about eighteen hundred of sperm, and six hundred and fifty barrels of whale
oil on board. We joyfully received the order to tear down
the try-works. All hands went to work with a will, and the
oily, sooty bricks were passed overboard. The pots were
secured below; the old chopped sheathing amidships was
torn from the decks, and the sheathing outside the gangway
removed. Every thing was cleaned up, and our deck-room
seemed boundless, now the cumbersome try-works were removed. All the dangers of the voyage seemed ended, and
we had only some ten or twelve thousand miles of sea to

navigate, and we should be home again.   But my mind looked forward with something of misgiving, for up to this time (thirty-eight months from home) I had not received a single word from my kindred; nor had I seen a newspaper from my native city; so that all at home was in a cloud of doubt and uncertainty.   Naturally my mind anticipated the continuance of a life which had become familiar and easy to me.   Having doubled the forecastle, the way was opening to whatever might be my deserts in the boats or on board the ship.

We now bore away to the north, to run to Talcahuana for repairs, and to recruit for the homeward passage. Much of the spare time was devoted to overhauling our clothing and increasing our warmth by doubling our flannel shirts, or placing one within another, and closely stitching them with blue woolen yarn, much in the manner of quilting.   Thus we succeeded in making an admirable garment for the cold weather off Cape Horn, and on the American coast in March.

As the ship is plowing her way to our port, I will take the opportunity to insert incidents in right-whale fishing which have come to my knowledge since the journal was written, premising that they have been received by word of mouth from the actors, who are whaling captains, now retired from the business, and living in safety and ease on well-earned fortunes.

In a peaceful, happy home on Long Island, surrounded by a beautiful family, I listened to the following account of an encounter with a fighting right whale.   I omit the name of the narrator, for I feel that the grand old man would shrink from the appearance of parading his whaling experiences. I call him an old man, as his snowy hair and beard indicate the snows of many winters; yet he has only filled forty-six years of life.   Gigantic in form and power, with a head to attract the sculptor's attention, and a countenance to arrest the eye of a woman, he modestly told me this story of a prolonged struggle for life with an enraged whale. As I regarded him, with the battle-fire lighting up his pleasant, beautiful eye, and as I measured his brawny figure, it seemed to me that he was just the man to plunge into a battle with the leviathan. In such contests he was mainly a victor; but he carries scars, and the snow-white hairs of premature age, to tell of the unequal conflict.

We had been conversing on his experiences with the vicious sperm-whale, and I asked him whether the right whale ever manifested the same fighting propensities. He replied that he had met with one remarkable instance in his own experience, and continued :

"My second mate had fastened to a large whale that seemed disposed to be ugly; so I pulled up and fastened to her also. I went into the bow and darted my lance; but the whale rolled, so that I missed the life and struck into the shoulder-blade. It pierced so deep into the bone (perhaps through it) that I could not draw it out; the whole body of the whale shivered and squirmed, as though in great pain. Then, turning a little, she cut her flukes, taking the boat amidships. The broadside was stove in, and the boat rolled over, the crew having jumped into the sea. I cut the line in the chocks at the same moment, to save being run under with a kink. The crew were soon safely housed on the bottom of the upturned boat, or swimming and clinging to the keel. The second mate wanted to cut his line and pick us up, but I foolishly told him to hold on and kill the whale; that we were doing quite as well as could be expected. But I had bragged too soon. Just then the whale came up on the full breach, and striking the boat, she went right through it, knocking men and wreck high in the air. Next the great bulk fell over sideways, like a small avalanche, right in our midst; and spitefully cut the corners of her flukes right and left. In the surge and confusion, two poor fellows went down: we saw no sign of them afterward, and the water was so dark, stained with blood, that we could not see into it.

"As the whale came feeling around with her nose, she passed close by me. I was afraid of the flukes, and got hold of the warp, or iron pole, or her small, or something, and towed a little way till she slacked speed a little. Then I dove under, so as to clear the flukes, and came up astern of them. I was in good time; for having felt the boat, she turned over and threshed the spot with a number of blows in quick succession, pounding the wreck into splinters. She must have caught sight of me, for she came up on a half breach, and dropped her head on me, and drove me, half stunned, deep under water. Again I came up near the small, and again dove under the flukes. From this time she seemed to keep me in sight. Again and again—the mate told me afterward—she would run her head in the air and fall on my back, bruising and half drowning me as I was driven down in the water.

"Sometimes I caught hold of the line, or something attached to the mad brute, and would hold until a sweep of the flukes would take my long legs and break my hold. The second mate's boat had cut long ago, and watched her chance to pick up the surviving crew, but had not been able to reach me; for when the whale's eye caught the boat, she would dash for it so wickedly that the whole crew became demoralized, owing to the loss of the two men, and the sight, to them, more terrible than to me, perhaps, of the peril the captain was in. To husband my strength, I gave over swimming, and, treading water, I faced the danger, and several times by sinking avoided the blow from her head. As a desperate resource, I strove with my pointed sheath-knife to prick her nose: I did all a strong man was in duty bound to do to save his life. The cooper, who was ship-keeper, ran down with the ship, intending to cut between the whale and myself; but we were at too close quarters. He was afraid to run me down, lest he might tear me with the ragged copper. Thus for three-quarters of an hour that whale and I were fighting: the act of breathing became labored and painful; my head and shoulders were sore from bruises, and my legs had been pounded by his flukes; but it was not until I found myself swimming with my arms alone, and that my legs were hanging paralyzed, that I felt actually scared. Then it looked as if I couldn't hold out much longer; I had seen the ship close beside me, and the second mate's boat trying to get in to me, and throwing me lines, or something to float on. But I failed to reach them. Now these things seemed very far off; that was the last I remembered, until I came to on board the ship.

"I was afterward told that the first mate, in answer to a signal from the ship, had come up, and seeing me feebly paddling with my hands and not answering to his hail, he put straight into the fight. The whale saw them coming, and made for them. The men sprang to their oars, and the mate had only time to seize my collar, while they pulled their best to escape from the furious whale. They thus gained time to take me into the boat, seemingly a drowned man. The mate had true pluck. Leaving me to the care of the crew on board, he put back for the whale. As he afterward said, 'She was too dangerous a cuss to run at large in that pasture-field.' Watching a chance, he got a 'set' on her over the shoulder-blade, and sent the red flag into the air. This tamed her; she sagged around for a time, and settled away dead. The mate then came on board and reported sunk whale; and I was put to bed, a mass of bruised flesh. It was several weeks before I was able to take my place in the head of the boat again."

A peculiar feature in right-whaling is the considerable number which sink on being killed. This rarely occurs with the sperm-whale. With the hump-back it is the rule, and therefore this fishing is carried on in shallow sounds and bays. On putting the question, "Why do right whales sink?" scarcely two men will give the same reason in reply. Captain West, when master of the *Adeline Gibbs*, in conversation with two Arctic whalemen, at Maui, gave the following answer: "To lance a right whale over the shoulder-blade, directing the lance downward, will kill it in the shortest time; but he will be almost certain to sink. Such a wound will be followed by a rushing escape of air, manifesting itself in large and continuous bubbles, rising through the water. When this occurs the whale is certain to sink." Therefore, he holds to the theory that whales are furnished with a sound, or air bladder, like fish, and that through no other cause than injury to this bladder could the whale settle instantly as it does. The two captains above mentioned stated that on their last cruises one had taken nine whales, without one sinking. The other had sunk eight whales, and prided himself on the fatal thrust of his lance over the shoulder.

It is also a curious fact in the history of whaling, that when our right-whalemen first met the Greenland whale in the Sea of Okhotsk, they did not recognize it as a whale worth the trouble of taking, but classed it among the hump-backs, or "sulphur-bottoms." Captain West informed me of a captain, whose name has escaped me, who, when he first visited the Northern seas, found himself surrounded by what he thought worthless whales, and so missed his chance to fill up at once. The whale he saw is known among American whalemen as the bow-head, on account of the higher arch of the upper jaw, as compared with the right whale. Large as is the head of the latter, that of the bow-head is larger and longer. The difference which first strikes the observer is the great prominence of the spout-holes of the bow-head; hence it is sometimes called the "steeple-top." As the whale lives on the surface, this steeple becomes the prominent point, as the hump of the spermaceti. It differs from its congener of the Southern seas, in having no barnacles along the edge of the lips. Upon the nose, or on the projection above the eyes, its bone is also longer; the blubber much thicker, softer, and richer in oil. In other respects it closely resembles the right whale.

The first discovery of the great value of this whale, as I am informed, was about the year 1846. The *Mount Vernon*, of New Bedford, Captain George A. Covill, was cruising in the Sea of Okhotsk for right whales, which were plenty, and the captain had his pick for most of the time. But one day his blubber-room was empty, and no sperm-whales were immediately about the ship, when a bow-head was discovered a mile to leeward. The first and second mates' boats were sent down, with the option of fastening or not, as seemed best. Their course was watched from the deck, when they were observed to heave up their oars at a short distance from the suspicious-looking monster, as though studying his motions. Captain Covill now directed his attention to more distant right whales. After a time the mates went on to the bow-head, and with little trouble killed him. When towed alongside, they estimated it as about equal to a seventy-barrel right whale. But they were pleasantly surprised by the great thickness of the blubber, and the length and weight of the bone. The prize tried out some one hundred and fifty barrels.

It was not until the next year that Captain Boyce, of the *Superior*, made the first cruise inside Behring Strait, where bow-heads were found in great numbers and of great size. Captain Covill took two whales at one lowering, which stowed five hundred barrels, and he estimated the tongues at twenty-three barrels each. He has found these whales less supple and dangerous than either the right or sperm. They are now only found along the edge of the ice. Alarmed by the persistent hunt of the crowd of ships, they are returning farther to the north, to find refuge in Symmes's Hole, or Kane's open sea, neither of which have been penetrated by our whalemen.

I may state, for the enlightenment of the gastronomer, that the thin edge of the right whale's lip is of a gelatinous nature, and when placed in the copper settler or cooler, so as to be surrounded by the boiling oil for about six hours, it becomes of the consistence of a jelly, which, eaten with salt, pepper, and vinegar, closely resembles pigs' feet. The tubular shells which are found on the nib of the nose are also eaten, when boiled in the same way. No part of the sperm-whale is eaten, however; but I suppose an excellent quality of glue might be made from the ten tons of white horse found in the head.

About the middle of November, being over three years from home, we dropped anchor in the land-locked harbor of Talcahuana, to refit ship for the passage round Cape Horn, and our long home voyage. Our poor ship presented a sorry sight, as we stood up the harbor. Time and the elements had done their work. The sails were patched and repatched; the newer cloths inserted contrasting, in their whiteness, with the older. Our rigging was frayed, and loose ends were flying crazily in the air. The paint of the spars was lost, while that on the sides was blistered and broken. The copper was much worn, and rolled up. Rough barnacles and waving grass fouled the bottom, and clogged the vessel's motion. Thus we presented a striking and painful contrast to the dandy clipper which left New London three years ago. Sorry as was our exterior, it was cheerful, however, as compared with the internal condition of affairs. The provisions we had brought from home were exhausted, and replaced by worse supplies picked up at Valparaiso. Our beef required much practice before it would remain on the stomach. Even when the offended nose endured, the stomach protested; and had it not been for the abundant supply of molasses to lubricate our gritty, sandy biscuit, we must have gone under. Our slop-chest was exhausted, and we made shift by patching and working old sail-cloth into our clothing.

Our voyage was a poor one, and the "lays" of the men were exhausted, and most of them were in debt to the ship. Our crew, short-handed and disheartened, were morose and quarrelsome, only a few of the original remaining. The ship so loved became almost a prison to me, and long since I ceased to keep a journal of the constantly recurring disagreeable incidents of the life about me. I became a human terrapin, shutting my shell, and waiting for the weary months to bring deliverance. We had all long since given up the expression "When I get home," and adopted the hopeless "If I get there." Now that the voyage was nearly over, I failed to find a joy in the thought of it, and time and events were indifferently accepted as matters of course.

In such moods, neither glad nor sorry, penniless, and without resources, we mechanically went through our duties, or wore away the tedium of liberty on shore. When they told me of the great earthquake of two years ago, which swallowed up the city of Concepçion, only a few miles from our last port, it failed to interest me. "Of course earthquakes will swallow cities," I muttered; "why not?"

Thus drearily our recruitment went on until the preparations of the ship were completed. A new set of sails were bent, the rigging was tarred down, the ends were stopped, and ratlines seized; and, as far as our lockers would afford, paint was renewed. We felt in a degree more decent as the *Chelsea* put on new clothes, and stronger morally as we scraped the fouling shells and grass from her bottom. Then, having a good supply of the fine fruits and vegetables of Chili on board, we hove the anchor and stood to sea, minus five of the crew, who, having nothing to draw at the end of the voyage, deserted. The two Spaniards shipped in Callao were discharged. We were still strong enough, as a crew merely, to navigate the ship; and as we were passing the Cape from the westward, and in midsummer, we had no concern.

We doubled the stormy point, with the rocky, mountainous cape in sight. A brisk southerly breeze, in twenty-four hours, wafted us from a degree north of the Cape in the Pacific to the same distance north of it in the Altantic. Running down the coast, and experiencing a La Plata thunder-storm, we touched the Brazilian coast, sending a boat into Pernambuco to procure a few supplies and some tobacco. We then bore away to the north, giving a wide berth to the West India Islands, and met inhospitable welcome in a three-days' gale, north of the Bermudas. We lost our flying jib and boom, with foretop-gallant-mast; and our decks were swept, and bulwarks and cook's galley washed overboard. Two of our boats were smashed on the cranes. This was, by odds, the severest gale experienced in the voyage, and served to stir the stagnating blood of all hands. Having something to fight, gave them a new interest in living, and made existence worth the struggle. As we neared our northern coast, we boarded several coasting-vessels, and obtained scant supplies of beans, tobacco, and other necessaries of life. Off the coast of Long Island we were for several days enveloped in fogs, and had to feel our way cautiously, by sounding, for the mud which marks the bottom off Montauk Light.

These were the most miserable days of the voyage. It was in the latter part of March; the weather was cold, and the fog penetrated to the very marrow of the shivering, half-clad wretches, who, barefooted, held the long watches of the wet decks. The watch below brought little comfort, as the forecastle was damp, and all our clothing and blankets were perfectly wet. At length the fog lifted, however, and the cry of "Land ho!" told of home in sight. But none rushed on deck to gladden their eyes with the low sandy shore which lay close under our larboard beam. "Land ho!" Of course the land was there; it always had been there; it always would be there. A week more or less, a day or so, what mattered it to the wearied souls who were coming, sore and worn, from a flight of ninety thousand miles, and of forty-one months' duration.

On a bright Sunday morning in the last of March, the sullen plunge of a single anchor in the mouth of the Thames announced the voyage ended. The sails were carelessly rolled up on the yards; no pains taken to dress the yard-arms neatly, pass the gaskets symmetrically, or to form the bunt ship-shape and sailor-fashion. At 9 A.M. the ship-keepers came on board, and at 10 A.M., while the shore-folk were warmly and decently clad, thronging from comfortable homes to church, a band of barefooted barbarians landed on the snow-covered, icy streets of New London. Our soiled, tattered clothing, our wild, haggard aspect, contrasted fearfully with the respectability—we were shocking!

A worthy man came to me, and taking my hand, asked my name. On being told, he said,

"Why that is my name also; I have a son on a whale-ship. Come right home with me; I guess I won't go to church to-day."

So he and his good wife turned about and took the poor waif, without questioning, to their blessed home; and will not the good Lord overlook the blank in their church pew on that morning? An unwonted tenderness stole over the

JUST LANDED.

rude sailor as the gentlewoman ministered to his wants, and, after he had done eating, with tears in her good, motherly eyes, she inquired whether we had seen the ship in which her boy was growing to be such a poor man as she saw before her.

Owing to difficulties in settling the voyage, some three

weeks passed before our accounts were balanced. Of some sixty-five dollars which came to me, after rigging myself and Charley Lings in blue jackets, trowsers, and pumps, and paying for our two passages to New York, there remained means to buy a ticket to Philadelphia, and a clean five dollars in my pocket.

After dark, on a Saturday night, I arrived in my native city, and entered the first tavern, not to drink, but to ascertain the whereabouts of some friends. An hour thereafter I entered a brother's door, to the surprise of his beautiful young wife, who little dreamed, when she accepted her new life, that such an invasion was at all probable. But she met the dispensation bravely, and we all sat up late, running over the incidents of the voyage. As I passed into blissful sleep, I knew that the voyage of the *Chelsea* was at an end, and that there were those yet left who could love the returned wanderer.

"NE PLUS ULTRA."

APPENDIX A.

At the back of Kelley's watch-maker's shop in New Bedford, there is a place of assembly for the whaling-captains of that city. Perhaps there is no other single spot on the earth so favorable for receiving information regarding the business, or where so many men of the largest experience daily meet.

Wishing to obtain their views regarding the habits, etc., of whales, I addressed a series of questions to Captain G. A. Covill, with the request that they should be submitted to the captains of New Bedford. The appended letter resulted:

"Since writing you, I have complied with your request by making known to the captains at Kelley's your desire to obtain reliable information concerning the habits of the sperm and right whale. I read your letter appealing to them for such information, and any other that would be useful to you in the work you have undertaken. All seem interested, and many express a wish that you may give to the world a book that will not only be interesting but truthful. All agree that such a book on this subject has never been published. To some of the questions you propose there is no disagreement of opinion, while to others there is quite a diversity.

"To your first question, all agree that the right whale is frequently seen making passage from one feeding-ground to another. He never crosses the equator, and is seldom if ever seen below lat. 25°. The right whale of the north latitude is very much larger than that of the south, the former averaging one hundred and fifty barrels, the latter about seventy barrels. The polar, or bow-head, whale of the Arctic resembles the right whale, yet differs from him in that it has no bonnet, or protrusion, with deep-set barnacles on its nose: the skin is smoother, the head longer, and the bone in the head longer and smoother, weighing from fifteen hundred to two thousand pounds, the length of the longest bone being twelve feet."

Question 2. "Opinions are about equally divided, many thinking that both the sperm and right whales can stay under water as long as they choose; others think they must and do seek the surface quite often, if not at regular intervals. I think the former have the best of the argument,

for they cite instances in their experience when whales, after spouting a
usual number of times, have gone down, and, notwithstanding that every
thing was favorable for seeing a whale five miles or more, no whale ever
appeared. As I told you when here, I have experienced the same thing,
and under the same favorable circumstances. I and others have known
whales to come up close to the ship, no whale having been seen before on
that day. Without going his length he would get through spouting, turn
flukes, and never be seen again."

Question 3. "The running speed of the sperm and right whales, when
gallied, is supposed to be from ten to twelve miles an hour."

Question 4. "When struck, he will frequently go twenty to twenty-five
miles per hour for a short time, when he will generally stop or 'bring to,'
and give the 'boat-header' a chance to kill him."

Question 5. "Sperm-whales have been known to run out three hundred
fathoms of line in four minutes, and sometimes to run out six hundred
fathoms in sounding."

Question 6. "Two captains say they have seen eighty-barrel sperm-whales
breach entirely out of the water. I know the men, and believe them."

Question 7. "To this question I will have to devote another letter. I am
acquainted with two or three captains who have had severe experience
with fighting whales. I will see them soon as possible, get their stories,
and send them to you."

Question 8. "Sperm-whales are sometimes taken on soundings on the
American coast, off the Galapagos Islands, and off Cape St. Thaddeus, in
from forty to ninety fathoms. I can not at this time call to mind by what
ships or captains they were taken."

Question 9. "I can not learn, and do not think, that the great squid of
the deep sea has ever been seen entire. Pieces of it are sometimes seen
half the size of a whale-boat."

Question 10. "Voyages are lengthened more on account of diminished
numbers of whales, than by their going in schools or their increased wildness.   · G. A. COVILL."

This testimony to the habits, etc., of the whale is so concisely
written that the letter is given entire; and it is satisfactory to find
the impressions of the journal so nearly correct. It will be noticed
that a whale leaping clear of the water is rare, yet it must be admitted that it is occasionally seen.

·APPENDIX B.

THE whale-fishery originated in Nantucket, in the year 1690, in boats from the shore.

In 1715, six sloops were fitted from Nantucket to follow the whale into deep water; no other ports being engaged.

In 1721, from a list given in M'Pherson's "Annals of Commerce," there were employed in the whale-fishery in Greenland and Davis Strait: from sundry ports of Holland, 251 ships; from Hamburg, 55; from ports in the Bay of Biscay, 20; from Bremen, 24; from Bergen, in Norway, 5; total, 355 ships.

In 1857, the whaling fleet of the United States consisted of 670 vessels; of which there were ships and barks, 617; the tonnage, 220,000 tons; the capital invested, $22,000,000; men employed, 18,000.

In 1852, only four ships were sent out from England, and the entire tonnage employed in whaling amounted to 16,113 tons.

In 1858, France had only three ships, measuring 1650 tons, and Holland had only three ships.

Thus the business had almost entirely passed into American hands. And it was without governmental support or encouragement, by bounties to owners or privileges to mariners, such as I have shown were continually held out by England. In proportion to the persistent policy of England to build up this splendid school for seamen at home, was her jealous hostility to the spontaneous growth of the business in America, and she has never lost an opportunity to strike at that wonderful prosperity. In the Revolution the little community of Nantucket alone lost by capture, 134 vessels, or about 10,000 tons, out of 14,867 owned in A.D. 1775; and large numbers of her young and hardy seamen, trained boat-steerers, and officers, perished miserably in the horrible prison-ships of England.

The war of 1812 fell with particular severity on this business, as seven-eighths of the mercantile capital was at sea on distant voyages, a large proportion of which could not return in less than twelve months. Many of the vessels were captured by British cruisers, and the business was broken up. With returning peace, the indomitable enterprise and energy of the American re-asserted its superiority in this congenial field of adventure, and soon the sails of our whalemen whitened every sea, until in forty years they had appropriated the business, and the fleets of England, Holland, and France had passed from the scene. But the time came when civil war crippled our hands, and we were powerless to protect a business which girdled the earth, and compassed every sea. Then a people who habitually shrunk from encounter with the whale, and who grudged our prosperity in a field they were confessedly incapable of, launched a swift steamer, manned, armed, and equipped for a piratical cruise, and coaled and refitted in their distant colonies. And, to England's shame and our great wrong, the accursed *Shenandoah* proceeded to war against defenseless whalemen, and amidst the ice of the Arctic applied the incendiary torch to thirty-four American whale-ships, regardless of the announcement, with evidence, that the War of the Rebellion was ended.

Thus at a blow was destroyed a fleet which England's entire marine could not have re-manned. To secure to herself a coveted carrying-trade through her *Alabamas;* to surprise in distant seas and ruthlessly burn our whale-ships, against which she could only thus compete; to destroy a business she lacked the courage to prosecute, were part of the bitter ends of British neutrality. Parchment patches over such rents may satisfy commerce, but the memory of the last war of England on American whalemen must remain as an heir-loom to the sons of every father who ever swung in a whale-boat, or wielded the harpoon and lance.

APPENDIX C.

To the sperm-whaleman who now sails to the distant grounds of New Zealand or Japan in pursuit of his gigantic game, the journal annexed may prove interesting, as it shows how near home the business was prosecuted, and how plentiful the sperm-whale once was directly at our doors. It is extracted from the log of the sloop *Betsey*, of Dartmouth:

"*Aug.* 2, 1761. Lat. 45° 54′ N., long. 53° 37′ W., saw sperm-whale; killed one.

"*Aug.* 6. Spoke John Clasberry; he had got one hundred and five barrels; told us Seth Folger had got one hundred and fifty barrels. Spoke with two Nantucket men; they had got one whale between them; they told us that Jenkens and Dunham had got four whales, and Allen and Pease had got two whales between them. Lat. 42° 57′ N.

"*Aug.* 22. Took a spermaceti, etc., etc.

"*Aug.* 28. Saw spermaceti; foggy; lost sight of him.

"*Aug.* 30. Saw spermaceti, but could not strike. Lat. 43°.

"*Aug.* 31. Saw spermaceti plenty; squally, with thunder.

"*Sept.* 2. Saw spermaceti; foggy and dark.

"*Sept.* 3. This morning at eight saw a spermaceti; got into her two short warps and the tow-iron,* but she ran away. In the afternoon came across her again; got another iron in, but she went away.

"*Sept.* 5. Saw spermaceti; chased, but could not strike.

"*Sept.* 6. Saw whales; struck one, but never saw her again.

"*Sept.* 7. Saw small school of spermaceti. Captain Shearman struck one out of the vessel, and killed her. Lat. 43°.''

It is evident that the methods of capture were very imperfect, from the great numbers seen, and the few captured.

---

* This was evidently before the tow-line was introduced in this fishery.

APPENDIX D.

In 1786, while the people of Nantucket were suffering from the effects of the late war with England, it was in contemplation to transfer the whaling business to France. The following are a part of the advantages offered by the French Government to the people of the island, who wished to settle at Dunkirk, and there establish the whale-fishery:

"You will communicate with all the prudence you are capable of to the select men of the island, and acquaint them with all the real advantages the town, port, and country offers for their establishment:

"The unlimited freedom it enjoys; the abundance and cheapness of all sorts of provisions; no custom-house, nor customs officers to embarrass a free trade; the small taxes; the regularity of the town; the manners and industry of the inhabitants; its situation; all of which render it the most eligible place in the universe for the people of Nantucket to remove to."

Grants, to wit:

"1st. An entire free exercise of their religion or worship within themselves.

"2d. The concession of a tract of ground to build their houses and stores.

"3d. All the privileges, exemptions, and advantages promised by the king's declaration in 1662, confirmed by letters patent in 1784, to all strangers who come to establish there, which are the same as those enjoyed by native subjects of his majesty.

"4th. The importation into the kingdom, free from all duties whatever, of the oil proceeding from their fishery, and the same premiums and encouragement granted for the cod and other fisheries granted to native subjects.

"5th. A premium per ton on the burden of the vessels that will carry on the whale-fishery, which shall be determined in the course of the negotiation, either with Mr. Rotch, or with the select men of the island.

"6th. All objects of provisions and victuals for the ships shall be exempted from all duties whatever.

"7th. An additional and heavier duty shall be laid on all foreign oil, as a further encouragement to them, in order to facilitate the sale of their own.

"8th. The expense of removing those of the inhabitants who are not capable of defraying themselves shall be paid by the Government.

"9th. A convenient dock shall be built to repair their ships.

"10th. All trades-people shall be admitted to the free exercise of their trades, without being liable to the forms and expense usually practiced and paid by the native subjects for their admittance to mastership.

"11th. They shall have liberty to command their own vessels, and have choice of their own people to navigate them.

"12th. They shall be free from all military and naval service, in war as well as in peace.

"The above is certified to by Abner Coffin, notary and tabellion public, by legal authority duly constituted, etc.

"NANTUCKET, *June* 15, 1786."

In thus granting privileges and immunities superior to the highest orders of nobility, the French Government evinced its anxiety to secure to the French marine and trade a share in a business its own people failed in acquiring. And it furnishes evidence of the reputation for skill, courage, and enterprise which our own hardy seamen had established for themselves, that they could obtain such terms from a proud and powerful government.

THE END.